Maree Anderson

Anne Kane

Nicole North

Alice Gaines

Volume 30

Secrets

Satisfy your desire for more.

SECRETS Volume 30
This is an original publication of Red Sage Publishing and each individual story herein has never before appeared in print. These stories are a collection of fiction and any similarity to actual persons or events is purely coincidental.

Red Sage Publishing, Inc.
P.O. Box 4844
Seminole, FL 33775
727-391-3847
www.redsagepub.com

SECRETS Volume 30
A Red Sage Publishing book
All Rights Reserved/July 2011
Copyright © 2011 by Red Sage Publishing, Inc.

ISBN: 1-60310-010-5 / ISBN 13: 978-1-60310-010-6

Published by arrangement with the authors and copyright holders of the individual works as follows:

KAT ON A HOT TIN ROOF
Copyright © 2011 by Maree Anderson

KELLEN'S CONQUEST
Copyright © 2011 by Anne Kane

SCOUNDREL IN A KILT
Copyright © 2011 by Nicole North

COX CLUB
Copyright © 2011 by Alice Gaines

Photographs:
Cover © 2011 by Tara Kearney Adkins; www.tarakearney.com
Cover Models: Taraneh Dugas and Jimmy Thomas
Setback cover © 2000 by Greg P. Willis; GgnYbr@aol.com

Printed in the U.S.A.

Book typesetting by:

Quill & Mouse Studios, Inc.
www.quillandmouse.com

Volume 30

Secrets

Satisfy your desire for more.

Kat on a Hot Tin Roof by Maree Anderson

Kat Meyer is clueless about the ancient curse that turns her into a cat between the hours of 11pm and 1am. *Feline*-Kat steals from people, but Kat believes her pet cat Cupcake is the one leaving "gifts" on her pillow. When Jace Burton wakes to find a naked and distraught Kat in his living room, he's inclined to believe her bizarre tale of sleepwalking. But how's he going to react when he discovers the truth?

Kellen's Conquest by Anne Kane

Orphaned as a child, Mia's most cherished dream is to settle down and have a family of her own. Kellen may be the sexiest man in the known worlds, but he's AlphElite and when they settle down, it's with one of their own kind. When someone sets him up to kill her, Kellen decides to kidnap her and keep her by his side until he's sure she's safe. They traverse the stars to find out who wants her dead, and more importantly, why.

Scoundrel in a Kilt by Nicole North

Brodie, Chieftain of Clan MacCain, is a dark, sensual Scottish scoundrel who loves nothing more than being a selkie shape-shifter, even if he has been cursed by a witch of the dark arts. Stunning modern day supermodel Erin Schultz blazes into his 1621 world like a falling star. Though he's certain she will shatter life as he knows it by breaking his curse, he can't resist her tantalizing seduction.

Cox Club by Alice Gaines

At the urging of her best friend, Andi Crawford visits an exclusive club in order to find some sexual satisfaction after her divorce. The last person she expects to find at a place like Club Cox is her overbearing ex-husband, Blake. But, he's there and as tempting as ever. Can she maintain her independence, or will she surrender to the intense physical pleasure only he can give her?

Contents

Kat on a Hot Tin Roof

by Maree Anderson

To My Reader:

When my kids were small, their favorite story was Slinky Malinki, about a cat-burglar of the feline persuasion, and I once owned a cat that used to carry stuff around in his mouth. So I was just waiting for an excuse to incorporate a clever cat-burglar into one of my stories, and voilà! *Kat On A Hot Tin Roof.*

My heroine, Kat, blames the "gifts" left on her pillow each night on Cupcake, her pet cat. And when she wakes up naked, curled atop her bed, she believes she's been sleepwalking—bare-assed naked sleepwalking. What other explanation could there possibly be? Hmmm. That would be telling ;-)

Oh, the endless possibilities for fun and embarrassment, LOL. Poor Kat. With all the weirdness in her life right now, the last thing she needs is a sexy alpha male, who sends her dormant hormones into orbit. So of course, that's exactly who rocks into town and turns her life upside down. And when Jace gets up-close-and-personal with Kat, he discovers there's far more to this cat-burglar caper than meets the eye.

I hope you enjoy Jace and Kat's story!

Buddha summoned all the animals to a meeting and promised to give each of the first twelve animals to arrive a designation representing a year on the Chinese zodiac. The animals were very excited. And none more so than Cat.

The night before the meeting, Cat was worried that he would oversleep. He took his concerns to his friend, Rat, and they agreed on a plan. Whoever woke first the next morning would wake the other, and then they would leave for the meeting together. But Rat broke his promise and left Cat sleeping.

Rat arrived at the meeting before any of the other animals, and Buddha gave him the honor of being the first animal of the Chinese zodiac. One by one, Ox, Tiger, Rabbit, Dragon, Snake, Horse, Sheep, Monkey, Rooster, Dog and Pig arrived, and each was allocated his place in the zodiac.

Cat woke up and found Rat gone. He ran to the meeting but arrived too late. It was over. And when he found out that Rat had gotten there first and been honored by Buddha, he was furious. Cat has never forgiven Rat. And to this day, if a cat finds a rat, he will do his utmost to kill him.

Chapter 1

Anyone spotting the cat crouched on the rooftop could be forgiven for thinking that it was a mini panther. It was sleek and muscular, and its short, jet-black coat had a glossy sheen that begged to be petted and stroked. But one glance at its copper-penny colored eyes dispelled any notion that this was a domesticated creature that would tolerate such indignities. It was wild. It had a mind of its own—a distinctly un-catlike mind.

And an agenda.

The cat didn't understand why it had been drawn to this particular house. Only that instinct had prodded and poked it until it had succumbed to the primal pull of a force it couldn't deny. It leaped from the rooftop to a fence paling, streaked across the inch-wide strip of wood capping the fence, then launched itself from the fence and hit the ground running. It darted across the grass, its lithe form wending between bushes and landscape plantings, barely raising a disturbance as it passed. At the side door of the house it came to an abrupt halt and paused, sniffing the air. Then it pushed its head against the cat-flap and prowled through into the kitchen.

It wasn't looking for food. Just as well, because there was no cat-lover residing here—no pets at all, in fact. And certainly no food left out for bold strays to sample.

The cat gathered itself to leap. In one smooth movement, it bounded from the floor to the marble countertop. It paused there a moment, whiskers twitching, ears alert for unwelcome intruders, before hopping into the sink and lapping at the tiny puddle of water.

Moonlight filtered through the open blinds, painting the pale walls with linear swathes of luminous silver. The glint from a moon-kissed trinket sitting on a saucer by the sink drew the cat's attention. It stepped neatly from the sink to the countertop and slinked over to investigate.

The cat sniffed the trinket, scenting human male—the same human male whose scent permeated the room. It sneezed and took a moment to groom its face and whiskers. With a final disdainful sniff, it scooped the ring into its mouth so that the trinket looped over one of its lower canines. And as noiselessly as it had entered the house, it departed.

Kat shivered. She curled up into a tight ball, wrapping her arms around her knees, but the chill licking her bare skin dragged her from sleep.

Bare skin….

She jerked to full wakefulness and blinked to clear the sleep-haze from her eyes. Crap. Not again! She uncurled her limbs and cast her gaze down her body even though she already knew what she would see. Or in this case, what she wouldn't see.

She'd stripped off her pajamas in the dead of night. Doubtless she'd also been wandering naked about the house. Doing goodness only knew what. Wouldn't be so bad if she had enough sense to crawl back under the covers after her nightly jaunts. But nooo. She had to lie there, completely exposed and vulnerable, until inevitably, the deepening chill woke her.

The last time she'd suffered this particular problem she'd been a twelve-year-old kid, and her nightly jaunts had lasted an entire year before ceasing as suddenly as they'd manifested. For a child on the cusp of womanhood it had been embarrassing enough, but for a twenty-four-year-old?

Little wonder she felt so lethargic these days, what with all the broken nights. Heck, she tucked herself in bed by ten-thirty every single freaking night because by ten she could barely keep her eyes open. Must be stress. But what the heck did she have to be stressed about?

She nibbled on her lower lip. Well, other than her grandma's escapades at the retirement village. And these bloody sleepwalking episodes!

Could be worse, she supposed. She could be the kind of sleepwalker who could open deadlocked doors. Or even tinker with security latches and crawl out windows. She had a vivid visual of herself waking up to discover she'd been parading naked up and down the street, giving anyone who cared to look a show they'd never forget, and her skin went clammy. The mere thought of making such a public spectacle of herself was enough to churn her stomach. Thankfully, her hasty extra security precautions had proven more than adequate.

A cool draft of air from the barely open window goosed her skin again. She rolled off the covers and was about to dive beneath them when a flash of gold nestled on one of her pillows caught her attention.

Aw, hell! Another gift. And not car or house keys this time.

She scooped the item from her pillow. Sitting cross-legged on the bed, she flicked on the bedside light and squinted at her "gift".

A man's ring. An old one by the looks of the worn band. She weighed it in her palm. Heavy, too. Probably worth a bit.

There was some sort of engraving on the inside of the band. An inscription? The lettering had been smoothed to illegibility by constant wear. Damn. There went her best chance of identifying its owner. She let the ring fall to the coverlet as she pressed the heels of her hands to her eyes. "Crap! I sooo don't need this."

"Mrrrow?"

Kat pried open her eyelids to glare at the cat that had been snoozing atop the throw rug an the end of her bed. "Cupcake, you pull another stunt like this, and I'm gonna swat your furry little feline behind. Then, I'm gonna remove that dingy old cat-flap and replace it with a fancy one that I can lock, okay? We'll soon see how you like being stuck inside and having to use a litter box!"

Cupcake blinked his amber eyes and yawned, displaying his canines. Then he buried his nose beneath his bottle-brush tail and ignored her.

Kat glanced at her alarm clock. Four a.m. She blew out a disgruntled sigh. No point trying to get back to sleep now. She scooted off the bed and planted her feet… right on top of her pajamas which had been haphazardly discarded on the rug beside her bed. In the exact same place they'd been left for the past few weeks. Ever since that night she'd been treated to a Chinese New Year dinner by a grateful client.

She gave herself a mental slap upside the head. Coincidence, nothing more. She could hardly blame the restaurant for a return of her childhood affliction, even if she *had* eaten some truly bizarre food. And even if she stretched the boundaries of her overactive imagination to its limits, there was no way that evening out could have prompted her too-lazy-to-lift-a-paw-unless-food-was-involved feline companion to morph into a cat-burglar the very next night.

It was just Cupcake's way of demanding more attention. Other cats brought in birds or mice, but Cupcake had obviously decided that keys, knickknacks, odd pieces of underwear, and even the occasional x-rated DVD, would garner more attention. And because Kat was completely unaware of her cat, or anything else for that matter, during her sleepwalking episodes, the sneaky furball had apparently decided that her mistress's nightly excursions were the optimum time for such thievery.

Cupcake didn't bring her a gift every night. But more often than not, there would be some offering left on a pillow. Hopefully, as soon as she got her shit together and quit this sleepwalking caper, her pet would quit bringing her these inconvenient "gifts".

Speaking of gifts, she would do a bit of work and then get started on locating the owner of this ring.

Kat stretched her arms over her head to work out the kinks in her back. While her printer spat out "Found!" flyers, she shoved on some clothes, tied her hair back with a scrunchie, and inhaled a glass of orange juice. From past experience, she knew that popping notices with a photo and a brief description of the found item in mailboxes, was far less time-consuming than knocking on doors and explaining her cat's latest bout of thievery to amused neighbors.

She grabbed her flyers and a fanny pack for some cash and keys, and let herself out of the house, locking the door behind her. A glance at her watch confirmed she had plenty of time to deliver the flyers and grab a coffee and a cinnamon roll at the local café before she had to meet with the mayor. Hey, it wasn't the healthiest breakfast, but Kat figured she deserved a treat.

Jace lay on his stomach, head buried beneath a pillow, trying his darnedest to ignore the eardrum-shattering blare of his lamentably effective cartoon alarm clock. A gag birthday gift from his baby sister, Jen. Evil brat. Groaning, he snaked out an arm and whacked the alarm with the flat of his hand, knocking the clock onto the floor in the process.

Oh dear, what a shame—

Darnit! Bloody thing was still shrieking like an angry ghost. Muttering a few choice imprecations, he rolled over to the edge of the mattress to peer down at the instrument of torture through sleep-bleared eyes. He snagged the clock from the floor and tried to wallop it into submission. By the time he realized the alarm wasn't actually set, and the shrill noise was coming from the bedside phone, the answering machine in the kitchen had picked up.

Shit. Probably something to do with work. He heaved himself out of bed and padded through into the kitchen. The aroma of freshly brewed coffee curled through his senses, and he sucked in a deep, appreciative breath. Automatic coffee-makers. Now *there* was a great gift. Typical that he'd had to buy it for himself. He made a mental note to think up something suitably annoying—and as practically unbreakable as his alarm clock—to give Jen in return.

The message was from a chirpy young woman confirming his eleven o'clock meeting with Pressfield County's mayor. Jace snorted. It should be illegal to be that chirpy at eight in the freaking morning. So much for thinking he could treat this contract like a bit of a holiday and sleep in.

He snagged a mug from an overhead cupboard, wincing when he knocked the still slightly swollen ring finger of his right hand against the shelf. Who would have thought catching a finger between a couple of hand weights could be so fricking painful? Lucky he'd managed to get the ring off over his knuckle before his finger swelled too much.

He didn't have much in the way of mementos to remind him of his grandfather, the man who'd raised him and Jen. Only the ring and the watch that Gramps had left to Jace when he passed away. Jace would have been pissed as heck—not to mention secretly heartbroken—if he'd been forced to cut the ring off his finger. Jen would never have let him hear the end of it. She was totally into the whole family heirloom being passed down from generation to generation thing.

From habit, he glanced into the mug he'd grabbed. It had happened to him only once, a few years back in a dive of a motel, but noticing a roach floating in your morning coffee *after* you'd taken that first sip, made a man cautious.

No potential floaters this time, just a bit of dust.

As he rinsed out the mug in the sink, he spotted a few short black hairs swirling down the drain.

Cat hairs?

There was a cat-flap in the kitchen. But Mimi Gallagher, his landlady, hadn't seemed the type to abandon a pet without making arrangements for it. And he'd seen no evidence of a stray lurking about the place. If he did find one hanging around, though, it would find itself taking a real quick trip to the nearest animal shelter. Jace was more your big dog kinda guy. Or, he would be, if he didn't live in an apartment and travel so frequently.

His desire for caffeine overrode all thought of abandoned pets and the weirdness of cat hairs in his sink. He filled his mug with strong hot coffee and wandered to the living room, heading for the white couch.

Huh. White. Impractical, much? Still, it was surprisingly comfortable, despite looking like it'd been plucked from some movie star's showcase mansion. The black carpet throughout was almost okay. If you liked that sort of thing.

He sprawled on the couch to drink his coffee.

This place had been a great find. Fully furnished and just right for his needs. And even though the ultra-modern décor reeked of some trend-besotted interior designer's influence, and wasn't at all to his taste, he could live with it for a few weeks. Mostly. The filmy drapes throughout the place really bugged the fuck out of him. A drape should keep out the light and insulate the interior of the room. These flimsy things did neither.

He drained his mug and, feeling restless, sauntered over to gaze through the barely-there silvery material obscuring the window and out over the lushly green lawn area. Outside, at least so far as plantings and hardscaping went, the Gallaghers had made good choices. Modern, easy-care and visually appealing. The three didn't have to be mutually exclusive.

As an architect, Jace had become adept at dealing with briefs from wealthy clients with crappy taste. He prided himself on mitigating their more embarrassing visions with something classy and tasteful. But on far too many occasions, he'd accepted an invite to walk through the finished building and nearly bitten through his tongue. Idiot interior designers who were allowed to run rampant and completely cock up the flow and feel of the building, tended to have that effect on him.

Movement snared his gaze. A woman strolling from mailbox to mailbox. A pretty damn hot woman so far as he could tell. She wore stretchy, butt-hugging exercise pants, and the butt those pants were hugging was nice. Very nice, indeed.

Ditto with the legs. Long. Toned. No stranger to exercise. He wouldn't object to having those gorgeous limbs wrapped around his waist.

He couldn't quite tell what the rest of her was like because of that hideous baggy sweatshirt—wait. Oh, yeah. Yeah, baby. That's it. Take it off for me.

She pulled the sweatshirt over her head and used it to blot her face before draping it around her shoulders.

"Now turn this way and come a little closer so I can see you properly," he crooned. "That's it…"

She bent to shove a flyer in the mailbox two doors down from his and then strode toward him, arms pumping, ponytail bobbing with each step.

Mmmhmm. A crop-top and a flat belly. Nice combo. He'd lucked out this morning because this babe was a sweet little package. Or should he say, *two* sweet little packages. Perky breasts. Just the way he liked them. Big enough to fill his palms but not so big as to be in-your-face distracting.

Jace's mailbox was next. Yeeha!

He got right up close and personal with the full-length window in his attempt to catch a better view of the features beneath those thick ebony bangs. And as he did so, he tangled his feet in the trailing hem of the drapes. Bloody ridiculous things. Whose dumb idea had it been to hem them longer than they needed to be so they dragged on the floor?

Without thinking, he yanked the drapes completely back just as the woman bent to stick a flyer in his mailbox slot.

Their gazes clashed. She straightened, the flyer still clutched in her hand.

Jace copped an eyeful of startled emerald eyes framed by dark lashes. Pale skin. Full lips. An exotic package and then some. A real honey. And with that killer body, way the heck, off-the-chart, hot.

Her kissable lips formed a perfect O.

Jace felt a familiar stirring in his groin and an unfamiliar pang in the region of his heart. Followed by an instant connection, too strong to be ignored, that sucked the breath from his lungs.

Her gaze left his face, licked across his chest, lingering on his pecs, his abs, lower…. And damned if his dick didn't jerk in response.

She stilled. Her gaze whipped to his face again. Those gorgeous eyes went all huge and shocky. And to his chagrin, she whirled and took off at a flat-out run.

What the—?

Jace peered through the window, but aside from the occasional slow-moving vehicle, there was nothing much doing. He glanced down at himself, wondering what had spooked her. Sure, he'd just rolled out of bed, but he wasn't *that* bad looking.

A car horn tooted. And when his befuddled brain finally kicked up a gear, he threw back his head and laughed. Way to show a lady you're interested, dude!

He turned away from the window and sauntered into his bedroom to fish out some boxers from the drawer before heading back into the kitchen. Wouldn't do to freak out the locals any more than he already had.

And it took another refill of coffee, the distraction of the local newspaper and an icy-cold shower before he could banish Miss Kissable from his mind and his erection subsided.

Chapter 2

Dammit, she'd only delivered half the flyers!

Kat brushed her hair back from her sweat-beaded forehead and tried to dismiss the way her hand trembled. But she couldn't. She was so freaking hot and bothered, not to mention wobbly-kneed, that she couldn't face retracing her steps and continuing her deliveries.

Her cheeks heated still more at the vivid memory of the buff naked guy standing framed in the window of the Gallagher's house. Omigod. Oh. My. God! She mentally kicked herself for bolting and not sticking around to watch more of the show. She was only human, and the encounter had been the closest she'd come to a naked man in two fricking years!

The Gallagher's new tenant was a first degree hottie.

The Gallagher's new *tenant.* She ground her teeth against a flush of anger that temporarily squelched her lustful thoughts. After all the trouble she'd gone to, undoing the previous designer's ghastly mistakes. All that angst over putting her own personal tastes aside, despite Mr. Gallagher telling her to ignore his wife's dithering over color swatches and pick something, fergodsakes, before he went nuts and called the whole makeover off because he just couldn't go through this again. All the sleepless nights spent trying to decipher Mimi Gallagher's vaguely expressed likes and dislikes, trying to accommodate both her, and her husband's, wants and needs and deal-breaker must-haves. All the little extras she'd shaved from the bill to keep the job within a truly stingy budget without stinting on quality. Like dyeing the ghastly lilac carpet instead of replacing it. And not even a month after their gushing praise of her work, they'd put the place up for rent and gone on extended vacation to check out buying something smaller and more compact, like a condo? Sheesh. Sometimes she wondered why she bothered.

Kat sucked in a deep breath and refused to let it get to her. She shouldn't take the Gallagher's decision so personally.

But now, as she tried to envision the interior of the house and bask in the pride of having done a bloody good job, all she saw was *him.*

Buff Naked Guy. His dark hair tousled from sleep and just long enough to curl around his nape. That electric-blue, piercing gaze. The uncompromisingly masculine features, saved from harshness by a dimple in his chin and a humorous quirk to his lips. Lightly tanned all over, from what she could see, with the perfect ratio of bulging pecs to chest hair. Just how she liked her men. Built, but not a muscle-bound gym junkie. Framed by the silvery voiles like some Greek god, just how she liked her…. Well, not that she'd ever admit to *that* particular fantasy.

And speaking of fantasies, who could forget his upstanding cock? Which had been every bit as impressive as the rest of his buff nakedness. Big. Thick. Hard. One hell of an impressive morning boner. Seemed such a pity to waste it.

Or maybe he wouldn't waste it. Maybe he'd clasp the root of his erection and stroke himself. Maybe he'd cup his balls with his other hand, squeezing them rhythmically in time to each long stroke up and down that broad shaft. Maybe he'd….

Maybe he'd think of her as he got himself off.

She moistened suddenly dry lips with the tip of her tongue. A warm throbbing ache, like the kind she got after a hard bout of exercise, centered in her pelvis at the thought of his cock and the pleasure that it—and the man attached to it—could give her. The crotch of her thong dampened, causing it to cling lovingly to embarrassing places, and she fought the impulse to slip her hand down her stretchy exercise pants and tweak the gusset of her thong away from her heated flesh.

The street was practically deserted, and that candy-cane-striped barber's pole outside Bill's Barber Shop was looking like a pretty awesome man-substitute right now. She was so darned revved up, that the first vibrator-less orgasm she'd had in far too long could all-too-easily feature that pole… with Bill and a bunch of his male customers, egging her on. And wouldn't that be just dandy? From buck-naked sleepwalking to public orgasms—way to go, Kat!

Sheesh. She sooo needed to get laid. Pity there wasn't a chance in hell of that happening any time soon. She increased her pace, eager to grab her breakfast and head home before her fantasies got the better of her.

By the time she reached the main street, she felt in control again. Mostly. So long as she didn't let her mind wander. Lately she had sex on the brain like some horny teenager!

After a short detour to dump the rest of her flyers in the trash bin, she pushed open the door of the Main Street Café. As was her habit, she took her time checking all the mouthwatering goodies displayed in the cabinets.

"Dunno why you bother, Kat. You and me both know you're gonna have the usual." Phil, the café owner, waved a bag with a cinnamon roll-shaped bulge in Kat's direction.

She stuck her tongue out at him as he handed over the bag. And just because she felt like being contrary, she made a production out of opening it up and checking the contents. "What if I'd wanted a date scone? Or a… a… bran and pineapple muffin?"

Phil stuck his hands on his hips and cocked his head to one side. "So, you wanna change your mind and go for something other than a large latté to go and a cinnamon roll? Miracles do happen I guess."

She shook her head and heaved a sigh brimming with mock tragedy. "Nope. I guess I am just that predictable."

"You're not predictable. You're just a sucker for my cinnamon rolls. Best in the whole damn city, my cinnamon rolls. How could you resist such temptation, eh?" Phil kissed his fingers, going for an over-the-top Italian gesture. Not that he was the slightest bit Italian. He handed over her latté. "Here you go. One and a half sugars. Only for you would I do half a sugar. I mean, who has *half* a sugar? Go the whole hog and shoot for two, why don't you? Half is like pretending you're just a little bit knocked up."

Kat took a sip of her coffee and closed her eyes in blissful acknowledgment of the perfect brew. "Oh, that's sooo good. Phil, you're my hero." She batted her eyelashes at him as she handed over all the cash in her wallet. Which just happened to be the exact amount he'd rung up on the register. "See? Predictable."

The café owner guffawed. "See you tomorrow."

"Maybe. I'm watching my weight you know."

Phil gave one of his famous snorts. "Little bitty thing like you? When you've got a gut like this, then you start watching your weight." He patted his ample stomach. "See you tomorrow, Kat." He grinned and waggled his caterpillar-like eyebrows.

She rolled her eyes at his presumption. Not that she could take offense, because he was probably right and she would indeed see him tomorrow. And the day after. And the day after that.

Abruptly depressed by how mundane and predictable and—let's face it— plain *boring* her life had become, she lost all desire to linger and banter with the only real friend she had in this town. Even the sexy thrill of copping an eyeful of Buff Naked Guy in all his glory seemed tawdry and pathetic.

"Yeah. See you tomorrow, Phil." She turned on her heel and smacked right into someone's impressively muscled, white-T-shirted chest.

"Steady!" Big hands clasped her upper arms as she hunched protectively over her precious coffee. "That was close. You okay, sweetheart?"

"Yeah, I'm okay," she said, checking that the lid was still sitting nice and firm on her takeout cup. "Should have been watching where I was going. Sorry."

The hands stroked slowly, and firmly but gently, down her arms, then released her. "No harm done."

Kat shivered pleasurably in the wake of those hands on her bare skin. His touch had conjured up shockingly vivid carnal thoughts. Thoughts that had her pressing her thighs together against a rush of lust that set her nerve endings afire. Her skin felt hot and tight, ultra-sensitized, like she was running a mild fever.

Whoa. What was *that* all about?

She blinked, shaking her head to clear the sensual haze, and finally got around to glancing up at the guy who'd nearly worn her coffee. Her gaze lingered on a beautifully-shaped mouth with a quirky slant to the lips, like he knew something she didn't... and was enjoying the heck out of the knowledge. And then she connected with a startling blue-eyed gaze. A purely masculine, smugly knowing, gaze.

Whatever she'd been about to say turned into a strangled gargle.

"Remember me?" he said. His voice was deep, whiskey-smooth with just the barest undertone of roughness, and Kat's eyes practically crossed at the thought of his body—specifically what he might *do* with that body—matching his voice. Smooth seductions. Slow and sensual stroking, taking his time to savor every little bit of her. Such a delicious contrast to the rough, needy, want-you-right-now sex she knew just by looking at him that he would take pleasure in. Backing her up against the nearest wall and ramming that gorgeous cock into her until she screamed. Yes, please!

"Mmmm. Buff Naked Guy." Her voice sounded like a sensual purr, and so unlike her normal voice that it jolted her from her little x-rated fantasy.

Buff Naked Guy? Oh, no. No, no, no! Please tell me I didn't just say that aloud?

He grinned at her, his gaze eating her up in such a wholly masculine, wholly appreciative way, that her insides turned molten. "I see you do remember me," he said.

Kat bit her lips against a groan of despair. Crap. She *had* said it aloud.

His grin got even wider. And his eyes gleamed with the surety that he'd affected her deeply, sexually. And was smugly pleased by it. "Thanks for the compliment." He stuck out a hand. "Jace Burton."

Swallowing the lump of embarrassment in her throat, she juggled her coffee and the café bag so that she could shake his hand. And she tried not to squirm as her traitorous, sex-starved female parts instantly reacted, inner muscles clenching and nipples puckering into tight little nubs when she touched him.

"Kaaat," she said, ending on a breathy exhalation that, even to her, sounded like a sexual invitation.

He didn't release her hand, merely raised his eyebrows. And when his thumb stroked her palm, the warmth blooming through her body made her gasp. His scent curled through her senses. Combined with his aftershave, he smelled so sexy, so deliciously masculine, so enticing, that she wanted to rub herself up against him and beg him to pet her.

"Just Cat?"

"Kat Meyer. With a K. For Kat, that is. Not Meyer. 'Cause there's no K in Meyer. Obviously." Jeez, Louise! How lame was that? How lame was it to yearn for him to call her by her full name, *Katalina*? To want to hear how it sounded on his lips, even though she'd refused to answer to that name since some dork spread it around she'd been named after a Playboy model.

And how lame was she, panting over a stranger like some hormonal, up-tight female who hadn't sex in far too long? Which she was, of course. But he didn't need to know that.

She shrank back from him, tugging on her hand, needing to distance herself from this far-too-disturbing-for-her-peace-of-mind man. Sure, only a few minutes ago she'd been bemoaning her dull, boring existence, but coming face to face with Buff Naked Guy wasn't what she'd had in mind to spice up her life. It was enough of a shock to accidentally see a guy completely naked—not to mention aroused—and be overwhelmed by instant lust and carnal fantasies before she was even introduced to him. Even more disconcerting was her wicked desire to lean in and press her aching breasts against his chest and whisper in his ear exactly what she'd like him to do to her.

With him still touching her, anchoring her to him, she could barely think beyond her own desires. But she clung to one important piece of knowledge—the only thing that stopped her from taking that final step and coming on to him. If she wanted to get laid with no strings attached, Jace Burton was sooo not gonna be the guy she would choose. He was too... too... overwhelmingly male. He struck her as a guy who liked to call the shots and dictate how the relationship was gonna progress. Whereas she didn't want to be dictated to. Nyuh uh, not this time. She didn't want to get involved with another jerk-off alpha male who would sweep her off her feet and then expect to have everything his own way.

Sure, she wouldn't mind jumping Jace Burton's bones and riding him till he begged for mercy. But only for so long as it took to get this needy, lustful yearning out of her system. And then she'd give him his marching orders and hopefully never see him again.

Yeah. Like that was ever gonna be a possibility in Pressfield County, where everyone knew everyone. The gossip mill was so efficient that three quarters of the townsfolk knew your business before you did, and the other quarter had made pretty solid guesses. They would have her engaged, married, and expecting her first child before she could even sort out her true feelings, just like the last time. And look where that not-so-subtle pressure had gotten her? Her ex had screwed her every which way. Sexually, mentally and financially. Heck, she'd only just finished paying off the debts he'd run up in her name and stuck her with. Was it any wonder she had no time for men?

Except.... Now look at her, practically creaming her panties because she'd seen the guy naked, and he was holding her hand? Pathetic! She was acting like some female cat at the height of breeding season. Next, she'd be on all fours, waggling her butt in the air, begging Jace Burton to pet her. What on earth must he think of her?

What on earth must Phil, and every person in the café, think of her?

Jace gave her hand a squeeze before letting it go, and damned if it didn't feel like he'd somehow branded her as his own. "Nice to meet you, Kat-with-a-K," he said.

Her pulse raced, and she could feel the flush painting her cheeks blooming on her neck and chest, too. The coil of desire pulsing between her thighs wound tighter and tighter, and she shifted from one foot to the other in an effort to ease the throbbing ache. Cursing beneath her breath, she beat down what she very much feared was a prelude to an orgasm, and managed a smile. "Nice to meet you, too, Jace."

Except it wasn't "nice". Nothing about this man was nice. He was sinfully sexy. He attracted her in ways that scared her. And that made him dangerous. Because he could potentially turn her boring little life right on its head.

Before she could make any more of an idiot of herself, she dived for the door and vanished through the exit.

Jace sauntered over to the window, staring after Kat until she rounded a corner and disappeared from view. And thought about going after her, but decided to play it cool rather than spook her again. It was a small town. He was bound to run into Kat Meyer again.

He approached the cash register and was about to place his order when the guy manning the register spoke up. "What can I getcha, Mr. Buff?"

Jace shut his mouth with a snap and frowned, wondering whether he'd heard right. From the combative gleam sparking in the guy's eyes, he had. He hazarded a guess that the man felt protective of Kat. And figured he'd better work fast to diffuse the situation, 'cause despite the bright white, freshly laundered and well pressed apron straining over a huge gut, this guy was no softie. And he really had his back up.

"That'd be Jace Burton, to you, my friend," he said, extending his hand. "Your friendly accidental flasher. Who rolled outta bed this morning, wandered into the living room and yanked open the drapes, completely forgetting he wasn't in his high-rise apartment."

The gleam turned into something a touch more welcoming, and the man gripped his outstretched hand, squeezing it hard enough that Jace smothered a wince before his hand was released. "Phil Goodkind. As in, all kinds of good home-baking and the best damned coffee in town."

If the food and the coffee tasted as good as they smelled, then Jace had to agree with that boast. He'd figured on grabbing something for lunch because he hadn't stocked the fridge, and when he'd spotted Miss Kissable, AKA Kat-with-a-K, venturing inside this place, his choice of café had been decided for him. He was about to order a sandwich when Phil got in first with another question.

"You flashed Kat, huh? How'd she take it?"

Jace met Phil's amused gaze. "She gave me a head-to-toe once over that'd make any red-blooded male want to jump her. Then she turned tail and took off like the hounds of hell were on her heels." He blew out a rueful breath.

"Not surprising considering the state I was in after she finished checking me out. If you know what I mean."

Phil's jaw dropped. Then he huffed out a great bellow of laughter which startled one of his patrons into slopping coffee from her cup onto the tabletop. "Sweet Lord above! That poor girl is wound tighter than a corkscrew. 'Bout time she got herself another boyfriend. Or better still, just got laid. What can I get you, Jace?"

"I'll have a hot-roasted pork on rye, and an Americano to go." What the hey. No such thing as too much coffee. Especially when it was good coffee.

"Bet our Kat won't be forgetting you in a hurry," Phil said, snickering.

"Yeah. Great first impression." And speaking of first impressions…. Jace scratched the bristles on his chin and made a mental note to shave before his eleven a.m. with the mayor. "Let's hope she doesn't hold it against me."

"Man, if you're real lucky, that's exactly what she'll do," Phil said, and winked.

Jace didn't know whether to laugh at the guy's sallies, or get pissed on Kat Meyer's behalf.

Before he could form any sort of response, Phil said, "Last guy she got involved with was a first degree asshole. Took her for a ride, and then some. It's made her antsy as heck about her taste in men. I told her she should just relax, have some fun. Yanno, enjoy herself for a change. But does she listen to me? Nope. She takes up jogging." He rolled his eyes. "That's our Kat. But we love her, warts 'n all. So, what d'you do for a living, Jace?"

"I'm an architect."

"Lemme guess. You're the guy the town council commissioned to design the new public library and recreation centre complex, right?"

"That's right."

Phil handed over Jace's coffee and sandwich, and rung up an amount on the till that seemed far too low to be accurate. "Coffee's on the house. My way of saying welcome to our neck of the woods."

"Thanks." Jace took a sip.

"Good, huh?" Phil's tone conveyed the smug satisfaction of a master barista who knew his way around a coffee bean.

Jace inhaled and sighed his appreciation. "Yeah. Real good."

"I roast my own beans. Be seeing you. And good luck with Kat. You're sure gonna need it."

Jace paused mid-step, intending to call Phil on his comment, but the café owner was already serving another customer and the two were chatting away like old friends. Which, given what he knew about small town life, they probably were. He exited the café and headed for home, his mind on the woman who'd run away from him. Again.

He wasn't used to women running from him. He usually had the opposite problem—getting rid of them. Because no matter how upfront and brutally honest he was about what he wanted in a relationship, his partners invariably expected more, wanted more from him than he was prepared to give. And there'd be the inevitable tears and recriminations when he showed them the door.

But that was big-city women, with big-city agendas that he couldn't begin to fathom. Maybe here in Pressfield County he'd find a woman who wanted what he did. Nothing more than a real good time for the duration of his stay.

Despite Phil's intimating that Kat needed to cut loose, Jace didn't believe that she could be that woman. Aside from the red flag of a disastrous past relationship, all his instincts told him a woman like Kat would never be just a temporary distraction. He would bet his right arm that she would end up being a keeper, one of those rare women who got under his skin and turned his life upside down.

Jace didn't need that kind of complication in his life right now. Maybe never.

Even so, thoughts of her filled his mind, and damned if he didn't get another cock-stand, just like some horny teenager. Shit. He hadn't factored this complication into his upcoming meeting with the mayor. At this rate, he'd be giving the entire presentation sitting down.

Jace peered at his reflection in the mirror and straightened his tie. Better.

A glance at his wristwatch showed it was quarter to eleven. Plenty of time.

He spent five minutes meticulously rechecking the files he needed for the presentation before packing up his laptop. His standard CAD software would be more than adequate to showcase his various visions for the buildings to the mayor and his cronies. And once they approved a preliminary design, Jace would commission 3D architectural renderings of both the exterior and interior of the proposed buildings. These would be displayed in the foyer of the council chambers so that the townsfolk could see exactly what their taxes and fundraising efforts had been poured into. Hopefully, the feedback from today's meeting would be positive. But if he was completely off-base and the mayor hated every single one of his designs, he could walk away with impunity. It wasn't like he needed the money.

He was only slumming in this sleepy, quintessential small town—the same kind of town he'd been raised in and gotten the hell out of, the instant an opportunity presented itself—because Jen insisted that the many accolades he'd garnered had turned him from a pretty decent guy into an arrogant SOB.

And he kinda suspected his sister was right on the money. The past few years had been full-on work, work, work, and he suspected that if he kept up this breakneck pace, he risked burning out. He'd decided he needed a change of pace, needed to interact with real people, instead of sycophants and rivals who praised him in public, but were secretly eager for him to fall from the lofty heights he'd worked so damned hard to attain. He needed to chill, relax, get away from it all. And his subordinates were a talented bunch in their own right, more than capable of picking up the slack in his absence.

As much as he loathed to admit it, since he'd arrived in Pressfield County a week ago, he'd slept better in that insipidly decorated bedroom than he ever had in his fancy apartment. In fact, he couldn't remember the last time he'd slept through the night without waking and inevitably giving up on sleep and switching on the TV or leafing through an industry magazine.

He hefted his briefcase and was pleased to note that his mashed finger hadn't given him much of a twinge at all. He swapped the briefcase to his left hand and checked out the injury. The bruising had faded to the merest hint of grubby-looking shadow and the swelling had all but disappeared. Excellent. His granddad's ring would be back where it belonged, safely on Jace's finger. But when he checked the saucer, where he knew he'd left it, the ring was gone.

He swore a blue streak as he scanned the kitchen. He even got down on hands and knees to pat his hands over the floor, but came up empty-handed. He forced himself to calm down and think logically. Must have stashed it somewhere for safekeeping, and it had slipped his mind. He could almost hear Jen teasing him about getting forgetful in his old age.

"Shit!" Nearly eleven already. If he didn't get a move on, he was gonna be late for the meeting. He didn't have time to look for the missing ring now, but when he got back he would search the house from top to bottom. Provided he didn't remember where he'd stashed it in the meantime. Which he was confident he would once he put his mind to it.

Grabbing his briefcase and his laptop bag, he sprinted for the door.

The mayoral offices were an easy ten-minute walk from Jace's house. He did it in five. And at a couple of minutes past eleven, he was shown into the meeting room by Mayor Evans's PA. Who just happened to be the same chirpy young woman whose phone call had awakened him this morning. She was also a very attractive young woman. And, by her blatant perusal of the fit of his trousers, she had definite potential for the kind of casual relationship Jace was looking for.

"Mayor Evans will be with you shortly," she said. "He's finishing a call."

"No problem. I'll just make myself comfortable." He was so busy communicating his interest in getting to know the young woman better that he didn't even register there was another person in the room until that person cleared her throat.

"Hey, Laurel. How about you quit drooling over Mr. Burton and I'll take it from here."

Jace's head whipped around, and he fell headlong into a highly amused, and somewhat resigned, deep green gaze. "Kat?"

"Hi Jace," she said. "Something tells me you're not here to take down the minutes of the meeting?"

"You two have met?" Some of the PA's sultry eagerness slid from her face.

"We sure have," Kat agreed.

"Twice, actually," Jace said, and thoroughly enjoyed the pink highlights which splashed across her cheeks. He knew that she was thinking about their first encounter. Because he was, too. He drank in the expressions flitting across her face. He knew exactly how she was feeling when she pressed the back of her hand to her forehead and let her eyelids drift down to hide just how totally turned on and revved up she was. Because he was totally turned on and revved up, too.

And when her gaze slid from his, and she cleared her throat, and then rose from her chair to grab a cup of water from the cooler, he got even more revved up. Her form fitting, just-above-the-knee skirt lovingly cupped her butt. Glimpsed through the slit in the back of the skirt, those superbly toned legs were sensational, even in low heels. He found himself wondering whether she wore hose or stockings. And hoping for the latter. With lacy tops. That he could roll down her legs. Or maybe not. Maybe he'd leave them on....

Kat took her seat and crossed her legs. Her skirt rode up her thighs. Jace almost quit breathing.

"I see," the PA said. Then, when neither party bothered to respond, she flounced from the room, shutting the door a little too firmly behind her.

Jace stared at Kat, who pretended not to notice and sipped her water.

Watching her toy with her disposable cup, lifting the cup to her lips to drink, licking water droplets from her lips, only made him hotter and harder. If that was possible.

The mayor, Paulie Evans, burst into the meeting room. "Sorry 'bout that, Mr. Burton. I couldn't get the wife off the damn phone. You know how it is. Shall we get started?"

"Get started on what?" Kat said, in a voice so husky and downright sexy that Jace's cock actually jerked and thickened, like she'd wrapped her soft little hand around him. Or better still, her lips. He swallowed a groan, shifting in his chair.

"Mr. Burton, I'd like you to meet Kat Meyer," the mayor said.

"You can call me Jace."

"I know," Kat murmured.

Paulie raised his eyebrows at her. "You all right, Kat? You seem a bit distracted."

She blinked, then flushed with mortification, exactly like a good girl caught behind the bike shed with a bad boy. And Jace knew all about that because he'd often been one of those bad boys.

"Sorry," she said. "Just, er, caught up in envisioning how some floor tiles I've found would look in the library entranceway."

Jace might have grinned at her obvious discomfort if the reason that she was present for this meeting hadn't just slapped him upside the head.

Damn. He smothered a wry chuckle, wondering why he felt so darned let down and disappointed. It wasn't like she'd just grown horns and a forked tail, and threatened to skewer him with a pitchfork.

No way was he keen to get into her panties now. She was a professional clash of ideas and opinions just waiting to happen. Especially if she'd been led to believe she would have input into the building design process.

He'd worked before with interior designers who thought their opinions deserved to be taken seriously. The result was inevitably a ton of extra problems. The only people he would tolerate interfering were builders—provided they knew their stuff.

So no way was sexy little Kat Meyer gonna poke her cute little nose into his business while he worked on this project. Not gonna happen. No fucking way.

Just like he wouldn't be fucking her, no matter how darned sexy, and sweet, and endearing, she might be. If they were going to be working together, it was imperative he keep their relationship professional.

Or at least that's what he told himself.

But, as he watched her nibbling on her lower lip, his cock had other ideas. And when she wriggled in her chair, obviously trying to get comfortable, and cast a glance at him from beneath her lashes and then blushed again, his brain hit him with a vivid image of advancing around the meeting table, grabbing her by her immaculate lapels and stripping off that staid, businesslike suit to rediscover the real woman beneath. The real woman that he'd seen this morning with her ripe breasts and taut belly and peach-shaped ass.

Oh yeah. He'd like to cup the firm globes of that lovely ass, lift her up and spread her out atop the huge table like some feast prepared especially in his honor. And then, when he had her arranged to his liking, he'd nuzzle and lick and lap his way down that hot little body. Bite, taste and tease until she squirmed and begged him to fuck her. And when he'd finished feasting on her, he'd unzip his trousers, pull out his aching cock, and—

"Shall we get started, Jace?"

Paulie Evans's question yanked him back to the here and now. And the realization that he had a hard-on tenting his trousers that wasn't gonna subside any time soon. Not with Kat's surreptitious gazes flicking him like electrically charged little whips. Not when every time he glanced her way, she wriggled beneath his gaze like she was somehow sensing and reacting to what he was thinking about her. And whenever she did that, all he could see was an x-rated image of her that was apparently permanently burned into his retinas.

It was the worst kind sexual torture. He had to get out of there.

"Would you give me just a couple of minutes, Mayor Evans?" he said, fumbling in his jacket pocket for his mobile. "I, er, have to take this call. It's my, uh, sister. Family emergency. Won't be a moment." Grabbing his briefcase and holding it so that it shielded his groin, he bolted from the room.

Chapter 3

Paulie Evans shook his head in mock despair. "Typical big city type. Man's wound tighter than an inner-sprung mattress."

Mattress.

Bed.

Jace on a bed.

Her bed. Oh yeah….

"I didn't hear his cell ring," Paulie said.

"Huh? Oh. He, uh, probably had it on vibrate." Kat clenched her thighs at the mere thought of anything with the ability to vibrate being anywhere near her right now. She was losing control, losing herself, her rational mind consumed by lust and desire and a throbbing, burning need to have sex. *Now.*

It was like she truly was in heat, a hapless female driven by the instinct to mate. She fought it, but it was a losing battle. Her pussy was throbbing and her panties were damp—again. There was a damned fine chance she'd come on the spot if Jace subjected her to one more of those I-wanna-lick-you-all-over looks.

Could he possibly be as turned on by her, as she was by him? Surely he wouldn't mind being fucked to within an inch of his life. He was a man, after all. Doubtless he would be more than willing to oblige her.

The thought was so tantalizing, so compelling, that she was out of her chair, across the room, and opening the door before it occurred to her that Paulie might consider her sudden departure rude. She swiveled to face him, leaning against the doorway to catch her breath. And she hit him with what she hoped was a suitably apologetic smile. "Sorry, Paulie," she purred. "I simply have to go to the little girl's room."

Paulie blinked. "Uh, sure thing, Kat." He began to rustle through some papers.

"Won't be long." She shut the door behind her. She sucked in a deep breath and caught a whiff of aftershave.

Gotcha! She headed for the bathrooms. That's where Jace would be hiding out. She knew it, could sense it. The phone call had been a fake, just an excuse to take a moment to compose himself.

The thrill of the chase thrummed through her veins, urging her into a run.

She burst through the door to the men's bathroom without a by-your-leave. And when she spotted Jace bent over a hand basin, splashing water over his face, she made a mewling sound of appreciation. His ass was simply sublime.

Jace glanced up. His eyes widened. He straightened and reached for a paper towel to mop his dripping face.

She slinked over to him and plucked the towel from his hand. She wound her arms about his neck, pressed her breasts against his chest, and rubbed her cheek against his.

"Kat, what the—?"

She cut short his protests with an open-mouthed kiss right on his lips. He tasted sooo good. She licked the seam of his lips, suckled his tongue, thrust her own tongue into his mouth. And when he responded in kind, she unhooked one arm from his neck and stroked it down his chest, down his abs, down the front of his trousers. She squeezed the hard length of his cock and felt it jerk in response.

Yes. He wanted her all right. Real bad. Just like she wanted him.

He grasped her ass, squeezed and kneaded, and she encouraged him with tiny growls of pleasure against his mouth as she unbuckled his belt and unzipped his fly. She yanked down the front of his briefs, eager to get her hands on him, eager to stroke his naked flesh.

When she fisted his cock, he wrenched his mouth from hers and snarled her name like a warning. "Kat."

"Jace." The head of his cock was velvety soft, the tip slick with pre-come. She worked him with her hand, tightening her grip when his shaft thickened and he thrust into her hand.

Her pussy throbbed, inner muscles tightening and releasing in a rhythm that demanded she do something to fill the emptiness inside her. All sense of propriety had fled. She didn't care if someone walked in and saw them. She didn't care what anyone might think. She didn't even care what Jace might think. She. Just. Wanted. Him.

Now.

"Are you sure about this?" he asked, his voice rasping and uneven. "Be very sure. Because if you keep on with that—God! I'm not… I'm not gonna be able to stop where this is leading."

She let go of his cock. Ignoring his groan of half dismay, half relief, she sashayed over to the door. She heard his sigh and a rustle of clothing, and knew he believed that she'd chickened out. Huh. Not a chance. She turned and leaned her back against the door. Thrusting out her hips, she skimmed her hands beneath her skirt and shimmied out of her panties. When she balled them up and chucked them at him, hitting the side of his face, she had his full attention.

She hitched her skirt up around her waist, dipped her fingers between her slick, wet folds, and looked him in the eye. "I need you to fuck me, Jace. I can barely think because I need you inside me."

He tucked her panties into his trouser pocket and strode toward her, unbuckling and unzipping as he went. He fished a condom from his wallet, letting the wallet drop to the floor as he sheathed himself. His gaze was hot and heated, and when he lifted her up so that she could wrap her legs around his hips, the musky scent of his arousal coated her tongue.

She nuzzled his neck, licking him, tasting him. Delicious. She ached for him to fill her. Her internal muscles clenched so strongly that she shuddered. "Fuck me, Jace. I want your cock inside me."

He slid his hands beneath her thighs, forcing them wider, positioning her so his cock nudged the entrance of her pussy. And then he lowered her onto that gorgeous, thick shaft of flesh.

Kat moaned against his neck as he filled her, stretched her. And clutched his shoulders as he pressed her against the door so that he could thrust into her. Ahhh. Yes. This was what she wanted.

"God," he said. "I fantasized about doing this to you."

His long, slow strokes teased her, stoking her lust. And every time his cock withdrew, she wanted him deep inside her again. "Harder. Fuck me harder." She bit his neck just hard enough to mark him with her teeth.

He held her still and rammed his cock into her. "Yesssss!" she hissed. "Like that."

She dug her nails into his shoulders, her body straining, thigh muscles clenching around his hips, inner muscles coiling tight, tighter. He pistoned his hips, thrusting into her pussy with such force that her butt slammed against the door.

"Jace. Oh God, Jaaace!"

One more stroke, this one so deep that she bit her lips against a yowl of pleasure. And then he emptied himself in her.

Kat came back to reality when Jace's cock slid from her pussy and he lowered her to the floor. She leaned back against the door and stared at him. Omigod. Oh. My. God. What the hell had come over her?

She couldn't think what to say, so she yanked down her skirt. He appeared to be at a loss for words, too, for he backed off and turned away from her to dispose of the condom.

While his attention was elsewhere, it was suddenly easier to run rather than face him. She hightailed it out of the bathroom and tried to calm the zinging of her stimulated nerve endings to manageable-in-public levels by smoothing her hair and scrubbing any remaining lipstick from her mouth with the back of her hand. Barely there, pale pink had been a fortuitous choice.

She paused with one hand on the meeting room door, swallowed a couple of times, and entered the room. Hopefully, Jace wouldn't be back for a couple of minutes, and that would be long enough to give her time to pull herself together before she had to face him again.

Shit! He still had her panties!

She shook herself like a wet cat. Too bad. Time to get down to business.

"Sorry about that, Paulie," she said, as she took her seat. "I have color swatches and samples if you'd like to take a look while we're waiting on Mr. Burton. And I've done preliminary costs based on—"

Paulie waved her to silence. "Look, Kat. If it were up to me, you'd be the only choice for this project. Which is why I gave you a head start by inviting you along to this meeting with our hotshot, big-city architect. So you could get a feel for him."

Kat's eyes almost crossed at his unfortunate choice of words, and all the heightened sexual awareness that she'd been so desperately suppressing smothered her in another breath-stealing wave. She muttered about the heat and fanned her face as she fought to concentrate.

"What exactly are you trying to say, Paulie? I thought I was the *only* choice for this project."

The mayor's gaze slid away. "Yes, well. I had it pointed out to me by Marina and Julia that there are certain ways of doing things. It's those two you have to impress. If they sway the vote you're screwed. And I won't be able to overturn a majority decision without causing a stink."

"Marina and Julia." Kat's breath hissed out from between her clenched teeth. "Do I even want to know who our two most contrary councillors are backing for this contract?"

Paulie gave her sympathetic eyes. "House of Hamilton Interiors."

Kat felt her hackles rising. Marina and Julia had recently had their houses redecorated by guess who. The three women were thick as thieves. "Gena Hamilton. After the mess she made of the Gallagher's place? You have got to be kidding me."

"I wish I was," Paulie said.

"God help us! We'll have a library that resembles the interior of some ruddy English country mansion rather than someplace comfortable, welcoming and kid-friendly. And I shudder to even imagine the rec center. It'll probably—"

Paulie held up a hand to halt her tirade. "As much as I don't personally get off on Gena's designs, she does run a very successful business." He leaned forward in his chair and pinned her with a disproving look that made her feel like a kid called to the principal's office.

Uh oh….

"And I'm no pussy-whipped pushover, either," he said. "If House of Hamilton Interiors does get this contract, I reckon I'm more than capable of toning down Gena's worst excesses, even if she is Sheriff Wade's sister. No way am I gonna let some hoity toity, wannabe society princess stick the town with something barely functional. Trust me on that!"

Kat could feel the lump of dismay forming in her throat. Paulie had tried to do her a favor, and instead of being professional and keeping her cool, she'd acted like a spoiled brat denied a treat. These days her temper flared at the slightest provocation. It was like she'd woken up the morning after that Chinese New Year's dinner a completely different person. Sheesh! She was never eating Chinese again.

She ducked her head and wondered how to smooth things over. But her innate honesty won out, so she just said what needed to be said. "Shit. Me 'n my big mouth. I'm sorry, Paulie. You know I'm grateful for this opportunity, and you know I respect the hell out of you. It's just…." She tugged on the end of her ponytail. "Regardless how I feel about Gena's designs, I have every confidence that you can handle her."

That last was a bald-faced lie. When Gena got the bit between her teeth there was no stopping her. Despite her sweeter than apple pie public face, the woman could do a first-class impression of pure bitch.

But, Kat wasn't going to roll over on this one. She'd been coveting this contract ever since the townspeople had started fundraising to replace the burned-out shells of the old library and rec center. Winning this contract would be a real feather in her cap. It'd be a step in the right direction, which was expanding her talents into commercial interior design. Sure, she loved working on private homes, but commercial was more challenging, more lucrative.

"The real bitch of it all is that Gena hasn't even shown the slightest interest in the contract until now," she muttered.

Paulie reached over to pat her hand. "It's all right, Kat. I know you have the best interests of the local folks at heart. But I gotta do this above board. We have to accept all proposals put forward and put them to the vote. So far, we've got three, and—"

"Three?" Kat winced at her own voice. It'd sounded like an outraged yowl. She took a sip of water and made an effort to modulate her tone. "Who's the other proposal from?"

"My wife's best friend's best friend," Paulie said. And had the grace to look shamefaced. "Sorry, Kat. I know this sucks, but if your proposal's solid, you'll be a shoo-in."

Kat wasn't so sure. But she smiled gamely just as Jace cleared his throat and re-entered the meeting room. Shit! How much had he heard? She didn't want him thinking that she was a prima donna or that Paulie was doing her favors.

"Sorry about that," he said. "The call took a bit longer than I expected." He didn't once glance Kat's way as he took out his laptop. While it powered up, he launched into an introduction of his vision for the new complex.

And when he pulled down the overhead screen and started his PowerPoint presentation, Kat could hardly believe that the clipped voice highlighting various architectural features belonged to the same man who'd just fucked her up against a door and probably still had her panties in his pocket. Talk about major personality transplant.

But that was good—real good—because now, listening to this cold, poker-faced professional, it was far easier to take a step back and convince herself she'd gotten him out of her system.

Relief coursed through her veins. Now she didn't have to worry about getting distracted. Now she could concentrate on the only thing that mattered: winning this contract from Gena Hamilton. She shoved all thoughts of Jace Burton from her mind. No more "Buff Naked Guy". He was "the architect". Nothing more.

Chapter 4

Jace found a vacant bench seat in the town square amongst a bunch of other people enjoying the sun and the fresh air. His stomach rumbled, and he took out the sandwich he'd bought from the café. As he ate, he reviewed the meeting. Paulie Evans had been impressed and enthusiastic about his preliminary designs, showing a definite preference for the same one Jace preferred. The man had excellent taste.

And speaking of excellent taste….

Kat Meyer had tasted damn fine—rich and exotic—and she smelled that way, too. Her scent and her taste still lingered, haunting him. As did the pair of her panties he still had in his pocket.

Damn the woman. She'd turned him into some besotted teenage boy who couldn't keep his dick in his pants. She'd seduced him, scratched her itch, and headed straight back into the meeting room to chat with the fucking mayor like nothing had happened and she wasn't bare-assed!

He'd figured two could play that game, so he'd done his best to ignore her. But damn, it had been hard—in more freaking ways than one.

She hadn't been fazed or had any difficulty keeping her mind on her work. She'd kept her delectable, incredibly kissable lips shut and busied herself with taking copious notes. She hadn't even voiced an opinion, despite being pressed by Paulie. And though he was relieved she hadn't waded in with some airy-fairy, ill-conceived plan for improving his designs, he couldn't help but wonder, had it really just been about sex for her?

Sure, he hadn't expected to her go gaga over his designs, but no feedback or reaction at all had been like a kick in his aching, sex-on-the-brain, crotch. His designs, all three of them, were fucking brilliant. And hot'n heavy sex in the bathroom aside, he'd expected at least a glimmer of approval from her.

But she'd given him nothing. Nothing except for occasional glimpses of cool, calm, professional eyes before she bent her head to scribble industriously on her pad. He supposed he'd gotten exactly what he'd been looking for. He'd been expertly seduced by one seriously hot woman, who was apparently eager for there to be no strings attached. What guy wouldn't be happy with that outcome?

Apparently, not him.

She'd acted like the sex meant nothing, like it was completely forgettable. Same with his presentation. It was a major blow to his ego, both on a professional *and* a personal level.

Dismissing the puzzle that was Kat-with-a-K Meyer from his mind, he strolled back to his house. And spent the remainder of the afternoon searching for his grandfather's ring.

Shit!

He moved the couch back to its original position, scrubbed his fingers through his hair, and threw himself full-length on the it to brood. In his mind's eye, he retraced his actions after he'd done that dumbass trick of catching his finger between the weights while unpacking them.

He'd examined his hand, seen the beginnings of some killer bruising and the first stages of swelling, and realized with a jolt that if he didn't get the ring off pretty fucking quick, he'd be up shit creek. So he'd sprinted to the kitchen sink, squirted a load of that nauseating floral dish detergent over his hand, lubed up his finger, and frantically tried to work the ring over his rapidly swelling knuckle. It'd hurt like forty bastards, and he'd cut loose with a string of curses that would have had impressed even his potty-mouthed sister, but he'd gotten the ring off. And then he'd rinsed it under the tap and plunked it on a saucer by the sink.

His next action had been to grab some ice and attend to his injury.

That had been five days ago. And he'd swear on his grandfather's grave that he hadn't touched the ring or moved it since. Of that he was one-hundred-percent certain, even if he couldn't be certain exactly when the ring had gone missing from the saucer.

He closed his eyes and pinched the bridge of his nose. And, as he did when he had a design problem to work through, let his mind drift toward a solution. Or, in this case, something that might explain the mystery.

An image of cat hairs swirling down the drain popped into his head. Rather than banish the image as inconsequential, he let the thought run its course.

Cat hairs.

Pet cat.

Stray cat.

Cat-flap.

Cat… burglar?

And hard on the heels of that flight of fancy came an image of Kat Meyer, dressed in some slinky, black Lycra outfit, prowling through his house. And into his bedroom. Where she stripped off that sexy cat-suit, climbed into his bed, and woke him in the best way a woman could wake a man.

Now there was a dilemma worth solving. How to get Kat Meyer into his bed. Or on the couch. Or even up against a door a second time. He didn't much care where. He just wanted her. Even though he knew it was a stupid-ass thing to want because every instinct screamed at him that pursuing a relationship with her would end up being complicated. And messy. And for once, he wouldn't be able to walk away with impunity.

Images of what he would like to do to her cascaded through his mind. Bending her back over his arm and suckling those handfuls of pert breasts. Delving his tongue into her navel and watching those taut stomach muscles clench. Licking the silky soft skin of her inner thighs and parting her folds with his fingers, opening her to his hungry mouth and thrusting tongue. Sucking her clit and licking her creamy pussy, screwing his fingers deep inside her, relentlessly, until she writhed and screamed and came—

The phone blared, jerking him from his steamy fantasy.

He didn't even remember shoving his hand down his pants. But there he was, sprawled on the couch, one hand fisted around his hard, aching cock.

Huh. A hand job. This was what Kat-with-a-K Meyer reduced him to.

He let the answering machine pick up the call while he got himself together. It was only his 2IC with an update on the project Jace had handed over to him before leaving for Pressfield County.

Jace rolled off the couch to his feet. He'd have a shower and get his shit sorted before he rang the guy back. And with the zipper of his pants rubbing against his still hard cock, he figured he'd better make it a cold shower. Again. All because of one hot-as-hell, green-eyed, pony-tailed woman, who was doing his head in.

And he'd only met her this morning. Shit. He was so screwed.

After a cold shower which left him in a foul mood, Jace headed for the kitchen to check the contents of the fridge. The vast, empty space reminded him he still hadn't shopped for groceries. With a resigned sigh, he grabbed a phone directory and turned to the takeout section.

He'd just decided on Chinese when a slight movement from the cat-flap in the side door caught his attention. Probably a stray gust of wind.

He wandered over to check out whether there was any way to secure it and prevent the hinged plastic door from flapping back and forth.

The cat-flap was sparkling clean, its plastic window free of grime. He caught a whiff of Windex. Seemed his landlady had polished the cat-flap *and* all the windows. He squatted on his haunches to examine the flap more closely and spotted a few short black hairs caught in one of the two sliding latches.

Just like the ones in the sink.

Probably a neighbor's cat. Or a stray.

Aha! The flap's latches could be set to different modes. He moved a latch and tested the flap by pressing on it with his palm. No movement. Problem solved. No more cheeky bloody moggies would be drinking from his kitchen sink.

Nothing like adding an item to the sheriff's "cat stash" to pour cold water on the heat of her unholy lust for I'm-Too-Sexy-For-My-Clothes Jace Burton.

As usual, Sheriff Wade and his deputy had acted like Kat's cat-burglar situation was the funniest damn thing they'd heard of in years. They'd been saving up a bunch of new "pussy" jokes especially for her next visit, and they hit her with them the instant she walked in the door. They were even running a betting pool on whether Cupcake's next underwear procurement would be boxers or a thong. Sheesh. How old were they? Twelve?

When the sheriff mentioned to be sure and tell Grandma Louise that he'd been asking after her, Kat got a bit of her own back by threatening to bring Louise down for a little chat with her two favorite men. The panic on their faces until she'd let them off the hook had been worth the lie. But, as she sauntered down the street toward home, the glee of having bested the two men seeped out of her. There wasn't a heckuva lot to rejoice over when you had a kleptomaniac cat to cope with and a grandma who liked to race mobility scooters. Oh, and you'd just had the best damn sex of your life with a guy you barely knew, and now you couldn't quit thinking about him.

It'd be just her luck to somehow bypass all her security precautions tonight, and for Sheriff Wade to discover her wandering naked around the streets in the wee small hours.

Yep. That would be the last freaking straw. She'd have to up-stakes and move across state because she'd never live that one down.

Kat rubbed her eyes and yawned. The first draft of her proposal was looking pretty darned good, but it still needed a heap of work. She might have made better progress if she hadn't been so distracted by thoughts of Jace. How was she ever going to face him again? She had no idea. Just like she still had no idea what on earth had prompted her to follow him into the men's bathroom and come on to him like a total slut.

Rampant hormones sure had a lot to answer for!

He was pretty impressive, though. Both personally and professionally. His designs were stunning, and his presentation had been incredibly detailed. She now had a more concrete idea of how far she'd have to make the allocated budget go. So long as she didn't go overboard with fancy, top-of-the-line fixtures for the main gymnasium's bathrooms and showers, the rec center would be pretty straightforward.

The library posed the biggest problem. She envisioned an area strewn with comfortable chairs and couches, plus sturdy desks for the computers. Add good quality, hard-wearing carpet, wall-coverings and blinds, plus furnishings for the staff area out back, and it'd be too easy to get carried away. She needed to be disciplined. And she needed to come in substantially below budget to have the best chance of winning this contract.

The screeds of numbers displayed in the spreadsheet on her computer monitor blurred, and she yawned again. Widely. And when she could no longer make the slightest sense of what she was looking at, she gave in to her fatigue and promised herself she'd get an early start tomorrow. She struggled from the chair, rubbed the circulation back into her numb backside, and stumbled into her bedroom.

Cupcake was curled up on the end of her bed, twitching and giving tiny mews as he dreamed of whatever it was cats dreamed. Chasing mice most likely.

Kat snorted softly. Oh, for the gift of a mouse rather than another piece of jewelry. Maybe overnight Cupcake would revert to being a normal cat again. One could always hope.

Much as it was tempting to do a face-plant onto the bed and sleep fully clothed, she stripped off her comfy sweatpants and T-shirt, and pulled on a pair of sleep shorts and a matching singlet. She climbed into bed, and the instant her head touched the pillow, exhaustion grabbed her and pulled her down into sleep.

She awoke in the dead of night. Naked.

Nothing unusual about that lately.

But this wasn't her bed. And *that* was definitely unusual.

Her sleepwalking excursions always ended with her crawling back to bed. So where the heck had she strayed to this time?

She patted the surface with her palms. It felt like she was lying on… leather? Her vision adjusted to the gloom, and she blinked at an expanse of white, highlighted by wan moonlight filtering through filmy drapes.

A white leather couch.

A frisson iced her spine and she rubbed her arms. This room was achingly familiar. So why did she feel so uneasy, so displaced?

She sat up and glanced around, mentally cataloging the contents of the room. From the white leather couch, to the four matching easy chairs, and even the thick pile of the plush carpet beneath her feet—

Omigod!

Panic clawed her mind, overriding all caution. She simply reacted, exploding into motion. And in her haste, she slammed her knee into a coffee table, its black lacquered surface relegated to a mere shadow by the inky blackness of the carpet.

She clapped her hand over her mouth to smother her scream of pain, and hopped about, rubbing her knee, as silent tears trickled down her cheeks. To her dismay, she stubbed her toe against a magazine rack, lost her balance and lurched into one of the beautiful standard lamps she'd been so thrilled to source at cost. She grabbed for it, but she was too slow. She could only watch in silent horror as it toppled to the carpet, landing with a shockingly loud *thud!* and the devastating tinkle of broken glass.

Chapter 5

Jace jerked to wakefulness with his heart thudding, wondering what had woken him. The silence of the house was soothing, and sleep beckoned seductively. Until he heard a dull creak. All houses creaked and groaned as foundations settled, and wood and metal expanded and contracted with changes of temperature. But this sound, this was like the creak of floorboards muffled by carpet…. When someone was walking on them.

He rolled out of bed, dragged on his jeans and tip-toed from his room. At the entrance to the lounge he paused, allowing his eyesight to adjust. There. A shadow that was completely out of place because it was in motion.

"Oi!" he bellowed, as he hit the lights. "What the fuck do you think you're doing in my house?"

A shriek echoed through the room, but with the brightness searing his eyes, he couldn't immediately focus on the intruder.

A moan reached his ears. The moan became a sob, which escalated into despairing howls of a distinctly feminine kind. They tore his heart to shreds because at some instinctive level, he recognized their owner.

After a moment of rapid blinking to clear the black blobs cavorting through his vision, he spotted her. She was crouched on the floor by the shattered remains of a lamp. His gut clenched at the shame and misery etched on her face. "Kat? What are you doing here?"

She buried her face in her hands and turned away from him. It was only then, when a corner of his bemused mind noted that the long, dark hair cascading down her back provided a perfect foil to the stark vulnerability of her spine and her pale skin, that he realized she was completely naked.

"What the fuck is going on?" he wondered aloud. And then regretted the words when he saw her body wracked by another huge, sobbing howl.

He skirted the broken glass and approached her cautiously, as though she were a wounded animal. "Kat. Sweetheart. It's okay. I'm not gonna hurt you, I promise."

She flinched when he touched her, but didn't protest when he tugged her to her feet. Heartened, he gathered her into his arms. "You wanna tell me what's up?"

"I-I have a p-problem," she said, snuggling into his chest and nuzzling him like a kitten.

His brain tossed up a few possible scenarios. A burning desire to retrieve her panties combined with chronic exhibitionism? Some weirdo prank she'd been dared to pull by her friends? Or perhaps she was a stalker-type whacko. None of them fit what little he knew of her, so he only said, "Oh?"

She shivered and burrowed into what scant warmth he offered. His arms tightened reflexively around her. "Spill," he said. "Whatever it is, it can't be that bad."

He hoped.

"I-I s-sleepwalk!" she said, making it sound like the eighth deadly sin. "I s-strip off my pajamas and w-wander 'round n-naked!" Her voice had risen to a wail that bordered on hysteria.

Naked sleepwalking? Jace loosed a burst of relieved laughter, which promptly choked off when she whacked him on the chest with her fist.

"It's not funny!" she said. And pulled from his embrace to stalk toward the kitchen.

He figured she was headed toward the side door. He followed, admiring the sway of her ass for all of five wonderful, world-stopping seconds before he realized that chivalry was not yet dead. Her hand was already reaching for the door handle when he said, "No, it's not funny. I imagine it would be pretty darn humiliating. Which is why you definitely shouldn't go wandering about like that a second time."

She paused, hand outstretched.

"Unless you just happened to drive to my place, of course. Can sleepwalkers drive cars while they're, er, sleepwalking, d'you think?"

Her arm dropped to her side. Her shoulders sagged, and the straight line of her spine curved into a protective hunch. "I don't know," she said, her voice barely above a whisper. "I don't even own a car."

Funny how the dirty mind Jen always enjoyed accusing him of having didn't kick in. He didn't imagine Kat running bare-assed through the streets—even though that image was a fantasy fit to make any red-blooded male go *Booyah!* Here he was with a naked woman in his house, a totally hot naked woman he'd been fantasizing about all freaking day, and instead of the mother of all boners, he had a gigantic case of protectiveness.

He could see her trembling and quivering like she was on the verge of shock, and even if she had driven here, no way would he let her get behind the wheel until he made certain she was okay. But if he attempted to touch her again, he suspected she'd bolt. And he'd have to go after her. And if anyone spotted them, he'd have to explain why he, a guy who'd only been in town a few days and was charging the folks of Pressfield County mega-bucks for his services, was chasing a naked woman he barely knew. At this hour of the morning, inventiveness wasn't really his forte.

"Right. How about I find you some clothes and we try'n figure out how you ended up here." Or more specifically *in* here. Because he knew darn well he'd locked both external doors before turning in for the night.

She angled her body slightly, just enough to meet his gaze over one shoulder. "That would be great. Thanks."

Her eyes sparkled with unshed tears, and the expression on her face.... Misery. Humiliation. Despair. Take your pick. Combine it with strained, far-too-pale features, and it was obvious she was traumatized.

He gulped and scrubbed his hands through his hair, hyper-aware that he didn't want to screw this up. "Uh, do you want to stay here while I get you some clothes? Or do you want to wait someplace else? Like, in the lounge?"

"I'll wait here."

"Okay. Won't be a minute." And true to his word, he broke all speed records getting back to his bedroom, grabbing clothing from his drawers, and returning to the kitchen. He found her perched on a stool behind the breakfast bar, staring out the kitchen window and facing away from him.

"Sweatpants and a T-shirt okay?" he said, coming up behind her and dropping the clothes on the bar. "Your, uh, panties are there, too."

When she didn't make a move, he backed off and headed toward the kitchen cupboards. "I have a hankering for hot chocolate. Want some? Reckon you could probably do with a sugar fix about now."

"Yes. Please. Thanks."

He set the mugs on the counter. "Uh, might just grab myself a T-shirt, first. It's a bit chilly. Be with you in a bit." He walked off without a second glance, and sure enough, by the time he'd grabbed a T-shirt, dragged it over his head, and returned to the kitchen, she was fully clothed. And squirming atop her stool like someone had their hands down her pants. In fact, her face was so flushed, if he hadn't known better, he'd have thought she was sexually aroused. Again.

He didn't push her, just let her be while he heated milk, grated chocolate into a saucepan, and added extra sugar because that was the way Jen usually liked it and sugar was supposed to be good when dealing with shock. When he'd stirred the mixture smooth, he tested the temperature with his finger. "Yeow! Shit! Guess that's hot enough, huh?"

He sucked his reddened, painful finger, and the faces he made provoked a tired smile from his unexpected guest. He poured chocolate into the mugs. "Let's go sit in the lounge. Those barstools are a mite uncomfortable."

He waited for her to choose the couch, then handed her a mug and settled into the easy-chair opposite. "So. Wanna talk about it?"

She curled up in the chair, cupped both hands around her mug and sighed. "Not much to talk about, really. Among other weirdness in my life at present, I've suddenly started sleepwalking again."

"Again?"

She took a sip of her chocolate and seemed to be contemplating whether to fob him off or spill. He could hardly blame her. They might have had sex, but he was practically a stranger.

"This whole sleepwalking nonsense happened once before," she said.

"When I was a kid. Lasted for a year and then I grew out of it, I guess. Evidently my embarrassing little problem has come back to bite me on the ass. With a vengeance. But it wasn't so bad this time because I've managed to limit my nightly wanderings to the privacy of my own home. At least, until now." Her attempt at a wry laugh was pretty pathetic. "Seems deadlocked doors and security latched windows just can't keep me in anymore."

"A genuine Houdini. Outstanding."

That got a proper laugh, and it warmed his soul that she seemed to be recovering from her shock. "You mentioned other weirdness in your life. Anything I can help with?"

She shook her head. "Not unless you know how to convince my cat-burglar to quit sneaking into people's houses and pinching their stuff."

Jace choked on his chocolate. "You have your own personal cat-burglar?"

She laughed at the expression on his face. "Yeah. A furry one. Cupcake—that's my cat—has started bringing me gifts. So far it's just been odd pieces of clothing, sets of keys, and other trivial stuff. But last night, he upped the stakes and left me a ring on my pillow."

Now that was one helluva coincidence. "You gotta be kidding."

She set her mug on the side-table and shifted position, hugging her knees in what struck him as a defensive posture. "It's not completely unheard of, you know. There're plenty of documented cases where domestic cats habitually steal items and present them to their owners. I searched the 'net and—"

"I believe you. And here's the thing. I've recently lost a ring that belonged to my grandfather. It just disappeared from the kitchen counter. I don't suppose—"

"It's a heavy gold band? And quite old? The engraving on the inside is nearly worn smooth."

"Sounds like mine, all right. It was my granddad's wedding ring."

"Oh, my. I'm so very sorry. You must have been frantic!" She flopped back against the couch and closed her eyes. "I handed it in to the sheriff. Filled out a report and asked to be contacted if someone claimed it. Took out an ad in the paper with a photo of it, too. Even did a mailbox drop with some flyers—"

"So that's what you were doing this morning when I—"

"Flashed me?" She opened her eyelids and a tiny smile ghosted across her face. But he noticed it didn't reach her eyes.

Fuck. He couldn't bear seeing her like this. He tried his best to make that smile real again. "So, your pussy stole my ring. What are the chances, huh?"

She pinned him with a haunted stare that made his gut clench. "Thanks for believing me. Because truly, this whole situation—my whole darn life, in fact—is too damned weird for words right now. I don't seduce guys in bathrooms. I just… don't do stuff like that. And it won't happen again. I won't let it!"

He didn't know what to tell her. Or how to fix her problems. So he fell back on a tried and true platitude. "As Gramps always used to say, everything happens for a reason."

"Yeah. I guess." She yawned, and seeing the dark circles under her eyes, it hit him how exhausted she must be. With her sleepwalking episodes disturbing her nights, she probably hadn't had a decent night's sleep in far too long. He had loads more questions he wanted to ask her. Chief among them being whether she might consider jumping him again, once she got to know him better. And then there was how she'd gotten into his house. But they could wait.

"Jace? Can I ask you a favor?" She sounded like a scared little girl.

"Sure thing."

"Can you walk me home?"

"Sweetheart, no way am I letting you walk home by yourself after what you've been through."

Considering what he really wanted to do was scoop her into his arms, lay her on his bed, and screw her senseless to help her forget about all the bad shit that was happening in her life right now, he figured that was a damned fine response.

His fuck-'em-and-leave-'em after they got all emotional stance had taken on a mighty big about-face. Kat might have pissed him off with her earlier attitude about that little mind-blowing bathroom encounter, but he now suspected that it meant more to her than she'd let on. Because when she'd needed help, the first person she'd asked had been *him*. Oh, not in so many words, but he knew a cry for help when it turned up naked in his living room.

Kat wasn't a potential good-time fuck-buddy. She was real. And damn, even though it scared him witless, he knew he wanted her in his life.

Jace spent the entire stroll back to his house thinking about Kat.

She'd confessed to decorating the house he was renting. Out of respect for her emotional state, he'd managed to bite his tongue and keep his opinions to himself. At least, until she'd also confessed how the décor didn't do much for her. Which had led to her briefing him on the trouble the Gallaghers had experienced with the previous designer, Gena Hamilton.

Kat had been forced to work with a restricted budget that would have made a nun weep. Dyeing the lilac carpet black had been a bloody clever idea, considering. It made him ashamed that he'd judged her so harshly.

Her own house had been another revelation. He'd half expected some girly, overblown décor. Or a painfully modern, painfully uncomfortable, minimalist nightmare. Instead, he discovered a house that he wouldn't mind spending more time in. The place was old and a bit neglected on the outside, and she'd obviously been short of funds when she decorated the interior, but she'd made it inviting and comfortable. And, just like Kat herself, a little bit surprising. Nothing too in-your-face, just eclectic touches of color here and there. He wondered what miracles she'd work with his own apartment.

Her little personal problem remained a mystery. He couldn't see how she'd managed to sleepwalk outside in the first place, given the sturdy security latches and deadlocked doors. Especially since both back and front doors had still been deadlocked when they'd arrived.

It'd taken her a good ten minutes of searching before she remembered where she'd hidden a spare key—taped inside a bird feeder that she'd had to stand on an outdoor chair to reach. The key was slightly corroded by the elements and so stiff in the front door lock that it was obvious it had not been used in some time.

The state of that spare key, and the fact that she'd had such difficulty remembering where she'd hidden it in the first place, made him disinclined to believe a sleepwalking woman could have let herself out of the house, used that particular key to lock up, then replaced it in its hard-to-reach hidey hole before wandering off on tonight's jaunt.

When he'd enquired after her usual set of house keys, she'd admitted locking them away in various places. Tonight's hiding place had been a filing cabinet drawer. Just one of her many precautions to ensure that she didn't do exactly what she'd somehow done—gotten out of the house and wandered naked and alone through the neighborhood in the dead of night.

It was a mystery, all right. One which made his gut churn when he thought about what might have befallen her.

Jace let himself into his house, yawned, and briefly considered heading back to bed. He glanced at his watch and realized his wrist was bare. Not surprising. Grabbing his watch from his bedside table had hardly been a freaking priority when he'd believed he had an intruder.

He wandered into his bedroom to check the time, and damned if he couldn't find the watch at all.

"Not fucking again!" He groaned and stalked back into the kitchen to brew some coffee in the hope it'd help kick-start his brain.

And that's when he spotted his watch, lying on the floor, tucked beneath the overhanging rim of a kitchen cabinet. Not too far from the cat-flap. Which, just then, was caught by another small gust of wind that made the plastic door flap ever-so-slightly inward before it banged to a halt.

What the fuck? He'd sorted that!

He fiddled with the cat-flap latches. Aha! Something he *could* explain. He'd screwed up and set the latches so that critters could get in through the flap, but not back out. He remedied that lack immediately. And double-checked that this time it was locked from both sides.

As for his granddad's watch?

He checked it over thoroughly. It was apparently unscathed and still ticking along nicely, thank God. But he had no fucking idea how it could have gotten there.

Chapter 6

Since there was little point trying to sleep with his mind racing ten to the dozen, Jace caught up on some work, then checked his emails. There were a couple from his 2IC—nothing major, just keeping him in the loop—and one from the mayor.

Interesting. He'd presumed that Kat's presence at the meeting meant she had the contract sewn up. Seemed there were two other parties making submissions, and all three proposals would be put to a vote.

Paulie Evans had provided a brief from each applicant. The link provided with Kat's information showed him a clean, professional looking website page for Kat Meyer, Interior Design, with a list of her qualifications, pricing and contact details, photos showcasing her work and glowing testimonials from previous clients.

The House Of Hamilton Interiors website was a fucking horror. Some people just didn't know when less was more… which was backed up by the photos showcasing a selection of Gena Hamilton's work. Her rooms were cluttered and so busy with color and texture that it was difficult to find a cohesive theme. The photo of Gena splashed across the Contact Me! page was a full-screen glamour shot that had been airbrushed to hell and beyond. That alone would have been enough for Jace to wipe the floor with any proposal of hers.

The last applicant had no online presence. No website, just an email—and a hotmail one at that. He scanned the scant information provided and wrote her off as a rank amateur, hardly a serious contender compared to Kat or even the Hamilton woman.

Jace leaned back in his chair. Kat was a talented designer who deserved a shot at something bigger and better than the limited scope a small town could offer. And he intended to make certain she got that contract fair and square. Even if he had to draft up her proposal and present it to the mayor and his councillors himself.

But for now, he'd settle for figuring out how the heck she had managed to get into his house. He was missing some crucial clue. The pieces to the puzzle were there, he just needed to put them together.

By half past eight he was going stir crazy, so he wandered over to grab a coffee at the Main Street Café and pass the time chatting with Phil. Okay,

okay. Peppering Phil with questions about Kat. And by the time the sheriff's office was open for business, he knew everything there was to know about Katalina Louise Meyer.

Her "little childhood problem" of buck-naked sleepwalking was widely supposed to have been a symptom of being raised by a single parent—the whole kids-acting-out-when-they-craved-attention thing. He also knew that the stress of dealing with Kat's little problem was the supposed cause of her mom disappearing when Kat was just twelve years old, leaving her to be raised by her Grandma Louise.

That was something she and Jace had in common, being raised by a grandparent. But Jace had been lucky enough to have a sibling. Kat had no one but her grandma. That had to have been hard on a young girl growing up in a small town.

At ten past nine, he pushed open the door to the Pressfield County Sheriff's Department and sauntered up to the counter.

The deputy sheriff looked up from his crossword. "What can I do for you, sir?"

"I understand Kat Meyer turned in a ring yesterday? I've come to claim it. The name's Jace Burton."

The deputy grinned. "I'll just go grab it from the cat-stash."

"The cat *what*?"

"The cat-stash. It's what we call the box where we store all the stuff Kat's cat has stolen. Usually it's just car keys, house keys, and the odd small ornament. But there's been a couple of DVDs, too. Cupcake sure has interesting taste when it comes to films." His grin spread all over his face. "Seems he doesn't much approve of porn."

The deputy walked over to a filing cabinet and fished out an archive box. "Can you describe the item in question, Mr. Burton?"

Jace did so. Even down to the illegible engraving. "It was my granddad's wedding ring. His wife had it engraved with the words, 'To my one true love, my darling Jasper. Love, Margie'."

The deputy squinted at the engraving. "That's enough to tug at the heartstrings of the most hard-hearted man alive. Reckon it could say that, too." He handed the ring to Jace. "And I reckon the best test is seeing how good a fit it is. If you've been wearing it for the past five years as you claim, then it should fit mighty well. Though, looking at that strip of untanned skin on your finger, I reckon you're above board."

"Very observant," Jace said. And slipped it on the ring finger of his right hand.

"Fits real good," the deputy said. "Looks like it belongs there, too. Which sure is good enough for me. Now if you'd sign the bottom of this form and confirm you claim ownership?" He pushed over a form.

Jace signed with a flourish. "Is Sheriff Wade here? I've been meaning to introduce myself to him. I'm the architect Mayor Evans brought in to design the new library and rec center complex."

The deputy extended his hand. "Mike Wells, at your service, Mr. Burton."

Jace shook hands with the older man. "Call me Jace."

"Sure thing, Jace. Sheriff's likely gonna be gone all day." The deputy snorted with suppressed laughter. "Kat put the fear of God into him when she threatened to bring her Grandma Louise down here for a chat. I'm pretty sure she was just pulling our legs, but Wade isn't taking any chances."

"Phil, from the café, mentioned that Grandma Louise isn't a woman to be trifled with."

The deputy's eyes sparkled with mirth. "Yep. She's a real hard case, for sure. Doesn't give a rat's patootie about giving us a piece of her mind if she thinks we deserve it."

"Do you reckon Kat takes after her grandma?" Jace couldn't resist asking.

"Well," the deputy leaned over the counter in a conspiratorial manner, "Kat's usually Miss Congeniality. But lately, when she gets real worked up about something? If you know what's good for you, you'll head for the hills. She's really on edge, you know?"

Jace snorted. They didn't know the half of it. Even he was hard put to reconcile the borderline nympho who'd jumped him in the bathroom with the vulnerable woman who'd sobbed her heart out in his arms. She was a bundle of contradictions. A real sexy, damned endearing, majorly addictive bundle. Which was why he was determined to stick around.

⁂

Kat had put aside her proposal and spent the afternoon at the retirement home, listening to Grandma Louise grump about all the daft rules and regulations she had to put up with.

"Time for lunch, Louise. Don't dive-bomb the other swimmers, Louise. We don't think it's appropriate for you to take over the aerobics class while the instructor's off sick, Louise. You know what I told 'em? I told 'em, 'Geez, Louise, how about you lot loosen up and join the fun!' I'm telling you, the staff round here might be a good few decades younger than us, but they're such boring old farts that I reckon they're all gonna die of old age before we do! If sitting 'round with a rug tucked over your knees is what old age is supposed to be, then I'm having none of it!"

Kat tended to agree. Not that she could admit it, because after a "friendly chat" from one of the staff members, Kat was supposed to be imploring her grandma not to encourage the residents to sneak out of their rooms at night and skinny dip in the pool.

She was tempted to suggest that her grandma move back in with her, but she knew Grandma Louise secretly enjoyed provoking the staff with her outrageous stunts. She reveled in her reputation for being a fun-loving old gal who could still catch a man's eye and give him a thrill he wouldn't forget in a hurry. She really did love it here at Sunshine Retirement Village.

By the time Kat had placated her grandma with chocolates and a brand new copy of her favorite video, she was wrung out. She kissed her grandma's cheek, promised to stop by again in a couple of days, and dragged her feet all the way home.

She was so exhausted she couldn't be bothered with anything more complicated than toast for dinner. And even then, she caught herself dozing off on the couch amidst fantasies of how wonderful it would be to have someone take care of *her* for a change. Someone who could rub her feet when they were sore, baby her with toast and hot chocolate when she was tired. Someone who could tuck her back in bed when she sleepwalked. Keep her safe, and comfort her when she awoke, disoriented and scared of what she might have done during her nightly wanderings.

Someone like Jace.

Enough! She hauled herself up and went through her nightly routine of checking that all the doors and windows were locked, and then locking away her house keys, before heading for her bedroom.

Before she switched off the light and snuggled down for the night, she gave Cupcake the usual lecture, which her cat ignored in favor sticking one leg in the air and proceeding to lick his unmentionables.

She sighed. "Don't pretend you can't understand me. Just, please don't bring me anything new tonight, okay? Let's try and make last night's giftless state a permanent one, hmmm? Because believe me, I hate the thought of locking you inside at night and dealing with litter boxes just as much as you do. But if that's what it's gonna take, then that's what I'll do. One last chance, okay?"

She thought her cat might have meowed in response, but she couldn't be sure because fatigue had already dragged her into semi-consciousness.

Kat's eyelids flew open. The only thing that was familiar was that she'd shucked her pajamas. This time, she wasn't curled up buck-naked on top of her bed, shivering her bare butt off. Nor was she lying on the couch in Jace's house, and even that, she might have handled. But this?

Not this. Not being ripped from a sensual dream, where Jace was petting her and she was making a rumbling noise like a purr in her throat, to find herself standing on damp, dew-kissed grass, directly outside the window of a house. Not glancing down to find her hand between her clenched thighs, like she'd been stroking and pleasuring herself, doing God only knew what else outside, where anyone might see.

What the fuck was happening to her?

It was all too much for any sane woman to cope with.

Her vision wavered and blurred. Her limbs turned to jelly, incapable of holding her upright. She sank to the ground with her heart pounding in her ears, its beat so loud and so abnormally rapid that she thought it would burst from her chest. And not even her brain shrieking at her that she recognized this particular garden, and this particular house, and that just through the window there was someone who would help her, if only she had the courage to ask, had the power to calm her rising hysteria.

She threw herself full-length on the lawn and howled her anguish to the world.

Chapter 7

Jace was out of bed and halfway to the door before he even registered what had woken him. Sounded like someone was hurting…. And that someone was in his backyard.

He flipped the latch, shoved open the door, and bounded out into the darkness. He didn't know quite what he expected—perhaps a victim of an accident or domestic violence. Or some drunken madwoman who'd stumbled into his yard and decided to make a scene.

From the corner of his eye, he registered the abrupt illumination as interior lights at the two neighboring houses flicked on, and his first thought was, "Shit, I'm buck-naked."

Next, was that even though the sound that had originally woken him had gotten quieter, he could still hear what sounded like a woman crying as though her world was about to end.

And just as an exterior light from the nearest house came on, and he heard voices, he spotted the source of those anguished cries.

Kat. Lying outside his bedroom window. Naked.

The couple next door had decided to investigate the disturbance. "What the hell is that?" Jace heard the guy say.

Fuck! He didn't hesitate, just acted on pure instinct and the desire to protect Kat from prying eyes and gossiping tongues. He ran to her, scooped her up so that her face was muffled against his chest, and dived back inside, shutting the door behind him with a nudge of his hip.

"Reckon it must be a cat," the neighbor's wife called out.

Jace bent his head and placed his lips to Kat's ear, murmuring that she was safe and everything was okay, while he waited in the shadows, his heart thumping and adrenaline coursing through his veins, hoping that she wouldn't scream the place down again. He seemed to have communicated his fears because her howls cut off, like she'd clamped her jaws together.

"Can't hear anything now, can you?" the woman called.

"Go on back to bed, honey," the guy said. "I'm just gonna check 'round back. Maybe do a bit of recon."

"Don't be long. It's two in the morning, and you've got to be up in four hours, so easy on the Rambo stuff, okay?"

Jace heard the slam of a window. He carried Kat into his bedroom. "It's okay, sweetheart. It'll all be okay." Provided she didn't let loose with another ear-piercing howl and bring the nosy neighbor knocking on Jace's door. Somehow, he didn't think claiming that his girlfriend had suffered a nightmare would cut it.

He laid her down in his bed and tucked the comforter up around her chin. It worried the heck out of him that she didn't say something—anything. She just lay there, staring at him with anguished eyes.

He stroked her hair back from her face. "It's okay, Kat. Your secret's safe. No one spotted you but me." He hoped.

"What's wrong with me, Jace?" she whispered. "Why is this happening to me?"

"Shhh. There's nothing wrong with you, sweetheart. Sleepwalking is nothing to be ashamed about."

"You didn't see what I was doing outside your bedroom window," she said, her lips quivering so badly he had to strain to understand what she'd said.

"Being a peeping Tom?" he joked.

"S-Something like that."

"Sweetheart, you can peep in on me any damn time you like." He bent to kiss her brow. "You just get some rest, okay? I'll grab some clothes and camp out on the couch. And just so we're clear, I'm a real light sleeper. No way you're sneaking past me!"

He'd started rummaging in a drawer for clothing when she called his name, and the panic in her voice rent his heart in two. "Jace. Don't leave me. Stay. Please?"

He closed his eyes and took a deep, bracing breath before he turned to her with what he hoped was a gentle, reassuring smile. "Sure thing."

He yanked on some boxers, and for good measure, a T-shirt, and climbed under the covers. Man, this was gonna be hard.

And it was harder, still, when she curled up like some orphaned kitten in desperate need of comfort, and he felt like a real shit for not giving her what she needed. And it got real damn hard, when he couldn't bring himself to deny her any longer, and against his better judgment, pulled her in to nestle against his chest.

And it stayed hard, as he listened to her breathing slow, and she gave a soft little sigh, and finally relaxed into sleep.

Jace cursed his unrepentant cock and tried not to think about all the things he'd like to be doing with it now.

Kat eased from slumber and stretched her limbs slowly, luxuriously. She inhaled a tantalizing scent. Healthy, clean male. Mmmm. She peeled open her eyelids and was confronted with the most delectable bare male chest.

Her pulse quickened. Lust surged through her body, laced with a need so hot and fierce that she whimpered and pressed her palms against her lower belly.

Jace. Only he had this effect on her. She wanted him. Needed him. He was asleep, but that didn't matter to her. She was gonna have him…. For breakfast.

She slid from beneath his arm in one quick, sinuous motion and tugged the sheet down to his knees. Kneeling beside him, she nuzzled and licked the taut planes of his abs, tasting him, inhaling his unique scent, rolling it around her tongue.

The hair on his belly arrowed toward his groin, and she rubbed her cheek against it, enjoying the scratchy sensation of the coarse hair on her skin and the smell of sex permeating the air. His cock reared up from between his thighs, firm and hard and just begging to be tasted. She ran her nails lightly from root to tip, her lips curving when his shaft jerked. Yum.

Tossing her hair over her shoulder, she bent forward, licked his tip, then sucked him into her mouth.

He groaned and thrust his hips, an unconscious demand to take all of him. She let him feel her teeth—the merest light pressure, more a warning than a punishment—followed by a soothing lap of her tongue. And then she increased her suction and pulled back, letting his cock slide slowly out until only the glans remained in her mouth.

She suckled him, flicking the rim of his cock with her tongue, teasing the slit.

His hips came up off the mattress. He shifted his legs wider. "Kat," he murmured.

Mmmm. An invitation that was far too good to pass up. She released his cock from her mouth and moved to straddle him.

Jace jerked from the best dream he'd had in his life when a soft hand grasped the root of his cock. Well, fuck me, he thought. Can't think of a better way to be woken up in the morning.

He was strangely unwilling to open his eyes. Because then he'd have to face reality and tell her to stop seducing him. He wasn't such an asshole that he could take advantage of a vulnerable woman.

Hang on. Did it count as taking advantage if she was the one doing the seducing? God, he hoped not. Because he didn't want her to stop what she was doing. And *he* sure as fuck didn't want to stop her, either. And while he wrestled with his conscience, she aimed his erection at the entrance to her pussy and took him inside her.

His eyelids shot open. Before he could protest—or beg, he wasn't entirely sure what was gonna come out of his mouth at this moment—her warm, slick flesh parted to accommodate his length and he was seated to the balls.

With her head thrown back so that her hair brushed her spine, her eyes shut and lips slightly parted, she was the most beautiful woman he'd ever seen.

And then she cupped her breasts, thumbs brushing across her nipples, teasing them into rosy, hard points.

He stopped breathing to drink in the sight of her, etching her forever in his mind. He grasped her hips to stop her from moving and give himself a small chance of redemption. Even though it would have killed him if she stopped now, his sex-saturated brain was finally getting around to telling him there were real-life considerations to think about here. Like her fragile emotional state. And the fact he wasn't wearing a condom. Pity he wasn't a complete prick, one of those guys who could just kick back and enjoy the ride, and not give a shit about the future.

"What do you think you're doing?" he asked, his voice raspy with frustrated lust.

She slowly opened her eyes and gazed right into his.

What he saw there, mirrored in their gorgeous green depths, was a raw sexual desire intense enough to rival his own. And more. Deeper emotions, yearnings and cravings for things that he'd convinced himself he didn't want, or need, in his life right now.

Fuck, when she looked at him like that, it smacked him upside the head just how much he did want those things. And needed them at least as much as he needed oxygen to breathe.

"I would have thought it was pretty darned obvious what I think I'm doing," she said.

Her gaze licked down his body as it had done when he'd pulled back the drapes and she'd first seen him naked. But this time, the sensation was far more intense because she was right here in the flesh. Touching him. Tantalizing him. Trusting him not to hurt her.

It took every ounce of willpower not to grab her, roll her over onto her back, and lose himself in her. Instead, when he felt her thigh muscles tense and she lifted herself up, obviously intending to give him the ride of his life, he grit his teeth, cursed himself for being a fucking fool, and tried to lift her completely off of his cock. But she was having none of that. She arched her back slightly, reaching behind her to grab his balls. And squeeze. Hard enough to give him pause.

"I trust you, Jace," she said. "And I'm asking you to trust *me*. I'm on the pill. I want this. I need this." With a final squeeze, she let go of his balls and slid down his length again.

His eyes practically crossed at the sensation of her inner muscles clenching him like a velvet fist. "God! Me, too."

"Happy, now?" she asked, squeezing him internally with a rhythm that drove him close to the edge.

"Fucking ecstatic," he said through tightly clenched teeth. "Or at least, I would be if I could be sure you weren't gonna run from me again the minute you come to your senses."

She rose up over him again, this time leaning forward and bracing her arms on either side of his chest. He didn't dare so much as twitch for fear that his cock would slip completely out of her. Her breasts swung enticingly above him. It felt like the worst form of torture not to raise his head and taste one of those rosy nipples.

"This morning, for the first time in weeks, I woke up feeling safe and protected. And I know exactly who to thank for that." She poked a finger at his chest. "You, Jace Burton."

To his relief, she sat back on her heels, and when he was fully sheathed inside her again, he groaned.

"And if that's not reason enough to seduce you, then how about this? The first time I saw you, my dormant hormones went into overdrive. Seeing your gorgeous big erect cock just about made me come on the spot."

The cock in question hardened even more inside her, provoking such a strong, tight squeeze of her pussy muscles, that his gasp was echoed by her own.

"I wanted so damn bad to stroll up to your front door and offer to make good use of that hard-on. I wanted so damn bad to fuck you, a complete stranger, that I turned tail and ran, rather than face up to how you made me feel." She leaned over him again, this time keeping her body close to his, brushing her taut nipples over his chest, and giving one of his a long lick.

"Oh? And how did I make you feel?"

"Wet." Lick. "Horny as heck." Nibble. "And confused as hell, because I didn't know what'd come over me." A long, luscious lick.

When he recovered his breath, he just had to ask, "And what had come over you?"

"You," she said. And bit his nipple. Then drew her nails down his chest, hard enough to score the skin, like she was marking him as her own.

He liked it.

Shee-it! He loved it. His brain went south. The woman was doing his head in.

"You, Jace Burton, are what has come over me."

"I see," he managed to say. And was damn impressed his response managed to come across as even semi-intelligent, considering what she was doing to him should have reduced him to a drooling mess.

"Good. Now quit asking dumbass questions. Shut up and let me fuck you."

He shut up and let her do just that. She rode his cock slowly, stoking the fire building in his loins with her hot slick pussy, intensifying the aching throbbing of his balls with each slap of her flesh against his whenever she ground herself down on him. He could bear it no longer. He grabbed her hips, taking control of the rhythm, moving her up and down his cock.

"Touch yourself," he whispered. "Touch your clit. I want to see you come."

A wicked smile curved her lips. She dragged her fingers through her wet, swollen folds, and her slumberous cat-like eyes met his, while she pleasured herself as he'd asked. And soon, the gasping mews that escaped her lips as she stroked her clit, drove him to piston his hips and thrust into her harder, and faster. Until she clenched around his cock, her hand movement suddenly jerky, fingers trembling and losing focus as her body stiffened, straining for release.

But he wasn't going to give her what she wanted, not yet. He reared up to tumble her backward onto the mattress. His hands pushed her thighs wide, and he thrust his cock inside her again, screwing deeper.

She moaned and tossed her head, and when she hooked her ankles around his thighs to keep him inside her, he slid his hands under her butt to tilt her hips so that he could thrust even deeper. She adapted to the new position, so he took his weight on one of his forearms, lifting up to give himself room to press his hand between their bodies and finger her clit, while he ground his cock into her.

"Ah, yes. God. Jace!"

"Fuck! That's it, Kat. Come for me."

The first ripples of pre-orgasm took her, and recognizing the signs, he flicked her clit with just the very tip of his fingernail.

"Jace."

He thrust into her hard and fast, and his name on her lips became a chant timed with each thrust, and each flick of his finger.

"Jace. Jace. Jace. Aaaah… Jace!"

He emptied himself into her, his cock jerking and throbbing.

She yowled his name one more time, then relaxed around him and beneath him, boneless with satiated pleasure.

He knew exactly how she felt. He had just enough strength left to roll off her, onto his side, and collapse beside her.

Jesus. Fucking amazing. And a whole bunch more adjectives he didn't have the brainpower to think of right now. He gathered her in his arms, settled her against his chest, and wondered how he was ever gonna let her go. And how bad it would hurt when he fulfilled his contractual obligations and had to leave both Kat and Pressfield County behind.

Chapter 8

Kat hummed beneath her breath, her happiness spilling over and making the people that she passed in the street smile. She didn't care what the neighbors thought if they'd spotted Jace grabbing her spare key from its hiding place, letting himself into her house, and then locking back up and walking away with a plastic carry-bag.

That carry-bag had contained a complete change of clothes, so she didn't have to walk back home in clothes that too obviously weren't hers. So people wouldn't speculate and gossip.

What a man. Jace's sexual prowess blew the socks right off her previous partners. Not that there'd been that many. But still. And she suspected he might well have ruined her for any other man.

Any other man….

She stumbled over a crack in the pavement, and some of her joy seeped from her heart. She didn't want any other man. She wanted Jace.

But she wasn't stupid. She knew the deal. As soon as he'd worked out the terms of his contract, he'd go back to his big city job, and his big city apartment, and his big city women.

She released her breath in a hiss at the mere thought of Jace with another woman. Oooh! She wanted to scratch something, scratch him! Instead, she dug her nails into her palms.

But she had no real claim on him, and he would soon forget all about the small-town girl who'd sleepwalked into his life.

Well, given that she sleepwalked buck-naked and had seduced him twice, it might take him a little longer than usual to forget her.

And dammit, she wasn't gonna think about bad stuff right now.

Jace was coming over tonight. For a sleep-over, he'd said, batting his lashes and making like some silly schoolgirl to make her laugh.

She knew his offer was twofold. One, to have his wicked way with her, which she was most definitely looking forward to, and two, to keep watch over her when she sleepwalked. He was going to try to discover just how she was getting out of her "locked tighter than a cat's asshole" house. Because, as he'd informed her this morning in no uncertain terms, "this wandering 'round outside stark naked just couldn't go on".

She couldn't take umbrage at his protective urges, not when he'd been crowding her into a corner of the shower cubicle and nuzzling that sweet spot just behind her ear, at the time he mentioned it. If she'd had any resistance to his suggestion after that, it had all melted away. Resistance tended to do that, especially when a sexy guy was sucking your nipples to aroused, aching peaks, lipping his way down your belly, then urging your thighs apart so that he could plunge his tongue into your pussy and lick you to yet another mind-blowing orgasm.

And boy, was it ever difficult to concentrate on her proposal with images of Jace's talented mouth and talented fingers—and hell, just Jace—filling her mind. After four hours of agonizing over how to justify the latest round of estimates without coming across defensive, she had only managed to sketch out one new page to add to her proposal.

She gave up. After filling the growling void in her stomach with a quick meal of instant soup and toast, she curled up on the couch next to her sleepy cat.

Cupcake definitely had the right idea, lazing around soaking up the late afternoon sun. Kat figured she might as well relax, too. Maybe read a bit more of the novel her grandma had lent her. Paranormal romance featuring were-wolf heroes wasn't really her thing, but it would pass the time. Then she'd get ready for Jace. Shave her legs, pluck her eyebrows. Go the whole hog with lacy underwear, perfume and a touch of subtle makeup.

The next thing she knew, someone was banging on her door.

She jerked upright on the couch and glanced at the clock. Seven already? She'd slept for nearly four hours? Crap!

Too much to hope that Jace wasn't one of those guys who was always on time and it was someone else. She rushed to the door and stood on tiptoe to peer through the peephole. Yep, too much to hope.

She flicked the latch and yanked the door wide. "Hi, Jace." A yawn caught her—and him—by surprise. "Sorry. Fell asleep on the couch. I just woke up."

"Yeah." He smoothed her mussed hair back with the palm of his hand and tucked a stray lock behind her ear. A slight frown creased his brow as he examined her face. "I can see that. Bought a bottle of wine to have with dinner." He handed it over.

She glanced at the label and raised her eyebrows. "How'd you know I like zinfandel?"

"Nobody has any secrets in this town. Least of all, you."

Yikes. She sure hoped that wasn't true!

Her dismay must have been written all over her face, for he cupped her nape and pressed a quick kiss to her lips. "Chill, sweetheart. I asked Phil from the café."

"Oh! Okay. Good." She stared at him through dazed eyes. He'd made her knees turn to water, and her brain a puddle of goo, with only a fleeting kiss? She struggled to engage her brain. "Um, yeah. Phil and I share a love of wine."

"So long as that's all you share."

She blinked as those sexily growled words penetrated her brain. "You can't be serious."

"Gotcha! Can I come in?"

She mentally slapped herself upside the head. Sheesh. She was forgetting her manners in a big way. But this gently teasing side of him was so unexpected that it put her off her stride. She sucked in a deep breath in an effort to get her shit together. "Of course you can come in."

"In that case." Without any warning whatsoever, he scooped her into his arms. "How about you get the door?" He angled her body so that she could kick it shut.

She hooked one arm around his neck, carefully cradling the chilled bottle of wine in the crook of her other arm. "Oooh! I've never been swept off my feet by a man before."

"Yeah. I kinda figured that. About time someone showed you some TLC, Kat Meyer." He strode into the kitchen and instructed her to leave the wine on the counter, then proceeded down the hallway. And right past her bedroom, toward the bathroom.

"Fancy a soak in that lovely big, old-fashioned, claw-foot tub of yours?" he asked.

Her heart fluttered with excitement and her nipples tightened. "How do you know I have a claw-foot tub?"

"I snooped."

The thought of him going into her bedroom, perhaps checking the contents of her underwear drawer, turned her on something wicked. A bolt of lust speared straight to her groin.

He deposited her on the chair placed strategically alongside the tub so that she could sit and keep an eye on it while it filled. Which, being a really big tub, would take a good twenty minutes.

He turned the faucets on maximum, fiddled with them for a bit, then turned his attention back to her.

"You almost seem like you know what you're doing," she said.

"I do. Gramps had a tub like this. I used to love wallowing in it—was about the only time I got some privacy, and my baby sister couldn't bug the heck outta me." He eyed her up and down, his expression speculative. "Which is why I know that we've got about twenty minutes to kill."

"Oh?" The word came out in a squeak.

"Oh." He stripped off her T-shirt and bent his head to nuzzle her breasts through her white cotton bra.

"There's something about plain white cotton underwear on a woman," he said. "So innocent." He reached behind her with one hand to unclasp her bra and tossed it to the floor. "But hiding something sinfully sexy beneath." His mouth closed over the tip of her breast, and the strong sucking pulls of his lips, and the slightly shocking sensation of his teeth on her nipple, made her wet and greedy for him again, even though she'd been thoroughly loved only hours previously.

She arched her back, encouraging him to take her breast deeper into his mouth. "Nice trick with the one-handed thing," she purred.

That clever hand stroked down her spine. It negotiated the waistband of her sweatpants and the barrier of her underwear with consummate ease, and cupped her butt, squeezing gently.

His mouth trailed butterfly kisses across her breast and her cleavage, then fastened on her other breast with a hungry pull that made her gasp. He had her sweatpants halfway down her thighs before she even registered what he was doing.

"Mmm. White cotton briefs, too. Sorry, sweetheart, cute as they are, these are gonna have to go." And they did. With barely any assistance from her slack-limbed self.

"Scoot your butt over to the edge of the chair, lean back and open your legs."

She complied. Because the hungry expression in his eyes as he looked at her, bed-head and all, made her inclined to let him do whatever he wanted with her.

"Wider."

She trembled but did as she was told. She was burning up, afire with passion and lust, unable to tear her gaze from his, and the wild, raw desire she saw reflected there. He was on the edge. If she wanted to provoke him into taking her hard and fast on the bathroom floor it would be child's play. And even as she reveled in that knowledge, she willingly ceded control to him and let him call the shots.

He knelt between her widespread thighs and brushed his fingers through her pubic hair. "God, you're so beautiful," he murmured, and pressed butterfly kisses to the sensitive skin of her inner thighs.

She tensed her thigh muscles against the desire to thrust her hips and clue him in to just how much she wanted him. He parted her labia with his thumbs, and licked her slit, a leisurely swipe of his tongue that had her whimpering.

He nuzzled her folds. "And you smell so damned good."

He hooked her legs over his shoulders and adjusted her position to his liking. "Did I mention that you taste fantastic?"

And then there was no more talking while he teased her mercilessly, alternating between licking and sucking and flicking at her clit with his tongue. When she writhed beneath him and her whimpers became cries that begged for more, he screwed two fingers into her sheath, pumping them in and out while his tongue continued to work its magic. She came with a series of gasps and shudders that wracked her body and lifted her hips completely off the chair.

Before she could even catch her breath, he'd turned off the faucets, proclaimed the water "just about right", and deposited her in the tub.

Kat gasped as the heat penetrated tender, still engorged tissues.

"Too hot?" he asked, testing the water.

"God, no. Just how I like it." She sank back against the edge of the tub, dangling both arms over the sides. "Heaven." And she didn't just mean the heat of the bath water.

He grinned in such a way that she knew he'd caught her meaning. "I love it when a plan comes together."

She gave him bliss-filled eyes. "You planned this, huh? Oooh. You're good, real good. Exactly what else do you have planned for tonight?"

"You'll see. Try not to fall asleep in the tub. I'll be back in a sec."

And he was, with two glasses of wine. He handed one to her and planted his butt in the chair. "Dinner's arriving in fifteen minutes. Hope you like pizza?"

"Mmmm." Kat sipped her wine and felt her whole body relax even further, even though she was naked in the tub, with a fully-dressed man watching her like he'd very much like to eat *her* for dinner. It was intimate, the kind of intimacy she'd never felt comfortable with before. But with Jace it felt different. Right.

"I'd planned to cook but pizza's good," she said. "So long as it's vegetarian and there's no olives. Can't stand olives."

He grinned. "I found that out when I told them where to deliver. The kid recognized your address and changed the order to vegetarian—hold the olives."

"One of the benefits of living in a small town where everyone knows you, I guess."

"Yeah. There is that."

She took another sip of wine and eyed him over the rim of her glass. "You say that like you've had personal experience with growing up in a small town."

"I have." He drank off his wine and poured himself another glass.

Hmmm. Now there was a telling reaction. "Don't suppose you fancy joining me in the tub?" she asked. And half of it was a ploy to diffuse his tension. But the other half, the greedy, needy half, was because she'd like to sit on his lap and watch his face as she slid down his cock.

"Sweetheart, I fancy it like crazy. But that pizza delivery boy is gonna be banging on your front door pretty soon. And what I plan to do to you is gonna take much, much longer than we have available."

She felt herself flushing from more than just the delicious heat of the water. The erotic promise in his voice, his tone, his words…. She really was in danger. In danger of losing her heart.

"Tell me about your childhood, then. It's only fair," she said quickly, when his expression started to go cold and closed and distant, like it had in the mayor's office.

"How's that?"

His voice was so tight and clipped, that she felt her resolve stuttering. But she battled on. "You've been talking to Phil. And when you picked up your ring, the sheriff or his deputy would've had a few things to say about me, too. You probably know everything there is to know about me, right? So it's only fair. C'mon, spill. I reckon you must have been the cutest little boy. Bet you got into a whole heap of mischief. Entertain me." She hit him with an over-the-top, seductress's come-hither expression, all batting eyelashes and pouty lips. "Or I'll just have to take drastic action and drag you in here with me. Which means the pizza delivery boy will just have to leave the pizza out on the porch and sing for his money. And I'm sure he'll hazard an educated guess as to why neither of us answered the door. My reputation will be ruined!"

The slight smile quirking his lips told her she'd nailed it, imbued her request with enough levity that he'd not treat it like an invasion of privacy. And her heart fluttered with excitement. She was going to learn about him in the best way, right from the horse's mouth.

"What do you want to know?"

Would "everything" be too much? she wondered. Yeah. Probably. Might scare him off. "You mentioned you had a sister. Tell me a funny story about you and your sister growing up."

He took another sip of his wine and stretched out his legs, making himself more comfortable in the wicker chair. She found herself fascinated by the play of muscles rippling his denim-clad thighs. For someone who spent hours behind a desk, he sure was built. She would bet he worked out. Seriously worked out, too. Those arms, the biceps—nicely showcased by a white T-shirt—did more than push pencils. He'd handled her weight easily, making her feel light as a feather, and delicate. Safe….

The fingers snapping in front of her nose dragged her from her daydream. "Are you sure you're up to this?" he asked. "You must be exhausted from all your nightly adventures."

"I'm fine," she said, blinking and trying to appear alert. "Don't leave me hanging. I'm dying to hear all about how you two tortured each other when you were growing up."

He smirked. "How do you know we tortured each other? We could have been best friends."

She sniggered. "Yeah. Right. Bet you drove your parents up the wall."

"I'm sure we did," he said. "Gramps claimed he could never figure out how such nice folks like my mom and dad could have spawned two such evil little critters as Jen and me. My dad winked at me and said it was genetic. And once he'd explained what 'genetic' was—I was maybe six—he blamed it all on Gramps."

He launched into a story about putting a frog in his sister's bed after she'd ratted him out for pinching an entire apple pie, even after he'd shared it with her. But she'd stuck a grass snake in his bed, paying him back for telling Gramps that she'd said a rude word. So they'd climbed into their beds that night and both screamed blue murder. And they'd gotten into even more trouble when their granddad finally got the truth out of them.

That story segued into another, and another, leading to a confession about the gag gifts brother and sister always tried to outdo each other with.

And after the laughter, he confessed the sorrow only hinted at before. How it had felt to lose both parents in the blink of an eye. To be called to the principal's office and see his sister already there and know something bad had happened. To be told about the car wreck and hug Jen tight and comfort her. And try to be brave, and not cry because boys weren't supposed to cry.

He'd waited there with his arm around his shell-shocked sister, wishing that everyone would just quit with the pitying looks and go away and leave them alone. And when his granddad had rushed through the door, sorrow and devastation etched on his tear-streaked face, Jace had learned that it was okay to cry. His granddad had loved his son and daughter-in-law, and he was hurting, and no matter what anyone thought, it was okay to show it. And the old man had enfolded him and Jen in his fierce embrace, and promised to take care of them.

"That's why this ring means so much to me," he told Kat. "Even though his estate was split equally between us, I signed the house over to Jen. She always loved granddad's house and it feels right to keep it in the family. Me? I had itchy feet and couldn't wait to get out and spread my wings. I didn't want the responsibility of a house. Gramps's wedding ring and his watch, and a bit of cash to get my business started, were all I wanted."

She opened her mouth to tell him she understood. That she, too, knew what it was like to feel stifled by obligation and family ties, but the doorbell rang. And the moment passed.

"Pizza," he said. "Be right back."

Jace made himself comfortable as possible in the old rocking chair in the corner of Kat's bedroom. He'd been right to suspect she was exhausted and in desperate need of rest. He'd returned, pizza box and plates in hand, to find her fast asleep in the tub. And the thought of her slipping beneath the water, drowning, had been like a swift kick in the gut that had left him gasping for breath.

What the fuck had he been thinking, suggesting she soak in the tub and then leaving her alone? Heart hammering, he'd cursed himself for all kinds of a fool before a burst of clarity calmed him down somewhat. She lived alone. She'd probably fallen asleep in the tub hundreds of times before. He hadn't been here to protect her then, and he wouldn't be hanging round in the future, either. What right did he have to worry about her?

But as much as he told himself that, he couldn't help it. She'd gotten to him. Lodged herself securely in his heart, in a place where only people he loved were lodged. There was only one other person inhabiting that private, secret place right now. His sister, Jen. The others were cherished memories and didn't take up too much room. But with the addition of Kat, he felt like his heart was full to bursting.

Gramps had told him real love between a man and the woman he wanted to spend the rest of his life with would have that quality. That it would fill him up and keep him warm at night.

After his own experiences with women, Jace had been inclined to believe that kind of love to be a rarity, something most people never experienced. And he'd never believed he would be one of the lucky ones. Until now.

Shit. No way. No way could he be falling in love with her. Jace didn't do falling in love. But it was frightening how quickly she'd become important to him.

Other than a sleepy murmur, she hadn't even woken when he'd plucked her from the tub, wrapped her in a towel, and carried her to bed. Right now, she looked like a pale, fragile angel, lying there in the vast bed, with her hair spread over the pillow....

If angels owned grumpy felines that is.

Cupcake hadn't been at all impressed to have his nap disturbed. He'd glared at Jace through slitted amber eyes, hissed his displeasure, then curled his bottlebrush tail over his nose and gone back to sleep. Hardly seemed the kind of athletic creature that would prowl the neighborhood and squeeze through barely open windows to steal things. That kind of caper seemed far too much like hard work for a slightly plump, lazy feline like Cupcake. Still, what the heck did Jace know about cats?

He had no intention of crawling into bed with Kat despite being sorely tempted by her soft skin, the warmth of her body, and the intoxicating vanilla scent of the shampoo she used. So he'd left the cat alone.

"But I'm warning you, furball," he muttered. "If I do ever end up in that bed, you're out on your furry ear. No way am I having an audience. So you'll be sleeping in the sitting room. You got that?"

His answer was the merest twitch of an ear.

He glanced at his watch. Almost eleven. And he hoped something happened soon, because damn, his butt was nearly numb.

Kat stirred. She sat up, eyes open, staring sightlessly in front of her.

Cupcake's head shot up, ears pricked.

Jace held his breath. He was on.

She scooted across the mattress and swung her legs over, planting her feet on the floor.

Cupcake hissed. All his fur stood on end.

"Sssh!" Jace rose from his chair, intending to grab the cat and toss him out of the bedroom. If Kat woke now, they'd have to do this all again tomorrow night!

But then Kat loosed an agonized yowl that made Jace's hair stand on end. Her shoulders hunched and she clutched her middle, rocking back and forth.

Shit. Sleepwalking wasn't supposed to be painful. Watching her suffer hadn't been in his job description. But as much as he yearned to go to her, he held back.

And as he watched, his attention riveted on her face, her eyes began to glow in the dim light. It was then he noticed that the pupils were slitted vertically, like a cat's eyes.

"What the fuck?" He blinked, unable to believe what he was seeing.

The hint of a muzzle bloomed, distorting her face. Her nose flattened and what he swore were whiskers sprouted on her upper lip.

"Son of a bitch!"

And as if offended that he could defile her essential feline superiority with anything remotely canine, she snarled at him, displaying long fangs. Then her head dropped forward onto her chest, hiding her face from his view beneath the curtain of her long hair. Pointed ears poked through that hair, situated on top of her head, not at the sides. Then the hair on her head was kind of sucked into her scalp—he didn't know how else to explain it—and replaced with a glossy black pelt, which also rippled over the rest of her body until she was completely covered with fur. Her spine bowed, then seemed to crumple. He heard the sickening popping of muscles and joints as her torso truncated, and limbs shortened and reformed. Hands and feet shrank into paws, nails became claws.

"Holy fucking shit!"

The cat that had been a woman surveyed the room. She hissed at Cupcake, displaying her fangs in a gesture that even Jace recognized as a display of dominance. Cupcake yowled. He leaped from the comforter like someone had lit a fire under him, and disappeared beneath the bed.

Jace could hardly blame him. Right now, he would dearly like to crawl under the bed and hide, too.

"Kat? Is that you?" He knew it was a stupid question because he'd seen her change! But a tiny part of him still hoped that he was mistaken, that he hadn't truly witnessed a woman shift into a cat. That he was dreaming.

Her eyes latched onto Jace's face. Eyes that smoldered with intelligence. Eyes that were the exact shade of green as Kat's.

And that was when all the pieces snapped into place. That was when Jace knew that Cupcake wasn't the cat-burglar at all. He knew exactly how Kat had been getting out of her house and exactly how she'd been getting into his. The ring. It had been her. His watch—after she'd stolen it, she'd discarded it on the kitchen floor because he'd accidentally set the cat-flap so she could get in, but not out, leaving her trapped in his house. The incident on the lawn—she'd been trying to get inside.

Kat meowed at him—whether an acknowledgment of what he'd seen, or a threat, Jace wasn't sure. Then she jumped off the bed and streaked out the bedroom door.

He remained rooted to the spot, staring after her.

And all he could think of was, *Fuck*. He sure hadn't seen that one coming.

Chapter 9

Kat awoke to a shaft of early morning sunlight washing her face through a gap in the blinds. She was naked, but *in* bed, not on top of it. Or worse, standing outside someone's bedroom window. Things were definitely looking up.

She yawned and stretched, and then it hit her that Jace might well have put her to bed after she'd sleepwalked. With him following her around to make sure she didn't do something outrageous, maybe things hadn't changed much at all. Eager to hear his verdict about her nighttime exploits, she bounced out of bed and shoved on underwear, jeans and a T-shirt.

Cupcake was in his usual spot, dozing on the end of the bed. She stroked his back and promised him some extra special cat food in his bowl this evening. Then she padded out into the living room, expecting to see Jace dozing on the couch.

But he wasn't there.

Or in the kitchen. Or even the bathroom.

Instinct had her heading back to her bedroom, and sure enough, there was a folded note left on her pillow. Some part of her brain had registered it was there even though her gaze had just skimmed over the white paper.

She unfolded it and scanned Jace's neat handwriting. *Busy with meetings all day. Meet me at my place at six. J.*

A frown knit her brows. She'd been expecting the kind of note that a man might leave his lover, not this terse little message.

A sinking feeling in the pit of her stomach had her clutching a pillow to her middle. The terror of waking up outside his house, naked and confused, crashed in on her again. Shit. Had she done something really awful? Too awful for Jace to cope with?

A shaky little laugh escaped her lips. Nah. From what she knew about Jace Burton and what she seen, that man could cope with anything she threw at him. She was being paranoid, reading too much into things. If she'd done something terrible or completely outrageous, he'd have stuck around to break it to her gently because that's the kind of man he was.

She shucked off her unease, grabbed a quick breakfast, and got stuck into her proposal. She managed a solid three hours before the phone's shrill tone almost made her jump out of her skin.

"Kat Meyer speaking."

"Kat, it's Tracy, from the retirement village. It's your grandma. There's been a little incident, and she insists on talking to you."

Kat suppressed a sigh. "I'll come right away. What's she done this time?"

A pause, and then, "It would be better if we spoke in person, I think."

"Oookay." Yikes. That didn't sound good. "I'll be there in half an hour."

Kat pumped her arms as she jogged up the hill toward the Sunshine Retirement Village. She'd figured rather than worrying about her own situation and whatever new stunt Grandma Louise might have pulled, she might as well get some benefit out of her unplanned excursion. So she'd changed into her exercise gear and blasted out the door like a woman on a mission. Which she was.

Not until she'd returned Phil's wave as she ran past his café, did it occur to her she hadn't bought her usual coffee and cinnamon roll for the past couple of mornings. How unpredictable was she? Woohoo! She smothered a gasping giggle. Phil wouldn't know what to make of that.

Or maybe he would. She wouldn't put it past Phil to have figured out that she had a man to occupy her. He had a scarily accurate radar for that sort of thing. He would know she didn't need the comfort of sticky sweet rolls for breakfast when she could have a man for breakfast instead.

Typically, that led to thoughts of having Jace for breakfast literally like she'd done only yesterday. And how delicious his cock had tasted. And how much she would like to taste him again. All of which meant that when she halted in the reception area to sign the visitors' book, she was red-faced from more than just the exertion of jogging.

"Is Tracy around?" she asked the receptionist. "She wanted to see me."

"Hi, Kat," the receptionist said. "I'll just page her for you."

"Don't suppose you know what Grandma Louise has been up to this time, do you? Tracy wouldn't say over the phone."

Her anxiety must have been obvious, for the receptionist said, "Don't fret, sweetie. Louise just had a little accident, is all. Nothing serious. But she wanted to see you, so Tracy thought it best to call you straightaway."

Kat's heart skipped a beat. "An accident? Tracy didn't say anything about an accident!"

"Nothing major. She took a corner too fast during the race and—"

"The race?" Kat groaned. "How many times do I have to warn her about charging round on mobility scooters? Those things aren't meant for speed."

"Oh, it wasn't a mobility scooter this time. It was—"

"A moonhopper," Tracy said, as she stepped out of the elevator by the reception area. She fixed the receptionist with a gimlet eye. "Thank you for filling Miss Meyer in, but I'll take it from here." And with that admonishment, she ushered Kat into the elevator.

"A moonhopper race?" Kat just couldn't imagine a bunch of pensioners bouncing along on big balls with handles. She didn't know whether to laugh or cry.

"Yes. Seems our aerobics instructor thought they might be a good substitute for Swiss balls because the seniors can hold on to the little horn thingies to help keep their balance." Tracy pushed the button to the second floor where Grandma Louise had her room. "Your grandma thought they'd be just dandy things to race with. And she was doing quite well, too. Leading the pack, in fact—"

"The pack?" Oh no. This was getting worse by the minute.

"About a dozen, all up. They got one circuit in before the dang things got a bit too bouncy, and your grandma ended up on her tushie. And she'd have been just fine, if George and Ed hadn't been hard on her tail and bounced right on top of her."

Kat covered her face with her hands. "Good grief. What happened?" The elevator doors pinged, and she followed Tracy out and down the corridor.

"George and Ed don't have much meat on them, so Louise got away with just a few bruises, a beautiful shiner, and a sprained ankle. The doc says she'll be just fine if she rests up for a couple of days. He's prescribed some pain meds and a light sedative to help her sleep, but she won't take them until she speaks to you. I think what's hurting worst is her pride."

"Because of the black eye?"

Tracy paused outside the door to room two-eleven, and grinned. "Nope. She bet George her bingo money that she'd whup his ass, and now she has to pay up."

Kat rolled her eyes ceiling-ward. "Save me."

"You and me, both! I'd appreciate it if you could have a wee word? Just ask her to tone down her antics for a little while. I turn a blind eye because, off the record, I reckon Louise is a fantastic role model for keeping active well into old age. But some of the other staff aren't quite so forgiving."

Kat nodded. "I'll see what I can do."

Tracy patted her shoulder. "Sweetie, if anyone can convince Louise to take it easy for a bit, it's you. She dotes on you." She knocked on the door and opened it a crack. "Louise? Kat's here to see you. Are you decent?"

"Only when you make me!"

Tracy smothered a chuckle. "See you later, Kat. Give me a call if you're worried about anything, okay?"

Kat nodded. "Will do. And thanks for looking after her."

"Katalina Louise Meyer." Grandma Louise's tone was decidedly snappish. "You going to stand there gasbagging, or come and pay your respects to your invalid grandmother?"

Kat rushed toward the bed to give a proper display of granddaughterly concern. She hugged her grandma carefully and was reassured when she got her usual rib-cracking squeeze in return. "Whoa. That's one heck of an impressive shiner, Grandma."

"Yep!" Her grandma's voice was chockfull of pride. "But do I get a steak for it? Nooo. All I get is some stinky bruise cream."

Kat perched on the side of the bed. "What's this I hear about you not wanting to take a sedative to help you sleep?"

"Oh pish posh! Plenty of time to sleep when you're pushing up daisies. Now, what's this I hear about you and that Jace Burton fellow?"

Kat felt her jaw sag. "How—? How on earth did you know about Jace?"

"Aha!" Louise folded her arms across her chest and grinned. "Wasn't entirely sure until now."

"Crap!" Sooo busted. And, since she knew she'd never be allowed to leave the room until her grandma knew all the excruciating details, she filled her in on everything.

Grandma Louise was quiet for a long moment. "You really like this Jace fellow, don't you?"

Kat could only stare wordlessly at her and gulp back her tears.

"There, there, baby," her grandma crooned. "Little wonder you're so on edge right now. But it'll work out all right. You see if it doesn't. And if he is fool enough to walk away from you when his contract finishes up, he'll be back. Just you mark my words. We Meyer women are irresistible!"

"I hope so."

"I know so. Now, dear, there's something I need to tell you. Would you mind shutting the door? Don't want any nosey parkers listening in on the big family secret."

Kat wandered over to nudge the door shut with her hips. Arms akimbo, she eyed her grandma. "What big family secret?"

"Well, it's more of a family *curse*. A very selective curse. I should have told you before, but I guess I just hoped we could get by. But with you getting *involved*—" she emphasized the word by miming speech marks with her fingers "—there's just no way 'round it. Shocking timing. But love never does much give a rat's patootie about timing."

Kat eyed her with concern. "Are you sure you haven't taken any medication already?" Grandma Louise was never this vague. Her mind was sharp as a tack and her tongue could cut you to shreds.

"You'd better sit down, dear. This is going to come as a bit of a shock."

Kat sank into the chair by the bed. Her mind reeled with all manner of horrendous curse scenarios, and it didn't help when Grandma Louise took a deep breath and appeared to be choosing her words.

"Best to come right out and say it, I guess. Katalina, you're a part-time cat-shifter."

Chapter 10

Kat released her pent-up breath in a snort. "I'm a what?"

"A cat-shifter," her grandmother said. "Like werewolves only with cats. And not during a full moon, either. More like, every twelve years."

Kat sniggered. "That's it," she said. "Absolutely no more paranormal romance novels for you! See what happens when you read that sort of stuff? It sends your already fertile imagination into orbit."

"Quit laughing at me, Katalina. You just zip your lip and listen to what I have to say, you hear?"

Kat subsided. Her grandma appeared to be quite agitated, and it wouldn't hurt to listen. She'd go find Tracy afterward, though, and discuss alternate medication. Whatever the doctor had prescribed must have been a tad strong. "Okay. I'm listening."

Grandma Louise settled back against the pillows. "Good. Now, according to family legend," she said, in the sing-song, storytelling style voice that Kat had so loved as a child, "in the 1890s, Catherine, one of your ancestors, went to live in Shanghai with her family. Unfortunately she fell in love with a man of Chinese descent. He used to call her his little cat and joke that he was a Rat, and he'd have to take care that she didn't eat him. Hah! If only he'd known what was in store for him."

Well, Kat thought, this sure is a new one. She didn't recall hearing any stories with a Chinese connection before.

"Foolish girl that she was, Catherine gave her virginity to this man, but rather than marry her as he'd promised, he chose to obey his family's wishes and take a Chinese bride. Long story short, Catherine was so incensed by his betrayal she visited a powerful magic practitioner and paid a small fortune for a curse that was supposed to give her lover bad luck for the rest of his life. But the curse backfired, turning Catherine into a cat and her ex-lover into a rat. And Catherine hunted him down and ate him."

Kat rolled her eyes. "Oh, please! You can't seriously believe in this nonsense."

"We can hardly disbelieve the evidence, can we?" her grandma said.

"What evidence?"

"The fact that all Catherine's female relatives born in the Year of the Rat, like she was—and *you* just happen to be—are cursed. The fact that every twelve years, timed to coincide with each Chinese Year of the Rat, you change into a cat and prowl off to harass your enemy, the Rat. The fact that ever since Chinese New Year, you've been changing into a cat at eleven each night, and then back into a human at one the next morning—that's the Rat's time of the day, you know. And you'll keep doing it until the Year of the Ox rolls around."

Kat stared at her, aghast. Could medication really provoke such a flight of fancy? Or was it something more sinister, some illness? No. Please, no. She pressed her fists against her roiling stomach.

"Don't you be looking at me like I've just grown ears and a tail. I'm not senile! Everything I've told you is true."

"But this is absurd!" She glared at her grandma, suspicion burgeoning. "This is all some joke, isn't it? Who put you up to this? Was it George?"

"No, dear. It's no joke."

Kat thought hard for a moment. "Okay, if I'm taking revenge on rats, why don't I just kill a bunch of rodents and be done with it? I assure you, I haven't been finding any dead rats on my pillow lately!" Hah! Let's see her grandma explain this away.

"That's because you're a vegetarian, dear."

"What does that have to do with anything?"

"You remember when you were twelve," Grandma Louise said, "and you cried buckets when your pet rat escaped? The truth is, it never escaped. You'd turned into a cat and you were a bit peckish, so you ate it. And some part of you must have known what you'd done because you went right off meat after that."

Kat lurched to her feet. "Enough. This is ridiculous! You can't possibly—"

"Katalina, sit!"

The order was a roar. Kat was so shocked that she did as she was told while casting worried glances beneath her eyelashes at her beloved grandma.

"Now, your cat-self is a picky eater like you," Grandma Louise said, frowning fiercely and wincing because of her shiner. "She doesn't much like the taste of rats, so she works off her frustrations by stealing stuff. It's usually only small, inexpensive things. But every now and then, she senses a man born in the Year of the Rat, and then she targets him and ups the ante. Makes his life a misery by stealing anything of value she can lay her paws on."

Prickles coursed down Kat's spine. And it was like her mind just opened up, allowing her to pluck a whole bunch of tantalizing little clues from various corners of her brain, and weave them into one cohesive whole. She suddenly understood why it'd never seemed conceivable to her that Cupcake had been the thief.

"I know you've been blaming Cupcake whenever you woke up in the morning to find gold cufflinks or some man's signet ring on your pillow. But the poor creature is innocent." Grandma Louise gazed at her with sympathetic eyes. "It's all making sense now, isn't it? It's why your mother left, too. She was weak. She couldn't handle what you are."

Kat could only nod, too shell-shocked to utter a word.

Grandma Louise yanked a video tape out from under her pillow. "Your mother taped this. When she left, she gave it to me for safe-keeping. You need to watch it so you'll finally believe."

Kat put the tape in the VCR and turned on the TV, and numbly watched a scratchy old black-and-white recording of her twelve-year-old self sitting up in bed, then morphing into a sleek black cat.

There was no denying it. She was a freak! Little wonder her mother had taken off and left her and—

Oh my God. Jace. He must have seen her change into a cat.

What the heck was she going to do about Jace?

Jace didn't know what the heck he was going to do about Kat. Given her panic, and her state of mind whenever she shifted back into a human, he firmly believed she had no recollection of changing forms or what she got up to as a cat. No one was that good of an actress.

She'd think he was clinically insane if he told her exactly what he'd seen. "Hi, Kat. Hey, did you know you turned into a cat last night? And when I finally got my shit together and thought to follow you, you were long gone. But hey, it all turned out okay, because cat-you turned up about an hour later with a stolen set of keys."

Yeah. Like that'd work.

Just like she would believe him when he told her that he'd broken a freaking speed record getting to his own house, hoping that she'd follow the pattern of the past couple of nights. And he'd never felt so helpless when she didn't show. He'd sprinted back to her house, calling, "Here, Kat! Here, kitty-Kat!" And he hadn't given a damn what anyone hearing him might have thought.

And waiting for her to return had been the worst hour of his damn life until he heard the cat-flap bang open. He'd felt a relief so profound that he'd had difficulty breathing. This must have been how his grandfather had felt, sitting up waiting for Jace or Jen to get back from some party. Nightmare.

He'd waited for Kat to deposit her prize on the pillow and change back into the woman he'd grown to care so much about in such a very short time. And then he tucked her up in bed, left a note in place of the loot, and walked out.

Coward that he was, he just hadn't been able to face her—didn't know how the hell he was gonna face her when she showed up at his place tonight, either.

He'd handed the keys in at the sheriff's office first thing in the morning and then kept himself busy with work.

Work. Yet another problem. If Kat got the contract, he'd be working closely with her. And if it wasn't already distracting enough having a sexual relationship with a colleague, keeping secrets from that colleague and worrying himself into an early grave about that colleague were just a fucking huge recipe for disaster. He wouldn't be able to focus one-hundred-percent on the job. And to a man like Jace, who'd built his business and his reputation on giving one-hundred-and-fucking-ten-percent to every job he took on, that was unacceptable.

But *this* situation he could fix. He'd pass the contract on to his 2IC. Stick around for another few days to oversee a smooth change of hands, then take himself back to his big-city apartment and his big-city job to lick his wounds.

Shit. His heart felt like it was being ripped from his chest, but he knew this was the right thing to do. He couldn't stick around for the duration and lie to Kat about what had happened to her last night. A clean break was the best way to handle this. He would make her think that now he'd gotten into her pants, he'd gone cold on her. Best for everyone if she thought he was a grade-A asshole who had just been using her. Best for everyone if she hated his guts.

In the back of his mind, though, he wondered what would happen if anyone else ever discovered her secret. Perhaps he should tell her the truth. Watching her recoil from him and treat him like he was a raving nut-job wouldn't be easy, but he had a thick skin. Even if she discounted everything he told her right now, something might clue her in later on, and she would realize he'd been telling her the truth. Besides, if some other poor bastard saw what Jace had seen and had the guts to come clean with her, he wouldn't be the first. It might just give the guy a bit more credibility with her.

He dialed the mayor's office and asked to speak to Paulie Evans.

"Jace! Was just about to call you."

"Nothing urgent, I hope."

"Just keeping you in the loop. Kat Meyer's pulled out of the running. Family stuff, apparently. Something to do with her Grandma Louise. She was pretty vague about the whole thing. Bit of a shock, though, given how keen she was. And given that I'd stuck my neck out for her." Paulie didn't sound very happy.

"I'm seeing her tonight," Jace said. "I'll see if I can change her mind."

"Good," the mayor said. "You do that. Otherwise we're gonna be stuck with Gena Hamilton or my wife's best friend's best friend. And I'm pretty sure that'll mean Gena's a shoo-in."

"Can't let that happen, can we?" Jace said.

"Glad to see we're on the same page."

Jace chewed the end of his pencil, considering his options. And wondering how the heck the woman who'd raised Kat since she was twelve years old could possibly not know about her granddaughter's "little problem".

Hang on. Kat had mentioned that she'd been twelve when she first started sleepwalking. Yeah, and he'd bet his granddad's gold watch that was no coincidence. What if she'd first changed into a cat around puberty, like around twelve-years-old?

Fuck! It all fit. He knew it from the frisson icing his spine and the sense of knowing that had settled in his gut.

He glanced at his watch. Three p.m. Plenty of time to visit Kat's Grandma Louise. Boy-oh-boy, the old girl had a heap of explaining to do.

Kat was tempted to pull her comforter up over her head and let her phone ring. But she'd never been one of those people who could ignore a ringing phone. What if the call was urgent?

What if it was Jace?

Her stomach rebelled at the very thought of confronting him, but she grabbed the receiver because she was sooo freaking brave. Yeah. Right. "Kat Meyer speaking."

"Kat, it's Tracy. There's some hot-shot architect named Jace Burton up visiting your grandma. Louise insists she's sick of being stuck in bed and wants him to take her outside for a spin in her wheelchair. You know how Louise is around a handsome man. I just wanted to check that you're okay with that. The guy says he knows you."

Kat's head was whirling. "Wheelchair?"

"The doctor insisted. It's just for a couple of days until we're sure her ankle's healed. Now, about this Jace Burton. You okay with him taking Louise around the grounds? Somehow I can't see her being able to twist him around her little finger." Kat could hear the smile in Tracy's voice. "He's got charm to burn, that man. Has her eating out of his hand."

"Uh, yeah. He's above board," Kat said, because she couldn't for the life of her think of anything else to say.

But she knew exactly what she had *do*. This out-of-the-blue visit was no coincidence. Jace was trying to find out what Grandma Louise knew.

Crap! Knowing her grandma, she'd take one look at him and figure if he was already involved with Kat and since he already knew about the curse, he'd make the perfect husband!

And Jace? Well, she squirmed just thinking about him and what his future plans might be.

Pulling on her running clothes, she sprinted for the door.

Kat signed in at reception and was told that Jace and Grandma Louise were still out on the grounds somewhere. She jogged through the gardens for a good ten minutes before she finally spotted them beneath the shade of a glorious old oak.

She slowed to a walk and as she approached, she could see that Jace was sitting at the foot of the wheelchair, gazing up at Grandma Louise with rapt attention. He loosed a bellow of laughter. "Oh no," she heard him say. "She didn't!"

"I'm afraid she did," Kat's grandma said. "Never could eat meat from that day forward. Drove me crazy up the wall trying to figure out how to get enough protein into that child. Didn't want her to end up stunted."

Kat cringed inwardly. Not the story about her pet rat's demise. "Grandma, how could you?"

Both of them glanced up. And both had guilty expressions on their faces.

"He already knew," her grandmother said. "He saw you shift."

"Yeah. And knowing sure made him inclined to want to stick around, didn't it?" Kat hadn't meant to sound so bitter, but she was hurting and couldn't help lashing out.

"I'm a fucking coward, I know," Jace said.

"Jace! Language!"

He hung his head. "Sorry, Louise."

To Kat's amazement, her grandma patted him on the head. "You've had a huge shock," she cooed. "Not surprising you'd forget to mind your tongue."

Aw, poor Jace. He'd had a shock. Well, what about her? What about finding out she was a genuine cat-burglar of the feline persuasion?

Jace stood and brushed some grass from the seat of his jeans. "Do you mind if I talk to Kat alone for a moment, Louise? There's something I need to say."

Kat's grandma smiled. "Go ahead, son. Just tell her exactly what you told me and everything'll be dandy."

He took a step toward her, and Kat opened her mouth to protest that no freaking way was everything "dandy", or ever likely to be in a million years, but she didn't get the chance. Jace cupped her nape and swooped in to plant a kiss on her lips. And not just any kiss. A kiss that quite literally made her toes curl in her sneakers. He possessed her mouth, licking the seam of her lips, thrusting his tongue against hers, coaxing a response from her.

And she couldn't resist. She kissed him back and gave it everything she had, everything she longed to say but was too scared to voice.

Vaguely, through a haze of wonder and desire, Kat heard her grandmother yelling, "Go, Jace!"

And when he pulled back just enough to stare into her eyes, she didn't try to hide what she felt for him. She let it all show. And hoped it would be enough.

"I love you," he said. "God damn it, I love you, Katalina Louise Meyer. Doesn't matter whether you're a cat or a woman, I love you. But there's one thing we're gonna have to get clear. Well, three things, actually."

"Oh?" she whispered, not daring to hope. "What might those be?"

"First, no way are you pulling your proposal. Because no way am I working with Gena Hamilton. You got that?"

He waited for her nod.

"Second, I'm twelve years older than you, and evidently I'm a Rat. That a problem?"

He waited for her to shake her head.

"And third is that tomorrow, we're getting a new cat-flap installed in your house—one of those ones you can lock so that critters can't get out. Because I'm not gonna lie awake worrying about you prowling round the neighborhood. And neither am I gonna go chasing after cat-you anymore, you hear me? Your cat-burglar days are over."

"I hear you. But what about your job and your apartment? Aren't you going back home as soon as this contract is over?"

He nodded. And her hope-filled heart plummeted right to her toes.

"But I want you to come with me. Just until we work it all out and decide where we're gonna live. Do you think we can work it all out, Kat? Do you think we've got a shot at making you and me, the cat and the rat, work?"

She smiled, her heart bursting with joy and love. And a big old dollop of sheer, unadulterated lust. "Oh, yeah. I reckon we've got a shot. No way are you getting rid of me and Cupcake that easy."

"Atta girl," her grandmother yelled, pumping her fist in the air. "So when's the wedding?"

Epilogue

It was nearly eleven in the evening, and George was sitting in his rocking chair, reading a book. Nothing unusual in that. He always had been a bit of a night owl.

He heard a scratching of claws and an imperious *meow*!

"Won't be a moment," he said, and hauled himself out of the chair to admit his late-night visitor. He waited for the cat to slink through the doorway, then checked the corridor before carefully closing the door behind her. The staff would chase her out if they caught her in his room.

When he'd settled himself back in his chair, he patted his lap.

The cat didn't need to be told twice. She leaped onto his knees and curled up into a ball.

George stroked the sleek black fur. "Promise you won't steal my cufflinks tonight. I need them for church tomorrow." He smiled to himself when she butted her head against his hand and rebuked him for his temerity with a tiny nip. "Now, now, Louise. Play nice or I'll yank your tail."

About the Author:

It's been my dream to be published in a *Secrets* anthology ever since I bought my first **Secrets** anthology—**Volume 6**, with stories from Angela Knight, Sandy Fraser, Alice Gaines and MaryJanice Davidson. I mean to say, what a line-up! How could I possibly resist adding that one to my must-reads pile? So when I found out that my novella had been accepted for a **Secrets** anthology, it was a real dream-come-true moment! I danced 'round the house in my PJ bottoms and my ratty old Huffer t-shirt, and I'm sure the "SQUEEEE!" could be heard across the ditch in Australia, LOL. And I must confess I was still in my PJs at 3pm, because I just "had" to email my friends and writing buddies. You just gotta love being an author and working from home ;-)

So I hope you enjoy my **Secrets** story. And please, feel free to drop me a line at maree@mareeanderson.com—I'd love to hear from you!

Kellen's Conquest

꙰꙰(꙰)꙰꙰

by Anne Kane

To My Reader:

I love to fantasize about what the future might hold for mankind. One thing I'm sure about is that love will still make it all worthwhile. I hope you enjoy reading Kellen and Mia's story as much as I enjoyed telling it.

Chapter 1

Year: 2478
Place: Earth Colony 6, Urali System

Mia looked around and rolled her eyes. Kellen's office looked the same as it had six months ago—sterile. The man needed a decorator, or at least a can of paint. Beige did not count as a color.

She crossed to the computer console, gliding on the balls of her feet. Her childhood in the projects had taught her the art of moving stealthily. Now, with a practiced flick of her wrist, she unwrapped the little dragon charm from around her neck. This charm, which she had named Spike, interfaced her neural implants with external systems using its A.I. base program. Its eyes opened, and pale green sparks glittered within the jewel-like lenses.

The computer's access port gaped wide for easy access. Mia hesitated uneasily and tucked a stray lock of hair behind her ear. Frowning, she took a moment to check the shadows for potential problems.

Kellen might be a lot of things, but he wasn't a fool. A sinking feeling landed in the pit of her stomach. She bit her lip and placed the little dragon on the computer interface board. Closing her eyes, she let her mind slip away and merge with the vast array of data banks.

Although she made her living as a data courier and thief, this wasn't theft. Not really. The file, the original idea, years of research and the design of the weapon all belonged to her. She'd just been too hasty when she departed, leaving the documentation and proof of her hard work behind.

Ah. There it is. Mia directed the download of the weapon specs through her implant to the little dragon, quickly running the data through a scanner to make sure the contents were intact. *Perfect.* She pulled her consciousness out of the computer.

"Not going to stay long enough to say hi?" The lazy drawl sent heat racing through her gut, even as she silently cursed the speaker. Kellen lounged inside the doorway, blocking the only way out. The smug look on his face confirmed what she already knew. *He set me up.* She'd waltzed into the lion's den like a naive idiot. Damn! She should have known better.

"Kellen. How nice to see you again." She forced her lips into a smile. She could only hope he'd lost a few brain cells in the months she'd been gone. "I'd love to stay and catch up, but I have a deadline to meet. You know what a stickler Marshal is for punctuality."

She waltzed across the floor, making sure her breasts bounced in their spandex prison. If she could distract him long enough, she'd be out of here. Just a few more feet. She edged past him and reached for the door handle, still smiling like a sex droid. It really amazed her how often that worked. Men could be surprisingly shallow at times.

"I don't think so, darling." The cold look in Kellen's eyes negated the amused tone of his voice. He snaked his arm out and caught her in an iron grip. "The last time I let you out of my sight, you didn't come home." He drew her back against his rock-hard erection and cupped her face with his hand. "I hadn't finished playing yet." He stared at her lips. "You owe me." He fastened his mouth on hers, his tongue roughly demanding entrance.

Mia whimpered as her treacherous body responded enthusiastically to his assault.

He had never been a gentle lover. Now his left hand dropped from her waist to her butt and drew her hard against the impressive bulge in his jeans. He ground his hips into her belly, fondling her breasts through the tight fabric of her uni-shirt.

Her nipples hardened and cream gathered in her sex. Her body remembered how much she enjoyed spreading her legs beneath him, how much she enjoyed having Kellen Tavish deep inside her.

She shoved her arms between his tight biceps and struggled to escape. *I can't do this.* She'd left him once. As much as she wanted to feel his cock inside her one more time and to hell with consequences, she knew her heart wouldn't survive leaving him again.

He was AlphElite, and she was just another female civi. She wasn't a breeder or soldier, only a female. She wanted so many things he couldn't give her. She wanted children, a home, and a family. She wanted all the things she'd never had and secretly longed for as a child. She wouldn't get those with Kellen.

He stood at the top of the proverbial food chain. No matter how wildly her traitorous body responded to his expert caresses, she knew he'd never pledge to her. Should he decide to pledge, he could command the attention of a dozen suitable mates, beautiful, rich influential females who would bring honor to his name and breed perfect AlphElite children for him. He considered Mia a toy, a pet he'd use and enjoy until he tired of her. As her handler Marshal enjoyed reminding her, she was a street brat, not a keeper.

"If you don't stop squirming, I may have to take you here on the desk." Kellen grinned, obviously remembering the many times they'd been too wild to wait until they staggered into the sleeping quarters. "Of course, I'm game if you are."

"Let. Me. Go." Mia bit the words out through clenched teeth. It wasn't fair, him having such a gorgeous body. Six-foot five, with wide shoulders, brawny arms and abs you could scrub laundry on, and his muscles rippled enticingly as he kept her locked against him. He didn't even notice her attempts to fight him off.

She aimed her heel at his instep, a maneuver one of her colleagues had assured her would bring any man to his knees. He shifted his weight, taking her with him. Her foot slammed down on the floor and a shaft of pain shot up her own leg. Not the result she'd intended.

Time to change tactics.

Mia turned full into his body and raised both arms above her head, sliding them around his neck. She lifted her head and eased her tongue across his mouth. *Mmmmm...that tasted good.* She nipped at his full lower lip. She loved those lips, especially when he used them on her.

She'd fuck his brains out and escape when he let his guard slip in the glowing aftermath. If she got to enjoy herself, well, all the better.

Unfortunately, he knew her too well. Grabbing one wrist, he twisted her around, binding her hands behind her back with a length of plastcreet.

Mia snarled in frustration. "Damn, you're an annoying mutant."

It embarrassed her to feel her sex creaming wildly in response to his touch. She'd have to start screwing around a bit, just as soon as she managed to get herself out of here.

He flipped her around to face him, held her by the restraints and stared off into the distance, his brow furrowed in concentration.

Uh oh. That look meant he was using his neuro-implants to contact someone. Probably not good news for her.

She tensed her hands against the restraints.

His harsh blue gaze snapped back to her.

She recognized that look, too. Seemed she wouldn't be going anywhere just yet.

He lowered her to the floor, his hands surprisingly gentle while he ripped the front of her uni-suit open and freed her breasts. Cool air splashed across her skin and her treacherous nipples stiffened in eager anticipation.

He pinched one nipple between callused fingers, growling his approval when she flinched and struggled to escape. Lowering his head, he sucked the other nipple into his mouth.

Oh, yeah, it had been way too long. She whimpered and arched her hips off the floor, begging for more. Chuckling like the smug male he was, he ripped the suit down to her crotch, sliding one big hand between her thighs. Rough knuckles brushed along her cleft, causing her to cream even more.

He liked it rough.

But then, so did she.

He palmed her sex, one finger casually flicking the hard nub of her clit.

A needy whimper escaped her clenched lips. She arched against him.

"Untie me." Her plea came out a husky whisper.

"I don't think so. I like you like this." He jammed one long finger into her slick sex.

She bucked under the sudden entry.

Kellen smiled, his finger stroking slowly in and out of her pussy. "Seems you like it too."

"Bastard!"

He raised one perfect eyebrow. "You started this."

His lazy drawl sent a flicker of heat thundering through her belly. He stroked one finger in her sex and circled the hard little button of her clit with his thumb.

She schooled her features to look bored.

He laughed and swooped down to reclaim her mouth.

As he kissed her, coherent thought vanished for a few critical seconds. She twisted her body sideways against the hard length of his cock. A swift intake of breath let her know he'd felt that move.

Mia wiggled her hands. The restraints didn't budge, the cool plastcreet expanding and contracting to prevent her from injuring herself.

Damn him to hell. She never did do submissive well. Kellen knew her better than this. Was he trying to piss her off?

He wiggled lower, pausing to catch her gaze before he pushed her legs apart and gave her a nice wet lick from anus to clit.

She yelped, every nerve ending on fire. While she gasped and struggled to peel her libido off the ceiling, he settled in to lick and suck with a vengeance, teasing her until she teetered on the edge of orgasm.

"Keeeeellen. Please," she panted.

He loomed over her, the head of his cock pressed against the tight entrance to her sex.

"Please what?" he ground out. His eyes were dark with arousal, his gaze searing her features. "Please fuck you? Please ram my cock into your tight little pussy till it tickles your tonsils?"

"Pleeaaase." She'd gone beyond making sense, beyond pride, beyond anything but pure feeling. It had been too long since she'd had him. Too long since she'd felt like this. "Please fuck me. Please!"

"My pleasure." He gave her a dark sadistic grin. His fingers dug into her waist. He worked his big thick cock into her swollen, waiting pussy one slow centimeter at a time, holding her hips down so she couldn't arch against him, couldn't take more of him than he was willing to give her.

Mia whimpered and moaned, twisting and bucking helplessly beneath him. She couldn't help herself. She wanted it all and she wanted it now. She wanted him buried in her so deep he'd never get out again.

As Kellen picked up the pace, his eyes went molten and glowed a sapphire blue.

"I missed you, you little bitch." He rasped the words between clenched teeth and rammed into her, seating his cock so deep his balls slapped her ass. "What the hell were you thinking, running away like that?"

Mia groaned. Now was so not the time for an in-depth discussion of their doomed relationship. Luckily, he didn't expect an answer. Frankly, at this point, she couldn't imagine why she'd left this luscious prick. No. Don't think about that. In that direction, a universe of hurt waited.

In and out he plunged his wonderful cock. That's all she could think about now. Harder and faster, he pumped his hips while she thrashed under him, meeting him thrust for hard deep thrust.

Heat coiled in her belly. The mother of all orgasms sizzled along every nerve ending. Each stroke of that delectable cock rocketed her closer to the edge.

Abruptly he pulled his cock from her dripping wet pussy and sat back on his heels.

"What the hell...?" She humped her body at him with instinctive need.

Ignoring her unspoken plea, he used his AlphElite strength to flip her over onto her belly.

She gasped.

He grabbed the back of her uni-suit and ripped the fabric away. Spreading her legs wide, he rammed his cock into her wet sex from behind, tilting her hips upwards to get maximum penetration.

DAMN! That felt good.

She braced her elbows on the floor as he reared over her, wrapping his arms around her torso to fondle her breasts, tweaking each nipple in turn until they hardened into pebbled points.

One thing about Kellen—he never disappointed her. He annoyed the hell out of her and made her want to kill him slowly and painfully, but he never left her wanting.

He resumed his steady pace and slid his delicious cock in and out of her pussy with agonizing slowness, making her aware of every luscious inch of him.

She couldn't hold back any longer. She climaxed hard, the waves of pleasure so intense they bordered on pain. She felt his hand sliding up to her neck. Just before everything went black.

Chapter 2

Where the hell am I?

Mia attempted to sit and choked back a squeal as pain hammered the side of her head. She promptly lay down again. Pain just wasn't something she knowingly courted. She concentrated on breathing while she waited for the pounding to subside.

Breathe in. Breathe out. It helped. A little.

Kellen! She'd been having mind-blowing sex with Kellen, and then….

She tried harder to remember but drew a blank. She couldn't recall anything but the sex. She couldn't even figure out why she'd been fucking Kellen. She had left him months ago. Maybe she imagined that. Maybe she'd been ill. Yeah, that must be the reason for her lack of memory. She was hallucinating.

Her hallucination opened the door and eyed her speculatively. "How do you feel?"

He actually sounded concerned. Mia frowned. Could hallucinations talk? A neon blue lizard streaked over Kellen's left shoulder and hovered above the bed. Its green eyes stared intently into hers.

"Hey! That's my dragon. Spike, get back here!" Mia grabbed for the impudent A.I. It easily dodged her awkward lunge and scooted over to land on Kellen's shoulder. If she didn't know better, she could have sworn the tiny dragon stuck a forked tongue out at her before burying its little face in Kellen's neck. So much for programmed loyalty.

She rubbed her head, relieved to discover the pounding had faded to a dull roar. Then, as understanding dawned, her chin jerked up. Kellen had used the pressure points in her neck to knock her out, and that was why her head ached. What the hell was he up to?

"Where are we?" She winced and lowered her voice. The pounding hadn't faded that much. "Why is Spike ignoring my orders?" She faked a steely glare. No need to let him know she was scared. "What the hell did you do?"

Kellen grunted and swiped a hand through his hair. He looked pretty cranky considering she was the one with the headache. "We're in orbit. I have a delivery to make in the Bakol system, and it seemed like a good idea to get off planet for awhile." He let his gaze slide over her, his expression dark and brooding. "I don't like people stealing from me." His gaze rested on her uncovered breasts.

Mia belatedly realized she was naked under the thin sheet. She pulled it up to her chin and stared mutinously into those cold blue eyes. "I didn't steal anything! I'd just retrieved the plans for my auro cannon when you came back to the office. They were my plans and they belong to me. That's not stealing."

Kellen shifted his weight restlessly, clenched hands betraying his tension. "Really? Then why didn't you just call me up and ask for them? Too complicated for you?"

"I didn't want to see you." Mia lowered her eyes sheepishly. It wasn't a confession she particularly wanted to make, especially under these circumstances.

"No shit. But somebody wanted me to see you." Kellen stalked to the bed and grabbed her chin with callused fingers, forcing her face up so she had to meet his irritated gaze. "Who sent you into my office? Don't you bother telling me no one, because someone made damn sure I knew there was going to be a break-in. You were set up."

Mia gasped. That just wasn't possible. She said, "Marshal sent me in. He said he could get me three thousand parsets for those plans, almost enough for me to retire."

Then she clamped her mouth shut. He didn't need to know her plans. He wasn't any part of them, now or in the future. She wanted more of a commitment in her life than he could offer, and she was damn well going to get it. Kellen could just go to hell and take all his AlphElite buddies with him.

His eyes narrowed. "You're trying to close me out. I'm not that easy to get rid of. Someone wanted me to kill you, and I intend to make sure that doesn't happen. I got an anonymous vid-call this morning. Someone claiming to be a friend said a Cyborg was going to break into my office and steal the main memory drives from the computer. They suggested I move the computer console out and set the room to detonate."

"Detonate?" she whispered.

A muscle twitched along his jaw and he bared his teeth in a predator's smile. "Cyborgs are tough opponents. A smart man would have taken the advice. If I had, you'd be dead. Unfortunately for my unknown friend, I was in the mood to kick a little ass." His grin gained a little humor. "That was before I found out whose ass it was. I can think of so many more interesting things to do with that cute ass of yours."

"But that means…." An icy chill danced down her spine.

She didn't want to go there. Marshal had been her handler since she'd lived in the projects. She trusted him, if only because she knew how much he valued the money he made off her. She shook her head. "Marshal wouldn't do that. He has no reason to want me dead." She glowered, daring Kellen to contradict her.

"Maybe, maybe not." He shrugged expressively. "How much would it cost to get him to sell you out?"

"He wouldn't. I can't make him money if I'm dead. A one-time payoff wouldn't get him enough to replace me." She wished she felt as sure as she sounded.

"That would depend on the payoff." Kellen reached over to swat her ass. She glared at him.

He laughed grimly as he jumped to his feet and strode away. "We leave orbit in fifteen minutes. Get your butt covered and up to the bridge. You can crew for me. You may as well earn your keep."

The door opened at his approach. He disappeared into the corridor, the traitorous little dragon still perched on his shoulder.

Mia glared after Kellen's retreating back. Who the hell does he think he is, a frigging slave lord?

The door slid shut with a swoosh, hiding him from her view.

Mia made her way to the bridge, not surprised the ship hadn't changed much since she'd last been on it. The walls were the same neutral color, and the floor still sported that ugly but serviceable plastcreet blend. She'd already concluded that Kellen wasn't the redecorating type.

He threw an impersonal glance in her direction before busying himself with the final checklists. "Belt in. We're revving up to break orbit."

Settling herself in the copilot's seat, Mia engaged the restraining harness and eyed the blinking lights on her console. It had been a long time. Back when they first met, she'd enjoyed crewing for Kellen. She loved the feel of controlling all that power, making the ship's huge mass respond to her command. She loved the freedom of space and the fact that Kellen trusted her with his ship.

Now she spun her seat in a half-circle and stopped in mid-motion, disconcerted to find him watching her with that predatory stare on his harsh face.

"What?" she snarled.

"You look good," he said softly.

Before she could react, think of a sane reply, he was all business. "Checklist complete. Flight plan uploaded into the computer. All systems are go. First and third thrusters are at max. Ready ignition sequence."

Her training kicked in without conscious effort. "Aye, captain. Ignition sequence ready." She keyed the thrusters and set the count in motion with the ease of long practice. "Launch minus ten and counting."

"Second and fourth thrusters, stand by for backup."

"Second and fourth, standing by."

"Brace for launch in five, four, three, two…."

Mia settled into her seat beneath the restraining harness as the ship shuddered and struggled to leave the planetary gravity field. The pressure thickened to an almost unbearable level.

She clung to the armrests and bit back a scream while the punishing force pinned her down like an insect. Then they were free, hurtling into the black void of space.

Her stomach lurched under the sudden transition to zero-g. The horrid sensation of freefall surrounded her. The harness kept her from floating away. A split-second later, the ship's artificial gravity field took hold and she fell back into her seat. She'd never gotten used to that part.

Mia sucked in a deep breath to steady her nerves and checked the glowing readouts that said they were on course. No warning beacons blared at them to stop. No surprise there. Kellen didn't have to answer to the Port Authorities. His AlphElite status gave him the cachet of diplomatic immunity for any flight plan he cared to submit.

She tapped the control for the harness and the straps folded back into their slots. The stars twinkling in the forward view port drew her attention. She sighed. The brilliant arc of the glowing nebula stretching across the black vastness of space always made her feel better.

Kellen switched control over to the A.I. interface before removing his restraining harness. He stood and stretched his arms over his head, working the kinks out of his muscles.

Mia turned. Her breath hitched in her throat at the sight of his deeply muscled chest bulging under that taut shirt. She straightened her shoulders. "Truce?"

"Truce," he agreed. "We need to find out what's going on. We have a better chance of that if we work together. Marshal wasn't the only one who knew you were going to retrieve the file."

"Yes, he was. I never discuss my runs before I go out. Not with anyone. You know that."

He crossed his arms and regarded her from beneath those incredible long lashes. "You said he could get you three thousand parsets for the file. That means he already had a buyer, probably someone who approached him." Kellen paused, went to the console and tapped his fingers by the main comp access. "Who knew about the file? Who was the buyer? Who would know you'd be the one he'd send in?"

Mia felt the blood rush from her head. She leaned against the wall to steady herself and did her best to present a brave face. Kellen was right. Marshal worked on percentages. If he named a price before a job, he already had a firm buyer.

"I don't know." She tried to think of anyone else who might have known about the prototype. "I never told anyone. Why would I? It's not the sort of thing that comes up in casual conversation."

"What about a debrief when you…." Kellen paused, his eyes narrowing dangerously. "When you ran out on me?"

"I didn't run," she corrected him. "I left. You don't own me." She thrust out her chin and squared her shoulders.

"However you phrase it, were you debriefed?" Kellen ignored her attitude and repeated his question, his eyes cold chips of blue.

Mia lowered her gaze. "Yes," she mumbled. "It's procedure, but I didn't tell them about the weapon. They didn't ask."

Kellen looked skeptical.

"They didn't!"

"Do they use drugs when they debrief you?"

"No! I'm not crazy enough to agree to that. They asked a lot of questions about your security, who you see and who comes to visit you. You were just my cover. They didn't think you had anything worth stealing." She felt her cheeks burn with a blush. "I'm sorry. I know you trusted me."

Kellen snorted inelegantly.

"I didn't trust you, darling. I knew what you were up to, but you were just too hot and sweet for me to send away. I always did have a sweet tooth. I made sure you didn't have access to anything critical and I ran damage control on whatever I let get out."

He had the audacity to grin at her, as if he expected her to be impressed with his ingenuity.

Mia sputtered. "What the hell do you mean you knew? I spent the last two years feeling guilty for leading you on and lying to you and you knew? You bastard." She raised her arm to slap his arrogant face, ashamed that she'd been soft enough to care about his feelings.

Kellen blocked the blow with a flick of his wrist and pulled her in close, preventing her from attempting another strike. "It seems we may have to work a little harder at this truce." He lowered his head to brush a feather-light kiss across her forehead. "I'm sorry. I didn't mean to hurt you."

Mia pulled out of his arms. Damn him to hell. She hated the way he could make her feel like a stupid female civi.

"I apologize," She said stiffly. "You were only pointing out the truth. I'm the one in the wrong."

Kellen sighed again. "I knew what the game was, and I played, too. Think about who else might have known about your weapon. We need to figure out this mess." He turned and stalked back to throw himself in the pilot's seat. "Whatever the issues between us, I don't want you dead."

Caught off guard by the honesty in his voice, Mia opened her mouth to reply but he cut her off before she managed to get a word out.

"You might want to clean up while I review the scan reports. We'll be switching over to FTL flight as soon we clear the Oort cloud around this system."

"In other words, get the hell out of your face." Mia muttered. Childishly, she stuck her tongue out at the back of Kellen's head.

"If you prefer." Kellen's hands flashed over the controls. Multi-colored lights flashed across the console in an annoyingly cheerful display.

Mia snorted and left the bridge. Double damn him. She'd forgotten about his enhanced hearing.

Mia stretched her arms above her head and turned on the shower. Fortunately, Kellen still liked his little luxuries. And real water, even reclaimed water, was a luxury in space. The warm liquid streamed over her body in a delicious spray. She opened the in-stall cabinet and perused the contents. A slight frown creased her forehead when she realized he'd kept it stocked with all her favorites. More likely, he hadn't bothered to throw them away when she left. She chose a jasmine-scented soap and luxuriated in the suds it produced, working them all the way from her hair to the tips of her toes. Her eyes closed and she inhaled deeply, the fragrance taking her back to a time when she'd dared to believe life could be different, that there could be a future for her with one of the AlphElite.

She sighed and turned so the water cascaded over her, rinsing the fragrant bubbles away. She was a big girl now. It was time to stop wallowing in fairy tales. She needed to figure out who could have set her up. Who would have something to gain by her death?

She stepped out of the shower stall, plucked a warm fluffy towel from the rack, and wandered back to the stateroom. Rummaging through the closet, she found an old exercise suit and slipped into it, taking comfort from its warmth. Feeling clean and decently covered, she headed down the corridor to the practice gym. It might be inefficient to work out right after showering, but she had to stay in shape and running had the bonus of keeping her calm. Now more than ever, she needed to center herself. She hadn't been ready for the disorientation brought by the reunion with Kellen.

The practice room was much as she remembered it. After doing a quick set of warm ups, she chose the treadmill. The corners of her mouth quirked upwards in an involuntary grin. No one had used it since she'd last been on-board ship. The machine was still set to her height and weight. Seems Kellen's reputation as a ladies' man was more gossip than fact. All she needed to do now was adjust the speed.

She'd paid a lot more attention to keeping in shape since she'd been out on her own. With no one to watch her back in a tough spot, she had to be sure she could get herself out of whatever trouble she landed in. Of course, she'd gotten herself into this particular mess, and it didn't look like she'd be getting out any time soon.

Mia palmed the activation control and started to run, keeping a steady pace and ignoring the twinges in her legs. Her mind wandered. Who was behind this?

No matter how hard she tried, she couldn't imagine Marshal setting her up. He was a cold, arrogant son of a bitch, but an extremely practical one. He stood to make a great deal of money on this deal and even more on her future escapades. It didn't make sense for him to set her up.

Perhaps the culprit was the client who'd ordered the run. But the client wouldn't know which agent the ORG would decide to send in. Ideally, nobody except Marshal and perhaps the head of the Outfit even knew she was an agent. None of this made any sense.

Was this whole conspiracy theory just a product of Kellen's less than trusting mind, or was someone really trying to kill her?

Kellen paced back and forth on the bridge. He couldn't think of one good reason why anyone would want Mia dead. Money and power were the two most common motives for murder, and they just didn't make any sense here. Mia had no money, no family, no power base of any kind. She was great at what she did, but there weren't any competitors who would profit by getting her out of the way. She was right about Marshal too. He had more riding on keeping her alive than anyone, so it would make no sense for him to tip Kellen off. But someone had. And that someone wanted Mia dead.

Kellen snarled in frustration. Doing was his strong suit, not sitting around playing what-if. He strode off the bridge and headed down to the exercise deck, needing to work off some of this tension before he attempted to deal with Mia again.

Heading down the portside corridor, he stopped abruptly as his enhanced senses detected the unlikely smell of jasmine. He closed his eyes, feeling his body harden at the remembered association. Jasmine had always been Mia's favorite scent. The master stateroom had retained that smell long after she had pulled her disappearing act. Some days, when he couldn't relax, when he kept tossing and turning in his big empty bed, he'd actually sprinkled jasmine scent on the mattress and tried to imagine her desertion had never happened, that she was still somewhere aboard ship.

Gods, he'd been in rough shape. And he ought to know better. AlphElite didn't believe in love. They knew it to be a fairy tale used to keep the civilians in line. Civilians made wonderful playthings, but that was all. When he pledged, it would be to someone carefully picked to breed him strong sons and heirs. He needed to keep his priorities straight here. Mia was a good fuck, the best he'd ever had. He'd find out who the hell wanted her killed and deal with them. Then he'd offer her a permanent position as his bed partner. It would provide her with stability and a secure future. She wouldn't have to risk her sexy neck stealing data anymore. And he wouldn't have to miss her anymore.

He resumed his march towards the exercise deck, pleased with his plans for the future. Pausing at the entrance to the exercise room, he took the opportunity to observe Mia before she became aware of his presence. She'd lost weight in the time she'd been gone. She looked leaner and harder than he remembered. Well-defined muscles corded along her arms and legs. He'd felt the addition of muscle on her small frame when they made love earlier.

He shook his head, disgusted with his mental slip. He really needed to keep his perspective here. They'd fucked earlier. That's all. Just a nice wel-come-back fuck.

His gaze slid possessively down her lean body and over her hips, taking in the long smooth length of her legs and the firm uptilted breasts restrained by a severe practice harness. A ghost of a smile flitted across his harsh features. She'd always tried to downplay the size of her chest. He thought it perfect, two nice handfuls of warm responsive flesh for him to play with.

He deliberately made noise when he entered the room, alerting her to his presence. He could tell the exact moment that she became aware of him. Her head came up and her eyes narrowed, sweeping nervously back and forth. She looked small and vulnerable, and somewhere in the vicinity of his heart he felt a familiar ache that had been missing since last he saw her. He'd be dammed if he'd let anyone hurt her now that she'd returned to his protection. Whether she was willing to admit it or not, she belonged with him. He would find the people responsible for threatening her and neutralize them.

He sauntered over to the treadmill, striving to look casual and in control. Even in that ridiculous exercise suit, she managed to look good enough to eat.

She acknowledged him with a curt nod, slowed the machine to a walk, and grabbed the towel dangling from the grip bar, using it to wipe the sweat from the back of her neck. "I didn't think you'd mind if I worked out for a bit. I like to keep in shape." Her voice wavered just a little.

He stared at her lips. She had such nice lips. Full and soft and very tempting. "Kiss me." Naked desire edged his voice.

The words hung heavily in the air between them. He watched her throat tighten convulsively as she swallowed. The pink tip of her tongue slid out to moisten her lips, and his groin tightened in eager response.

He leaned closer, the scent of jasmine filling his senses. He knew he should leave her alone. He knew he was playing with fire. She'd run out on him once. She hadn't planned on returning. She could run again.

He didn't care.

He wanted her.

He wanted her spread naked beneath him, begging him to fuck her.

He repeated the demand. "Kiss me, Mia."

She hesitated, and for a moment he thought he'd have to have to make the first move. Then her eyes closed and she swayed towards him. He wasn't sure if she crossed that last few feet of deck herself or if he met her halfway. Her lips opened, ready for his assault, and he took complete advantage. His arms went round her and drew her hard against him, letting her feel for herself how much he wanted her.

Her body melted, molding itself tightly to his hard frame. She uttered a soft cry and parted her lips, inviting him to plunder the depths of her mouth.

He put a tight rein on his lust, forced himself to slow down, to inhale her intoxicating scent. His tongue probed the depths of her mouth, dueling with hers, withdrawing for a minute to trace the outline of her lips, taste the faint traces of her mint lip balm before returning to plunder anew.

She responded eagerly, wrapping one long leg around him and grinding her hips into his, her body instinctively seeking release.

His cock jerked, eager to accommodate her. He ground his jean-clad erection against her, letting her know how much the feel of her eager body aroused him.

His hand went to her nape and tilted her head back while his questing tongue tasted the faint trace of sweat lingering in the hollow of her neck. He felt her pulse beating erratically under his tongue, betraying her arousal. He ran one big hand down her spine to cup her ass, kneading the firm flesh through the snug fabric of her exercise suit.

"Damn you, Kellen. Why didn't you just let me go?" She breathed the question into the hollow of his neck, sending a shiver of lust straight down his spine. "It's never going to work between us."

He brought his head up to reclaim her lips, silencing her protests and her doubts. He ran his hand along the front of her exercise suit, opening it with practiced ease and releasing the catch of the practice restraint. Her glorious breasts spilled into his waiting hand. He brought his other hand down so he could cup both of her breasts, holding them up to suck first one, then the other into his mouth, teasing the nipples into hard little nubs.

He raised his head and stared directly into her mutinous eyes. "I'm not letting you go," he warned, his voice hard and implacable. "You know you want me every bit as much as I want you."

He scooped her into his arms, his AlphElite strength making light of her weight. Walking over to the padded floor mats, he carefully laid her down, placing his own body on top of her so that she couldn't escape. When he ran his thumb across one sensitive nipple, Mia whimpered, arcing upwards in a silent plea.

He smiled grimly. She could protest all she wanted, but her body betrayed her needs.

For now, that would have to be enough. The threat to her safety would force her to stay at his side, giving him time to convince her that she needed the arrangement to be permanent.

Chapter 3

Two standard weeks later, entering the Hubrian system.

Mia keyed her breakfast order into the galley computer, hesitating between fruit or a cereal. She chose a fruit/yogurt combo.

"Coffee?" She glanced over at Kellen who was busy checking computer readouts.

"Hmm?" Kellen glanced up absentmindedly. "Oh, sure. Black." He went back to checking the readouts against the star map on the console in front of him.

Mia laughed at his preoccupation. It amazed her how quickly he'd managed to take her presence for granted. It felt like she'd never left. She grabbed a second mug of the thick black liquid. For one mischievous second, she was tempted to add a sweetener. *Would he even notice?* She resisted the impulse and placed the coffee down in front of him.

Collecting her own mug and the yogurt mixture, she sat opposite him, propping her feet on the seat across from her. The yogurt slid down her throat smoothly, the taste tart, and she made a mental note to make sure to top up the supply when they made port. They'd have to stop soon. She'd already noticed a shortage of some staples.

Kellen continued to key the data into the console. Without glancing up, he reached for the coffee mug and swallowed half the contents in a single gulp. Mia's mouth curved upwards in amusement. They could have been an old pledged couple breaking their fast for all the attention he paid her. The thought pleased her far more than she cared to admit.

Spike zipped in from his morning rounds and landed in Mia's lap, settling his small form comfortably before he began to preen his metallic scales in imitation of a flesh-and-blood creature.

"Good morning to you, too." Mia cocked her head and studied the little creature with interest. Kellen had attempted to convince her Spike was just a machine, that the little dragon didn't have real thoughts or feelings. She wasn't buying it. Spike had way too much personality not to be self-aware. Not that she always appreciated his choices, she thought wryly. The A.I. often sided with Kellen against her. But now she stroked his scaly wings absently as she sipped her coffee.

Sisl dacr derkepen. Spike broadcast his cheerful gibberish in a general pattern. Mia wondered if it bothered the little creature that no one answered his telepathic renderings.

As domestic as this scene was, she had to focus. They still weren't any closer to figuring out who wanted her dead. Maybe Kellen was just being paranoid. It surprised her that she hadn't heard from Marshal, but then again, he'd probably assume she hadn't retrieved the weapons data yet. She rarely gave him an ETA for her return, and he knew better than to expect one.

Kellen signed off and turned his attention to the galley computer. With a quick flick of his wrist, he input his breakfast order of steak, eggs, and bacon. Not even a token vegetable.

He looked over at Mia. "Tomorrow, around midday."

"What's tomorrow?" She cocked her head, giving him a puzzled look. She knew he sometimes forgot she didn't have the neural implants that allowed the AlphElites to communicate without words.

"Planet fall. We're dropping the shipment on Hubri3 tomorrow. We should get there around noon local time. We'll need to top up our supplies, too."

A shrill chime interrupted them, signaling his meal was ready. Kellen removed the plate from the alcove and eyed the bloody red meat the food comp had produced. "Never did figure out how to work this damn thing properly." He looked hopefully over at Mia. "I don't suppose you know how to make it cook the meat? I'd like a meal incapable of running away before I finish eating it."

Mia suppressed a giggle. Seems the big he-man has kitchen issues. She took the plate from his hand and put it back in the alcove. "Burn it," she instructed.

Ten seconds later the plate reappeared, the bloody steak transformed into a charbroiled masterpiece.

"The original programmers were Kai," she explained. "They like their meat dead, but just barely. If you fed them this, they'd call it burnt." She retrieved her mug and took a sip of the cooling coffee. "How long will we be on Hubri3?"

"We won't be. I will." Kellen dug into his food with alacrity. "This is really good. Thanks."

Mia raised her eyebrows and stared at him in confusion. "And where will I be?"

"Right here on board ship where no one can hurt you."

She scowled. "That's ridiculous. You can't keep me out of sight forever." She paced across the room, her attempts to loom over him spoiled when he stood. Really! If reincarnation existed, she planned to come back as a 6'5" Amazon.

"Not forever. Just till we figure out who wants you dead."

Kellen's I'm-talking-to-a-brain-dead-Barbie tone of voice immediately put Mia's hackles up. Short and female did not translate as stupid. She resisted the urge to stomp her foot in irritation.

"And what about the people who want you dead?" she asked.

Kellen blinked, looking confused. "Who wants me dead?"

"I do, for one," she snapped. "Have you any idea how annoying you are when you start with that alpha caveman crap? I'm more than capable of looking after myself."

"Which is why you ended up on my ship without being consulted?" he inquired dryly. "I'm trying to protect you. Someone set me up to kill you, and I, for one, would like to get to the bottom of that before you start waltzing around the universe like it's your own personal playground." He grabbed her wrist and pulled her hard against his body. His eyes narrowed. "You can get that mutinous look of your face. I want you alive and kicking, and I plan to keep you that way whether you like it or not."

His mouth came down to claim hers, hard and demanding, not taking no for an answer.

Mia, taken off guard, kissed him back. He grunted and the kiss softened, deepened, demanding submission and catching her up in feelings she didn't want to explore too closely.

Mia waited a long half hour after Kellen debarked before she exited the ship's airlock. She snorted in a very unladylike fashion. What made him think he could get away with handing out orders? The more time that went by uneventfully, the less convinced she became that someone wanted her dead. It could all be one big misunderstanding.

Still, she made sure he'd had enough time to leave the spaceport before she strolled off the ship. She'd been making do with Kellen's clothing long enough. She wanted something to wear that actually fit her.

Flagging down a flitter, she asked to be taken to the nearest shopping district and used her cred-chip to pay for the transport. She'd never been on this planet before and examined with interest the wares displayed in the gaily colored bazaar. A shop to her left had a selection of colorful outfits that appeared suitable for her needs. She headed in that direction, anger disappearing at the thought of a new wardrobe. A little retail therapy went a long way.

It didn't take long for the helpful attendants to find enough outfits to satisfy her feminine longings. She almost blushed as the giggling salesclerks carefully folded and packed the scraps of lace that were her new undergarments. She couldn't wait to see Kellen's face when he saw her in that black lace.

Loaded down with purchases, Mia left the shopping district and looked around, hoping to spot an empty flitter for the return trip to the spaceport. Not one in sight. She sighed. The thought of walking back to the ship with all these parcels didn't thrill her.

She'd gone several blocks before an uneasy feeling settled between her shoulder blades. She looked around cautiously, but nothing looked out of place. Assorted beings hurried about their business, none seeming the least bit interested in her. She smiled nervously at her own imagination. Kellen's paranoia must be contagious. Still, she reached into her front pocket and fingered the reassuring bulk of the thazere she'd liberated that morning from the weapons locker.

Scanning her surroundings again, she spotted a reptilian sentient several blocks behind her. An icy shiver of fear danced down her spine. Something about Krictlins always made her nervous. Despite their sentient status, they held themselves apart from other species. They rarely exhibited any type of emotion, even in a fight. Over six feet tall with massive heads and bodies and incredibly quick reflexes, Krictlins could be defeated by few species in hand-to-hand combat. She walked a little faster.

Four blocks later, she could still see the Krictlin behind her. Mia tasted fear sharp and acrid on her tongue. She might be a great thief and fast on her feet, but a data thief didn't need to excel at hand-to-hand combat. She knew she couldn't take down a Krictlin. They were also the one species, with their thick scaly covering, that she couldn't instantly neutralize with her thazere. At best, it would slow the creature down.

She rounded the next corner, hoping to lose the reptile, only to find herself in a deserted cul-de-sac with no houses, no shops, and no witnesses. Glancing back, she saw the Krictlin had closed the gap. She guessed him to be less than a hundred feet behind her. Adrenaline flooded her system. To hell with the new wardrobe. She dropped her packages and ran.

Before she'd gone more than ten feet, the Krictlin grabbed her arm and jerked her around to face him. The creature hissed, whether in triumph or anticipation, Mia had no idea. She struck out hard with her left foot while fumbling for her weapon.

He released her arm, slipped under the blow, and backhanded her across the face. She staggered under the strength of the blow, losing her grip on the weapon, and grunted as pain exploded in her head. The thazere went skidding across the ground and out of reach. The creature grabbed her arm and twisted. Agony ripped through the muscles and radiated upwards to her shoulder.

Mia clubbed him with her fist and succeeded in freeing herself. Shocked by her success, she pranced backwards, afraid to turn and run. Why had that worked? Was he toying with her?

"Shesssss sssscared." The sibilant hissed with excitement.

Mia felt the blood drain from her face as she realized her fear aroused the Krictlin. He was toying with her. She glanced to either side, searching for anything she could use as a weapon, but found nothing. Damn. This isn't fun anymore.

She aimed her best roundhouse kick at the thing's head and only succeeded in hurting her foot. Limping, she swung at him with her left hand and again the reptile ducked the blow.

The Krictlin hissed in earnest now, forked tongue flicking in and out in excited jabs, beady eyes flat and dead-looking. "Issss going to kill youssss ssloowwwlly."

The anticipation in his voice belied the total lack of expression on the scaly face as the monster advanced on Mia. She backed away slowly, aware she didn't have much room left. The cul-de-sac ended with a high brick wall blocking the way out. She wondered if Kellen would ever find out what happened, or if he'd just think she'd run out on him again.

Impotent anger surged through her. She might die, but no way would she let this damn slimy reptile get her without a fight. Gathering the tattered remains of her courage, she attacked.

For a few minutes, she thought she had a chance. When she punched the Krictlin in its soft belly, he rewarded her with a pained grunt. She managed to duck under its return swing and elbow it sharply in the ribs. The reptile bent over in response, and Mia slapped an arm down hard across the back of his neck. But the reptile turned at the last moment, and the blow glanced off his scale-protected shoulders. A shaft of pain shot through her wrist.

He slapped her across the head with an open hand, and she went down. He pounced, pinning her arms at her sides.

Mia squirmed, attempting to slip out from under the monster. but the weight of his bulky form held her down. She tried to slam her head into the soft flesh of his throat. The reptile jerked his sideways, avoiding the blow. His nostrils flared, his breathing slow, deep and evilly disgusting.

Mia closed her eyes and frantically tried to think of some way to escape.

"Why the hell don't you ever listen?"

Kellen—thank the gods! He sounded close, and he sounded furious.

Her eyes jerked open, but she couldn't see past the reptile on top of her. The beast jerked upright and turned, hissing angrily. "Mine!"

"I don't think so." Kellen crouched in a fighter's stance, a long wicked knife held loosely in his right hand. "I haven't finished playing with her yet, and I don't share so well." His left hand wove back and forth in a hypnotizing pattern. He circled the reptile warily, going left to force the monster to concentrate on him and loosen his hold on Mia.

She took the opportunity to scramble to her feet, fleeing down the cul-de-sac towards freedom. She stopped just short of the corner and turned.

"Who sent you?" asked Kellen, his tone neutral.

The Krictlin ignored the question, its beady eyes following Mia. "She is mine. I will kill her slowly. It will be good. He promised me."

"He lied. Didn't he tell you I would kill you to protect her?"

Kellen's tone seemed mild, but death lurked in the depths of his eyes. Mia shivered. She'd seen him like this before. When he went into a killing rage, he became calm, the opposite of the Berserkers of Old Norse legends. The Krictlin didn't stand a chance of surviving.

"No! Ssshe isss mine." The attack came quickly, large claws tearing a bloody furrow down Kellen's forearm.

Kellen retaliated with an upward slash of the knife, scoring a deep wound on the creature's belly. He danced out of range, amazingly quick on his feet for such a large man.

The Krictlin roared and attacked again, swinging its powerful forearms wildly. Kellen ducked under the attack and slipped out of reach after inflicting another deep wound with his knife.

Mia watched in guilt-ridden horror from the entrance to the cul-de-sac. This was all her fault. She should have obeyed Kellen and stayed aboard the ship. His arm dripped a steady stream of blood. The combination of his blood on the ground and the ick flowing from the many wounds on his opponent affected the combatants' footing.

Her pulse accelerated. Kellen was tiring. His slashes became slower, his footwork clumsy. The reptile renewed its attack despite its own gaping wounds.

She gasped, fearing Kellen wouldn't be able to avoid a particularly savage swipe, and let her breath out in a sigh of relief as he slipped the blow. He retaliated with one of his own. The two fighters continued to circle each other warily.

Kellen pivoted on his left foot, coming up under the Krictlin's guard. Both hands on the knife, he drove the vicious blade deep into the space between the two top vertebrae. The Krictlin hesitated for a moment.

Mia sucked in a painful breath. Unbearable tension held her immobile.

The eyes of the reptile became opaque, losing their evil glint as the scaly body slid bonelessly to the ground.

Chapter 4

Kellen jerked his knife free. Wiping the gore off on his pant leg, he shoved the weapon back into the scabbard strapped to his thigh and turned to face Mia. She probably didn't know it yet, but she could be in more trouble from him than she'd been from the lizard.

"Don't you ever do that again." He stalked towards her, heedless of the steady drip of blood from several deep lacerations. "When I give you an order, you will damn well obey it."

She'd almost gotten herself killed, something he didn't even want to contemplate. When she disappeared six months earlier, she'd ripped his heart out. He couldn't take too many surprises like this one. If he had to, he'd keep her tied up and restrained on the ship.

Her eyes, staring up at him, were wide with alarm. "I needed some clothes." She gestured weakly towards the abandoned packages.

Kellen had no idea what the hell she was talking about, nor did he care. He grabbed her by the arm and headed back towards the spaceport, dragging her behind him.

"Hey, stop that!" Mia stumbled after him, trying to keep her balance while attempting to pry his fingers from her arm. "I can walk by myself."

He ignored her protests. He planned to blister her adorable backside with his bare hands once they were safely back aboard ship and off this gods-forsaken planet. She deserved a damn good spanking for that one horrible moment when Spike had come winging into the storerooms to tell him the Krictlin had attacked her.

He didn't slow down until they were onboard. He placed his hand palm down on the identi-pad and keyed the locks to privacy. Retaining his hold on her arm, he strode down the central corridor to his cabin and threw her onto the oversized bed so hard she bounced.

Turning on his heels, he stalked back out of the cabin. "Door lock override. Authorization alpha tango three-nine-five." The recessed panel slid shut with a snick, the locks engaging smoothly. That should keep her out of trouble while he got them out of orbit.

He made his way to the bridge and started the countdown sequence. He'd flown without a crew before. He could certainly do it again. Right now, they were both safer with the length of the ship between them.

Blood dripped from the deeper gash on his arm, falling to the floor with a sticky plop. With a frustrated snarl, he stood and pulled his shirt over his head, wrapping it snugly around his forearm to staunch the flow. He'd deal with his wounds once he felt he'd put a safe distance between the ship and anyone pursing them. He eased himself back into the pilot's seat.

"Engage auto navigation."

"Engaged." The smooth voice of the computer's auto navigation system answered instantly. At least the ship obeyed orders.

"Prepare to break orbit."

The launch sequence progressed without a hitch, and once the ship had left orbit, he turned over control to the autopilot. The ship settled onto course, hurtling smoothly through the vacuum of space. Kellen refrained from transitioning to FTL flight since it made communication difficult. He needed to contact his team.

He checked the readouts, adjusting the fuel mixture slightly. Setting the scanners to the maximum sweep, he searched for other ships in the area. He hadn't detected any sign of someone following them to Hubri3, but that attack hadn't been random. The Krictlin had obviously been lying in wait for Mia. She'd just made it incredibly easy for him by leaving the ship alone.

He smacked his hand on the console in frustration. He had no problem with hunting, but he didn't enjoy being the prey. He needed to call in his team for a little brainstorming.

But first, he needed to check up on his crew. A slight smile teased the corner of his mouth. She'd had enough time to work up one hell of a temper by now.

Mia paced the decking and glared at the locked door. *How dare he manhandle her like that!* The passage of time had done nothing to calm her down.

"Get back here, you big jerk." She pitched a pillow at the door. It slid to the ground with a very unsatisfying whoosh. She knew she should be grateful to him for rescuing her, but right now, she wasn't feeling particularly grateful. He certainly knew how to bring out the worst in her.

She felt the vibrations underfoot that signaled the engines were powering up to break orbit. He wouldn't be back any time soon. Hurrying to the jump seat in the corner, she managed to strap herself into the restraining harness just as the pressure started to build. *Inconsiderate jerk.* He could at least have warned her before they broke orbit.

When the gravity field stabilized and her stomach returned to its proper place, Mia released the harness and resumed her restless pacing. Sooner or later, he had to come back and deal with her. A smart man would make it sooner.

A quiet click signaled the door locks disengaging. The door slid smoothly into its recess in the wall and Kellen stalked into the cabin.

Mia opened her mouth to tell the big jerk what she thought of him, but snapped it shut at the sight of the deep red blood dripping steadily through the tourniquet on his left arm and onto the floor. She scrambled off the bed and rushed to his side, anger forgotten.

"You're hurt!" She reached for his arm and pulled the shredded shirt away from the gashes made by the Krictlin. She peered worriedly at the ugly wounds. "They look awfully deep." Then she pushed him to the bed. "I'm going to get the medi-kit and fix you up."

He must really be in pain, she noted wryly. He stayed meekly on the bed with his mouth shut while she bustled about in search of the medical supplies. She finally found the kit thrown haphazardly into a cabinet and returned to kneel at his feet.

Rummaging through the medi-kit for disinfectant, she slid an apologetic look up at him. "This is going to hurt."

Kellen grimaced. "People don't usually warn me before they hurt me. Just do it. You'll probably need to tape some of them shut. It feels like he sliced me to the bone." He reached down and ran his fingers absently through her hair, winding the strands between his fingers as he gritted his teeth and stared fixedly at the wall.

Mia swallowed convulsively, bracing herself. She didn't want to hurt him. As gently as she could, she cleaned the wounds one at a time, wincing at every flinch. Some of the cuts were deep enough to concern her. That he'd managed to get back here without blacking out from loss of blood amazed her. Then again, the AlphElite didn't like to acknowledge weakness. Their recuperative powers were awesome. He'd probably be back to his normal bossy self before the cycle finished.

She picked up the antiseptic, studying Kellen's face to gauge how much more pain he could endure.

Too rugged to be handsome, his face bore the wounds of past battles. An old scar zigzagged along his left cheekbone and his nose, broken more than once, sat slightly off center. She could spend the rest of her life waking up to this face.

Mia blinked and gave herself a mental shake. *Where the hell did that come from?* His AlphElite status meant there couldn't be a future, not for them. She had too much pride to settle for a position as his bed partner.

Sternly she forced herself to concentrate on the task at hand. As she carefully doused the slashes with disinfectant and taped them up, she worried her bottom lip with her teeth. Finally satisfied that he'd survive, she looked up to meet his deep blue eyes. "You can let go my hair now."

A ghost of a grin flitted across his face as he focused on her. "You look good on your knees." He withdrew his fingers, smoothing her hair with gentle hands.

She wrinkled her nose. "Yeah? Well, don't get used to it. I'm not the kneel-worshipping-at-your-feet kind of crew." She rose gracefully from the floor. "So do you think the lizard targeted me specifically, or was I just in the wrong place at the wrong time?"

Kellen reached out and enclosed her wrist in one big hand, pulling her onto his lap. Wrapping her in his warm embrace, he nuzzled her neck. "I don't know for sure. I need to contact my team and see if I can find out what the hell's going on. They're vicious, but Krictlin don't go around attacking people for no reason. The creature said, 'He promised me'. I want to know who he is, and if he's the same person who warned me about the break in." He rubbed his chin back and forth on her collarbone in a gesture she found oddly comforting.

"I should have kept the Krictlin alive to answer some questions," he added with a shake of his head. "Hindsight has always been one of my strengths."

Mia said, "So I guess restraint isn't, huh?"

He lifted one hand to cup her breast, stroking the tight nipple through her shirt. "Sometimes restraint isn't called for."

She considered objecting, but anything she said would have sounded hollow. Feeling more than ready for a little distraction, she eyed the growing bulge in his pants. *Maybe a lot of distraction.* She caught his gaze, raising one eyebrow suggestively. "So you're not planning on tying me up again?"

Kellen's smirk held the promise of seduction. "Only if you want me to." He tracked one finger across her breast.

"Nope. That'd make it way too easy for you to catch me." She slipped off his lap and scooted out the door, laughing over her shoulder. "They call this game tag. You're it!"

Chapter 5

Mia fled down the corridor, laughing out loud when she heard Kellen scramble clumsily to his feet. It didn't hurt to keep him on his toes. He needed to lose some of his damned arrogance.

As she turned the corner into the exercise room, she could hear Kellen start after her. Skirting the exercise equipment, she headed for the shower area and suppressed an insane urge to giggle. It might be a delayed reaction to the attack, but she felt like a teenager hiding from her boyfriend.

She looked back over her shoulder. Kellen had gained ground fast. An evil leer adorned his face. She squealed, more in anticipation than fear. Ducking under the heated towel rack, she dodged through the open shower stall and into the dressing area.

She skidded to a stop.

The exit door she'd been heading for had vanished. A nicely flowered laminate wall stretched across the space in front of her. Kellen had done some remodeling in the last few months. She heard him slide to a stop behind her and felt herself getting slick and excited.

"You know what happens when the big bad wolf catches the little girl, don't you?" Kellen drawled in a seductively low voice.

Mia turned to face him. Gods, he looked magnificent. Even with one arm taped together, he made her mouth water and her pussy clench in eagerness. His pants stretched painfully tight over his massive erection, leaving little to her imagination.

He locked her gaze with his and stalked forward slowly, every muscle tensed, ready to spring. She found herself hoping he'd pin her against the flowers on the new wall and fuck her brains out.

He stopped in front of her, legs braced wide, arms crossed with deceptive casualness across his massive chest.

Mia swallowed hard. He looked big and intense and way too in control. She glanced down at the straining crotch of his pants. Make that enormous and tasty, in a scary sort of way.

"Hey, you." She winced. Talk about cheesy.

"Hey, yourself." The edgy growl in his voice sent shivers of anticipation through her.

He closed the space between them in one big step. Placing a hand on the wall on either side of her head, he pinned her in place, his splendid body crowding hers, making her feel small and feminine and incredibly horny.

He leaned down, slowly covering her open mouth with his. Roughly, his tongue probed, dominant and demanding. His hands swept through her hair, cradling the back of her head, tilting it up so he could better plunder her mouth. He moved one hand down, caressing her spine, her back, roaming possessively over her body as his mouth branded her as his.

Mia lifted her arms, gripping his shoulders to hold herself upright. The man could make her resolve melt with a single kiss! No one should be able to kiss this good. Her body swayed forward in invitation, her thighs brushing his. His bulging cock pressed aggressively against her belly.

Mia dropped one hand to stroke the thick length of him through his pants. "I want this inside me."

Not taking his mouth off hers, Kellen swept her into his arms and strode back to the exercise area. With careless strength, he lowered her onto the floor mats and stood as he stripped off his clothing and tossed it aside. Naked and magnificent, he towered over her.

Hot damn, he looked good enough to eat. Mia felt heat race through her body to pool low in her belly. She eyed the big cock bobbing unashamedly above her. Maybe just a little taste.

A tense smile lurked at the corner of his mouth.

"Strip." He growled the order.

"What?"

"Strip!" he repeated, raising his eyebrows as if daring her to defy him.

Mia had no intention of defying him. She supposed she ought to feel humiliated, being sprawled at the feet of a naked, demanding male. But she was more than ready to put that cock of his to good use. She grasped the lower edge of her shirt and pulled the sheer fabric over her head in one smooth motion, allowing her breasts to spring free, their nipples coming to attention under Kellen's hot gaze.

Hearing his low rumble of excitement, she undid her pants and pushed them over her hips, teasing him with a slow sensuous wiggle of her ass.

Kellen dropped to his knees at her feet. Grabbing the pants in one big hand, he yanked them off and tossed them aside. An ankle in each hand, he spread her legs and sprawled between her thighs on the mat. He draped his injured arm across her hips to hold her in place while he reached out with the other hand to fondle her breasts, rubbing the nipples between his fingers. Fondling, kneading, massaging, he played, gentle and firm in turns until Mia squirmed and whimpered mindlessly.

He lowered his head and ran his clever tongue around one swollen nipple, then the other. He let his hand drift lower, caressing her belly, the hollow of her hips, the dark triangle covering her mound. Using two fingers to gently part her labia, he stroked his thumb maddeningly over her clit. She arched up into his hand, seeking relief.

Kellen obliged her by sliding first one, then two fingers into her creamy core, stroking and plunging, circling and thrusting, taking her higher and higher until she exploded in a wild orgasm. He took his name from her lips, covering her mouth as she screamed out her pleasure.

His kiss, hard and demanding at first, softened as she drifted back to reality.

"I missed you," Mia whispered softly, floating dreamily in the aftermath of her orgasm.

"Nice to know." Kellen stroked a stray lock of hair from her face.

Mia lifted herself to her elbows and looked down at Kellen's cock, still rock hard and standing at full attention in its nest of dark curls. "I suppose I could do something about that for you," she offered.

"Really? What do you have in mind?"

"Oh, I don't know." Mia tilted her head sideways. "Maybe a little blow job?"

Kellen grinned. "I don't think a little anything's going to help." He put one hand behind her neck and urged her face down to his groin. "But give it your best shot."

Mia stuck her tongue out at him, then circled the thick base of his cock with one hand and slowly licked her tongue along the entire length. Encouraged by the groan that maneuver elicited, she took the big glistening tip in her mouth, licking and sucking with enthusiasm. While she worked her tongue back and forth on the shaft, she used her free hand to caress his taut balls, drawing ragged breaths from him.

"Stop."

Letting the big cock slide from her mouth with a wet pop, Mia looked up questioningly.

Kellen didn't elaborate. But his hands bit roughly into her shoulders as he dragged her head up so he could reclaim her mouth. What had started as an aggressively dominant attack quickly turned to a slow sensuous invasion as his tongue danced erotically around hers.

With a quick shift of his hips, he rolled over, trapping Mia beneath him. Raising himself up on muscular arms, he slowly lowered his body over her until the head of his erection prodded her mound.

"You feel so good." He thrust slowly through her tight creamy folds, forcing his huge erection deep into her eager pussy until she could feel his balls slapping against her ass.

She started to close her eyes, loving the sensation of his cock filling her so incredibly full.

"Don't." Kellen's voice held a sharp note of command. "Look at me. Watch me fuck you. I want you to see how much I enjoy you."

He pulled out, then thrust again, establishing an easy rhythm that quickly threatened to drive Mia to the brink of insanity. All the while, his gaze stayed locked on hers.

He thrust harder and faster, ruthlessly pounding his shaft through the slick wet folds of her pussy. Mia felt as if she were on fire, the heat radiating from her sex to her thighs, her belly and her nipples. Her nails dug bloody furrows into Kellen's back as her hips thrust upwards in time with his thrusts, forcing him ever deeper into her velvet sheath.

"Kellen, Kellen." She chanted his name mindlessly, spiraling ever higher. It felt so damn good to be back. She didn't know how she'd ever work up the strength to leave him again.

Her orgasm came hard and fast. Mia screamed as she felt herself climax, muscles spasming, clamping down hard on Kellen's cock, milking every last drop of his seed as he followed her over the edge and shifted to collapse beside her, wrapping her in his big brawny arms.

She felt safe in his arms. She didn't want to think about danger or the ORG or why someone wanted her dead. She just wanted to snuggle against his familiar bulk while she drifted off to sleep.

"Kellen?" Her voice came out low and husky.

"Yeah?"

"Thanks for killing the Krictlin for me."

"You're welcome, honey." He hesitated a moment. "Mia?"

"Yes?"

"The next time I give you an order, you damn well better obey me."

Mia turned her head so she could look into his eyes. Her mouth curved softly. "Yes, master!"

"If only you meant that," Kellen said. "Go to sleep."

Chapter 6

Mia woke alone. Well, not entirely alone. The little A.I. dragon perched on the headboard above her.

"Morning, Spike." She stretched her arms over her head. She felt good this morning. Even the fact Kellen had managed to program her own A.I. to spy on her couldn't ruin her mood. "Where's the big boss this morning?"

Spike chirped cheerfully, and the image of the bridge filled her mind.

Spying could work both ways. She said, "Well, I guess that means I have the shower to myself."

The bruises the Krictlin left on her face had turned interesting shades of blue and green while she slept. They felt tender under her questing fingers, but she considered herself lucky she hadn't broken any bones. She felt some residual stiffness in her joints, but a good hot shower would cure that. She'd always been a quick healer. She sauntered off towards the exercise room, grabbing a piece of fruit from the bowl Kellen kept on the table at the foot of the bed. When she'd finished her shower, she dressed casually and headed up to the bridge.

Kellen greeted her with an easy smile. "Morning, sleepyhead." Although she noticed he heavily favored his injured arm, he ignored her colorful face and nodded to the displays flashing at the navigator's station. "Thought I'd have to crew for myself again."

Mia smiled back at him, grateful for his tact. "Can't have that. Lady knows where we'd end up with you reading the star charts." She slid into the navigator's chair, palm down on the access panel so the ship could identify her. After a brief hesitation, the displays turned green, the security subroutine accepting her DNA.

She paused, fingers hovering over the input loops, her eyebrows raised in question. "You haven't taken us into FTL flight. Where are we headed?"

"Just waiting for confirmation on that." Kellen listened to his internal network link for a few minutes, eyes vacant as he communicated with his team.

Mia averted her gaze and studied the console in front of her. It always bothered her when he communicated through his implanted link, although she tried not to let it show. It reminded her of the huge gulf between them, something she had conveniently forgotten yet again. Idiot.

"Tangot Base. We're going to meet up with the rest of my team and see if we can come up with a plan to flush out your secret admirer." Kellen reached up to rub the back of his neck. "A couple of the guys heard there's a bounty out on you." He threw her a look she couldn't decipher. "Four thousand parsets." He paused. "Preferably alive, but not absolutely required. And the client name isn't listed."

Mia's jaw dropped. She stared at him, speechless. What the hell had she done to get a bounty on her head? She'd probably pissed Kellen off more than she'd pissed off any other person in the universe, and even he didn't want her dead.

"You're joking, right?"

Kellen shook his head. "Nope. Dead or alive."

Mia tried to wrap her brain around the thought that someone had offered hard currency to have her killed. "If a bounty's offered, there must be a name attached. Some way to collect."

Kellen shook his head again. "Just a number to call when you've been, um, detained. The offer came down through the Miner's enforcement stream, so it's legit. They wouldn't pass on an offer if they doubted the source."

"That's ridiculous. Someone can't just decide to kill me without any explanation." Finding out someone wanted you dead sure smacked down a good mood in a hurry. "It's not fair!"

"Honey, life isn't fair. You should know that by now." Kellen stood and moved in front of her. He took her chin in his hand, raised her head so he looked directly into her eyes. "Don't look so worried. I'm not going to let it happen. We'll find out what's going on and who's behind this. Now plot us a course to Tangot Base."

He kissed her roughly, his mouth hard and possessive. His hand left her chin, wandered down to caress her breast.

Some of the tension drained out of Mia. It would be OK. It would. Kellen wouldn't let some nameless, faceless monster hurt her. She opened her mouth, kissing him back.

Kellen broke contact and returned to the pilot's station. "You belong to me. You have since the first time I took you." He turned those glowing sapphire eyes on her. "I may not be a pleasant man, but I promise you, no one is going to hurt you so long as I'm around."

Mia stared at him open-mouthed. Breathe, she told herself. That hadn't been a declaration of undying love, just Kellen being his typical caveman self. Someone had threatened to take away his favorite toy. That pissed him off. He hadn't asked her to pledge. She swallowed hard. A change of subject would probably be good right about now. "So who are we meeting at Tangot?"

"As many of my team as we can get there. I've sent out a broadband summons, but I'm not sure where everyone is. Mac and Bree are playing at asteroid mining at the far end of the nebula, so I doubt they'll make it in, unless they've already started back. I had to piggyback their call onto the outbound base system. Jake, Tyson, and Ayden are all in the area and will be there." He shook his head. "As usual I haven't the faintest idea where the hell the Sciber twins are."

"Probably out drinking, carousing and generally raising hell. Isn't that what you AlphElites do on downtime?" Mia winced inwardly at the thought of Kellen carousing without her.

"Yeah." Kellen smiled ruefully. "I couldn't raise them, but that could just mean they got lucky and tuned out their neural implants for awhile."

Mia nodded, her fingers flashing quickly over the comp display, locking in their course. "How long do we have? It'll take a bite out of our fuel reserves to transition back into FTL."

"I told them we'd meet in two days."

"Okay. We can probably stay in warp and get there in plenty of time." She modified the input data in front of her and relaxed.

She really enjoyed crewing for Kellen. With just the two of them onboard, the atmosphere felt relaxed, cozy, almost homey. It had been that, the feeling of being at home, which had prompted her to leave Kellen after their last voyage. All the coziness felt way too domestic, and that scared the shit out of her. Now she'd come back, and nothing had changed.

"Don't do that!" Kellen growled, annoyance edging his voice.

Mia's head snapped up. "Do what?"

"Thinking. You're thinking. That always lands us in trouble."

"Well, excuse me." Mia said stiffly. She'd forgotten what an arrogant jerk he could be at times.

"You looked like that right before you ran out on me." His look dared her to disagree.

"Well, maybe I was thinking you're a big, macho AlphElite jerk. Which, by the way, you are."

Kellen shook his head. "Maybe, but you're not going to walk out on this big jerk again. Got that?"

The flash of pain Mia saw deep in those blue eyes stopped her retort before it left her mouth. For just a second, Kellen had looked vulnerable. Hurt.

She said in a hard voice, "I never wanted to leave, you idiot. It just wasn't going to work out, and the longer I stayed, the worse it would feel when I had to go." She didn't know why she felt compelled to explain herself now, but she didn't want to be the cause of his pain.

He scowled at her, all domineering male. "Well, you don't have to go, and it's going to work if I have to restrain you to my quarters and have Spike guard you day and night." His voice got low. "I will not let you leave this time. You're mine. You stay with me."

Well, it certainly didn't take long for his caveman side to surface, Mia thought, but that vulnerable look had been real. It hadn't occurred to her she'd hurt him. Maybe she should have talked things over with him before she left.

She glanced at his cold profile. Or maybe not. Talking had never been Kellen's strong point. Orders. He was good with orders.

And with those big callused hands of his, a treacherous little voice in her head piped up. He had real talent with his hands. She snorted. Even her subconscious sided with him.

But typically, Kellen had returned his focus to the issue at hand. Her attack. "We need to look at this logically." He tapped his fingers on the console. "Someone has put a sizeable bounty on you. They aren't broadcasting who they are, or their reason. Why? Why don't they want you to know who's gunning for you?"

"It's someone I know?" Mia ventured. "I'd be able to do something about this if I knew who put up the bounty."

Kellen looked over at her, his brows creased in frustration. "There has to be a reason. You may not know what it is, but there has to be something. How about an old lover looking for revenge? Did you see something you shouldn't have on one of your little forays? Do you have something someone else wants? Think."

"Well the first one's out. You're the only one I've screwed in the last five years." Mia cringed as she realized what she'd just admitted. She concentrated on the readout in front of her, not daring to look up and see if he'd noticed.

Kellen stood and began pacing back and forth. "So tell me what you've been up to for last couple of months. Professionally, I mean."

Mia mulled over her last few jobs. "I've had only two data acquisition projects in the last year. Mostly I've been couriering files between clients. You know, information they feel is too sensitive to put out on the airwaves where it might get intercepted." She shrugged dispiritedly. "I've been on dozens of different worlds and about as many ships. If this is about something I saw, it's not something I realized I shouldn't have seen. Hell, maybe whoever is behind this has the wrong person."

"Tell me about the projects." Kellen crossed his arms over his chest. "Maybe I'll pick up on something you've missed."

"Well…." Mia frowned as she recalled the details. "The first went down about a year ago. Marshal had me infiltrate the Myacan governor's ball. I acquired a list of the Myacan weapons caches in the Orion system from the computers at the embassy. The Uralian government wanted to check the Myacans private records against the ones they provided to the United Interstellar Council." She almost smiled as she remembered how easy it had been to break into their systems. The Myacans had incredibly outdated techno security. Any newbie in the ORG could have gotten the list.

Kellen shook his head dismissively. "I doubt it's the Myacans. They're pacifists by nature. Their weapons are all defensive. Hell, they've never even used capital punishment. I find it unlikely they'd put a bounty on anyone. Did anything happen at the ball? Think hard. Did you see anyone out of place? Anyone talking to someone they normally wouldn't."

Mia thought for a few minutes, but couldn't dredge up anything useful. "I don't think so. The evening followed the same basic political ass-kissing agenda as usual." She frowned. "I guess that's not much help."

Kellen shrugged. "It tells me we should look elsewhere. What about the other project?"

Mia shook her head. "Not much chance of me seeing anyone out of place on that one. I retrieved data files from the asteroid belt on the far side of the nebula. The inhabitants are all androids and remote-control mining machines." She stretched her arms over her head, arching her back to relieve the nervous kink in her neck. "The data was dropped before I showed up. I have no idea who dropped it or what it contained. I just picked up the parcel and brought it back. They set up a blind drop on this end as well, so I couldn't identify the terminal contact."

"Doesn't sound like anything worth killing over," he admitted, still pacing. "There has to be something we're missing, something important. Were any of those courier jobs sensitive or top secret?"

"Not that I know, but then, most of those files are encrypted. I have no idea what's in them."

"Which makes it even more unlikely they figure into this."

Mia nodded in agreement. "This whole thing is unlikely." She started ticking off points with her fingers. "One. I don't have any family, so that rules out the whole Freudian thing. Two. You're my only ex-lover, as well as my current one. You swear it isn't you. Three. Money can't be the motive. I'm not worth anything if I'm dead." She looked down at her hand ruefully. "Two fingers left and I'm out of ideas. Good thing I'm not trying to make a living as a detective."

Kellen stopped his pacing and reached out to ruffle her hair with his fingers. "It's okay, darling. We'll figure it out." The corner of his mouth turned up in sexy grin. "And until we do, you have to do whatever I tell you. So you see, there's an upside to everything."

Mia rolled her eyes. "Only you could come up with a line that corny. Go pilot something, will you."

Kellen bent to drop a kiss on the top of her head and crossed back to his own chair. "You know you find me irresistible."

And that, thought Mia, summed up her biggest problem. She did find him irresistible.

Chapter 7

"Do you always get through planetary security this easily?" Mia toyed with the little dragon draped dormant around her neck. No one had questioned her right to carry an A.I. Everyone from the stationmaster on down to the cargo crews were respectful and courteous with Kellen. They'd waltzed through entry protocols without challenge.

"Why would anyone want to keep a handsome stud like me off-planet?" Kellen countered innocently as he draped a protective arm around her shoulder.

She curved her mouth in sardonic appreciation. He certainly didn't have an ego problem. She marveled at the way his arm had already healed from the wounds inflicted by the Krictlin. His genetic mutations certainly held advantages over straight humans when it came to regenerative abilities.

"What did you tell your team about me?" She tried hard not to sound nervous. She'd deliberately managed to avoid the team when she'd been living with Kellen. She found the thought of meeting seven other men as dominant as Kellen intimidating, to say the least.

"The truth. You're a ruthless thief who stole my heart." His teasing tone helped settle her nerves. "Lucky for you, they don't believe anything I tell them."

Mia swatted his butt as they entered the bar. "Smartass."

Kellen grinned. "Yeah."

"Hey, boss, over here." A tall muscle-bound blond rose from his seat at the far side of the bar. His smile widened appreciatively as he sized up Mia. "I see you brought a little toy along for us."

"She's off limits, so keep you paws to yourself." Kellen tightened his grip on Mia's shoulder, drawing her even closer to his side, then gestured rudely and made an unlikely suggestion about the man's parentage.

She gulped down a giggle. He was so sweet when he got protective. Could the testosterone levels get any higher? Smiling sweetly, she stuck out her hand. "I'm Mia. Pleased to meet you."

The blond took her hand in both of his and brought it to his mouth, kissing the back. Then, releasing her, he swept a low bow. "Ayden Smith. I'm honored to make the acquaintance of such a classy lady." Grinning at Kellen's scowling face, he relinquished her hand. "Kellen seems a little protective. Perhaps it's best if we don't push him."

Mia couldn't help herself. She laughed.

Kellen cuffed the other man good-naturedly. "She's not interested, so go slink back to your corner."

Ayden winked unrepentantly. "You want to dump this cretin, you just give me the word." He flashed a white-toothed grin and slid into his seat.

"I'm not sure I want you to meet the rest of these rogues." Kellen pulled out a chair for Mia and grabbed one for himself, swinging it around to straddle it backwards.

"Jake and Tyson." He nodded to two dark-haired men on the far side of the table. "They're the snipers of the team. Once they have you in their sights, you're dead meat walking."

The two men exchanged grins in smug acknowledgement of their prowess. Mia relaxed in her seat, noting the competent, self-assured look of the men. They were all AlphElite. The difference showed in every look, every move they made.

"The big bear beside you is Mac," Kellen continued. "He's the communications wizard. Makes sure we all know what's going on. The bald one beside him is Bree. He's our techie guy. Knows all about the electronic stuff."

She lifted a brow as she realized Kellen had missed someone. "So what does Ayden do?"

"Mostly pisses me off. He's also magic with explosives, so we let him hang around."

Ayden inclined his head, acknowledging the introduction. "The twins are the hand-to-hand experts." Ayden leaned forward and grabbed a mug of local beer off the table. "Haven't heard from them yet. If we need them, they'll be here."

Kellen stared at his men. "So what do we know so far?" He rested his big hand casually on Mia's thigh, absently stroking slow circles. He was staking his claim.

Ayden spoke up. "The bounty on your lady friend was posted on the day you took off from Colony 6. The details are layered pretty deep, but Bree here managed to get us a name." He studied Mia's face. "Ever hear of Guye Defalcio?"

Mia blinked. "Guye Defalcio? He's head of the ORG. He can't be behind this. I've never even met him."

"Well, he seems to know who you are," Bree said. "I did a pretty complete job of hacking into his system. He's been watching you for a long time. Notes on his comp indicate he's set you up a few times, hoping to get you killed." He slid an apologetic look over at Kellen. "Seems he hoped Kellen here would do you in on your last job. He had you sent in, and then he made sure Kellen knew about the break-in. This guy really doesn't like you."

Mia's brow creased in a puzzled frown. As head of the ORG, Guye Defalcio might technically be her boss, but she'd never met him. What reason could he possibly have to want her dead? That didn't make any sense.

Kellen focused on Bree "You sure about this?"

"Oh, yeah. The man keeps meticulous records. Looks like he's obsessed with your lady friend, but…." Bree paused, shrugging his massive shoulders. "At the same time, I got the feeling there was something off, something missing. Like he never gave any reason why he wanted her offed. Everything in his records is detailed, precise, and logical, except when it comes to her. This thing he has for Mia just doesn't add up."

Kellen turned to Mia. "You sure you don't know him?"

She shook her head. "Never met him."

He turned back to his team. "Okay. What else do you have? Maybe we can figure this out." Kellen hesitated. "Or just figure out how to neutralize him. I really don't need to know why he's doing this."

Jake spoke up. "He's a loner. No siblings. Pledge mate died in a mining accident shortly after she gave birth to their son. The son's dead, although I couldn't find any details. Defalcio has been with the ORG for twenty years, the last seven as its head. I didn't get a lot of personal info from the files. He doesn't seem to have any close friends. His reputation says he's cold, calculating, and does whatever it takes to protect the ORG." Jake looked meaningfully at Kellen. "From what I've read, he wouldn't hesitate at murder if he felt it was necessary."

Kellen's eyes narrowed thoughtfully. "Any way we can get an image of him?"

"Sure," Bree spoke up. "Bound to be one or two on the 'net. Why?"

Kellen looked over at Mia. "You said you don't know him, have never seen him. If you don't know what he looks like, it's possible you've seen him somewhere he didn't want to be recognized. That would explain the bounty."

Mia nodded slowly. "I suppose."

Bree eyed the A.I. draped around Mia's neck. "If your little buddy there interfaces me with the galactic data net, I should be able to snag you a holovid of him."

In response to a cue from Mia, Spike's eyes snapped open, the jeweled irises focusing on Bree. Kellen nodded, and the little dragon unwound his tail from Mia's neck and flew over to land on Bree's head.

Bree grinned happily and tilted his head, pulling aside the dark mop of hair that covered the data port behind his left ear. Spike inserted the tip of his tail into the port, and Bree's eyes rolled upward, his body twitching as his consciousness joined with Spike to surf the net.

For the next twenty minutes, his body jerked and twitched, sweat running down his frame. The team kept a casual eye on him to make sure he didn't fall or hurt himself. They were familiar with his techie pursuits and waited patiently for him to find the information they needed.

When Bree's eyes rolled down to normal, he gave a slight shake of his head, careful not to dislodge the A.I. He lifted his left hand and aimed the implanted data chips under his fingernails at the center of the table. A holographic image appeared, depicting a tall man with all the physical characteristics of an AlphElite. The image ran in place, turning to flashing a haughty look over its shoulder before the holograph looped and began to run again.

"Thanks for the ride, buddy," Bree grinned happily as Spike withdrew his tale and returned to wind himself back onto Mia's neck. "There's no rush in the universe better than surfing the net linked to an A.I."

Kellen studied the hologram for a few minutes. "Ugly brute. He's definitely one of us." He turned to raise a questioning brow at Mia. "Well?"

Feeling numb, she stared at the image of the man who wanted her dead. She shook her head. "Nope. I've never seen him."

Kellen squeezed her shoulder comfortingly. "Don't worry. He's not going to hurt you."

She was about to reply when she heard a loud voice from the far side of the bar. "Hey! Mia!"

The greeting caused all seven of them to turn and stare.

"It's Marshal." Mia leaned closer to Kellen. Her handler showing up in this bar at the far side of the nebula seemed quite a coincidence. Spike stirred at her neck, his jeweled eyes snapping open in reaction to Mia's fear. "How did he know where to find me?"

"Very good question." Kellen's eyes narrowed speculatively. "He's coming this way. Let's see if we can find out." He casually removed his hand from her thigh and draped his arm around her shoulder. "Relax. He can't hurt you with all of us right here."

Mia stroked the little A.I., more for her comfort than his. She looked at the men sitting around the table with her. None of them had moved, but she felt a tension in each that hadn't been there before. Their casual poses suddenly seemed less relaxed, more watchful. She looked up at Kellen's rugged face. She saw determination, anger and a hint of something she couldn't identify. He would protect her. She had an odd feeling of family, something she'd never experienced before. She could get used to it.

She watched Marshal approach. He seemed to be his normal self, glad to see her, but his smile wavered a bit when he took in her companions.

"I thought you were dead or something." Marshal stopped beside Mia's chair. "You haven't checked in for over two weeks." He leaned one hip against the table, his gaze traveling from Kellen to the rest of the group. "Aren't you going to introduce me to your friends?"

Mia didn't answer immediately. Everything about Marshal seemed off, his smile, his voice, the way he moved. She tightened her hand on Kellen's thigh, hoping to communicate her uneasiness.

Kellen shifted in his seat, placing himself firmly in Marshal's line of sight and positioning Mia slightly behind him where he could better protect her. "You may have heard of me. I'm Kellen Tavish. Mia and I were close awhile ago. Getting reacquainted now." His cold gaze didn't waver from Marshal's, nor did he offer his hand.

"We're all getting to know one another," Ayden said, slouching in his seat and intent on cleaning his nails with one very long, very sharp knife. Mia wondered where he'd had it stashed.

"Mac and I like her already." The smile on Bree's face could freeze an arctic dragon in mid-flight. "We'd take it real hard if anything were to happen to her."

Marshal's eyes darted to Jake and Tyson. They stared back with deadpan eyes, not bothering to introduce themselves.

"Don't mind them." Kellen's voice stayed calm and polite. "They're not used to being social. We try to civilize them, but it's an uphill battle." He bared his teeth in a predatory smile. "So how'd you track us down?"

"Just coincidence." Marshal shifted uneasily. "I got this far and decided to stop in for supplies before heading out system." A tick at the corner of his mouth betrayed his growing agitation. "Mia going AWOL left me shorthanded. I've got some deliveries to complete in the outlying systems."

"Well, don't let us keep you. You must have a schedule to make." Ayden's voice dripped ice.

"Just leaving now." Marshal lifted an eyebrow at Mia. "Don't suppose you want to come along?"

"Thanks. But no." Mia's guts churned. Something was definitely wrong. Spike unwound himself from her neck and broadcast warning vibes at an alarming rate.

Marshal acted as though he expected Kellen's team to pounce at any minute, yet he made no move to leave.

He was the type of man who liked to be in control. He snapped out orders, expecting immediate obedience. This polite banter was out of character. Mia shifted closer to Kellen, instinctively seeking his protection.

He tightened his arm around her while he addressed Marshal. "Seems someone's put a bounty on Mia. Any idea what that's about?"

"Bounty?" Sweat beaded Marshal's brow. His gaze darted nervously from man to man. "Nope. Didn't hear a thing."

Odd. He didn't seem too interested in the threat to his most lucrative operative, Mia thought.

Marshal went on hastily. "I've got that schedule to keep, so I'd better get moving." He straightened abruptly, turning to leave. "Nice to meet you all."

The next few moments passed in slow motion. As soon as he finished speaking, Marshal twisted back to face the group. He pulled a thazere from his pocket and pointed it directly at Mia's head.

Before she could react, Kellen's left fist shot out and caught her handler squarely under the chin, spinning him around to Ayden. Ayden grabbed Marshal by the neck and tossed him across the table to Jake. Jake wrapped one beefy arm around Marshal's head and twisted, neatly snapping his neck. He tossed the corpse to the floor like so much refuse. Mia, speechless, just sat there as Spike whirred his anxiety.

The whole episode had taken less than a minute.

"I can't believe the man could be that dumb." Bree shook his head. "We warned him."

Kellen bent to retrieve the thazere and looked up at the bar's muscle-bound enforcer who had rushed over at the sounds of a fight. "Set to kill," he noted. "Clear case of self-defense."

The enforcer nodded in agreement, grunting as he shouldered Marshal's remains. "Some bipeds are just too stupid to live," he noted sourly. Without further comment, he hauled the corpse off to the disposal unit.

"This is getting more than annoying." Kellen took a long drink of his beer. "We need to get to this Defalcio character and find out what the hell his problem with Mia is. Then we deal with him."

As she started to laugh, all the men turned to look at her. Realizing she sounded hysterical, she buried her face in Kellen's broad chest, the laughter quickly turning to sobs.

"It's okay, honey." Kellen stroked her hair soothingly.

She lifted her face from Kellen's comfort. "Someone I've never met wants me dead. The man who's been my handler for most of my adult life just tried to kill me. A bunch of men I just met today killed him. 'Okay?' I don't think so." She choked back another sob and wiped her eyes with the back of her hand.

Kellen continued to cradle her as he turned his attention to the men at the table. "We need a plan. Any suggestions?"

Mac looked thoughtful. "If we knew the location of the ORG headquarters, we could launch a raid. Grab Defalcio, bring him in to question." He looked over at Mia. "Don't suppose you know where the headquarters are?"

Mia shook her head. "I think they're based on a mobile platform. The signal moves around a lot. I got my orders from Marshal, and debriefs were always done aboard ship." She shivered as the mental image of Marshal, his neck broken, flashed in her mind.

"Maybe we can locate the ship and blast it out of existence." Ayden grinned cheerfully. "That could be fun."

Kellen threw him a quelling look. "Wouldn't work. We'd have to be sure we had the right ship, and that Defalcio was on board. There's too much chance we'd blow up a ship full of innocent civis.

"Spoilsport." Ayden pretended to pout.

His clown act had the desired effect. A ghost of a smile flickered around Mia's mouth.

"We could put out a bounty on Defalcio," Bree suggested. "Maybe that'd piss him off enough to get careless, show his face."

Mia leaned against Kellen's chest, one hand nervously toying with Spike's tail. She worried her bottom lip with small white teeth. "One of you could take me in to collect the bounty. Not for real," she amended when six sets of eyebrows shot skywards at the same time. "Set a trap. If he wants me, he has to show himself."

Dead silence greeted her suggestion. Her plan sounded perfectly logical, if you ignored the inherent danger. The rest of the team turned to Kellen, waiting for his reaction.

"Are you insane? Or just suicidal?" Kellen slammed his palm on the table. "We are not going to use you as bait for some lunatic."

"It might be the only way to flush Defalcio into the open," Jake said logically.

Ayden frowned and tipped his chair back. "We'd all be there to cover her."

"No way," Kellen snarled, daring anyone to defy him.

"Kellen." Mia kept her voice soft, but a steely conviction underscored her words. "It's not your choice. I appreciate that you care about me and want to protect me, but I'm not a child. I make my own decisions. I want to do this." She reached up, gently stroking one rugged cheek. "I need to find out why this man wants me dead. And I need to know it's over, that I can get on with my life and not always be looking over my shoulder."

Kellen looked down into her eyes. She could tell he really wanted to say no. Finally, he gave a reluctant nod.

She planted a big wet kiss on his cheek. "Thank you!"

Kellen looked rattled as he returned his attention to the team. "So that's decided. Now how are we going to make it work?"

Mia watched as Kellen turned the ship's controls over to the A.I. interface and strode across the bridge. "Come on." He released her harness and pulled her to her feet. "We've got some time until we get to the jump-off point."

With one finger he tilted up her chin, and she could see the sympathy shining in the depths of his blue eyes.

They'd returned to the ship after the meeting with his team to make preparations and set the plan in motion. But now that they were committed to action, terror threatened to paralyze her. She couldn't believe she was just going to waltz in for a face-to-face with the man who wanted her dead.

She was about to say this when Kellen lowered his head to take her lips in a long slow kiss that seared her to the very soles of her feet. *Damn, the man knew how to kiss.* His practiced tongue sought hers, initiating a duel that sent liquid fire racing through her veins.

She raised her arms, wrapped them around his neck, and returned his kiss with a passion edged with desperation.

Kellen took his time, not rushing her, softly cherishing her with his lips and tongue. His hot mouth coaxed a response from her. Slowly, her fear receded, replaced by an aching need that only he could satisfy.

He lifted his head, mouth curving in a wry smile. "This is really becoming a bad habit."

She raised a brow. "What?"

His eyes danced with laughter. "Kissing you." He scooped her into his arms, making her feel very small and very feminine. Striding down the corridor to his stateroom, he tossed her onto the sleeping platform, stopped briefly to strip off his clothing before he pounced, wrapped her wrists in one big hand and pinned them to the bed over her head.

When his gaze dropped to her chest and the nipples that had pebbled in anticipation, she felt a blush stain her cheeks.

He fastened his mouth on hers, and suddenly nothing else mattered. Only this man. Her lover. He opened the front of her suit to let her breasts spill free. She arched her back, wordlessly begging him to touch them. If this were all she could ever have of him, this physical union, then she would make it be enough. She refused to let him go again.

He lowered his head, his tongue tracing the outline of the sensitive mounds. "You are so sexy." He scored one swollen nipple with his teeth. "I can't believe I ever let you get away."

Mia needed to hear this, to know that he cared about her more than her lack of status. She inhaled deeply until his spicy male musk, so very familiar, filled her senses. She moaned and squirmed under the assault of his practiced hands and mouth.

He licked and suckled her breasts while his hand ventured lower, stripping off her suit and exploring every curve, every hollow, every inch of her writhing body.

He nibbled a line from her breasts to her navel, stopping to tease the faint indentation with the tip of his tongue. She twisted and squirmed beneath him, molten heat following the path of his tongue.

He released her hands while his mouth continued its downward path, murmuring his approval when she gasped beneath him. She loved his mouth, the way it could look so stern with AlphElite disapproval one moment and so sexy and inviting the next. He could drive her crazy with his tongue alone.

"I love the way you taste when you want me." His breath feathered across her as he spread her thighs and leaned close to nuzzle her mound, watching her with those molten eyes. The sensual hunger visible in them caused her pulse to rocket.

He lowered his head to lick at the sensitive folds of her entrance. His tongue flicked the hard nub of her clit, wringing a breathless gasp from her lips. Her entire body jerked as flames seared through her. Then he dipped his tongue into her aching core, caressing, teasing, tasting.

She couldn't stay still, bucking and squirming beneath him as her body spiraled out of control. Honeyed heat raced down every nerve.

"Come on, baby, come for me." He plunged a finger deep inside her, stroking the sides of her tight channel.

She wound her fingers through his hair, holding him to her as wave after wave of her orgasm rocked through her. "Oh, gods, Kellen."

Not giving her time to come down, Kellen pulled himself over her and thrust deep inside her silken sheath. Her inner muscles clamped around his invading shaft, drawing it deeper into her, rejoicing at the tight fullness. Mia wrapped her legs around his waist, trapping him inside her body.

He lifted himself on muscular arms and she met his gaze, watched the blue of his eyes intensify as he thrust into her, burying himself over and over again inside her creamy core.

He kept his gaze locked on hers, and in the depths of his eyes, she saw passion and want and need. And love. He might not be willing to give voice to the words, but it was there, unmistakable, enveloping everything else.

She matched him thrust for thrust. Tiny flames licked over her nerves, searing a path from her breasts to her belly to the junction of her thighs. She writhed, whimpering and moaning as sensation after sensation drove her higher and higher until the world exploded in a million fragments of incredible light, and there was no more Kellen, no more Mia.

Only the two of them, together.

Finally Kellen dropped onto his side, holding Mia and rolling over carefully until she lay sprawled on top of him. He nuzzled her neck, placing a kiss in the tender hollow of her throat. "You look very satisfied."

She smiled. "I feel very satisfied." She traced the line of his jaw with her finger. "You know exactly what to do to make me lose control. I should be terrified of you."

He raised an eyebrow, that sexy grin of his causing her heart to do a little flip. "But?"

"But I know you'd never hurt me. Or let anyone else." She laid her head on his chest and closed her eyes as his arms tightened protectively around her.

Tomorrow, she'd worry. For now, it was enough that Kellen held her close against his heart.

Chapter 8

Mia's face was so clear, so trusting, so full of faith. Kellen wanted to wrap her in his arms and hide her in the safest place he could find in the universe. But deep in his gut, he knew she was right to confront the danger head on. And if he wanted them to have any kind of a future together, he needed to acknowledge her courage.

A loud pinging noise sounded as the ship signaled its final approach to the planet. Kellen reviewed the readouts and slid into the pilot's seat. He adjusted his restraining harness before switching the systems from autopilot to manual. Only under extreme circumstances would he let the ship go through docking procedures on auto. He didn't trust landing or takeoff to the auto programs. Too many things could go wrong, and he believed sentient reaction time, good old gut feelings, would give him the edge.

His fingers flew over the input screen, adjusting the speed and angle of approach. Satisfied with the ship's performance indicators, he told Mia, "Time to buckle in."

She'd been edgy and restless for the last few days. He wished he could make her feel better, but this plan didn't thrill him much either. He just hadn't come up with a viable alternative.

Mia settled into the navigator's seat and buckled the restraining harness. Kellen resisted the urge to check to make sure she'd tightened the straps properly. *She's an adult. Let her be.*

He put his doubts aside and concentrated on landing the ship safely. "Initiating docking procedures." He spared a brief thought for the team. They had arrived yesterday and should be in place by now.

Implants would be their only means of communication unless it became necessary to abort the mission. If things went sideways, all bets were off. They'd use whatever means were available to warn the team off. AlphElite loyalty demanded that they leave none of their operatives behind. Standard operating procedure.

Because Mia didn't have the ability to communicate telepathically, Kellen would rely on Spike to keep tabs on her. He could easily access the A.I.'s neural network and use it to track Mia.

Defalcio had agreed to meet Kellen at Sudds, a mercenaries' club in the upper section of the main city. Jake and Tyson had already settled into the club's visitor's quarters, posing as a couple of well-to-do friends blowing off some steam. They would fade into the background long before Kellen showed up to make the exchange.

Mac and Ayden were going in together. The two of them would ham it up, just a couple of miners on leave burning through their cred-chips before returning to the asteroid fields. No one would pay much attention to them.

Bree was to remain at the docking bays and make sure their ships were fueled and ready to take off once the mission was complete. If the twins ever showed up from whatever hellhole they'd disappeared into, they would provide extra cover.

The bridge deck tilted sharply to the left as the ship initiated its final descent through the outer atmosphere, the artificial gravity field lagging a few seconds behind. He pushed all thought of the upcoming mission aside and concentrated on piloting the ship.

Kellen checked the restraints on Mia's wrists for what seemed like the tenth time since they'd docked. They needed her to appear as a captive, but in case of trouble, he wanted the restraints loose enough for her to escape quickly. Spike hung dormant around her neck, ready to activate when needed. A short-handled laser hugged the small of her back, and she had a pair of compact thazeres strapped to her inner thighs. *Gods, he hoped they wouldn't be necessary.*

As soon as the ship secured its umbilicals to the assigned docking bay, he'd switch the controls to autopilot. Dealing with security and landing clearances was tedious at best, so he might as well let the ship's computer handle that particular drudgery.

Even after all the planning, with the rest of the team close by and ready to assist, Kellen's nerves had him strung so tight he might go berserk at the slightest provocation. There were too many variables, too many ways this scenario could go wrong.

Mia swallowed hard. "I'm starting to think this isn't such a good idea. Defalcio must really hate me. What if he shoots me on sight?"

Kellen checked the charge before sliding his weapon into the underarm holster. "It's a little late for second thoughts. I agreed to meet him in a public place so the rest of the team can protect you. If the bastard so much as blinks wrong, one of them will take him out. But I'll still need to find out why this is happening. We need to know he's just one nut after you. We don't want to find out after he's dead that there are ten more like him on your tail."

He ran big hands up and down her arms. "If there's the slightest chance he's going to hurt you, he's dead meat. The team will take him down, and they're good. They never miss." He drew her against his chest and buried his face in her silky soft hair, inhaling her sweet scent. "I have no intention of letting Defalcio harm one pretty little hair on your head."

Mia smiled. "I trust you. And your team. I just want it to be over. The waiting is getting on my nerves."

"It'll be over soon, honey." He held her out a bit so he could look down into her eyes. "Some day you'll be telling our grandchildren about this."

"Our grandchildren?"

"You didn't think I'd go to all this trouble just to let you get away, did you?" Kellen heard himself saying. He added gruffly, "I thought we'd start out with half a dozen sons. Enough to keep you busy and out of trouble." He reached to snag a stray lock of hair and tuck it behind her ear. "There'll be no girls until they've got enough brothers around to protect them."

"Yeah, right." A wistful smile turned up the corners of her mouth. "Somehow I can't picture us as a mommy and daddy team."

Kellen caught her chin, held her pinned. He could tell she didn't believe he'd forgo AlphElite status to bond with her, and who could blame her? But now wasn't the time for that particular discussion. Still, he couldn't let it go. "Use your imagination. Haven't you ever wondered what it would feel like to hold a child of ours in your arms?"

He was waiting for her answer when the electronic voice of the autopilot broke the spell. "Security screening completed. Initiate compression equalization?"

"Initiate." Kellen dropped his head to give Mia a quick, hard kiss before returning to the pilot's chair to run through the post-docking checklist. When he'd satisfied himself the ship was secure, he keyed in the shutdown codes. The ship would be running on minimum systems until he returned to power it up. It saved wear on the systems and made it impossible for anyone without the codes to hijack her.

Now that they were so close to their target, Mia looked scared. He didn't blame her. "Let's get this show on the road." The words came out a little brusquer than he intended, but she took a deep breath and nodded.

Kellen used his implant link to notify the team that he and Mia were on their way. Jake transmitted assurance that Defalcio had only one person visible with him. Kellen knew there would very likely be others nearby. It would be foolhardy to expect someone of Guye Defalcio's stature to go anywhere without adequate backup.

When they reached the club, Kellen put a restraining hand on Mia's shoulder. "It has to look like you're under my control." He produced a thin length of flexi lead. Attaching one end to her bound wrists, he coiled the other in his hand.

"As long as it doesn't give you any ideas." She raised her eyebrows suggestively while a hint of a smile ghosted across her mouth. "I don't intend to play submissive just for your enjoyment."

Kellen grinned despite the tension. "We can discuss that later."

"The hell we can." She twisted her wrists in front of her.

Kellen entered the club with Mia trailing behind at the end of the flexi lead. A quick look around assured him the team was in place and had seen them enter. When he spotted an employee, he motioned the man over to give his name and explain they were here for a scheduled meet with Guye Defalcio.

The man eyed Mia, taking in the restraints and the flexi lead in Kellen's hands. He smirked, coming to the obvious conclusion that she was a pleasure-slave being delivered to her new master. "Follow me. Mr. Defalcio has been waiting for you."

He led them towards one of the semi-private alcoves at the far end of the room. Strategically placed plants effectively blocked their view of the area.

At their approach, a burly giant of a man materialized from behind the greenery, his hand fingering the holster at his hip.

Their escort held both hands up in a conciliatory gesture. "Mr. Defalcio is expecting these people." Taking the coin Kellen slipped him, he bowed in the direction of the alcove and melted back into the crowded common room.

The bodyguard sized Kellen up insolently, ignoring Mia. Kellen stood his ground stoically, refusing to be intimidated. After a tense but silent battle of wills, the guard jerked his head towards a small table with a pitcher of bluish liquid on it. "You wait here. I'll tell Mr. Defalcio you've arrived."

Kellen used his free hand to move the chairs so that his back was to the wall, Mia beside him. He didn't want her blocking his view.

He took advantage of the wait time to familiarize himself with the lay-out of the bar. The door they'd entered was at the far end of a dozen tables crowded with serious drinkers. A stone bar ran down one side of the room, every seat occupied. The only women in sight were working. Definitely not the sort of place one chose for a romantic rendezvous. He noted Ayden and Mac at the pool tables to his left. They were joking and clowning with each other, but had maneuvered themselves into the optimal position for backup if things turned ugly.

He saw Jake nursing a drink at a small table to his right. Familiarity with the two snipers made him look left and up to find Tyson. Sure enough, he could see him leaning over the second floor railing, his eyes scanning the crowd with deceptive calm, a long-necked bottle held casually in his hand.

When the bodyguard reappeared, Kellen sent a heads-up to the team through his link.

The bodyguard gestured towards the alcove. "Mr. Defalcio will see you now."

Kellen stood and tightened his hold on the flexi lead. Mia rose obediently, but he felt her tension and wanted to tell her, *Don't worry. No one is going to hurt my woman.*

He led the way into the alcove, noting every item available as a weapon, every avenue of escape. A low circular table surrounded by well-padded seats filled most of the space. Walls on three sides provided partial privacy.

Tyson's calm voice floated through his neural implant. *I've got a lock on*

Defalcio. Don't get in my line of sight.

Kellen shifted his position, giving the sniper plenty of room should he need it.

From the corner came a cynical voice. "So this is the little bitch. It's about time I finally put an end to her."

Kellen studied the man lounging on the far side of the table. As large as Kellen, though not as well muscled, he had short dark hair like Mia's, cut military style. His eyes were flat and cold, eyeing her as though she were a particularly obnoxious bug.

Kellen moved forward, partially blocking Mia from view and diverting Guye's attention to himself. "What'd she do to you?"

"Does it matter?"

"Not for this kind of money. But I'm curious."

"Oh, she's worth every bit of the bounty." A distasteful grimace crossed Defalcio's face. "She's the spawn of the bitch who took my son from me. He died to protect her and this—this creature. Died like a civi on a dirty, backwater planet at the edge of the known worlds." The hate in his voice was almost palpable. "Imagine how I felt when I learned he'd died, but that the bitch he spawned had survived. I vowed I'd find her and send her straight to hell."

At both his revelation and his hatred, Mia gasped. Then she straightened and glared at him. Kellen shot her a look of pride before turning back to Defalcio. "You're her grandfather?"

"No!" Defalcio spit out the word, horror clear on his face. "My son was AlphElite. He had an impeccable pedigree. He graduated at the top of his class from the best military school in the Urali System. He'd been pledged to a female of suitable breeding and good background. I set up the match myself. Their offspring would have been the best of the best."

He locked his malevolent gaze on Mia. "He joined the ORG, as he should. His team went on tour to the Urali System. That's where he met the conniving bitch. He should have just used her. That I could have understood."

Mia stirred beside him, ready to attack, and Kellen tugged on her flexi lead. Calm, he told her without words. She stilled.

Defalcio shifted his gaze back to Kellen. "You know how it is. Civi females are damn good fuck buddies. Nice tight cunts, high tits, squirmy little asses. You're AlphElite. You've had your share, haven't you? But that's it. You don't pledge to them. You sure as hell don't breed them."

Kellen had to go on playing his part, so he forced the words out. "Yeah. I know what you mean."

Mia, to her credit, stayed still.

Defalcio shook his head distastefully. "When my son came home, I knew he'd changed. He looked happier than I'd ever seen him. I thought the tour had affected him, bonded him with his team. I should have paid more attention." He slammed his fist into the wall, anguish on his face. "He didn't even have the guts to tell me to my face. He quit the ORG, left me a note, and crawled back to that bitch. He threw everything away for her. He threw his life away." Defalcio moved out from behind the table, his gaze locked on Mia. "His bitch may be dead, but you aren't. You look just like her. Did you know that? You couldn't have been more than four or five when I finally tracked them down. I ordered the hit on that planet. Jorge shouldn't have been there. I arranged for him to be off-planet. I set up a business deal he couldn't pass up. Damn him, he must have sensed something, because he went back. He had that ability, could sense things before they happened. They told me he tried to dig her out of the hovel with his bare hands. It collapsed with him still inside. My people reported Jorge and his bitch both died. No one said anything about a kid."

He smiled, an expression of pure evil, and his attention snapped back to Mia. "Seven years ago I became head of the ORG. I sifted through the personnel rosters. Just routine, familiarizing myself with the operatives. I saw your file image. You looked like her come back from the dead. I knew that couldn't be possible, so I checked your history. I couldn't believe my luck. It all pointed to you being the bitch's spawn. After all these years, I could finally take my revenge on her for destroying my son. I could destroy her child, as she destroyed mine." His eyes shone with manic glee.

Kellen fingered the weapon at his hip. Defalcio focused his malevolent gaze on Mia, who looked defiant but said nothing. He ignored Kellen completely.

Ayden's disembodied voice came over the implant, his tone neutral. *Two bodyguards down, one still standing, behind to your left. Can't get him without the target making my position. Jake and Tyson are in place, ready if you give the signal.*

Do they have a clean shot? Kellen didn't want to chance taking down any bystanders.

He noticed Mia tensing up. He'd warned her to follow his lead and keep a low profile, but the realization that her parents' murderer stood right in front of her, gloating about his despicable crimes, could be more than she could handle. She looked as if she was seconds away from launching herself at Defalcio barehanded.

Kellen gave another sharp tug on the lead, shooting her a quelling look when she turned her head to glare at him. He didn't need her putting herself between Defalcio and the snipers.

Give me a minute. Ayden sounded eager for action. *Okay, Jake and I both have beads on the target. Tyson's in place to take out the last guard.*

Roger that. Kellen replied through the implant. *Stand by.* For a moment he was tempted to give the signal and finish this with a clean kill. Listening to Defalcio's evil ramblings left a bad taste in his mouth. He spared another glance at Mia.

"I deposited the bounty to your Embank account, as agreed." Defalcio's gaze didn't leave Mia. "Do you want to verify the money's there before you leave her?"

"That won't be necessary." Kellen's voice came out a strangled hiss. Keeping himself from giving the order to shoot took real restraint, not one of his better qualities.

"Did you do her on the way over?" Defalcio flicked a glance at Kellen, snapping his fingers and holding out his hand for the flexi lead.

The man was clearly insane.

Kellen glanced over at Mia. Despite his earlier warning, she'd curled her hands into tight fists. That icy look in her eyes usually preceded murder and mayhem. He judged the distance between them, getting ready in case he had to tackle her to keep her out of trouble. He said easily, "It's none of your business what I did."

Defalcio smiled. "It doesn't matter, you know. I intend to let the guards have at her as soon as I bring her to headquarters."

Okay, he's got to go down. Tyson's voice came over the link low and heated.

Ayden's answering snarl crackled through the link. *Shooting seems too good a death for a snake like that.*

Jake piped in calmly, *He's like a rabid Vsuian moonhound. Nasty and contagious. Take him out quick and clean.*

Defalcio spoke again in a low, vicious voice. "I want to watch her suffer before I dispose of her."

Kellen had heard enough. He couldn't imagine how Mia managed to hold herself back. *You guys still got him in the crosshairs?*

"Roger that. It'd be an honor to drop the bastard."

Kellen dropped the flexi-lead.

Defalcio took a step forward, grabbing for it. He stopped at the audible snick of a thazere powering up.

Kellen aimed his weapon at Defalcio's head.

Defalcio looked up, sudden understanding warring with the fury on his face. He shook his head. "You stupid bastard."

Kellen kept his gaze locked on Defalcio, his voice icy calm as he addressed Mia. "What do you want me to do?"

Mia let out a strangled growl, tension visible in every line of her body. "Kill him." Her voice was soft, sorrowful, but she needed to say the words.

Her choice. Her decision.

"Are you sure?"

She gestured at the impotent rage on her grandfather's face, the insanity shining in his eyes. "Yes."

Kellen squeezed the trigger.

Chapter 9

Of course, the rat wouldn't stand still and let himself get fried to a crisp. A little violence and betrayal like this would be a normal part of his day. He knew how to deal with it.

Defalcio threw his hefty bulk directly at Kellen. The two well-built Alph-Elites collided with a meaty thud. Defalcio grabbed Kellen's gun arm and used his forward momentum to twist it sharply, ruining Kellen's aim.

Kellen grunted and clenched his teeth as intense pain shot up his recently healed arm. The gun skittered across the tiled floor and a sizzling sound heralded the appearance of a smoking hole in the inner wall.

"You idiot. You let that bitch get to you." Defalcio's voice dripped with contempt.

Tyson's voice came through the link without emotion. *Want me to take him out?*

No. Kellen scowled. *His ass is mine. He threatened my woman. You're here to protect Mia.* He blocked the pain and dropped to a defensive crouch. His focus narrowed to Defalcio. Studied him, looking for weaknesses. He circled slowly to the right, away from Mia.

A muffled thud sounded to his left.

Last guard neutralized. Mac's voice this time. *Not a clean hit. You've got an audience.*

Defalcio broke eye contact, searching for the source of the noise.

Kellen grabbed the drink pitcher from the table and smacked it across the side of Defalcio's head. Blue liquid splattered and pooled on the floor.

Defalcio staggered. His attention snapped back to Kellen. He slapped the pitcher from Kellen's hand and aimed a vicious kick to the knee.

Kellen dropped and rolled, avoiding the blow. He came to his feet smoothly and kept his eyes on Defalcio. *I'm taking this asshole down.*

Defalcio kicked out. But his left foot went high, missing Kellen's face. Barely. The man knew how to fight.

Kellen circled, keeping eye contact. Defalcio's were as cold and cruel as a pit snake's.

You might want to hurry up and finish him. Crowd's getting restless. Tyson again.

"Quit whining, Tyson. Jake sounded amused.

Kellen ignored their banter.

He faked a grab with his left hand, followed with a right jab to the face. He didn't connect. This wouldn't be easy. Just as well. He smiled grimly. He wasn't in the mood for easy.

Defalcio ignored the feint, twisted to the left, took his own jab at Kellen's face and grazed his mouth with big knuckles. He tried to take him down by hooking a leg, but missed.

Blood sprayed from Kellen's split lip in a crimson arc. He lifted his hand and wiped blood from his eyes. Glancing back at Mia, he tried to convey confidence with a cocky smile. *Looks worse than it is.*

He jabbed a right fist to the other man's jaw.

Defalcio swiveled to block and misjudged the distance. He overextended, leaving his right side vulnerable.

Kellen came back with a low kick that swept his opponent's legs out from under him. Then he smashed his right fist into Defalcio's ribs. The sickening snap of breaking bones filled the air.

Defalcio fell to the floor, his face contorted in agony.

Kellen bared his teeth in a predatory smile.

Rolling over awkwardly, Defalcio came to his knees. He drew a laser from an ankle holster. One arm held his injured ribs as he struggled to bring the weapon to bear.

Kellen pivoted. Kicked. Went for the killing blow, putting all his weight behind it.

Defalcio's head jerked back as his neck broke with an audible snap. His jaw dropped in disbelief, his eyes glazing over. He dropped to the floor with a loud thunk.

It's over. He's dead.

Kellen became aware of his surroundings, of the circle of onlookers. A few just watched. Others bounced on the balls of their feet, spoiling for a fight.

Tyson and Jake, eyes constantly moving, kept their weapons panning the crowd in a silent warning not to interfere. Mac and Ayden stood back to back with Mia sheltered protectively between them.

Mia.

Her eyes wide with shock, she stared at the corpse of her grandfather. An agonized sob escaped her lips, and she trembled violently. She looked so small and vulnerable.

Kellen's heart ached for her loss. He grabbed her in a giant bear hug, palming the back of her head gently as she buried her face against his chest. "I'm so sorry, baby. We didn't have a choice."

"I know," Mia whispered. "It had to be done. He hated me so much."

"He was crazy. You saw that." Kellen dropped a tender kiss on the top of her head. "None of this was your fault."

Mia burrowed closer and took a deep breath. "I know."

"We might want to get out of here." Mac squatted beside the body, making absolutely sure Defalcio was dead. "I'm betting he had some kind of warning system set up. We'll be lucky if it's ten minutes before this place is crawling with trigger-happy ORG agents, not to mention drunken rednecks that just plain like to fight."

"Good point." Kellen gently pried Mia from his chest. "We have to get out of here and back to the ship. You ready to move?"

Mia scrubbed her face with the back of her hand. She nodded, avoiding eye contact with any of the men. "Sure. Anytime."

"Okay then, let's roll." Kellen and Mac tucked Mia between them and moved into the main area of the club with measured steps. Jake brought up the rear, weapon out and ready. Ayden and Tyson took up point positions, one to either side, weapons at the read as they swept the room with cold eyes.

"Hey!" A burly miner, his belly full of false courage, stepped in front of the group to block the exit. "You guys think you can just walk out of here with the pretty little bitch?" He leered drunkenly at Mia.

Kellen drew up straight, but before he could move, Mac stalked forward to face the miner.

This one's mine. "And as a matter of fact, yes, we do." His eyes narrowed with concentration, Mac thrust his fist straight at the miner's throat.

The man dropped to his knees, gasping for air and clutching his ruined windpipe with both hands. A well-placed kick sent him sprawling sideways.

Show off. Tyson's amused drawl relieved the tension.

"Anyone else have a problem?" Mac glared around at the motley collection of bar patrons.

No one spoke. No one dared look directly at the irate mountain of a man. Mac's mouth curved in a slow, predatory smile as he said through the link, "I haven't had this much fun in ages."

"Okay, you're the man. Now let the kiddies go and let's get our asses back to the spaceport." Kellen's eyes panned the crowd. "I don't see any ORG agents, but they've got to be here somewhere."

They're setting up an ambush at the spaceport. Bree had no trouble communicating despite the distance between him and the team. *They've already tried to board Kellen's ship. Security held, so they're deploying at the outer edge of the ring.*

How many? Kellen started the group forward again. Knowing where the ambush was settled his nerve. First priority was to get clear of these civis. Never underestimate the capacity for violence in a crowd of redneck miners.

I count ten, Bree replied. *You're outnumbered, but they don't know you've made them. I'll provide distraction when you're ready. That'll give you an edge.*

Mac dropped back beside Mia as the group moved towards the exit. The crowd parted to let them through, no one anxious to be Mac's next target.

Tyson and Ayden moved ahead, watching for signs of a trap. When they reached the door, Tyson opened it and Ayden slipped out, weapon swinging in a wide arc as he searched for threats.

Ayden turned back to the others. "Exit clear."

The two stood to either side of the door, covering the team as they left.

Kellen kept Mia close to his side. She responded like a robot to his prompting, her eyes blank with shock. She had never been this quiet, but he didn't have time to worry about her state of mind right now. He hoped she'd hold together long enough to get back aboard the ship.

They had six city blocks to cover before they entered the outer ring of the spaceport.

Tyson. Mac. Take forward point. Check out the alleys and cross streets. Kellen hated the sprawling urban setting. Too many places to hide.

Roger that. The two snipers moved forward cautiously, checking out each alley and cross street ahead of the team.

Nothing moving out here. Mac held up a hand to signal the next alleyway was clear. *Not even the proverbial mouse. I'm guessing they all went to ground when the ORG moved into the spaceport.*

Kellen nodded. *We need to get past them.* He looked down at Mia. "You stay between me and Ayden. When we get to the outer ring, Bree will create a distraction and lay down cover fire. We'll need to make a run for the ship." He paused and gave her shoulder a quick squeeze, making sure she understood. "No matter what happens, keep running."

Mia nodded. Pulling the compact thazeres from the holsters at her thighs, she gave him a ghost of a smile. "Ready when you are."

Kellen's heart skipped a beat. She was tough. She'd be okay.

But first, they all had to get out of here alive.

"Got them in sight." Tyson and Mac both went to their knees, blending into the buildings around them as they froze in place. "Ahead of us, to both sides." Grudging admiration edged the words. "They've left us one way in, and if we take it, they'll nail us."

Bree? Kellen pulled Mia into the shadow of a sidewalk café. *You got something for our friends out here?*

Roger that. You all in place? Bree asked.

Just kicking back waiting for the fun to start, Kellen confirmed. *What'd you have planned?*

Fireworks off to the right. That'll make it look like you're coming in from that side with guns blazing. It won't fool them for long, so you need to hoof it in here ASAP. I've got the forward laser array set to cut both sides of the path. Stay in the center and you'll be fine.

Silence reigned for a few short seconds.

Bree's voice came gleefully across the neural network. *And action—*

Explosions ripped through the air, brilliant flashes lighting up the sky to their right.

Go! Go! Go! Kellen grabbed Mia by the arm and started to run. When a figure in fatigues popped up in front of them, Kellen shot him between the eyes without missing a step.

"To your right! To your right!" Mac flashed a warning while coolly firing at a shadow that materialized on the path ahead of them. An agonized howl rose as the agent went down hard.

Kellen felt an energy blast graze his shoulder before he located a third ORG agent and blasted him with the thazere.

Shit. He nailed me. Kellen blocked the pain and kept on running, shielding Mia's body with his own. *If I go down, you get Mia out of here.*

Mac and Tyson made it to the ship's access port and took cover to either side, pinning down the remaining ORG agents with precisely aimed shots. The rest of the team swarmed up the last few yards of the path and scrambled into the safety of the ship. The two snipers backed in behind them and slapped the control panel.

The access port whooshed shut, the airlock engaging with a loud thump.

"We did it!" Mac and Tyson high-fived each other, jubilant grins plastered across their faces.

Mia threw herself into Kellen's arms and burst into tears.

Chapter 10

Kellen held her gently, close to his heart, and looked helplessly over her head at the rest of the team. The sympathy and understanding on their faces reassured him.

"You go take care of her." Ayden nodded at Mia. "We'll get the ship up and out of here." He turned to Bree. "Is she ready to fly?"

Bree nodded. "The sooner the better. I doubt the ORG is going to take kindly to us hanging around." He turned to address Kellen. "Okay with you if I captain the ship out of here?"

Kellen nodded curtly, his attention focused on Mia. "I'm taking Mia to the stateroom. Let me know when we're in the clear."

He strode down the corridor to his sleeping quarters, Mia cradled possessively against his chest. Entering the stateroom, he laid her gently on the sleeping platform and then hesitated. She'd stopped crying, but she hid her face behind the dark curtain of her hair to avoid looking at him. He didn't know if she blamed him for killing her grandfather, or if the whole damn mess was just too much for her. Somehow she'd become the most important thing in his life, more important than his ship, his career, even his AlphElite status.

His jaw dropped as realization hit him. Her grandfather had been a vicious man, but he had been AlphElite. That meant she could claim AlphElite status for herself. They could formally pledge.

Just as quickly, he realized it didn't matter. It had never mattered. He loved Mia, had loved her before she'd walked out. He didn't care about her parents or her status. He wanted her, Mia, and he wasn't about to let her get away again.

He crouched beside the bed and took her chin gently in one large hand, tilting her head so he could look directly into her bottomless green eyes. She looked so fragile, so sad. His heart ached for her suffering. He searched for words to comfort her.

"I'm sorry things turned out like this. I know how much it would mean to you to have family." He searched her face for forgiveness, afraid he wouldn't find it.

"Some family." Mia shook her head sadly. Tears glittered on her lashes. "It isn't your fault. He was insane. He wanted to kill me. My own grandfather."

Tears threatened to well up again. "He didn't care about me. He didn't even think of me as family."

She put her hand on Kellen's shoulder, running her fingers across his collarbone. "He was so filled with hate." Her brow creased in bewilderment. "Why do some people hate so much?"

Kellen shook his head. "I don't know. It's like a sickness. His hatred hurt him as much as anyone."

"Kiss me," she said.

He lowered his mouth and trailed his tongue across her lips, teased them open. His tongue darted in, stroking, tasting, exploring the sweetness of her mouth. He took his time, not pushing, taking only what she offered, until she moaned in surrender, her arms coming up to wrap around his neck while she tangled her fingers in his hair.

He repressed the urge to shout with joy. *She doesn't blame me. She still wants me!*

He sank onto the bed beside her, unwilling to let her go. She looked so beautiful lying there beside him. His heart ached at the sight of her. Her dark hair spread over the pillows in silky disarray, and her eyes were smoky with the beginning of passion. Her lips, full and enticing, begged him to kiss them again.

With infinite tenderness, he took his time, worshipping her without words. Stroking. Licking. Caressing. The smell of her arousal rushed through him, flooding his body with liquid heat. He could feel her need in the way her body moved restlessly under his hands.

He uncovered her breasts, reverently cupping them in his hands while he worshiped them with his tongue, stroking them with gentle fingers until the nipples rose in taut, hard points. He paused to remove the rest of her clothing with reverent care.

Taking his time, he ventured lower, licking at her belly, tasting the thin sheen of sweat on her hips and circling the pert dimple of her belly button. Lower still, he licked and nipped at the tender skin of her inner thighs. He cupped her sex with his hand, using two fingers to spread her labia so he could insert another finger into her slick channel to test her readiness.

She creamed, arching her back. Catching her gaze, he lowered his head to cover her pussy with his mouth. His tongue swirled around the hard little bud of her clit before delving deeply into her heated core. He returned one hand to her breasts, stroking, teasing, and pinching. He held her down with a brawny arm across her hips while she came, screaming out his name as she thrashed under his mouth.

While she still quivered in the aftermath of her orgasm, he stood and quickly shed his clothing. Spreading her legs, he lowered himself over her, his cock probing at the apex of her thighs while he held himself over her with his muscular arms. He paused.

"Will you pledge your life to me?" It wasn't really a question, not quite a demand. He cupped her tight little ass in one big rough hand, angled her hips up to meet his rock-hard cock. He locked his gaze onto hers, waiting for her answer.

"That's not fair." The radiant smile on her face told him what he wanted to know. "You know I can't resist you when you're naked."

He nudged her swollen, wet pussy with his cock. "Say it," he demanded. "I want to hear you say it."

"Yes." She breathed the word out softly, her eyes shining with love. "I'll pledge my life to you."

He entered her in one swift thrust, burying himself to the balls in her tight sheath. "I love you so much." He nipped at the tender lobe of her ear. "You're so soft and silky and tight. A perfect fit."

Mia moaned and arched against his big male frame. His huge erection stretched her slick channel, filling her deliciously. "I love you too." She rolled her hips up to meet his thrust.

"Thank the gods for that." Kellen withdrew, then slowly pushed his way back in, arching his back to watch in fascination as her tight pussy swallowed him, inch by inch.

The mewling sounds she made as she took him into herself were incredibly erotic, making him even harder. He wanted her so badly, he couldn't restrain himself much longer. He picked up the pace, ramming his big cock faster and faster into her tight channel.

She matched him, thrust for thrust, stroke for stroke. Digging her nails into his back, she drew him even closer. The slick walls of her channel tightened around him, holding him trapped deep within her, squeezing his cock until the world exploded around them in an incredible climax of pure feeling.

꙳ᎨᏦᏝᏋᎦ꙳

"So when are you going to dump this wimp and get yourself a real man?" Ayden waggled his brows at Mia, ducking a backhand swat from Kellen.

"Oh, he's not so bad." Mia sat on Kellen's lap, wriggling her backside enticingly. "He has some real talents."

"Such as?" Jake managed to look interested.

"Well, he's a good cook. He makes the best breakfasts." She turned to drop a kiss on the tip of Kellen's nose.

"He cooks?" Jake looked astonished. "In all the years I've known the man he has never cooked. He can't even get a decent meal out of the auto-dispenser."

"You didn't deserve my cooking." Kellen said smugly, wrapping Mia in a bear hug. "Mia does."

Love! Mia savored the feel of that single word. *He loves me.* She could feel it in the way he held her, see it in the way his eyes blazed with fire as he watched her, and hear it in his voice every time he said her name. *He loves me.* Mia couldn't believe how happy she felt, basking in Kellen's unashamed affection.

The team split up after escaping from the planet, scattering to lay low while the ORG swept the galaxy looking for them. Just last week, the newly appointed head of the ORG announced they were abandoning their search as a useless drain on resources and were moving on to business as usual. Now that the danger was over, the team had decided to get together to celebrate.

"I'm guessing you're not going back to work for the ORG?" Bree asked.

Mia shook her head. "No. I think it's time for a change of employment." She wrinkled her nose. "I suppose I should send in my official resignation."

"No need. I'll just insert the appropriate notarizations into your records. It's easier that way, no awkward questions. I can authorize a nice severance package and an impressive letter of recommendation, just in case you decide to go back into that line of work." He smiled cheerfully. "Sometimes my hobbies come in handy."

"Most of your hobbies are illegal," Mac pointed out.

"But handy," Bree reiterated.

"Very handy," Mac conceded.

"So what do you plan to do next?" Ayden asked Mia.

"She's going to look after her pledge mate." Kellen nuzzled the top of Mia's head. "That'll be a full-time job."

"Your pledge mate?" Ayden looked puzzled for a moment and then understanding dawned. "Hey, you two are getting hitched!"

Mia grinned. "See, Kellen. I told you Ayden isn't as dumb as he looks."

Ayden looked offended, spoiling the effect when he winked at Mia. "I do not look dumb!"

Mia laughed. She couldn't help herself. With Kellen by her side, all of her dreams were coming true. She'd always wanted to belong to a family and now she did. They may not be a normal family, but they accepted her, cared about her, and protected her. It was enough.

And soon, she and Kellen would be starting their own family. A secretive smile lit her eyes as she let one hand stray down to cover her belly protectively. Perhaps they already had.

About the Author:

Anne Kane lives in the beautiful Okanagan Valley with a bouncy Jack Russell terrier, a cantankerous Himalayan cat, a geriatric guinea pig and too many fish to count. She married her high school sweetheart and has two handsome sons and three adorable grandchildren. By day, she's a respectable bean counter, but after hours her imagination soars and she writes romances that span the galaxy and encompass beings of all sizes, shapes and origins. She first started telling stories as a child and she just can't seem to stop.

Scoundrel in a Kilt

❧❧❧❧❧

by Nicole North

To My Reader:

Nothing's hotter than a Highland hunk in a kilt... except when he takes off that kilt. I hope you enjoy my wicked, dark shape-shifting selkie scoundrel, Brodie, as much as the time-traveling heroine, Erin, does. This is the third tale in my shape-shifter series. The first was *Devil in a Kilt* in **Secrets Volume 27 Untamed Pleasures**. The second was *Beast in a Kilt* in **Secrets Volume 29 Indulge Your Fantasies**. The selkie is an ancient Scottish legend and I loved putting my own sexy spin on it.

I dedicate this story to my wonderfully supportive husband. I love you!

I also dedicate this story to my amazing critique group and friends, Rebel Romance Writers: Terry, Carol, Randy, Betty, Judy, Tammy and Pam. I also dedicate this story to another fantastic critique partner and friend, Vanessa. You've all been an incredible help to me. Thank you!

Chapter 1

Scotland, present day

"I'm in hell," Erin Shultz muttered between chattering teeth. *Frozen hell!*

"Concentrate, Erin!" Sam, the creative director of the photo shoot called, his voice carried away by the icy Highland wind whipping off the Atlantic and across the castle's roof.

Didn't he know it was damned hard to concentrate on edgy poses when one's nipples were in danger of freezing and falling off? The thin silk dress, studded with millions of sequins, didn't do a thing to deflect the wind.

"We're looking for ethereal but sexy," Kincaid, the fashion designer and client, reminded her. "Mythical but earthy. Pretend you're a mermaid."

A mermaid? On top of a castle? That made a lot of sense.

Determined to get a great photo even if it killed her, Erin focused on her stiff facial muscles. *Move, damn you!*

Three more blinding flashes.

"That's a wrap!" Sam waved.

Erin dashed inside the castle, grabbed her coat from the female assistant, and wrapped her shivering body within the heavy wool. "Thank you. I have to find some heat."

"Kincaid isn't impressed by your photos, Erin." Sam's voice echoed from behind her.

Her stomach dropped as she spun to face him. "He loved my look before. I thought those last few shots were great."

Sam's hard gray eyes and tight ponytail made his expression appear more severe than usual. "We're scheduling a re-shoot for tomorrow. Something isn't translating into the pictures this time. Are you distracted? What's going on?"

"Nothing. I'm fine." Why did he bother asking? He didn't care about her financial problems. "I'm simply not used to working in such extreme cold," Erin said. And the world was indeed a cold place.

Sam patted her back. "Do better tomorrow."

She nodded and watched him walk away. Her eyes burned and her throat ached. *How could I screw up so badly?*

She descended the narrow spiral stairs to a corridor. Spying a lit fireplace in a bedroom where a photo shoot had taken place earlier, she slipped inside. Holding her hands out to the fire, she absorbed the divine heat and scanned her surroundings. Nothing in the room was modern, from the ancient, velvet-draped bed to the chests and candlesticks.

Sam and Kincaid strode by the room, footsteps echoing. "If her photos are topnotch tomorrow, I'll still want her to walk in my runway show in Glasgow," Kincaid said in his highbrow British accent. "If not, I'll have to find another blonde…" Their voices grew distant, then a door slammed.

Nausea latched onto Erin's already empty stomach. *What am I doing wrong?* Maybe she was over-thinking it. She needed this job and many others to help get her finances back on track and pay for medical school. She'd lost most of her savings in the damned stock market. She'd always invested wisely, as her financial advisors suggested, but she may as well have gambled away her life savings in Vegas. Her dream of becoming a doctor was even further away than it had been five years ago when she'd been "discovered" by a top agent and decided to take a few years off from school.

And now the problem with her photos. This seemed minor, but it could have far-reaching repercussions.

If she didn't get to the van soon, she'd have to hike a half mile in four-inch heels and chilling winds. Striding toward the door, she accidentally kicked something with her toe—a piece of metal—and it clattered a few inches. She bent and picked up a tarnished brass key. It appeared ancient and felt warm to the touch.

Heat and happiness spread through her. Energy buzzed along her nerves. Strange. Erin clasped the key within both palms. The feeling intensified.

"Hello, dearie."

Erin jumped. A gray-haired matron, broom in hand, stood in the room's entrance. A nametag on her shirt read Louise.

"Hi."

"Are you enjoying your visit to Farspag Tower?" she asked in a strong Scottish accent.

"Yes, thank you. I found this on the floor." Erin relinquished the key and the icy chill and anxiety almost overwhelmed her.

"That old thing? Take it if you wish." When Louise placed the key back into Erin's hand, the astounding positive feelings returned.

"Wow." This tiny piece of metal was better than a double espresso or an anti-depressant. Anticipation filled her, and she was unable to hold back a smile. "This isn't a valuable antique?"

Louise shrugged. "I've never seen it before. Perhaps 'tis the key to your future."

An eerie thrill raced through Erin. She didn't know whether to run away or laugh.

"'Tis yours, dearie. Enjoy. And come back to visit us sometime." Louise patted Erin's hand, then shuffled to the far corner and started sweeping.

"Thank you." Erin slipped the key into her coat pocket and hurried down the narrow stairs to catch up with the photographer and his crew.

In the dim light of the high-ceilinged great hall, her heel caught in a gap in the stone floor. Her heart in her throat, she grabbed for the ancient oak table, hit her shin on one of the benches and bit back a curse. All she needed was a massive bruise to add to her troubles. She yanked her shoe from the crevice, slid it on, and sprinted for the door. The pain in her shin disappeared faster than she could've imagined. Had the key caused this?

Maybe it would also bring her good luck at tomorrow's shoot. She hardly noticed the biting wind as she raced across the stone-paved car park and climbed into the van. A feeling of warmth and well-being enveloped her.

"Why are you smiling?" Fellow model Britnee sneered as Erin settled into her seat. "Sam said you're going to have to bring it tomorrow or you're out."

"I will." Erin smiled wider, because the key made her feel that good, even with her nemesis taunting her.

"Maybe it's time to retire. Or go catalog," Britnee said.

Oh, the arrogance of teenagers. "Bite me."

Ten minutes later, Erin arrived at the reception for Kincaid in the small pub on the ground floor of their inn at Dunmory Village. Would she have to face him and his disapproval again? Maybe she would skip it. But the delicious scents of steak and roasted potatoes lured her in and made her stomach growl. She hadn't eaten since breakfast. She placed a few appetizers on a tiny plate.

She craned her neck, searching the room for her friend Katie, but couldn't find her.

Erin sneezed and one miniature meat bridie tumbled to the tartan carpet. "Oh no. I can't get sick," she muttered, pressing a napkin to her tickling nose. She swallowed and pain seared across her throat. "Dammit!"

"Something wrong, Ms. Schultz?" Kincaid asked, approaching.

"No. Sorry." He might cancel everything and hire another blonde if he thought she was sick. "I'll do much better tomorrow… with my pictures, I mean."

"I certainly hope so," he said, lifting a brow before sauntering away.

An ache of dread filled her stomach, and she felt like that ugly, gangly teenager again. The one dubbed alien giraffe by all the cool kids, while her mom was dying of cancer.

Hoping to find a dark corner to hide in, she turned and smashed into a tall man wearing a lot of plaid and carrying a pint of ale.

"Och!" He stared down at his ale-drenched traditional kilt and ivory linen shirt. Bits of flaky bridie crust clung to his plaid sash.

"Oh, no!" Could her day get any worse?

He glared at her. Déjà vu immobilized her. She'd seen him before, but where? A fellow model? He certainly could be a model with those dark, exotic eyes, high cheekbones, and sleek-muscled physique. He looked like he'd stepped straight off a runway in Milan or Paris.

"I'm sorry. I'll pay for cleaning—" She pressed the napkin to her nose just as a sneeze erupted. "Excuse me."

"Ne'er mind!" The kilted guy stomped off. He didn't even offer a *bless you.* Fine. She couldn't help that she was sick. A fit of coughing took hold. And if he was too arrogant to accept her apology, then screw him. She hated egotistical men, even if one happened to be a walking erotic dream.

She sneezed twice more.

What was she doing at a party? She ditched her empty plate and slipped up the narrow staircase to the small room she shared with her friend and fellow model, Katie.

"Why weren't you at the party?" Erin asked, closing the door. "Still getting ready?"

Katie ran a brush through her long black hair. "Yes, for a date. I just finished packing. We leave for Glasgow tomorrow, remember?"

"Yes. You have a date?"

Katie grinned, her too-cute dimples showing. "I met a guy. He's taking me to a pub tonight to hear live music. It's a kickoff to the Celtic Festival that begins tomorrow."

"He doesn't by chance wear a kilt, does he?"

"He's Scottish, so he probably will wear one. Most people will be in costume."

Figured. Not that she ever wanted to see the impatient jerk again. But for the first time, Erin found she envied Katie's long, silky black hair, hollow cheeks and perfect eighteen-year-old skin. Being twenty-four in the modeling world was becoming difficult. She was ready to get on with the next chapter of her life and follow her true dream. She'd made a vow to herself and her mom. She'd simply thought modeling would be a fast way to gain financial stability.

Erin dug out a bag of chocolate-covered almonds and slumped in a chair. "I have to redo my shots in the morning. If they look like crap, I'm fired."

Katie's mouth dropped open. "Why? What happened?"

Erin chewed a mouthful of nuts and swallowed. "My expression was wrong, or something. Kincaid wasn't happy."

"Kincaid is an ass!" Katie said.

"I know, but he's an important ass."

"He's only one designer. If he fires you, there are thousands of others who would book you in a heartbeat."

"You're so sweet. Thank you." She loved Katie for her pep talks, but it would take more to get her over this hurdle. "Achoo!" She grabbed a tissue. "Oh yeah, and on top of that, I'm coming down with a cold or flu. I almost froze solid out there in the wind." Katie had been fortunate enough to pose inside by the fireplace.

"I know what would help." Katie pointed to the mini bar.

"Getting drunk?"

"A hot toddy, as my grandma used to say. She would put lemon and honey in it, but everyone knows what the active ingredient is." She held up a miniature bottle of amber-colored liquid.

"Scotch?" Erin grimaced. "Not my thing."

Katie removed the lid and handed it to her. "Trust me. If anything can fight off a cold by morning, this would be it."

"Why not? I'm desperate." Erin downed a swallow. It scorched her sore throat and she almost choked. Coughing, she grabbed a bottle of water and drank half of it. "Yuck! That doesn't go well with chocolate-covered almonds." She squinted at the whisky label through watery eyes. *Farspag Tower*, it read just below a picture of the castle where she'd spent a miserable day.

"You'll think it has magic in it." Katie grinned. "Drink all three little bottles. It's not that much."

"Clearly an acquired taste." She forced down another sip. "Ugh!" At least she'd sleep. By the time Katie left fifteen minutes later, Erin had polished away two mini bottles of Scotch and started on the third.

I will get better. I will get better. She lay on the bed feeling as if she were floating. Heat flowed through her veins like lava and her coat felt sweltering. She struggled out of it and flung it to the chair. The mysterious brass key fell from the pocket. Clutching it to her, Erin again tested its effect. It took away her anxiety and made her feel happy. Nice.

After finishing off the third bottle, she fell into bed. The covers were cozy and her pillow soft. She exhaled a contented sigh. She'd forgotten to take off her dress, but was too sleepy now to move.

Images swirled in her mind. A man materialized. A tall man with black hair and wicked dark eyes—the one who'd been in the pub. "Leave me alone. I don't date or dream about male models. Especially arrogant ones." She'd had enough of those types five years ago.

Torches flickered on the walls of the dim room. Torches? Wait a minute. This wasn't her room.

"Dream… just a dream," she whispered.

The hottie moved toward her and his kilt fell off. "Whoa." Such a muscle-chiseled body. Yes, he had to be a model who worked out two hours a day and ate no fat. "Not interested," she mumbled. But that didn't help. A part of her refused to listen, and she couldn't take her eyes off him. This guy was different, his gaze more intense and focused, as if she were someone important to him.

"You've got the wrong woman, Highlander."

Slowly, he climbed onto the bed and lay down next to her, his warm breath tickling her ear. Chills skittered down her neck. It had been a long time since she'd been in bed with a man. A year or more?

"I don't have time for this," she whispered.

"I'll make it worth your while, lass." What an accent he had, thickly Scottish. Glancing down, she saw something equally thick. She hadn't seen an erection that big in… ever.

"You've been eating your oat cakes, I see." Her words came out slurred. She really shouldn't have drunk three bottles of Scotch on an almost empty stomach.

He murmured something in a language she didn't understand, then kissed her ear, her cheek. His lips were hot and tempting.

"Go away. I'm sick. I have to sleep and recover. I have a hard day tomorrow." She shook her head, blinked, and he disappeared. Yes, she was in her room again with the red glow of the digital clock showing just past nine p.m. A few seconds later, the wicked Scot returned.

"'Tis only a dream and willna disrupt your sleep." His deep voice and accent could seduce the granny panties off a nun.

She deserved a fantastic dream, didn't she? To make up for the past year of celibacy. And a horrid day.

"Aye, you do," he murmured.

She found herself being sucked in by his hypnotic chocolate gaze. "Don't read my mind. You're only a figment of my imagination and you'll do what I say."

"Indeed?" Smiling, he slid his fingers into her hair, pressed his lips against hers and teased her mouth with seductive flicks of his skilled tongue. Each brush spiked unfamiliar arousal through her deprived body and held her enthralled. She had forgotten how sharp, breathless and controlling desire could be. Holding onto his muscled arms, she tugged him closer, inhaled his musky scent. All scrumptious male.

Who are you? Her voice would no longer work, but did it matter anyway? He was a dream—nothing more. His kisses delved deeper, became more erotic, and need ached inside her. He made her ravenous.

Sliding his searing hand down her suddenly naked body, over her hip and along her thigh, he touched her just the way she wanted. The slow, light strokes set her skin on fire like the whisky burning in her veins.

Dare she go after what she wanted? She ran her fingers down his chest and hard, rippled abs.

He purred. "Aye, lass, touch me."

"Are you real?" she whispered.

"What do you think?" He curled her hand around his rigid cock, springing upward toward his navel. His hand guiding hers, he urged her to squeeze and stroke slowly up and down. Wow, he felt amazing. Sleek and powerful. Like someone she wanted to crawl all over and munch on. She gently nipped at his jaw, the rough stubble scratching her lips.

Growling, he slipped a hand between her thighs and moved upward to cup his palm against her mound. His fingertip dipped into her wetness, finding her clit to fondle and taunt.

"Oh!" Pleasure spiraled outward and her legs fell apart wide.

"Is that good, princess?" he asked.

"Yes. Fantastic."

He kissed and nibbled at her neck while he busied his fingers in ever bolder and tempting ways, spreading her sex lips, caressing her wet clit in maddening circles. She thrust her hips toward his hand, seeking penetration. He slid a finger into her and she cried out.

"Yes, more," she moaned.

He removed his finger. And disappeared.

"Don't stop." She gasped. "Where are you?"

A loud pop sounded and pain shot through her head. "Ouch!" What had the bastard done to her?

Holding her head between her palms, she shivered, her eyes tracking back and forth as the pain evaporated. Icy cold surrounded her. Now she lay on something hard, rough and wet. A rock? The full moon gleamed over a dark ocean and waves crashed below, spraying chilling salt water over her. Freezing wind whipped at her hair.

What the hell?

Chapter 2

Ròncreag Isle, West Coast, Scottish Highlands, 1621

Who or what was stealing the female selkies?

Brodie, Chieftain of Clan MacCain and member of the Ròncreag selkie tribe, stood on a cliff on the south side of the island, gazing through the darkness toward the sea. Even with his keen eyesight, he saw naught—no ships, galleys or lanterns on a vessel that would indicate fishermen were kidnapping them. The culprits were probably the Orkney tribe of selkies. Maybe they were running out of females.

Screaming from far below echoed upward. "Help! Help me!"

"What the devil?" Brodie climbed down to another part of the cliff. In the moonlight, he saw what appeared to be a woman—nay, a mermaid with a blue tail—on a giant rock that jutted up from the sea. "Mermaid?" He had never in his life seen one.

Her banshee-like screams would frighten off any thieves this night.

Or was she somehow linked to the selkie disappearances? A spy? He would rescue her and find out who'd sent her. He descended the narrow pathway toward the ocean. The autumn night wind felt refreshing on his bare skin.

"Oh my God! Please let this be a horrible nightmare!" the female yelled.

Because of his superior selkie senses, he heard her words clearly over the crashing waves. But her unusual, accented English was difficult to decipher.

He jumped into the icy water and swam out, fearing the mermaid would flee before he arrived. He hoisted himself onto the rough rock behind her.

"Are you hurt?"

She squealed, faced him and drew back. "You! From my dream. What did you do to me?"

"Dream?" Saints, she was the most beautiful lass he'd seen since Elspeth had betrayed and abandoned him. Nay, this one was even lovelier. Like Elspeth's, the mermaid's hair was white-blond, but short, and her eyes ethereal blue. Shimmering sea-green and blue scales covered her from her breasts on down.

"How did I arrive here?" she demanded, her teeth chattering.

"Swam? Who sent you?"

"No one sent me. I don't even know where the hell I am!" She swallowed hard, her eyes scanning the cliff behind him.

"'Tis Ròncreag Isle, Scotland."

Her hair was dry. She couldn't have swum here, unless she'd been here a long while.

"I'm freezing. Can you help me?"

"Aye. Come."

"I can't get into the water! I'll die from exposure. It's like the freakin' Arctic out here!"

A mermaid who refused to get into the water? Hmm. He offered his hand. "Trust me."

"Where's your boat?" Her hand touched his. "Oh, you're warm," she said, wriggling closer.

Then, he saw she wasn't a mermaid at all. Her bare, pale feet stuck out from the bottom of the tight gown that sparkled like stars. Was she an angel or a fairy? Or a selkie spy sent by the Orkney tribe? If that were the case, why would she be so susceptible to cold? Nay, she did not have the selkie scent. She smelled human and very tempting, almost as if she were aroused, or had been recently. In any case, she was shivering and he had to get her warm.

"Hold onto my shoulders while I swim to shore," he said.

"I don't know if I can—"

"Aye, you can." He turned his back and she clung to his shoulders. "Hold tight, but dinna choke me. Ready?"

"Yes." Her voice grew high and squeaky.

He inched back into the water and swam toward the craggy shore. Her light weight didn't hinder his progress overmuch, but her breasts rubbing against his back distracted him. He could never again trust a human woman, but this didn't dampen his lust for her. He muttered a curse when his tingling shaft grew rigid as the rock he now hoisted them onto.

Sensual pursuits had not interested him as much over the past few weeks, not since his friend, Torr, and that irritating old wizard, Finnian, had tried to convince him he should give up his selkie abilities. Even though these came from a witch's curse, Brodie enjoyed the selkie powers and lifestyle. And now the selkies needed his warrior skills more than ever, to save their women.

"Climb up," Brodie told the lass, taking her hand and urging her off his back and onto the rocks.

"Ow, ow, these rocks are sharp! How did I arrive here without my shoes? How did I come to be here at all? I'm supposed to be in bed, asleep."

"I dinna ken." Brodie pushed to his feet and stood upright beside her. She was exceptionally tall for a lass, but also slender.

"Brrr! It's so cold!" She visibly quaked.

"Take my hand."

When she did, her shivers stopped. "How do you do that?"

He shrugged. "So, you're human?"

"Umm, *yeah*. Aren't you?"

Her impertinent tone made him want to shock her into silence with a ruthless kiss. What would she taste like?

Nay, he could not indulge. She might be a danger to his whole tribe. "Which clan are you from?"

"I'm not from a clan. I'm from Wisconsin. Yikes, you're naked! And—and...." She motioned toward his erection.

Aye, he couldn't help but be aroused. He found her keenly appealing.

He turned. "Climb onto my back again and I shall carry you up the cliff."

"Are you out of your mind? What if you drop me?"

He snorted. "I'm no' going to drop you, lass! I climb these rocks all the time."

Erin surveyed the guy's sexy bare ass in the moonlight and considered her options, which was only one if she wanted to survive this freezing cold without cutting her feet on the rocks. "Okay, you promise not to drop me?"

"Aye. Hurry."

She yanked up the confining tail of her sequined gown and stepped onto a rock, the jagged points stabbing the tender soles of her feet. "Ow! Damn!" Four-inch heels a size too small she could take, but not rocks. Grasping his strong, broad shoulders, she wrapped her legs around his trim waist and clung to his back like a monkey. He held one hand around her thigh and scaled the crag like a professional rock climber. Squeezing her eyes shut and pressing her forehead against his upper back, she tried not to imagine crashing onto the boulders below. How had he made her feel warm just by touching her? It made no sense. Was this a lucid dream, a delusion, or something more sinister?

When he slowed and his muscles relaxed a bit, she opened her eyes. He ducked and carried her into a pitch-black cave.

"Where are you going? I hate caves!"

"Shh. 'Tis safe and warm here." He continued around two bends and into a torch-lit area. He lowered her to the ground in a "room" that contained a makeshift bed of furs. A woman lay there asleep. A fire burned in a pit in the center of the floor, the smoke trailing upward. Further back, steam arose from what appeared to be a rock-surrounded hot tub sunk into the floor.

"You give new meaning to the term caveman," Erin said. "Who's that, your wife?"

"Nay. 'Tis only Margaret." He wrapped a scratchy plaid blanket around Erin, ignoring his own nudity.

Only Margaret? What did that mean? Didn't matter. Erin simply wanted to get out of here and back to civilization, or the real world, whichever applied.

"I remember you from the pub. I'm sorry I caused you to spill ale on your kilt."

He frowned. "Pray pardon, but I dinna ken what you're speaking of."

So, he was determined to continue acting. She rolled her eyes. "Never mind." This had to be an elaborate scheme or joke. "How much did they pay you?"

Giving her a perplexed glance that was too exaggerated to be real, he poured wine from an ancient bottle into a tarnished silver goblet and offered it to her.

Was he serious? "No, thanks. I've already had too much to drink."

"'Twill warm your blood and calm your nerves. You're in sore need of it."

"How do I know this isn't drugged or poison?" Then she wondered if the whisky from the tiny bottles had been drugged. Had it made her hallucinate? Was this a bad LSD trip? She had never experimented with any sort of illegal substance.

Mr. Hottie drank a sip from the goblet. "Would I do that if it were poison?" He handed it to her.

"Tell me the truth. Was I drugged, or did Kincaid put you up to this so I couldn't make my photo shoot in the morning?" This guy was clearly a model, earning a bit of extra cash by playing a giant practical joke on her. "Or was it that little bitch, Britnee? If she gets me out of the way, she has the runway job in Glasgow, right?"

He studied her a long moment, eyes narrowed. "I dinna ken who or what you're blathering on about. But you're sounding a wee daft."

"Me, daft? You're the one who's playing dumb. Who are you?"

"Brodie, Chieftain of Clan MacCain."

"Chieftain? Right. Trying to move from modeling into acting? You're pretty good, I have to say." His accent was far more pronounced than Mel Gibson's in *Braveheart*.

"And what is your name?" Brodie asked.

"I'm sure you know."

"Nay."

"Erin Schultz."

"A pleasure." He bowed.

Her gaze skittered down his body again. She'd known many male models like him, men who loved nothing better than to strut around in the raw. All those quick clothing changes backstage before anyone and everyone made nudity nothing unusual. Still, this guy was something to look at, and he knew it.

"How far is Farspag Tower from here?" she asked.

"My tower is just beyond the minch." He motioned to his right.

His tower? Minch? "What is a minch?"

"'Tis a narrow channel of the sea."

"How long will it take? I need to be there by morning."

"Why?"

"I have an important photo shoot, as I'm sure you know."

He frowned, observing her as if she were a nut… or dangerous. "Shoot? Are you carrying a pistol?"

"No! A camera… taking pictures." She sighed. "Never mind! Will you help me get back there by morning or not?"

"I shall try, but I make no promises," he said in a hard tone.

"Fair enough. Thanks."

"Drink the wine. Are you hungry?"

Though her stomach ached with hunger, she shook her head and sipped the wine. No way in hell was she going to eat haggis or whatever boiled animal part he threw in front of her. She swallowed, realizing her throat no longer hurt. "Hey, I think I'm better." Her nose wasn't stuffy. "The whisky must have done the trick!"

The red-haired woman on the pallet sat up and glared. "Who is she?"

"Erin. I found her outside on the rocks. Be civil to her, Margaret," he said in a stern tone. "I shall be back in a trice." He moved toward the exit. What kind of place was this that the guy went around naked everywhere in the cold?

"Where are you going?" the surly Margaret asked.

"To find a galley to take her to the mainland." He disappeared through the opening.

This seemed to appease his girlfriend. And it certainly appeased Erin. Maybe she would make it to the shoot in time to keep the job.

The woman, wearing a long white nightgown, arose. When she faced Erin, she didn't look as young as before. She appeared to have aged twenty or thirty years. A few gray strands wove through her red hair. Erin blinked hard. She had to be hallucinating. Maybe this was all a nightmare.

She pinched her forearm. "Ouch." Not a nightmare. And the wine she was gulping certainly tasted real.

"Where did you get that?" Margaret snapped.

"The wine? That guy, Brodie, gave it to me."

"From here?" She held the bottle aloft.

Erin nodded.

The woman slapped the goblet from her hand.

"What the hell?" Erin gaped, readying herself to kick the woman's ass if necessary. She'd taken kickboxing, fencing and a little self-defense.

"That is no' for you."

"Well, excuse me," Erin muttered.

"Dinna provoke me, wench!" The woman growled, evil green eyes turning black.

A shiver traveled through Erin. "Fine, whatever, Margaret. Let's just chill, okay? I don't want to be here any more than you want me here."

"My name isna Margaret. 'Tis Lady Wilona MacRae. But you willna remember it." Sneering, she poured herself a goblet full of her prized wine and guzzled.

Okaaay, you greedy psycho.

The wine Erin had drunk heated her veins and warmed her clear to her toes. It was even making her a bit lightheaded. Dammit, she had no tolerance for alcohol, plus her stomach was empty. Those chocolate-covered almonds had done nothing to curb the flow of the alcohol. Glancing at the exit route, she hoped Brodie would return soon so she could get away from this crazy bitch.

"Are you wanting Brodie for yourself?" Wilona asked.

"Are you kidding? That arrogant narcissist?"

The woman's eyes narrowed. "You speak in a strange manner. Where do you come from?"

"Originally, Wisconsin."

"A land far, far away."

"You could say that."

"I ken why you've come." Wilona didn't appear happy with whatever twisted idea she'd conceived.

"Do you? Please enlighten me, because I'd love to know."

Ignoring her, Wilona placed her goblet on a trunk and lifted her hands toward the ceiling. She chanted and droned in a foreign language. The ancient sounds sent a dark shudder through Erin. A cold wind gusted through the entrance, whipping at the fire, swirling smoke and dust around the cave.

"Shit!" Erin shrank back into the corner, crouched and covered her face. *Where am I?*

The wind calmed and she peeped through her fingers. A naked, blond model-hunk strode in the door. "You summoned me, m'lady?"

You've got to be kidding me. Erin snorted.

"Indeed I did, Jamie. Tie her up." Wilona held out a length of rope.

"What?" Erin croaked, a chill slithering through her.

"Aye, m'lady." The blond took the rope and advanced toward Erin.

"Are you insane?" Erin screamed and scuttled away. "Why are you tying me up? I'm not doing anything. Brodie! Help me!"

"Remain calm. I willna hurt you." Charming blue eyes twinkling in the firelight, Jamie helped her stand and stroked a hand along her cheek. "A bonnie lass." His voice was seductive, almost hypnotizing, and for some reason she trusted him. He bound her wrists in front and led her to the center of the cave, near the pleasing warmth of the fire. There, he raised her hands over her head and attached them to a hook on another rope.

Wilona said something in the strange language, and Jamie glanced back at her.

"Do it," the harridan ordered.

What is going on? A strange, feverish excitement engulfed Erin. "Let me go." Her voice emerged as a distant whisper, even to her own ears. Had she been drugged?

Jamie caressed her cheek, ran his thumb over her sensitized lips. "I'm sorry, but I must do as my lady commands."

"What... why?" Erin wasn't sure what she wanted to ask. Her thoughts swirled around, making her feel pleasantly drunk. The damned wine.

Arousal shimmered through her. No, she didn't want to feel that way. This guy was a stranger, and she did not warm up to strangers that easily.

He circled behind her, breathed into her ear and stroked his fingers over her bare back where her gown dipped down.

Desire flamed within her. *What is happening?* She never got turned on this easily. And certainly not by an arrogant male model. Sure, in her dream she'd allowed herself to fall under Brodie's seductive spell.

But this was no dream!

At least, no dream like she'd ever had. Something was wrong. Her skin was on fire and yearning for a touch. Any touch. His fingertips felt like heaven stroking up her back with luscious tingles. He moved in front of her again and gathered her gown into his hand, tugging it slowly upward. Then his burning hand on her thigh, fingers spread wide, slid up to her hip and leisurely down again. She shivered and closed her eyes to better savor the sensations. Though she knew she shouldn't, she grew wet and craved more.

"Touch her," the woman commanded in the background. "Take her. She wants you, Jamie."

No, no, no. I don't. But some part of her did. Desire thrummed through Erin like a drum beat. This was a completely unnatural kind of arousal for her. She wasn't normally attracted to models, but now she'd become a sex-starved nympho. Though she tried to stop them, her legs spread. Her body wanted this, even if her rational mind didn't. His fingers teased her inner thighs for unbearable long moments, then finally slid over her mound and between her legs. She moaned, closed her eyes, and Brodie's face and sexy dark eyes appeared in her mind. Yes, she would fantasize he was touching her, just like in her dream. He had skilled hands.

"Brodie?" she whispered.

Chapter 3

Brodie heard Erin breathe his name as he reentered the cave. But the sight that greeted him—Erin's dress hiked to her hips, Jamie's fingers covering her mound, stroking, sliding—drove both lust and anger through him. For a long moment, he could do naught but stare. Her long legs spread wide, back arched, Erin was the most sexually alluring sight he'd ever beheld. Instantly, he grew hard and craved her.

Why had she whispered his name?

"Your wee whore appears to enjoy Jamie." Margaret stopped beside him, displaying a sneering smile. Whatever was going on, she'd arranged it, he was sure.

Possessiveness and jealousy rarely showed themselves in the Ròncreag selkie society. But Erin was not selkie. She was human, and since he'd saved her life, it was his duty to protect her, even should that mean protecting her from herself. Besides, he had an erection that wasn't going away. For some reason, Erin aroused him quicker than anyone in a long while.

"Out," Brodie said. "Both of you, out."

Appearing startled as if coming out of a spell, Jamie removed his hand, allowing Erin's skirt to fall.

"Me?" Margaret blinked with feigned innocence.

"Aye, and take Jamie with you."

"You canna want her. She'll spread her legs for anyone. She could never be faithful."

A spark of rage lit within him. "Out! Now!"

Margaret's gaze turned darker and more hostile. "Come, Jamie. You can keep me company." She gathered her things.

"I didna ken she was yours," Jamie muttered as he passed by.

Mine? Nay, Erin was not his, but something about her captured his interest and aroused him beyond comprehension.

Once the two selkies exited, Brodie returned his attention to Erin. His seething anger transformed into sharp lust. Her dress now concealed her lovely legs. The position, back arched, her hands tied above her head, caused her breasts to thrust out provocatively. Through the shimmering dress, her nipples protruded, tempting him. He had the mad urge to suck them. Worse, he craved dropping to his knees before her, sliding her dress up and sampling her musky essence. Would she taste sweet and tangy?

She still breathed hard with arousal. With lowered lashes and dark blue eyes, she watched him. He had only just met her, so why did he care what kind of faithless wanton she was? And how could he desire her so intensely?

He moved forward, taking in the rosy flush of her cheeks. "Enjoying yourself, I see."

"Untie me." Her voice was husky and breathy.

"Why should I?" Standing next to her now, he smelled her musky-sweet arousal, even more spellbinding than he'd imagined. Lust seared him and his cock grew harder. He suddenly wished he wore clothing to hide his uncontrollable reaction to her. As it was, she glanced down at his bare erection, standing at attention.

Her eyes darkened and her lips parted.

Why the devil did she have to look so damned tempting, like a carnal feast waiting for him?

Though he wanted to devour her, some part of him hated her. She was too much like Elspeth. "You will spread your lovely thighs for anyone, aye?"

"No. Bastard."

He chuckled, though there was little humor in it. He knew of no other lass who would dare insult him while tied up and at his mercy. "You're brave and hedonistic. Are you sure you're no' a selkie?"

"A what?"

Moving behind her, he saw the only things holding her gown in place were the shoulder straps. He took his dagger from the trunk and carefully cut the thin strips of material.

"What are you doing?"

"Quiet." He peeled the soggy fabric down her hips.

"You ruined the dress, you ass! Do you realize how much—"

He reached a hand around and pinched her hard nipple between thumb and forefinger. Not enough to cause pain, just enough to get her attention and make him want to bite her.

She squeaked.

"I said quiet," he murmured near her ear. The lush floral scent of her hair combined with her female musk made him ache. His cock pulsated and he allowed the head to brush one shapely cheek of her derriere.

A purr escaped on her breath and she arched her back, pushing her sweet arse toward him, offering herself. Growling, he stroked his cock down her crack, leaving a trail of glistening pre-cum. She gasped. How he longed to bend her over, slide into that cunny and take her from behind.

Instead, he suppressed his urges and circled in front of her. She wore some kind of strange string garment, its only purpose to hold a small patch of blue fabric over her mound. He cut it off, flung it away, then lay the dagger aside.

What a breathtaking sight she was, every man's fantasy. The face of an angel. High, perky breasts that would fit his palms to perfection. Hard, rosy nipples begging to be sucked. A narrow waist, flared but slim hips, and legs that reached from here to England. A man might give his very soul to possess such a woman. But what of her mind, her heart, her soul? Dark as midnight, in his estimation. She would not know of honor and fidelity. She would only know of selfishness and taking her own pleasure. Aye, the face of an angel, but the soul of a she-devil.

Why did he care? All he should care about, all he would focus on was what he could see before him. Lust incarnate. The blond hair of her mound was short and sparse, allowing him a clear view of the wee slit where her glistening arousal seeped out.

"Like what you see?" She yanked on her bonds.

Brodie shrugged one shoulder in a lazy manner. "'Haps."

"You do. You like it a lot. Your cock couldn't get much harder."

He sent her a bitter grin. Nay, she was no demure lady. Elspeth, at least, had been modest and pure when he'd met her. Erin was quite the opposite. Most likely, she sold her body on a daily basis, wherever she came from.

"Are you always so wanton?" he asked.

"No. I don't know what's… come over me. The wine. I started feeling extremely aroused after you gave it to me."

"Wine?" Frowning, he crossed to the table, lifted the bottle and sniffed. He detected a bitter scent. "'Tis tainted."

"Poison?"

"Nay. It contains some sort of herbal potion. 'Haps a lust potion."

"An aphrodisiac?"

"Aye. But how did it get in there?"

"What's-her-name—your girlfriend—did it. She told me it wasn't for me and slapped it from my hand. Then she called in her blond boy-toy to tie me up and molest me. And instead of rescuing me, you enjoyed watching."

"You didna appear to *want* to be rescued." Nay, she had liked Jamie's hands on her, even though she had said Brodie's name. That had to mean she desired him. Saints! The realization made his cock harden even further and his balls tighten.

"Bottom line, this is your fault. So do something about it!" Erin demanded.

"And what would you have me do, princess? Appease your lusts?" He gave her a mock bow. "Service you?"

Her eyes narrowed. "Untie me, for starters!"

"I am enjoying too much holding you captive."

"You narcissistic, conceited, cocky, irritating bastard!"

Brodie snickered, and Erin wanted to do nothing more than slap that smug grin off his face.

The stupid aphrodisiac in the wine had made her so horny she couldn't stand it. No, she was not a wanton, as he'd called her in antiquated terms. In fact, she had not even been interested in sex during the last year or two, instead focusing all her energy on modeling. But now, because of the potion, she ached inside and moisture dribbled onto her upper thighs. Her body yearned for Brodie—even if she did hate him. He'd given her the potion, cut her clothes off, and now would do nothing but stare at her with that dark, lustful gaze as if she were a stripper.

Maybe she should play the part. Then, at least, she'd feel some satisfaction instead of this torturous frustration.

"You want me, Mister I'm-too-sexy-for-my-kilt? Come get me," she breathed. "I'll make you feel good." She had never imagined saying those words, but that's how she felt at the moment—hungry for raw, down-and-dirty sex. And Brodie looked as if he'd be good at it with his sleek, honed muscles and impressive cock. "I'm hot and wet and waiting for you," she whispered, wondering what it would take to break his inflexible control.

His expression hinting at annoyance, he moved so close to her that the heat from his body warmed her, made her feel as if she were melting. His musky male scent was seduction itself. She craved his sensual lips on hers. His face almost touching hers, he inhaled, then moved down and brushed his lips over her nipples.

Arousal zinged through her. She cried out, thrusting her breasts toward him.

He flicked at one hard nub with the tip of his tongue.

"More," she urged. "Suck them."

"No' until you beg me." Nothing could ever be so wickedly provocative as his midnight eyes staring directly into hers. So close. His tempting mouth hovering over her breast.

"Please," she whispered.

"A wanton such as you are can do better than that, surely."

"Damn you!" Tears stung her eyes. She didn't understand what was happening to her. She had never begged for sexual favors in her life.

With a devilish smile in his eyes, he grazed his smooth lips and scratchy beard stubble over her nipples in blatant torture. Electrical impulses snapped through her and she trembled.

"Please. Suck my nipples. I'm begging you, Brodie." *Oooh.* If he didn't, she was going to die.

But he did, drawing one into his hot mouth with firm pressure. Lightning bolts of arousal shot toward her core, so intense she thought she might come. He switched to her other nipple while gently fondling the one he'd abandoned. The double stimulation drove her over the edge. Her body convulsed, pleasure streaking through her in long burning waves. Her screams echoed from the walls, but she could do nothing to control her reactions or her body.

When she became aware again, she found she'd encircled his waist with her legs, ready to impale herself. But he wouldn't let her. Instead, he held her aloft and released her bound wrists from the hook overhead. His forearm beneath her derriere, he carried her to a pallet and laid her down. Crawling upward, he tied her wrists to something over her head.

She wanted to protest and demand her freedom. But his cock distracted her, jutting out, swaying with his every movement. She drew in his masculine scent, both spicy and earthy, and despite having just climaxed, she yearned as never before to indulge in oral sex. She had only tried performing it once in her life, and had failed miserably. Probably because she hadn't really wanted to do it back then. She'd been pressured into it by her self-centered boyfriend.

But now, scoping out Brodie's delectable erection, she found she wanted to give it another try. While he was focusing on the rope, she lifted her head and placed one wet lick on his cock. He jerked, shifting his attention to her, his dark, hooded eyes boring into hers for a long moment.

He didn't move. "Do that again."

"Say please."

"Nay. You say please."

She licked her lips, deliberately enticing him. "Why should I?"

"Because 'twould give you much pleasure to lick my cock. Aye?"

She shook her head, when in reality she craved him, yearned to explore the shape and feel of him with her mouth, discover the flavor of him.

He inched slowly closer, his prick protruding toward her lips. "You started this, brazen lass. Dinna lose courage now."

"I could bite you," she threatened.

"You willna bite me hard," he said, equally threatening.

"I might."

"Nay. You can give me a gentle, sweet love bite, though. Right here." He stroked his massive shaft down and up once, then allowed the head to protrude from his fist.

"You'd like that, wouldn't you?" she asked, trying to hide her increasing arousal at the erotic sight of him holding his dick that way.

An eager little growl escaped his throat.

When she lifted her head, his cock was an inch from her mouth. She flicked out her tongue again, barely touching the tip. It tasted of salty seawater. Moaning, he inched closer. She opened—she couldn't help it. The wide head slid into her mouth. The masculine taste of him flooded her with more moisture. She stroked her tongue over the tip and around the ridged sides of the head. Oh, he was big and so hard.

She glanced up into his eyes, almost closed now. He drew in a hissing breath and held it. She sucked at the head and he pushed slowly in. Her jaws stretched. Growling foreign words, he withdrew and traced her lips with the tip, then teased it back inside. She sucked harder.

"Och, 'tis good."

Wanting to devour him, she let him feel the edges of her teeth scraping gently against the flared ridge at the back of the head.

He groaned deeper in his chest and his abs trembled. His whole body stiffened and he thrust gently, going to the back of her throat and withdrawing again. She stuck out her tongue and he allowed her to lick his silky shaft all the way to his balls and back up again.

With another string of blunt foreign words, he rose and moved away.

"Where are you going?" Why did he always have to stop just when she was getting into it, even in her dream? "Come back."

Nay, Brodie could not do it. One part of him would relish spilling his seed into her mouth while she drank him up. Another part of him felt such an act would be demeaning to her. Despite her words, she was no whore. More like a princess she seemed, and with an air of near innocence. Something about her spoke to him on a deep level. Her wanton behavior was probably due entirely to the lust potion he'd given her by accident. His fault. He could not take advantage of her in a vulnerable state.

With his dagger, he cut the rope from her wrists, freeing her, and stepped away.

"Thank you."

She was the most beautiful, enticing lass he had ever encountered. Her big blue eyes were bewitching. And those lush lips, so full and pouting—he wanted to lick and suck them. Her facial shape was perfection.

But perfection was always misleading.

Why the devil did she have to be human? If she were selkie, he would've already taken her. The last human he'd been with had been Elspeth. He'd loved her, but she had proved herself a faithless bitch, running away with his enemy. So beautiful, so cunning and traitorous, like the siren who lured sailors to their deaths.

Every time he looked at Erin's blond hair, he thought of Elspeth and the same pain seared his gut. He would not fall under the spell of another human who could rip his heart out.

Erin was wet and aroused, but he did not believe his eyes when she slid her hand between her legs and stroked the lips of her quim. They appeared swollen and hungry. Eager. He yearned to fuck her until they both collapsed from exhaustion. The potion had made her insatiable, but the effects would be temporary. What would she be like after that? Would she hate him for giving her what she'd asked for? Worse, would he become addicted to her?

"Brodie. I want you," she whispered, her lashes lowered, her eyes dark.

I want you, too. And that's what he hated most. He felt he'd die if he couldn't have her. That she had that much power over him already warned him. She could destroy his world.

She arose from the pallet and moved toward him. "Why are you torturing me?" she asked, stalking him like a hungry tigress.

"Torture?" What about him? He was near dying with lust. But his selkie instincts sensed danger.

"Yes. I want you," she breathed against his chin. "Now."

A renewed surge of desire immobilized him. He could not remember being this aroused in his lifetime. He should go for a swim in the icy cold ocean, but likely that would do naught to curb his appetite. And he had to protect her from lascivious male selkies who would take advantage of her, himself included.

He should not have untied her hands, for she now ran her fingers down his chest in tantalizing temptation. Her female fragrance reached him. This was the same hand she'd used to stroke her sweet cunny. He seized her wrist and lifted her hand. Aye, the scent of her was rich, irresistible, like sex and berries. He sucked two of her fingers into his mouth and the flavor of her tangy sex juices near drove him mad. Hunger clawed up from his soul. What spell had she cast over him?

He withdrew her fingers and captured her mouth in a deep, voracious kiss. Her tongue swept against his in a tormenting dance. "Mmm, saints!" He wanted to eat her up, savor every inch of her, nibble and bite. She tasted like perfection.

Wrapping her fingers around his straining cock, she squeezed and stroked. Pleasure ricocheted through him. He muttered Gaelic curses. Restraining her hands, he carried her back to the pallet. How could he stop himself from taking her, hard, fast and furiously?

"Lie still," he ordered, pressing his palm to her chest to hold her in place. He dropped his other hand between her spread legs and stroked two fingers along her sex lips, so drenched, swollen and eager. He slid his fingers into her snug passage.

She gasped and lifted her hips.

"Aye." He pushed his fingers deeper. She rode them, uttering little whimpering sounds that made his cock pulsate. How he ached to fuck her hard and deep. She was tight, but she could take him. Thrusting those two fingers, he dropped to his elbows and licked the wee firm nub of female flesh. She tasted like the best of carnal delights. Immediately she screamed, climaxed, her juicy pussy shuddering and gripping his fingers. How unbelievable she would feel squeezing his cock.

But he could not risk the consequences.

He slowly drove his fingers in and out, sliding easily now in her slickness.

"Oh, Brodie," she breathed. "You're good!" She raised her hips, undulating. "Yes, more." Indeed, she was insatiable. He flicked her with his tongue, then sucked the tiny sensitive bud forcefully. She cried out and shattered within his hands once again.

How he loved making a woman come. Especially this woman.

He had indulged in many sexual pleasures with the female selkies, but never had one of them been so lusty as this human. Her response was due to the potion, but still, he could not believe her responsiveness and desire. She climaxed several more times, and he never tired of tasting her delicious sexual essence.

Finally, she fell asleep. He covered her with a blanket and rose, reluctantly. He should damned well be considered a saint after that. He could have had her ten times over. Should have.

Muttering a string of Gaelic curses, he strode to the hot spring and lowered himself into it. Here, he would relieve his own frustrations without getting caught up in her. He had a suspicion she would steal his soul if he let down his guard.

Hours later, Brodie rested on the furs beside Erin, watching her sleep, listening to her deep breaths. Her long, dark lashes lay fanned against her ivory skin. Something blue glittered on her eyelids like fairy dust. She looked like a painting, not real at all. And she possessed some manner of magic, though he had not yet figured out what. A magic that had ensnared him.

He glared at her plump, rosy lips. The memory of those opened wide for his cock to slide between sent lust surging through him. Cursing, he squeezed his eyes shut. Though he had given himself a barely satisfying release earlier, he was now granite hard again.

"So," someone said behind him.

What the devil?

Margaret stood at the edge of the pallet and glowered at him.

"I asked you to leave." He rose to face her.

Margaret folded her arms and dropped her gaze to his suddenly dwindling erection. "I dinna wish to. If I have to share you with that human, I will."

He sighed. How could he get her to understand he was no longer interested in her?

"How are you able to change your age?" Erin asked in a drowsy voice.

Brodie glanced down, wondering how long she'd been awake.

"Is your new lover a lunatic?" Margaret asked Brodie.

"Nay." He gave Erin a quizzical look. Why had she asked such a strange question?

Erin sat up, covering herself with the blanket. "What was your name again?"

"Margaret."

"No, you told me a different name before."

She shook her head. "I am Margaret."

"What was in the wine?"

"Naught. 'Twas just wine. A very good year, aye?" She smirked.

"Did you put a potion in it?" Brodie asked, knowing full well she had.

"Nay. I hope to see you later, Brodie." Margaret gave him one last glare and strode out.

"She's a weirdo," Erin whispered. "I'm telling you the truth. She had a different name before and looked twenty years older. She lifted her hands and chanted, then that blond guy appeared. She's like the wicked witch of the west."

"Witch?" A cloud of dread suddenly overshadowed him. "What name did she tell you?"

"I can't remember. It's on the tip of my tongue, and it's driving me crazy."

"Wilona?"

"Yes! That's it."

"Damnation!" He glared at the exit tunnel. Why had he not suspected? Wilona MacRae was the witch who had cursed him into selkie form. If she could change her age and human appearance so profoundly, her black magic had to be growing stronger. Who knew what she would do next? If she was jealous of Erin, she might even try to kill her.

Chapter 4

"What's wrong?" Erin asked, wondering at Brodie's dramatic reaction to his girlfriend's real name.

"I must take you off the isle and to the mainland," he snapped.

"Great! I can still make the photo shoot."

Brodie paced away. His bronzed skin over chiseled muscles fascinated her. Her memories of what had happened earlier seemed like fevered dreams. Her face burned when she recalled all the erotic pleasures Brodie had given her, and how she'd begged for them. He'd used his fingers, his mouth. Why had he not taken her up on the offer of actual sex? Since he was more bad boy than gentleman, he had to have ulterior motives.

"Come. I must take you to Farspag Tower for your own safety. If she is truly Wilona MacRae, she is a witch. She uses her magic for evil and her own twisted—" Brodie stared up at the ceiling abruptly, as if listening. "What, Finnian? God's blood!" he shouted. He strode to the other side of the cavern. "Damn the man," he muttered. "I'm coming! Give me a minute, would you?"

Brodie had gone as insane as everyone else in this wacko place. No, it was likely part of the practical joke.

"Come, lass. Get up. You must put on your gown."

"I can't. You cut it off me and ruined it."

"Bring it along, then. You can repair it later."

"You can repair it! And what am I supposed to wear in the meantime?"

"Naught."

"I'm not strutting around naked the way you do!"

"I'm no' strutting around." He had the gall to look miffed. "And we must hurry afore Wilona casts some sort of damnable spell on you." He flipped up the lid of his trunk. "Here, wear my shirt and plaid." He brought the items to her and they looked exactly like the ones he'd worn in the pub.

Ignoring his chatter about magic and spells, which was clearly part of whatever role he was playing, she unfolded the plaid. "I'm supposed to wear a man's kilt? What are you going to wear?"

"A sealskin."

"A what?"

"I dinna have time to explain it all now, but I must tell you one thing. Try to understand."

"What?"

"I'm a selkie."

"What the hell is a selkie?"

He rolled aside one of the large rocks near the corner and snatched an article of clothing from beneath it. This garment appeared to be made of thin black leather or vinyl. A wetsuit perhaps.

"Come. I'll show you."

"Wait! I'm not dressed." The voluminous linen shirt hung to her knees, and the cuffs below her hands. And considering how tall she was, that was saying something. The plaid was simply a big wool blanket.

"Here, let me help." He took the plaid and loosely wrapped it around her. He glanced into her eyes, his gaze potent and compelling.

What was it about him? In her profession, she had seen all manner of gorgeous men, but none drew her like he did. She sensed a great depth in him, and a troubled spirit. *He needs me.* Whoa. Where had that insight come from?

"Hold the edge." He adjusted and fastened a leather belt at her waist, making the plaid into a long skirt.

"Cool."

"I shall keep you warm."

"Umm… no. I meant…."

But he was not listening. Instead, he crammed her sequined dress into a drawstring sack and looped it over her neck and shoulder. Something about wearing his clothing—that he put on her—was unbelievably sensual. His appealing, musky scent was all around her, against her skin.

Brodie took her hand and led her outside the cave. The sun had just risen over the watery horizon. Or was it low in the sky? She didn't know east from west.

"What time is it?"

He shrugged. "About an hour 'til dusk."

"Dusk? Dusk! I missed the shoot and the van to Glasgow!"

"You slept a long time, lass. Slept like the dead, after I made you come about a dozen times." He smirked.

Her face heating, she smacked his arm. "Why didn't you wake me?"

"There was no reason. You needed rest."

"Dammit! I needed that job more."

Tightening his grip, he led her away from the cliff and toward a small beach where massive black rocks protruded from the beige sand and turbulent white-capping waves. Strong winds whipped her hair back. Beyond the black boulders, the dark blue ocean and distant misty gray islands were breathtaking. It appeared a picturesque, primordial landscape.

"Look at all the seals!" She gaped in awe at the dozens of animals lounging on the sand off to the left. "I've always wanted to see seals in the wild but never did. How awesome."

Brodie slid her a worried glance. "Now you ken what a selkie is."

"A seal?"

"A person who changes into a seal."

"Stop teasing me!"

"We dinna have time for this. Listen, lass," he commanded in a stern tone. "There is no boat here on the isle at the moment. I'm going to put on my sealskin and shift form into a seal. When I do that, you're to get on my back and hold on 'round my neck. I'm going to swim with you to the mainland. It's a far-piece, so dinna be frightened. As you might imagine, seals are excellent swimmers, and fast."

"What? What!" *The Twilight Zone* music played in her head.

"You heard me. Now dinna be afraid."

"You're crazy! There is no way you can swim all the way out there. I can barely see the mainland from here. You'll drown both of us."

"Trust me."

"Right." *Idiot!*

"You trusted me last night when I rescued you from that rock in the ocean. And you trusted me when you were tied up. When you were so aroused you begged me to do wicked things to you, but I was a gentleman. Nay, a *saint.*"

Heat rushed to her face. "Do you have to keep bringing that up? I was drugged!"

He lifted a brow and stepped into the thing he called a sealskin. It looked like a sleek and velvety wetsuit, blackish gray in color.

"Remember, dinna fear me no matter what. I'm still Brodie, and I'll get you to safety. When I turn into a seal, I canna talk like a human, but I can understand language. You're to climb onto my back and hold on. Understand?"

She rolled her eyes. God, was this guy deluded. "Okay, fine, whatever, fantasy man."

He pulled the wetsuit up over his trim hips, hiding his abundant package, which he was so obviously proud of, then slid his arms into the sleeves. He faced away from her and pulled the hood over his head. Amber light flashed, bright as the sun. She shrieked and covered her blinded eyes.

She squinted, opening her eyes cautiously. The intense light was gone. Brodie was gone, and in his place was something that looked like a seal. She stepped forward to examine it. Yes, it was a seal.

"You weren't kidding, were you?" she whispered.

The seal shook his head.

"Brodie?"

The seal nodded.

"Okay, I've officially gone insane." She glanced around the beach. "Brodie, come back here!" This was a magician's trick, right? No humans anywhere, just a bunch of seals lounging in the late afternoon light, watching her. Something poked her leg and she jumped back. A seal nose with big whiskers, inky black eyes and a sleek head.

"Brodie?" No way. That couldn't be Brodie.

It nodded again, then motioned with its head.

"Where do you think you're going?" The distant shout echoed over the beach. Wilona, in her youthful form, scrambled down the cliffs and stepped onto the sand, the wind tearing at her hair, her plaid dress and wrap.

The seal—Brodie—let loose a series of loud barking sounds and scuttled toward the woman. She backed up a few paces.

"How dare you threaten me, Brodie? You're mine. I made you, and you'll obey me! Shift back into your human form."

The other seals roused from their stupor and the whole herd of them advanced on Wilona.

"Back!" she commanded. But the animals didn't obey. She fled the beach and climbed the cliff, yelling foreign words. A second later, she disappeared and a huge black bird flapped up from the spot and sailed into the sky.

"Holy crap!" Erin searched the cliff with her keen gaze but saw no remaining sign of Wilona. She had not just changed herself into a bird. Had she?

The black bird—it had to be a vulture—circled, then drew in its wings and dove toward Erin. Screaming, she ducked and crouched on the wet sand. Talons snagged in her shirt and feathers brushed her head. She rolled and kicked, then somehow ended up on her feet again. The bird flapped away and circled.

"Bitch!" Where was a rock or stick when she needed one?

Brodie-the-seal again nudged his nose against her.

"Okay, okay, dammit! Whatever drug was in the wine evidently had hallucinogenic side-effects. Maybe if I talk to myself I won't go completely insane."

Brodie scurried into the shallow water and waited, the waves washing around him.

"This is going to be cold!" Her bare feet were already too numb to feel the icy water when she splashed in, but to be immersed in it up to her neck would be horrible. "What if I pass out from hypothermia?"

The seal shook his head and moved into the waves.

"You better not drown me, seal-man!" She couldn't believe she was going to trust a seal to transport her across a couple miles of open ocean. But what choice did she have? The Wilona-vulture wheeled overhead, circling closer and closer, beady eyes on Erin. Scurrying through the frigid surf, she raced after Brodie.

How very odd to wrap her arms around this big seal's neck. She locked her hands together at the front of his throat and he glided into the ocean. A massive wave approached and she held her breath. The water crashed over them, but she didn't feel its chill, much like last night when he'd rescued her from the rock.

Brodie swam, the muscles of his seal body flexing. A moment later, he lifted her above the surface while he slid effortlessly through the water. She felt as if she rode on a kneeboard or a raft behind a boat.

The giant bird circled overhead. "Wilona's still up there, waiting for her dinner."

But Brodie paid her no mind. He concentrated on swimming. And she had to admit he was unbelievably fast. The bird dove into the ocean and a moment later a fin appeared. A shark fin.

Erin screamed. "Shark! Shark!"

Brodie increased his speed. Then she noticed all manner of seals and dolphins swimming behind them, leaping through the waves, and… "Orcas?"

The pod of huge black-and-white killer whales swam in formation, as if providing an escort and guarding them from the shark.

"Wow!"

Before she knew it, they approached the shore of the mainland. Once in shallow water, she stood, yanked up the bottom of her kilt and splashed onto shore. No longer in contact with Brodie, she was freezing and shaking so hard she could barely stand upright.

The seal barked at his friends and scampered in after her. On the narrow strip of sand, the golden light flashed again, but she forced her eyes to remain open. She had to see what kind of trick this was. Brodie stood upright, pushed the hood back and peeled the sealskin off his human body, revealing those awe-inspiring muscles and bronzed skin. She couldn't see the sleight of hand. How had he done it?

"I still can't believe it," she said, her teeth chattering. "You were a seal?"

"Aye, believe it."

"How?"

"A little over a year ago, Wilona placed a curse on me."

"Why?"

"No time to explain now. I must hasten you to Farspag Tower before she catches up." He ushered Erin toward another cave—not surprising. Once inside, he dragged a leather satchel from a shelf and removed plaid clothing and an ivory shirt, a kilt outfit much like the one she wore. So Mr. Stuck-on-himself was finally going to wear real clothing? Shocking.

"Do you have dry clothes for me?" she asked, chilled to the bone.

"Nay. I'll keep you warm until we arrive at the castle. Then you can change."

"So, hurry before I freeze to death." She removed the heavy waterlogged sack from her shoulder. The saltwater had probably ruined the sequined gown inside. Not that it mattered now. She'd missed the photo shoot and in all likelihood would not be part of any of Kincaid's runway shows. Her current situation pushed all her real-world problems to the back burner anyway.

"Come." Picking up the wet sack and lacing his warm fingers with hers, he led her from the cave, along the windy shore and onto a narrow path that trailed toward the cliff top. She basked in the warmth of his touch, heating her from head to toe. In the near darkness she stumbled and fell, narrowly missing striking her knee on a boulder. After helping her stand, he swung her into his arms and traversed the path. She'd never had a man carry her before. Never imagined she'd like it, but the gentle way he held her made her feel cared for.

She slid her arms around his neck beneath his long wet hair. He seemed so wild, sexy and appealing. His male scent, mixed with the salt air, did crazy things to her libido. She wanted to lick his neck.

"I can walk, you know," she said.

"This is faster. You might hurt yourself if left to your own devices."

"Humph! I'm not that clumsy."

"You're a tenderfoot." He winked.

"Well, I don't go barefoot much."

His teasing grin disappeared. She followed his gaze upward to see what had changed his mood so abruptly. A tall castle stood at the top of the cliff, dim light shining from the narrow windows.

"That's Farspag Tower!" she said. Thank God, she was back in civilization. It wasn't too far from the castle to the village and the inn where her clothing and luggage awaited her. At least, she hoped her stuff was still there and that the crew or Katie hadn't taken it with them. Would they have the police out searching for her? She hoped her disappearance hadn't caused too much of a stir.

When Brodie reached the top of the cliff, the trail leveled out and changed to mud and grass, then cobblestones. He didn't put her down, and she was glad. Walking barefoot over cobblestones would be difficult. He carried her along the stone wall and approached the closed iron gates.

"Guard!" he called through.

A kilted man rushed forward. "M'laird, pray pardon. We were no' expecting you." The guard, with a large sword in a scabbard at his side, opened the gate from the inside and bowed.

"Robert." Brodie strode through. "My thanks. I'm going up the back stairs."

"Aye, m'laird. As you wish." Carrying a torch, Robert escorted them past several more of these kilted, guard-looking types, all of whom bowed and maintained curious, almost fearful expressions.

What the hell was their problem and why were they all in costume? "Oh yeah, the Celtic Festival." Erin looked to Brodie for confirmation.

He retained his frown, flicking an irritated glance at her. Then, staring straight ahead again, he carried her along the side of the castle.

"Oh, I get it." In order to keep up the pretense of the whole reenactment thing, she was not supposed to mention the festival. She knew some Ren Faire people in the States got so into reenactment they believed it was all real.

Robert's keys jangled as he unlocked a door made of bars, then a narrow wooden door. "Have a care on those steps, m'laird."

Brodie grunted and stepped inside the dark space. Robert closed the door behind them. A lone candle on a table barely illuminated the stone steps.

"Don't drop me, please," she whispered.

"Still, you dinna trust me?" Brodie growled in her ear. The challenge in his tone contrasted with the sensuality of his warm breath.

Her heart lurched and arousal burned through her quick as a dynamite fuse. "Yes." She slowly turned her head, allowing her lips to brush his. Pausing, he pressed her against the solid stone wall and kissed her. Devoured her lips in such an erotic way, it brought back memories of how he'd consumed another part of her last night with flicks of his tongue and gentle nips. He'd created a sexual storm like she'd never before experienced.

Tightening her arms around his neck, she returned the kiss, craving the taste of him and the way he teased her tongue with his own. He was so hot and yummy, and her connection to him primal. Unexplainable. She hardly knew him on a rational level, but when it came to the sexual, she understood him. Knew what would make him moan, knew he would touch or kiss her in a way to spike her arousal.

He maneuvered between her legs. And through the scratchy plaid, his massive erection ground against her itchy, wet crotch. She yearned to feel him sliding into her, spreading her wide. He would quench this aching, burning need.

"Mmm, yes. Brodie, please." She licked at his lips.

He muttered terse foreign words and turned his face away. "Cease, lass!" He shifted her around so that he cradled her in his arms once again, and moved up the stairs with determination. In the dimness, his face was stern, his jaw clenched hard.

"Damn you," she muttered. "Why do you do that? Get me so horny I can't stand it, and then stop? Every freaking time?"

He growled more Gaelic words.

"Thanks for the explanation!"

"Quiet," he ordered in a low but harsh tone and set her to her feet on a landing. He inched a door open and peered through. "Follow me," he whispered. "Make no sounds."

"Why?"

"Shh."

What was the big deal? She saw no need to hide from the festival people.

He took her hand and led her along a narrow corridor. A floorboard popped.

"Damnation," he muttered, yanking her forward and into a dark room. He closed the door behind them. A loud thump followed.

"What are you doing?" she asked.

"Barring the door."

"Why?"

"You'll ken soon enough." He strode around the room as if he could see.

The room smelled smoky and a dim glow came from the hearth where he knelt. He rose with a lit candle, which helped illuminate the space. A gigantic four poster bed sat in one corner, heavily draped with hangings.

"This is that room—I think," she said. The antique trunks and wooden chairs were moved around a bit, but it seemed similar.

"What are you speaking of?"

"The room where I warmed by the fire and found the brass key."

"You have been in my bedchamber afore? Who allowed you in?"

"Chill. Okay? The door was open. And if this is your castle and your bed-chamber, why the hell are we hiding?"

"Ne'er mind about that. When were you here?"

"Yesterday."

"Who did you speak with?"

"A lady named Louise."

"I dinna ken a Louise. You're either lying or daft. I dinna ken which yet."

"Neither. Thank you very much."

A knock sounded at the door. "Brodie?" a woman in the hallway called.

He muttered foreign words Erin could only guess were frustrated curses. "Who is that?" she whispered.

"My mother. Stay in this room. Dinna leave for anything. I'll have some-one bring you food and dry clothing."

"I don't understand. Why do I have to stay here?"

"If you go outside, Wilona will try to kill you."

A shiver skittered through her. She didn't want to have another run-in with that weird and dangerous woman.

He opened the door to leave.

"Will you come back?"

He nodded.

"Brodie, who is this?" A dark-haired woman with a strong English accent pushed into the room. She wore an Elizabethan-looking green velvet dress embellished with gold embroidery.

"'Tis Erin. And Erin, this is my mother, Lady Sarah MacCain."

"From which clan?" Lady Sarah asked.

"Erin is no' Scottish."

"What is she, then?"

"American," Erin said, fed up with them talking about her as if she weren't there. "But I think my heritage is German and English." Why was she even bothering to play along with them?

"English? I'm English, as well," his mother said. "Are you a lady?"

Was she asking about her sexual practices? "I'm a woman."

"Who is your father? What is his title?"

"Title? He used to be regional sales manager for a company that makes cheese, but I haven't seen him in almost twenty years. Why?"

Through the open doorway, Erin noticed a sudden movement. An old man with a long white beard, black robes and a monk's hood stood there, staring at her with intensity. Then a small smile twitched his mustache. He looked like someone out of a fantasy movie.

"Oh, Brodie," his mother whined. "She is not appropriate at all. She's a commoner. Her father makes cheese."

"Cease, Mother. 'Tis no' what you're thinking. I rescued her. She's cold and hungry. Have someone prepare a tray of warm food for her and bring her dry clothing." He urged his mother from the room, closed the door and locked it.

Was that woman really his mother, or only pretending? They did have similar coloring. And she appeared to be the right age, if she'd had him young.

Was this an honest-to-God home with a family, or part of the Celtic Festival? Maybe they rented out the castle for photo shoots and movie sets to help make ends meet. The family probably left for the day during such events.

Erin hadn't noticed any modern conveniences in the castle yesterday, like lights on the ceilings, phones or outlets. But somehow, the camera crew had obtained electricity. She'd noticed extension cords on the steps. Other than that, she hadn't inspected the place, but now she did.

No outlets in the walls. No lamps. No phones. No TV. She searched the entire room, behind the bed, and found nothing modern.

Though weird, it was nothing to be alarmed about. Simply a historically accurate castle. One Brodie's family, or the National Trust, had preserved, complete with a full staff of costumed employees to make all the tourists feel they'd slipped back in time for a few hours. Yes, she'd heard of castles that held medieval banquets. People, mostly Americans, paid a lot of money to be a part of that. The employees playacted the entire thing, with ladies, lairds and servants, and in connection to the town's Celtic Festival, it would likely get even more elaborate.

That explained it. Ren Faire extraordinaire. She released a breath and sat on the edge of the bed. But that still didn't explain how Brodie appeared to shift into a seal and back. Had to be illusion. Or how Wilona appeared to shift into a bird. Tension latched onto Erin's body again.

"Dammit!" She leapt up and paced. "I need to call the agency. Or Katie." Someone had to come get her out of this freakish nightmare.

She banged on the door. "Hey! Brodie!"

Chapter 5

"I must talk to you, m'laird." Finnian trailed Brodie's quick stride down the castle's corridor.

"What do you want?" Brodie wished the old wizard would give him one moment's peace.

"She's the one. That is the lass who will break your curse."

Brodie halted abruptly and turned. He didn't have to ask Finnian how he knew any of the rubbish he blathered on about. He claimed to use a scrying stone to see the future, but Brodie didn't believe any of his predictions. "I told you, I dinna want the curse broken."

Finnian's bushy white brows lowered. "How can you say that, Laird Brodie?"

"I'm a selkie and proud of it." He continued on toward the library.

When Elspeth had betrayed him—at the same time the curse had been placed on him—he'd retreated to the land of selkie, away from his clan, who'd looked on him with either doubt or fear. Elspeth had smashed his pride, as well as his heart. He didn't wish anyone to know how much she'd hurt him. With the selkies, he had his pride at least. They did not doubt him. They accepted him as he was and respected him.

"But you were chieftain of this clan first. Are you no' proud of that?" Finnian asked, still dogging him.

Brodie glanced back to find five other men following them, along with his mother.

"M'laird? Brodie!"

He strode into the library alone, slammed the door and barred it. "Damnation, 'tis like a prison here." He dropped into the old leather chair behind the desk cluttered with moldering estate books and papers. His father's, all of it. Although it had been four years since his father's illness and death, Brodie still did not feel as if he were truly chieftain.

Naught but one problem after another. Decisions to be made. A clan of over a hundred people to lead. When all he craved was the water sluicing over his skin. He thirsted for the taste of salt water in his mouth. Even the silence of this room, minus the rhythmic ebb and flow of waves, hurt his ears. He knew it was the curse that caused this uncontrollable yearning for the sea.

The past year, while he'd been a selkie, had been the best of his life. Finally, he was free. Up to that point, his entire life had been devoted to duty, his father grooming him to be chieftain. And yet, his father had never thought he would be good enough, or disciplined enough for such a task. He'd been right, of course. No matter how hard Brodie tried, he always fell short of his father's expectations.

He opened a drawer and pulled out a missive from his friend, Gavin MacTavish. Now there was a man who took his duties to his clan seriously. A hollow emptiness filled Brodie, for some part of him yearned to feel that way as well. To enjoy leading and spending time with his people.

He read the missive.

Brodie, Chieftain of Clan MacCain,

There is hope. The curse that afflicts us can be broken, and in my case has been broken. I am now a man whole again with no remaining ill effects from Wilona MacRae's curse. The requirement is love given and received in equal parts, with complete trust and without reservation. Wilona and her accomplice, my cousin Alpin MacTavish, are headed in your direction. I am also sending this missive to Torr. If either of you can stop these two villains, please do.

Gavin MacTavish, Chief of Clan MacTavish.

Brodie threw the paper on the desk. This missive had come several weeks ago and he had hoped to ignore it. Torr's curse had been broken when he fell in love with and married Brodie's sister, Catriona. Alpin MacTavish was dead, but Wilona was still creating chaos.

The bar across the door flew upward and clattered to the floor.

"What the devil?"

The door pushed inward. Finnian entered and barred the door again. "Pray pardon, Laird Brodie, but I must speak to you. 'Tis of utmost import."

"Using your magic, I see." Brodie sighed.

"When I must. I ken you enjoy being a selkie, but—"

"I make my own choices."

"Aye, you do. You're the chieftain. But you're strongly drawn to this lass you've found and brought home. You want her. I know it." Finnian's eyes gleamed with insight.

"Cease reading my mind."

"I dinna have to read your mind to see this. I was young once. I ken what goes on betwixt a man and a woman." Finnian sent him a mischievous grin, almost hidden in that long white beard and mustache. "You wanted her in the cave, but you wouldna take her."

"God's teeth, Finnian! 'Tis no' your concern. Have you been looking in your scrying stone again, spying on me?"

"Why is it you wouldna take her as she begged you to do?"

Brodie muttered some choice Gaelic curses. Finnian must have been eighty or ninety years, but his mind worked like that of a quizzical adolescent. And because of this, he thought he could get away with anything. "There is naught wrong with your hearing, auld man."

"I know why. You think your curse will be broken if you bed her."

"I told you, I make my own decisions." Brodie threw the bar from the door and exited into the crowded corridor. He would not stay here to be trapped and picked at. They all wished him married and tied to this castle, never to leave. Nay. He loved his freedom too much.

"Step aside," he ordered. Once a path cleared, he passed those lining the corridor, all waiting for an audience with him for one problem or another. He could not abide it. Shaking off the hands that grasped his plaid, he strode through the great hall and outside to the cliff's edge. Inhaling the salt air, he felt a bit of his sanity return and the tension drain from his shoulders.

Aye, he desired Erin more fiercely than he'd ever desired any woman, but he could not give in to it. Taking her would mean something far more profound than a swift tumble in the heather. Already, something about her haunted him.

Through the darkening twilight, he noticed people on the narrow strip of beach below. They were naked and holding black sealskins. Selkies would not show up here unless something was wrong. He hoped with all his might that more females had not been taken.

Brodie descended the path and approached the three male selkies—the leader Dominic and his two brothers. "What has happened?"

"Five more females were abducted during the night," Dominic said.

"'Slud. Did anyone see who took them?"

"Nay. This time they were taken from the Bairn Caves on the north side of the isle."

"Bairn caves?" Brodie said. "You mean they were mothers?"

"Aye, stolen from their wee infants."

"Damnation! What of the guards?"

"Only females are allowed to guard them. They were taken, too."

"Are you certain the Orkney Tribe wouldna do this?"

Dominic shook his head. "The leaders deny it. We've always had peace and civil inter-mating."

"'Haps some outlaws of their tribe, then? Or selkies from another isle."

"'Tis possible. We're hoping you'll be willing to continue helping us. You are a trained warrior. You could teach us how to fight and better defend ourselves."

Because the selkies were lovers, not warriors, they were unaccustomed to dealing with violence. They had lived in peace on their islands for millennia, and now to suddenly have someone threatening their existence by stealing their females had to be a shock.

"Aye, of course I'll help." Brodie moved toward the cave to retrieve his sealskin. He regretted that he had not told Erin where he was going, but for now, she was safe in the tower. As soon as he was able, he would return for her. And figure out what to do with her.

Scuffling sounded outside the bedchamber door. Erin moved closer, hoping to dart out when they opened it. But when the door swung inward, she saw two large guards in the corridor, along with the ancient Gandalf look-alike—Finnian—and a short, middle-aged woman dressed as a maid in dull, frumpy clothing.

"Go on now, talk to her." Finnian prodded the woman into the room and slammed the door behind her.

Now what? Erin wondered. And where had Brodie run off to?

"I'm Aggie," the woman said in a resigned tone. "I work for the family."

"Hello, Aggie. I'm Erin."

"Are you hungry?"

"No, thanks. A woman brought a huge tray of food earlier." Erin had eaten all the bread and cheese she could hold, along with a little red wine, and avoided the mystery meat. After that, they'd allowed her a basin of water, soap and a cloth to bathe herself in, primitive style. Her new clothing was dreadful Ren Faire garb—a dingy old linen smock, tied-on skirts, and a belted plaid overdress. A far cry from haute couture, but it was warm and dry.

"Can I go downstairs?" Erin asked.

"Nay." Aggie circled her, looking her up and down as a farmer might inspect a cow before purchase. "Are you a virgin?"

Erin gaped. "That's a bit personal, don't you think?"

"Humph. I'll take that as a *nay.*"

Erin scowled, too speechless to do anything more.

"Have you ever been in the family way?" Aggie asked.

"Excuse me?" Surely she didn't mean….

"Have you given birth to any bairns? Had any miscarriages?"

"No!"

Aggie squinted up at her. "What happened to your hair?"

Erin fingered the strands of her straight blond hair, cut only a week ago by one of the top hairstylists in New York. But she was sure the salt water and mud hadn't done wonders for it, nor had the soap they'd given her. "I've had no opportunity to wash it with actual shampoo since my imprisonment."

"'Tis a mite short for a lass."

Erin released a long breath and prayed for patience.

"You might do," Aggie muttered.

"Might do what?"

"You might make a suitable wife for Brodie. But I have my doubts."

Erin almost choked. "Wife? No way. No way in hell! You people are nuts."

Aggie eyed her. "'Tis no' a lady what uses such salty language. But your impudence does remind me of my wee Catriona." She grinned fondly. "Where do you hail from?"

Erin threw up her hands. It was the hundredth time someone had asked her that, and she was tired of it. "Never-Never Land."

"Humph."

"What is going on around here? Can you explain that at least?"

"Master Brodie, the poor wee laddie, is cursed. And we but want the best for him. He must come back to us."

"Brodie? A poor wee laddie? Are we talking about the same tall man with dark hair?"

"Aye."

"How can you call him wee?"

"I helped birth him. Bathed him when he was a wee bairn. And that's who I see when I look at him." She beamed as if she were his mother.

"So, he's cursed you say? How?"

"Didna he tell you?"

"No, he said he didn't have time. I only know he turns into a seal. Or at least, he somehow creates that illusion."

"He is cursed into the form of a selkie. Indeed, a seal."

"How? Why? When? Where?"

"A little over a year ago, he was involved in a skirmish. A young laird was killed, the son of Wilona MacRae. 'Twas in no way Laird Brodie's fault, but she blamed him and his two friends and took her revenge. Now the curse must be broken, whether Brodie wishes it or no'."

"Why wouldn't he wish it?"

Aggie shrugged. "I dinna understand how, but he enjoys being a selkie."

"Okay." Erin frowned. "So, how does it work?"

"A woman must break the curse." Aggie looked at her pointedly.

"Me?"

Aggie shrugged. "Finnian says so. But the auld man is daft."

"How would a woman do that?"

"'Tis for me to know and you to find out. But it seems to have worked for those other two strapping lads, Gavin and Torr."

"They were selkies, too?"

"Nay, they were cursed to shape-shift into the form of other animals. But since their marriages, they are cured."

Holy crap. This was the weirdest place on earth. "Well, I can't marry Brodie. Sorry, but I hardly know him. And he's so moody, arrogant and bossy, I'd strangle him in a week's time." Yes, he was hotter than molten rock, had a talented mouth and hands, but that wasn't enough to base a marriage on. "Besides, Brodie doesn't like me."

"Did he say that?"

"Didn't have to." Nope, he was always scowling at her as if she'd killed his favorite pony or done something equally horrid. Even though at other times, he seemed attracted to her, during their foreplay, for instance. Still, he'd refused to have sex with her.

"Clearly, he's a guy with a hell of a lot of issues," Erin said. "I don't need that. I've got enough crap in my life, what with my career going to pot." If she could even salvage it now. The Kincaid show was out. When she got back to civilization, she'd have to see what the agency could do. If she only had a phone.

Aggie looked perplexed, then shrugged. "You're bonnie, so no matter how odd you are, Brodie will warm to you, given time. I've no doubt of it."

"Odd? Me? You people are all far beyond bizarre." Dammit, why would no one listen to her? She had to escape and return to the village before she lost her mind.

At dawn, a woman entered the bedchamber and built a fire in the fireplace. Erin pretended to be asleep. She couldn't believe they'd kept her locked in this room since last night. The authorities were going to hear about this.

When the woman closed the door on her way out, Erin waited for the lock to click. It didn't. This was her chance!

Erin flung back the covers and leapt from the high bed. Feeling like a teen readying herself to run away, she placed pillows under the covers to resemble her sleeping form.

Her eyes were scratchy and burning from lack of sleep, but she had to escape this freakish place. She couldn't believe the noisy partying going on downstairs last night. They'd played bagpipes and fiddles, and had a merry old shindig until all hours. They could've at least invited her.

She belted the plaid around her waist, over the woman's smock they'd given her yesterday. The top of the plaid material was long enough to pull over her head like a shawl. Since it was surely frigid outside, she wrapped another of Brodie's plaids around herself like a cloak. She pulled the old leather men's boots from beneath the bed where she'd found them and put them on, praying she wouldn't catch a foot fungus. They were too large, but she could manage if she tied them tightly.

Where had that rat-bastard Brodie gone, anyway? Was he still inside the castle, or had he escaped back to his precious island? She wanted to strangle him for abandoning her here, locked up with these psychos. But she also wished she could've told him goodbye. No time to worry about that now.

She inched the door open and stepped into the empty, dim corridor. Listening for the sounds of her jailers, she crept along the floor and down the steps.

Several people lay sleeping on the floor of the great hall, their snores echoing off the high ceiling. They'd probably drunk so much booze at last night's party, they'd slept wherever they passed out. One man lay before the entry door. No chance of opening it without waking him. She tiptoed by the men, following the smell of baking bread down another set of narrow winding stairs into the hot kitchen. No electric stoves here. It appeared they did it all the old-fashioned way, with a fire-heated oven and a huge black pot hanging over another fire. Two of the women, dressed as servants, eyed her. She would have to play along and get into Ren Faire mode, which she knew squat about.

"I'm the new servant... umm... Fiona. Just hired yesterday," she said in what she hoped was a Scottish accent. "I was sent to help out and check for eggs... under the hens, you ken."

One of the women motioned toward a doorway. Outside. Freedom!

"I thank you." She bobbed a curtsey and rushed toward the door.

White mist enshrouded everything outside. She crept along a stone pathway. The stench of animal dung was strong on this side of the castle.

Through the thick fog, she edged around the stone walls of the castle. Finally, she arrived at tall iron gates. "Locked, dammit."

"And where might you be going, lassie?"

Erin almost jumped out of her skin.

The giant, bearded, sword-carrying dude appeared out of the swirling mist.

"Umm. Brodie—I mean Laird Brodie—commanded me to meet him at the shore. Down there." She pointed in the direction they'd come from before.

The guard considered her with a skeptical glare, then shrugged and unlocked the gate. "Have a care on the way down. 'Tis slippery and the mist makes it nigh impossible to see."

"Aye, and thank you, kind sir." Cripes! She probably sounded like a bad actor. Thank God he'd believed her.

She made her escape at a controlled, leisurely pace. Once out of his sight, she followed the wide muddy driveway instead of the tiny trail that led to the shore. Where was the paved drive and highway? With all the mist, she couldn't tell if she was on the wrong side of the castle or where. It was only about a half mile from the castle to the village of Dunmory. But how could she tell if she was going in the right direction? After exiting the gates, she should turn right to go to the village. But at the moment she was in the middle of a grassy area. Piles of cow poo lay here and there. Trying to dodge one, she stepped in another.

"Shit!" She wiped off her leather boot in the grass. "Where is the road?" She went right a short distance, then circled left again. Wait. She stopped, eying the muddy narrow road marked with hoof prints and some kind of narrow wheel tracks. Maybe it would lead her back to the highway. She followed along beside it.

Had she walked a half mile? The fog was still thick but glowing more brightly, which didn't help with visibility. Beyond about eight feet in front of her, all she could see was white. If she had been walking toward Dunmory, she would've reached it by now. She'd probably gone in the wrong direction. At this rate she'd be lost before the fog drifted away, and by then, she'd be a mile off course.

Two kilted men emerged gradually from the mist ahead of her. She froze. Judging by their costumes, they were friends of the maniacs at the castle. Maybe sent after her. She sprinted away from them across the pasture, leaping over piles of cow dung, her loose boots flapping on her feet.

One man yelled in Gaelic and footsteps pounded behind her. She glanced back but could see only white mist.

Sounded like a damned ancient army chasing after her. Hoof beats and shouting and clanging metal. With another backward glance, she saw more of them looming out of the mist, some on horseback. Hell!

Her boot almost flew off, and she stopped to yank it back on. A man's large arm locked around her waist and lifted her off her feet. She kicked at the smelly man, but her boots flapped about.

She elbowed him in the stomach. "Let me go! I'm not part of your Celtic Festival."

"Calm, lass. We'll no' hurt you. Who are you and where are you going?" He loosened his hold and she scrambled away from him.

"I'm going to Dunmory. My friends are waiting for me there. Could you point me in the right direction?"

"Weeel, I'll tell you one thing, lassie," the bearded man said. "You're headed in the wrong direction. Coming from Farspag Tower, are you?"

"Umm. No."

He snorted. "You must be. There's naught else out this way. Friend of Brodie MacCain?"

Would claiming friendship to him help her or hurt her? "I know who he is."

The man spoke low to another one. They sent her lusty-eyed looks and chuckled.

Oh crap.

"If you come with us, we'll help you reach Dunmory."

She doubted that. "I'll find it on my own. Thank you. I'll just wait until the fog lifts."

"What kind of neighbors would we be if we left you in the middle of a pasture? We wish to help you. 'Tis much too easy to stumble into the bog and drown in the peaty mud."

"Aye, or fall off a cliff," his friend added cheerfully.

Sounded horrid. "I'll just stand right here in this safe pasture and wait for the mist to drift away."

"'Tis no' safe. There's an ornery bull hereabouts someplace. He loves naught more than to chase folks and run them to ground with his big horns." The man eyed the thick cloud cover for a moment. "And indeed, we're expecting rain."

Ha. Bastards. They were manipulating her. Still, the idea of being chased by a mean bull didn't appeal.

"All you have to do, lassie, is follow us. We'll lead you to the village."

The wind had picked up and the fog was drifting away, but a slight misty rain took its place. Dammit, they'd been right. She tugged Brodie's plaid tighter over her head.

The icy wind blew harder.

"This weather will only get worse," the man warned. "We canna in good conscience leave a lady such as yourself out here in bad weather. You'll catch your death. Follow us." The man and his cronies turned and ambled back the way they'd come.

No, she didn't trust them, but neither could she stay out in this cold rain and wind. She trailed behind them at a distance until they reached the muddy road again. From time to time, they glanced back with smarmy grins. As the fog dissipated, she surveyed the area. Where was the village? The field where she stood—or was it a moor—rolled. To the left, beyond a high cliff, lay the ocean. In the distance to the right was a mountain made up mostly of rock, gravely scree gathered at the base, with thick mist hiding the top of it.

"Where the hell am I?"

"Did you say something, lass?" the man called back.

"No."

"No' much farther and we'll be there."

Minutes later, some kind of structure, a stone wall, materialized out of the misty rain. She didn't remember a wall on the outskirts of the village. Behind the wall, more rock walls rose up into what appeared to be a castle. Was this Farspag Castle again? Would she never escape the place? At least she was no longer lost in a dung-filled pasture. Rain soaked the plaid covering her head and she wanted to get inside some kind of building ASAP.

She glanced around. Why did everything look so different? This wasn't Farspag Castle.

"What is this place?" she called to the men.

"'Tis but a tower. Dunwield. We must pass through this land to reach the village on the other side."

She stopped. "I'll go around."

"'Tis no' possible."

He was such a liar! There was no walled castle one had to pass through between Farspag and the village.

She reversed direction on the muddy road but could not run because the muck sucked at her loose boots with every step. The wind off the Atlantic buffeted her, gusting stinging rain into her eyes. She swayed, almost blown down by the wind. What was this, a hurricane? She turned her face away to draw breath. Hands grabbed her upper arms. She was lifted up and thrown over a meaty shoulder.

She screamed and kicked. "Put me down!"

His hold tightened around her legs as he carried her, head dangling. "Daft wench! The gale is worsening. We must go indoors."

Well, crap. What other choice did she have? At least maybe these guys wouldn't hold her prisoner like that Farspag clan.

"I can walk!"

Mr. Stinky—and boy, did he have horrid body odor—carried her through tall iron gates and up steps. Inside the castle, he set her on her feet in what could only be another great hall, with another full cast of Ren Faire actors. Not again! Her head swam from being upside down. She blinked, trying to orient herself and stop swaying.

A rotund man rose from a table elevated from the main floor on a platform. He licked the grease from his lips and chewed. Crumbs littered his bushy beard.

"Chief MacPeter, we found this lass roaming on the moors."

"Who is she? Where does she come from?" he demanded around a mouth full of food.

Talk about authenticity. Plus, this place stank to high heaven.

"She came from Farspag Tower, m'laird."

"Farspag?" the chief growled, his eyes turning sharp and mean.

"She is a friend of Brodie's."

"Is that so?" Chief MacPeter dusted off his hands, moved around the table and approached her. His stench reached her well before he did.

"Oh dear God," she muttered, then held her breath.

"She's damned tall for a lass." MacPeter scowled up at her. "And naught but skin and bones."

"Aye. But a great beauty," the one who'd brought her said. "And I wager, you could fatten her up."

Several of the men laughed.

MacPeter grunted, his gaze running up and down her body. "Her clothing offends me. It reeks of Brodie MacCain."

You're the one who reeks! Brodie, on the other hand, smelled great last time she'd sniffed him.

"Take her to the solar where the women are," MacPeter said.

"Aye, m'laird."

"Tell Maude to ready her for my bed tonight." MacPeter started back toward his table.

"What?" Erin's voice echoed off the ceiling. She must have misunderstood.

All went silent.

MacPeter paused and glared back at her. "You will warm my bed this night, lass."

"No!" She ran for the closed exit door. Two brawny guards blocked it like stone statues. "Please, I just want to go to the village. My friends are waiting for me there."

"Tie her up and take her to my bedchamber!" MacPeter ordered.

Chapter 6

Gale-force wind and rain whipped across the entrance to the cave of the female selkies on Ròncreag Isle.

Brodie! Finnian's psychic yell lanced through Brodie's head. Disoriented, he stumbled back and caught on the wall.

"Damnation! What?" Brodie should've throttled Torr for leaving Finnian at Farspag to torment him.

The lass, Erin, ran away this morn and is in danger. MacPeter took her hostage.

Icy fear slithered through Brodie. "How did this happen? She was locked up at Farspag."

She escaped. Come now, Brodie! MacPeter will kill her.

Brodie growled curses, trying to use anger to drive out his fear for her. "I must leave," he called to the male selkies. "I'll return as soon as I'm able and we'll continue the defense training." He took his sealskin and descended the blustery cliff to the sea. "She canna obey anything I say. Hellish lass!" He slipped into his sealskin and dove into the violent ocean in seal form.

⁂

"Give her to me! Now!" Brodie yelled to MacPeter through the Dunwield castle gates, fifty of Brodie's best men standing behind him, armed and ready for battle. Only a couple of hours had gone by since he'd learned of Erin's capture, and he prayed she was well. The gale had passed and everything gleamed wet in the sunlight.

MacPeter strolled forward with three of his men, but stopped before he reached the closed gates. "Were you planning to marry the lass?"

"Nay. I am her guardian until I can return her to her family in England." He hoped MacPeter believed that lie.

"She's going to be my bride," MacPeter said. "We shall have a trial marriage. I must first see if she is fertile and whether my seed will grow in her belly."

Brodie wanted to throw his sharpest *sgian dubh* at the bastard's throat, but restrained the impulse. Instead, he tried for cool and rational. "She willna agree to it. 'Twould be illegal."

"Oh, she'll agree," MacPeter said in a smooth, deadly tone. An evil grin split his round, bearded face.

"If you hurt her in any way, I'll kill you," Brodie promised with utter sincerity. Already battle lust stormed through his body. His stomach ached with stark terror for Erin's life.

MacPeter laughed. "Young Brodie is threatening me," he told his men, shrugging. "I dinna need marriage. She will be my whore. When I tire of her, I'll send her back to you."

"Return her to me. Now!" If MacPeter or any of his men had raped her, Brodie would start a damned war on her behalf. To hell with the consequences.

"You took my promised bride away from me and gave her to your unworthy friend," MacPeter said. "I seek a replacement."

Brodie clenched his teeth, wishing he could smash the older man's face. "My sister was never betrothed to you. 'Twas illegal and my mother's doing. Catriona had been promised to Torr since she was a mere child. She was never yours. And as I said, I am no' here to provide you brides. You must find your own."

"But I have."

"The lass you hold captive now is not yours, nor mine to give." Brodie glanced back at his men, wearing leather-studded armor, each bearing a sword or ax along with daggers, bows and arrows. "Release her, or prepare for battle!"

Screaming sounded at the castle's portal. Women ran out, then Erin emerged, brandishing a basket-hilt sword in both hands. Saints, she was magnificent, like a Celtic warrior goddess, her blond hair gleaming in the sunlight, her face a mask of fierceness. And she still wore his plaid. That sent a surge of possessiveness through him.

"She is—" *mine.* Brodie clamped his mouth shut before the word sprang out. Where had such a thought come from? Damnation, he was doomed to lose something in this debacle—either his heart or his selkie abilities. Or both. Either way, he had to keep Erin safe.

MacPeter laughed, his eyes lighting. "She's a Highland lass, surely! Look at how she defends herself."

"But no' yours." Brodie drew his sword and motioned his archers forward. "Erin, come. We leave now!" To MacPeter, he said, "Open the gates and allow her to pass through."

MacPeter's face reddened, his eyes narrowed with dark malice, but he remained still.

"She is under my protection. Dinna challenge me!" Brodie waved Erin forward. "Let her pass."

If MacPeter made one wrong move, Brodie's archers would fill him with arrows, and that would be the end of the swine. His glare moved over Brodie's men, calculating, assessing.

"Very well," MacPeter finally said and motioned for one of his men to unlock the gates.

Erin dropped the sword and rushed through the open gate. When Brodie saw that her hands were tied in front of her, he was overcome with respect for her and the way she'd fought her way out.

Relief flowing through him, Brodie tugged her to the far side of his horse, and his men closed ranks, further blocking her from MacPeter.

Daft lass! Brodie wanted to grab her and shake her, and at the same time, hold her close, but he forced himself to do neither. He was not sure he could control his actions. "Did any of them hurt you?"

"No. Thank you for helping me."

Still, she looked terrified, her skin pale, her bright blue eyes wide. He'd fallen short of his duty. He should've been there to prevent this altogether.

His hands savoring her small waist, Brodie lifted her to his horse and swung up behind her. To keep her from falling off, he wrapped an arm around her and tugged her tight against his chest. Relief sighed through him. Some instinct within him said this was exactly where she belonged.

"Cut this rope off me, Brodie," she said, lifting her hands.

"That can wait." He flicked the reins. "I need to get you away from this place."

"Will you take me to the village? To Dunmory?"

Nay, I will not, was his first thought. Then he remembered he should help her return to her home. "Why?"

"My friends are waiting for me there at the inn."

"What friends?"

"Katie. Sam."

Brodie still didn't know where she'd come from or why she'd shown up here in the Highlands, but he didn't like the idea of her joining a friend named Sam at an inn.

"Nay. You're lying."

She twisted around to glare at him, her tempting lips only inches from his. "I'm not lying!"

He ached to kiss her into silence and submission. A couple of his men snickered. Brodie glowered at them. "Stay back twenty paces," he ordered. "I need to speak to the wench in private."

Wisely, they clammed up and dropped back.

"Why did you sneak out and leave the safety of Farspag?" he demanded in a low voice near Erin's ear.

"Duh! How would you like to be held prisoner by a bunch of Ren Faire fanatics?"

What in blazes was she talking about? "I dinna ken what renferfantatics are, but I was trying to protect you. I just rescued you from a true imprisonment."

"Humph. Good thing I took fencing a few years ago or I would never have escaped that pigsty of a castle. You couldn't even get inside the gates, Mr. Chieftain."

"I would have gotten inside the gates, lass. Have no doubt of it."

"I don't want to stay at Farspag any longer. I want to go back to the village, or back to Glasgow. Or basically anywhere there's a freakin' phone, car or airplane so I can go home."

Half of what she said made no sense. Wherever her country was, they'd butchered the English language. He had been to Glasgow, of course, but the city was no place for a lone woman, especially a beautiful one, to be walking around unescorted. He should want her to go back to her home, but of a sudden, he found he did not want to let her go yet. During the short, hellacious time he'd known MacPeter had captured her, Brodie realized he had some sort of twisted attachment to Erin. Desired or not. 'Haps he wished to know whether she might want him despite having no lust potion in her blood. Or mayhap he simply wanted to discover what manner of magical powers she held.

"Nay. You must stay at Farspag a while longer, until I find out your purpose," he said, feeling a bit guilty and selfish. He wanted to know her better, wanted to explore desire with her again. He craved the taste of her.

"My purpose? My purpose!" she yelled. "I'm not here to be your damned slave. You can't keep me prisoner!"

"Shh." He clamped a hand over her mouth. "Hold your tongue or I'll tie a gag on you." He would not have his men witness the disrespect she showed him. A mere lass did not talk to a chieftain in such a way.

She bit his palm and he snatched his stinging hand back.

"Listen, lass. You're pushing your luck. And I'm no' above giving you a sound thrashing on your luscious arse to keep you in line."

He should not have said that. Now all he could think about was her sweet derriere with its firm curves and smooth skin sitting tight against his groin. Pleasure tingled through his cock, hardening it further and causing it to press firmly against her.

With an appealing female growl, she elbowed him in the stomach, but not hard enough to hurt. He tightened his arms around her and held her bound wrists in one hand so she couldn't move.

Farspag came into view in the far distance. He glanced around to find his archers still guarding his back, the rest of his men following.

"Can you cut this rope off me now?" she asked minutes later.

"You dinna want my dagger near your wrists while we're riding like this. 'Twould be dangerous." Truth was he wanted her tied. He liked her being a wee bit helpless and under his control. He needed to teach her a lesson. She smelled so good she distracted him, made him think of yester eve and the time they'd spent alone and naked in the cave.

When they arrived at Farspag, he had a pike-hard erection and hated himself for it. But with her wee arse rubbing against his cock the whole way, what had he expected? As the horse trotted through the gates, Brodie leaned forward to get one last whiff of Erin's hair. He wished to bury his nose in it while he buried himself inside her. Heaven on earth.

He drew up, leapt down, and helped her dismount. When her bewitching blue eyes met his, for a moment it was as if he'd been struck by lightning. The breath left his lungs.

"Thank you for rescuing me," she said. Her gratitude appeared genuine, and he had a mad craving to kiss her.

"How could I no'?" he murmured, moving his face closer to hers.

"Brodie!" The female shout from near the castle's portal snapped him out of his fantasies.

His sister, Catriona, rushed across the stone-paved barmkin toward them, bright red hair and emerald green dress gleaming in the sun. Her husband, Torr Blackburn, waited by the entrance. With his long chestnut hair, dull-colored plaid kilt and brown doublet, Torr was more subdued in both his manner and appearance.

Hell and damnation, what were they doing here? Brodie could easily guess, because the last time he'd seen these two they were trying to convince him he needed wedded bliss like they had. And love to break the curse.

He lifted Erin into his arms and headed toward the entrance of the tower.

"What are you doing?" she whispered. "I can walk."

"Shh."

"Brodie?" Catriona chased after him. "Will you not untie her and introduce us?"

Torr stood aside with a smirking grin.

Brodie gave him a nod of greeting. "Welcome. Come inside and refresh yourselves." He carried Erin across the great hall, ignoring anyone who stared, and up to his bedchamber. He kicked the door shut and tied her to his bed using a length of leather cord.

"You promised to untie me, you ass!"

He barred the door. "You do idiotic things when you're free. You're lucky MacPeter didna torture, rape or kill you. I willna allow you to be used against me."

"How could I be used against you? That's stupid!" Erin's glare cut into him.

"MacPeter could capture you again and hold you hostage, or for ransom."

"So now you're holding me hostage!"

"Nay. I'm only trying to save your life. If MacPeter had his way, you'd spend the rest of your days under him in bed. Does that appeal? Do you get wet and wanton for him?"

"Ewww, no!" She cringed. "I would've killed him if he'd attempted to force me."

Brodie would have killed him, too, but it couldn't come to that. Whether she cooperated or not, he had to keep Erin safe.

"Did MacPeter or any of his men touch you?" He had to make sure.

She shook her head. "No, they didn't. One of his women servants gave me a bath. That's all."

Thank the Saints. Some of the tension left his body. It would kill him if someone hurt her. "The biggest danger to you is yourself," he said. "You're reckless." Then he remembered his father used to say the same thing about him. Reckless. Never thinking of the consequences. Could he and Erin share such a thing?

"I can't wait 'til the day I can tie you up and torture you!" She yanked at her bonds.

Perversely, her threat aroused him even more. Before he realized it, he kicked off his boots, removed his sporran, and almost unclasped his belt. Then he stopped short. The side of her smock was ripped open, revealing a tempting line of smooth pale flesh and the side of her breast. Lust raged through him. He leaned over her and took her mouth in a punishing kiss. She refused to open, clenching her teeth together and turning her head aside.

"Look at me." He nudged her face back. "You will obey me from now on."

"No! Bastard! I don't obey anyone, certainly not you!"

Damn, but her rebelliousness made him even harder. "Then you will no' be getting loose this day."

"Like hell!" She kicked at him, her too-large boots flying off in the ruckus. He grasped her ankles, pushed her legs up and insinuated himself between. Sitting on his knees, he captured her thighs in a leg lock. Her plaid skirts and smock drifted up, revealing all her tempting feminine delights to him, her pink cunny, juicy and swollen. Waiting for him.

With much impatience, his cock jerked. Saints! How could he resist her?

Erin took in Brodie's wide shoulders and biceps flexing beneath his thin linen shirt as he held her thighs in place, spread apart. His midnight glower moved from her eyes, down her chest and to her exposed crotch. Her sex tingled, excited by his wicked perusal. His frown and guttural foreign words grew darker by the moment. She then noticed the front of his kilt tented by his massive pole. No matter how much he irritated her with his bossy, controlling ways, she still hungered for him. Not just sexually. She hungered for him emotionally. Though he'd closed himself off, deep down she knew he was someone who could understand her and accept her as no one ever had. And the way he'd come to her rescue with a whole freaking army told her he cared more than he was willing to admit. A thrill shot through her.

He licked his thumb and stroked it up along her slit to her clit, where he circled round and round, gently massaging.

"Wow," she breathed. That felt fantastic. She gasped and arched her back.

His thumb prodded into her opening, then retreated. So good. She ached to feel his amazing cock spreading her while he gave her devouring kisses.

Watching his fingers again, he rubbed her sex lips and licked her juices from his thumb. "Mmm. Sweet."

"Brodie," she whispered, craving him more now than she had in her aphrodisiac-fevered dreams.

He swiped his thumb through her moisture, over and over, teasing, tantalizing, while he gazed into her eyes. His were deep and dark, revealing a glimpse into his tormented soul. She yearned to give him what he wanted, to ease his turmoil. Clearly, they both wanted the same thing.

"Please, Brodie. I want you."

He clenched his jaw and his breathing changed. He caressed her clit in a circle that made her delirious. She spread her legs wider. The tingles of orgasm began faintly. He pulled back to suck her juices from his thumb.

"Don't stop," she begged. "More, please."

"You are too damned tempting."

"Good. Give in to temptation. Looks like you have a boner the size of the Eiffel Tower under that kilt."

"A tower?" He lifted a brow, a faint grin softening his lips. "You're such a brazen wench."

"You love that about me."

"Aye, I do." His thumb barely grazed her, but the effect was like a jolt of electricity. She jerked. He stared at her crotch again, his fingertips teasing. "You're so wet, lass."

"You make me hotter than anyone ever has." Maybe she shouldn't have admitted that, but it was true.

"What of your past liaisons?"

"So insignificant I don't remember them. Why do you care?"

"I dinna."

But she saw a rare vulnerability in his eyes. Why was he lying?

"Yes, you do. That's why you came over to MacPeter's to fetch me. You want me. You just don't want to admit it."

"Quiet."

"Take me," she whispered. "I want to feel you inside me." What would it take to break his inflexible control? "Fuck me, please."

He growled, glaring at her.

Abruptly, he unfastened his belt and threw his kilt aside. When he'd pulled his shirt over his head, he knelt between her thighs, naked and gorgeous with all those sleek muscles, his cock jutting upward. His frown turned sensual and tortured, as if he yearned for something he shouldn't.

"Yes, Brodie. Please."

He hissed Gaelic words between clenched teeth, which only made her hotter. She lifted her hips, offering herself, so desperate for him she'd do anything.

Looking into her eyes, he teased the tip of his cock along her slit, spreading her juices. She squealed and thrust her hips, needing far more.

"Shh. We dinna want everyone to hear you," he murmured.

"I'll be quiet. Now, please. Fuck me."

Moaning, he placed the tip in her opening. "You do beg in a most tempting manner." When her hips flexed again, lifting toward him, his cock slid in an inch.

"Oh, yes," she hissed. He was so big and rock hard. "More, please."

"Och. Your wee cunny is squeezing me," he said in a raspy whisper, along with words she didn't understand. Dropping his gaze to their joined bodies, he moved shallowly within her but drove deeper with each thrust.

"Oh, yes. Brodie, more," she encouraged. He felt so amazing, filling her, spreading her aching vaginal walls, sliding deeper than she had ever been penetrated. Once he was imbedded to the hilt, he halted, hovering above her, the gorgeous muscles of his chest, abs and arms flexing. His jaw clenched; his dark gaze locked to hers. He dipped his head to take her lips in a possessive tongue kiss that tasted of sex. His hips moved, his pelvis, in an erotic withdrawal and thrust. One. Another. Gradually gaining speed. The pleasure heightening with each slick lunge of his cock. She could think of nothing but the awe-inspiring feelings he was unleashing within her. Ecstatic, fiery sensations darted from her head to her toes. Nothing in her life had ever been this intense. She heard herself crying out, screaming, but could do nothing to stop it.

"Shh, Erin." Holding her head, almost lovingly, between his warm palms, he closed his mouth over hers, devouring, catching her cries. His thumbs gently stroked her cheeks, her ears. Yes, finally, all she could see, feel and taste was Brodie, just as she wanted. All of him invaded her senses, her body, and she welcomed him. Never had she imagined enjoying a man this much. She would never get enough of him. She had no control over her body or mind at the moment. He was master of it all, of her. The sharp tingling swirled upward, round and round, higher and higher. The feeling of her spirit somersaulting through the air filled her and then ecstasy was grinding through her.

"Och." He murmured unusual words as he pounded into her hard, through her orgasm, intensifying and lengthening the pleasure. He muffled her screams and gasps with his lips. Abruptly, he withdrew, his hot cum shooting against her thigh.

Chapter 7

Minutes later, after washing himself off at the basin in his chamber, Brodie tugged on his shirt and belted his plaid in place. Saints, he was so stunned he could hardly speak or think. Erin was astonishing. Such a sensual lass. Unusual. He had been with a lot of women, but never one who enthralled him. And never one who had given him such fierce pleasure.

Just in time, he had withdrawn and spilled his seed on the coverlet, accidentally dousing her thigh and derriere in the process. Hell, he could not get her with child and trap them both, even if he was near obsessed with her.

"Untie me, Brodie. Please."

He could not resist that cajoling, wee-lass expression on her face. Aye, she'd probably like to clean herself up. Taking his *sgian dubh*, he carefully cut the ropes binding her.

"Thank you," she whispered, rubbing her wrists.

"They're chaffed and raw." The sight of her injury stung his conscience. Why had he not taken better care of her? He retrieved a small jar of herbal salve from his trunk and sat on the bed beside her. "Let me put this on. 'Twill help with healing."

"What's in it?" She sidled closer to him, her breast brushing his arm through the shirt. A sense of warmth, affection and comfort beset him. He did not share these things with others, but now he yearned to with her.

"The salve?" she prompted.

"Herbs and such."

"You're a font of information."

He could not help but smile. "Aye." He coated a fingertip with the aromatic salve and massaged it into the scrapes. "Your skin is so soft and sensitive." Like warm silk. He lifted her arm and kissed the inside of her forearm, wishing he could kiss every delectable inch of her. Aye, he could easily go another round already. Saints! He placed her hand on her lap and rose instead.

"That feels better. Thank you."

When she gazed up at him with those big blue, trusting eyes, his chest ached.

Hell.

He put away the salve. "I shall return later."

"When? Can I go downstairs?"

He tried to ignore the way her voice tore at his conscience. "Later." He exited the room and locked the door with the key.

"Why are you locking her in?" his sister asked, suddenly appearing in the corridor.

"Stop lurking about, Catriona. 'Tis obvious. I canna allow her to escape and be captured again."

"She's smart enough not to."

"You ken naught about her. You havena even met her."

"But I want to!"

"Later." He strode away from her.

"Churlish boar-pig," Catriona muttered behind him.

Torr waited by the library door. "Could I have a word?"

"Aye, if you make haste."

"Where are you off to?" Once they'd entered, Torr closed the library door behind them.

Brodie had to return and help the selkies, but he didn't want to share that with any of the humans, not even his best friend. "Whisky?" He poured himself a wee dram.

"Aye, thanks."

"I'm glad to see you, of course, but what are you doing here?" Brodie handed him the glass. "I suspect 'tis no' a social call."

"Finnian sent a missive."

"The meddling wizened pine-knot. What did he want?"

Torr sipped his whisky, letting the silence stretch out. His green eyes were too damned all-seeing and all-knowing. "I'm thinking you ken what he said."

"You've turned into a matchmaker, too? I never thought to see the day. My sister has unmanned you." But his friend did indeed look happy, as if he had nary a care in the world.

Torr snorted. "Dinna be daft. You ken 'tis your destiny to have the curse broken. And to accept the love of a woman."

He knew no such thing. Brodie couldn't love someone he couldn't trust, and trusting a woman with everything in him was nigh inconceivable now. He had trusted his former betrothed that much, and all had been shattered. For him to step onto the same unstable, boggy ground this soon after the first debacle would be lunacy.

A knock sounded at the door.

"Now what?" Brodie muttered. "Come!"

The door opened and his friend he hadn't seen in over a year walked in.

"Gavin?" Brodie and Torr said at the same time. Gavin's black hair was a mite longer, and his red-and-blue plaid new. What surprised Brodie most, however, was his smile.

"Aye." Gavin's pale blue gaze moved between them. "Do I look that bad, then?"

"Nay." Torr strode forward and shook his hand, then gave him a brotherly hug. Brodie was in no mood for it. There was only one reason his two formerly cursed friends were here, and he didn't like it. Even now they were discussing the curse. His gut clenched. Damn Finnian. Why couldn't the old coot mind his own affairs?

Brodie threw back the whisky and swallowed. The fiery liquid burning all the way to his stomach, he poured himself another and one for Gavin.

When he faced his friends again, they watched him expectantly.

He handed Gavin the whisky. "Good to see you, my friend." Brodie had not yet grown used to the straight, thin white scar down one side of Gavin's face from forehead to jaw. He'd sustained the sword slash during a skirmish just before he'd last seen him. But Gavin looked the picture of health and happiness. Marriage apparently agreed with him.

"So, both of you decide to pay me a visit the same day," Brodie said. "This has Finnian's moldering scent all over it."

"He said you found the lass on a rock in the ocean." Gavin's sharp gaze narrowed and pried at him.

"Aye. So?"

"How'd she get there?"

"Dinna ken. Perchance a galley brought her."

"Or 'haps she's from the future as my wife, Shauna, is," Gavin said.

"What?" Torr laughed.

Gavin raised his right hand. "I vow 'tis the truth. She's from four hundred years in the future. Is there anything unusual about this woman you found? Does she speak in a strange way and use words you dinna understand?"

Brodie shrugged and sipped the whisky. True, Erin was very bizarre in her manner and speech, but that didn't mean she was from the future.

"'Twill do you no good to run from destiny," Torr said.

Devil take destiny. Brodie did not believe in such blather.

"Have either of you seen Wilona of late?" Gavin asked.

"Nay," Torr said. "Last Catriona and I saw her, she turned into an owl and flew away."

"I've seen her," Brodie confessed.

"Where?" his friends asked in concert, maniacal gleams in their eyes.

"On the isle where I stay often, with the selkies. She's been posing as a beautiful young selkie. I didn't recognize her, she'd changed her appearance so much. But 'tis her, I know it now. She tried to attack Erin as I was bringing her here."

"Saints! We can't kill her until Brodie's curse is broken," Gavin said. "Or it will never be broken."

Brodie considered. Maybe he should kill Wilona. Then he'd always be a selkie. Nay, he could not murder her outright, even if she was a witch of the Dark Arts. Besides, if he was always a selkie, would Erin still like him?

What the devil was he thinking? He didn't give a damn if Erin liked him.

"What is your plan, Brodie?" Gavin asked.

"I must keep Erin safe until I can return her to wherever she came from. I must not let Wilona hurt her, nor the MacPeter take her hostage again."

"You canna keep her prisoner in your bedchamber forever. I tried that with Shauna." Gavin grinned. "Didna work."

"'Tis almost time for supper," Torr said. "'Haps you should allow Erin to eat with the rest of us in the great hall. She would enjoy meeting Catriona and Shauna."

Brodie snorted. "'Tis never good when a gaggle of women get together."

Erin carefully descended the narrow spiral stairs, holding to the rough stone walls for support. Her borrowed women's shoes, which Aggie had found someplace, were unstable and too tight besides. Brodie and his wardens had released her from the bedchamber cell so she could eat dinner with everyone else. She didn't yet know if this was a reward or more torture. Mainly, she hoped to find a sane person to take her from this place.

As she entered the great hall, all eyes locked on her. With Aggie's help, she had repaired her sequined gown during her hours of confinement and now wore it. She scanned the two dozen people but did not see Brodie. Where was the sexy knucklehead?

A tiny, wide-eyed girl pointed at her gown, which shimmered and sparkled in the candlelight. "She's the fairy queen!"

Voices whispered and murmured through the silence of the great hall. "Nay, she's a mermaid," a teenage boy said.

Erin frowned. What the hell? She was not playing along with their Ren Faire nonsense.

Two smiling women approached from her left. "Mistress Erin, I'm Catriona, Brodie's sister." She curtsied.

"So nice to meet you." She hoped this girl, at least, was sane. With her flaming red hair and light blue eyes, she didn't look a thing like Brodie. Could she really be his sister, or was this a role?

"And I'm Shauna," said a dark-haired woman who appeared to be around her own age, early to mid-twenties. Surprisingly, her accent was American, unlike the rest of these actors, but her plaid dress was certainly Highland.

Erin shook both their hands.

"Won't you sit with us during supper so we can talk?" Catriona asked.

"I'd love to." *Please God, don't let them serve sheep entrails.*

Erin seated herself at a table made of wide boards, which had been polished smooth by eons of use. The two women sat on the bench on either side of her.

"Where's Brodie?" Erin asked. "I have a bone to pick with him."

Catriona smiled. "I suspect he's in the library with our husbands. The three of them are the best of friends."

"Ah." So that explained why the two women had latched onto her.

"And everyone has a bone to pick with Brodie, including me," Catriona said.

"What did he do?"

"What did he not do is a better question. First, he kept you locked in his bedchamber all day and wouldn't even let me meet you. What a heathen. He's the most stubborn man God ever created."

Erin nodded. "For sure."

"He refuses to fall in love so his curse can be broken."

Well, at least everyone here told the same story about curses, etcetera.

Brodie's hawkeyed mother seated herself at one end of the table. Erin was thankful she didn't have to sit beside her.

"You sound American," Shauna said. "Where are you from?"

"Wisconsin."

Shauna's eyes widened. "Early twenty-first century?" she whispered.

"Um, yes."

"You do know we're in 1621, right?"

"Well, I didn't know what year this Ren Faire was supposed to be, but 1621 sounds about right."

"No. I mean it's really 1621. This isn't a Renaissance Faire."

"Right." She thought she'd just met the sanest person here, but instead, Shauna was the most delusional.

"You don't believe me." Shauna looked too serious by far. Not even a teasing glint in her green eyes. "I'm from the future, too. We're both time-travelers."

"That's crazy." Couldn't be 1621. No way in hell.

"Have you seen anything modern since you've been here? Electric lights, phones, a car, or even a freaking bathroom?"

Erin swallowed hard and shook her head. She'd thought they'd been trying to torture her by making her use the garderobe privy, which was a stone outhouse on an outside wall of the castle. "So this isn't just a really accurate—"

"Nope. I also couldn't believe it when I arrived earlier this year."

"But I thought I was in the back of beyond. You know, the boondocks of the Highlands. Where they took their Ren Faires and Celtic Festivals extremely seriously."

"I'm sorry to say this is the real deal."

"But how? Why? What's going on?"

"How? Magic. Why? That's more complicated, but I suspect it's your destiny to fall in love with Brodie because—"

"You're going to break his curse!" Catriona said, looking positively thrilled.

"How do I get back to my regular life?" Erin asked Shauna.

"I have no clue," Shauna said. "At first, I wanted to go back, too, because

I didn't want to leave my parents, my sister, my apartment, my career. I was a college professor. But then I fell completely in love with Gavin, and I couldn't bear to leave him." She shook her head, strong emotion in her gaze. "My life is here now, and I'm so much happier than I was in the future. Hmm, that sounded weird."

"But is there a way to get back?"

"Possibly."

"Do not tell her," Catriona said in a panicked whisper. "You cannot leave, Erin! Please. We've been waiting for you for months. You're the answer to my prayers."

Erin hadn't expected such a vehement response. "Why?"

Catriona glanced behind herself, then moved closer and spoke in a low voice. "Brodie will not take his place as full-time chieftain of this clan until his curse is broken. He's put the whole clan at risk. The clan needs his protection and leadership. As a selkie, he yearns for the sea more than anything, but if he has you—if he loves you and you love him—the magic will happen. No more curse. You have a grand destiny!"

God, this was disturbing. Erin frowned and glanced at Shauna.

"I understand your frustration and confusion. I was there a few months ago. Finally, I accepted it. I had to give up my career—which still irks me—but I love Gavin more than anything. It's been worth it."

"I'm a fashion model," Erin said, "and I wanted to go back to school to become a doctor. That's my dream, and I'm not about to give it up. Besides, scientists say time-travel isn't possible."

"Guess they were wrong. Hey, maybe you could be a doctor here. I'm sure they could use your help."

"I don't have my degree."

Brodie and two other tall, gorgeous men in kilts approached the table and took seats on one end, capturing everyone's attention. Brodie's dark gaze homed in on Erin. She wanted to throw a wooden spoon at him. It was his fault she was here, dammit. She wanted no part of curse curing, unlike the two women beside her. Catriona giggled and Shauna was clearly sending a silent communication to the blue-eyed devil with a slash-scar down his face. He winked at her.

So they were in love. Fantastic for them. But Erin couldn't do it.

Her gaze drifted back to Brodie and her heart flip-flopped. He was big, commanding, dark and fierce. *No, stop looking at him.* She fixed her gaze on the table before her. This whole situation was too huge for her. What the hell business did she have traveling through time and getting mixed up with a real Highland chieftain who was a real freaking selkie? None!

When she remembered the amazing sex they'd had a few hours ago, she couldn't believe that was her, either. Feeling such overwhelming intensity and hunger for this man.

So they had phenomenal sex. That was no reason to fall in love. Was it?

A small wooden platter plopped down in front of Erin. She jumped and sent a glare up at the servant. The platter contained generous helpings of brown bread, mystery meat and a chunk of something white. Oh yum. She wasn't about to be the first to try it. She glanced along the table. All grew silent and a thin man dressed in black, apparently a priest or minister, said grace.

Brodie bowed his head and sneaked a glance up at her. Their eyes met and the wicked look he sent her should've singed her. The priest would surely consider it sacrilege if he knew about it.

Erin quickly dropped her gaze and squeezed her eyes shut. *God help me* was the only prayer she could formulate in her mind, for she'd been dragged into something she couldn't control. And was involved with someone she couldn't control.

Chapter 8

From the other end of the table, Brodie watched Erin eating a berry tart dessert at the conclusion of the meal. A bit of the flaky crust clung to her upper lip. He had the foolish compulsion to march over there and lick it off.

Nay!

Damnation, she would be the death of his freedom, the finish of being a selkie—if he wasn't most careful.

"Such a dark glower at a beautiful woman?" Gavin sat down beside him again after having gone off to talk to his wife in the corner. Comparing matchmaking notes, no doubt.

"Aye, that's just it. The more beautiful a woman, the more evil in her soul."

"Humph." Gavin sipped his ale.

"The curse has warped his thinking," Torr muttered on his other side.

"Shauna talked to Erin," Gavin said, low so no one else would hear. "And they are from the same time period, early twenty-first century."

"How is that possible, then?" Torr leaned forward.

Gavin shrugged. "Magic? We learned that the ghost of my great uncle somehow helped Shauna reach me."

"Finnian mentioned something about our dead ancestors helping us as well," Torr said.

"That makes no sense at all. None of it." Brodie hoped his dark scowl told them how much he hated this conversation. "Listen to yourselves. You're blathering on worse than Finnian. Where is the auld coot, anyway?"

"He disappeared after he learned you'd given Erin a good swiving," Torr said.

"What? How the devil...?"

"Everyone inside the castle and out heard her cries of passion." Torr smirked.

"Damnation," Brodie muttered. He hadn't wanted any of them to know he'd given in to temptation.

Gavin grinned and held his ale aloft in a toast. "To your upcoming nuptials."

Brodie muttered Gaelic words that told Gavin to go swive himself.

Torr snorted with laughter.

"Until you come to your senses," Gavin said, "I'll spend the rest of my time with my sweet, beautiful wife that I love, and who loves me." A devilish smile spread across his face. "She ne'er tires of showing me how much."

"I could've done without that bit of information," Brodie grumbled.

Gavin pushed himself up and sauntered away. At the side of the table, he leaned down and whispered something into his wife's ear. She blushed and chuckled. Catriona and Erin rose and drifted into the corner, their heads together. Catriona was no doubt poisoning Erin's mind in some way.

Brodie muttered a curse beneath his breath and drank a hefty sip of ale.

Gavin and his bride did look happy, sitting close and cozy on the bench. Gavin fed her bites of pastry with his fingers and teased her.

Brodie shifted his gaze to Erin and their eyes met. That instant of eye contact was like a battering ram to his stomach. She was so damned beautiful, but equally untrustworthy. Like mouth-watering poison. And in truth, he craved her. What they had done earlier... Saints! He was hard again just remembering sliding into her tight, wet passage. 'Twas heaven being inside her, driving into her while she squirmed, moaned and screamed, expressing her pleasure in the most vocal way possible. Now his fully erect cock pushed hard against the back of his leather sporran, the pressure stimulating him further. His long linen shirt kept the scratchy wool fabric of his plaid from abrading his overly sensitized shaft.

He was not hungry for food. He was hungry for her. The bad thing about being a selkie was that his lusts ruled him. Selkies would rather have sex than eat when they were starving. Then again, 'haps selkies were not so different from human men.

From the corner, Catriona and Erin sent covert glances his way during their private discussion. "Methinks your wee wifey is stirring the pot," Brodie told Torr.

"Doubtless," Torr agreed. "'Tis what she does best. Well, one of the things...." He cleared his throat. "Ne'er mind."

"I wish you'd take Catriona for a stroll outside and get her away from Erin."

"Why?"

"I dinna like it when people conspire against me."

Torr snorted. "Catriona has tried to find you a woman for months. And once she does, my life will be a hell of a lot more pleasant. So, dinna expect me to help you escape matrimony."

Brodie's heart hitched at that m-word. "I thought you were my friend."

"Indeed, I am. But sometimes you dinna ken what's good for you."

"You see the way Brodie watches you?" Catriona asked.

Erin glanced at him where he sat at the table in the great hall. "You mean like he wants to choke me?" His dark glare would probably terrify a weaker woman.

"Nay, he does not! He's falling in love with you."

Erin rolled her eyes. "Please, girl. I'm not buying what you're selling. Brodie is not capable of that emotion."

"He is. He was in love last year and betrothed to a woman named Elspeth. But, because of the curse, she left him for another man."

The poor guy had a broken heart. No wonder he was surly. "Clearly, she damaged him beyond repair."

"She wasn't the right woman for him. Too timid to put him in his place. But you are not."

A deluge of icy water gushed onto Erin. She shrieked.

Shivering, she jerked around and spied two teenage boys holding big empty buckets. "Why the hell did you do that?" she yelled.

"She didna turn into a mermaid," one muttered.

"The two of you, out!" Brodie stomped into the fray, pointing a commanding finger toward the door.

The boys dropped the buckets and fled.

"Bastards!" Erin yelled after them, and to everyone else in the great hall, she said, "I'm not a mermaid, okay? And I'm not a fairy queen! I'm just a regular woman. Everybody got that?"

Silent and slack-jawed, they gaped at her.

Brodie stopped beside her, his expression concerned. "Are you well?"

Nodding, then shaking her head, she yearned to launch herself into his arms and cry her eyes out. But she wasn't quite that whiney. So what if this was one of the worst days of her life, first getting captured by a bunch of barbarians, then learning she was stuck four hundred years in the past? She was still her model-self, hiding her true feelings and displaying the emotions those around her expected.

"Brodie, you stay here. I'll find something dry for her to change into." Catriona urged her up the spiral staircase.

Before Erin reached the top, she couldn't see for the tears flooding her eyes. What was wrong with her? She didn't cry. Never! But suddenly a feeling of helplessness overwhelmed her. What was she going to do? She was in 1621. No friends, no family, no way to earn a living, no home. Not since she was a teen had she depended on anyone. She'd learned to cook at a young age and take care of her little sister while their mom was out working two jobs. And now she didn't know if she'd ever see her sister again, the one person in life she was closest to. Her dream of becoming a doctor felt completely out of reach at the moment.

Catriona helped Erin into Brodie's room and pulled her into a comforting hug. This only made Erin sob uncontrollably. Painful emotions poured out. The true magnitude of the danger she'd been in at MacPeter's castle. They could've all raped her or killed her. During this time period, women had very few rights, and if that bastard had killed her, no one would've known or cared. Except maybe Brodie.

To add further madness to mayhem, she might be falling for Brodie, a warrior with all the sweetness of a barracuda.

"There now, Erin." Catriona patted her back. "Everything will be well."

Once her tears stopped and Erin got herself under control, Catriona handed her a hanky.

"I'd like to talk to Shauna," Erin said, needing to find a way out of this place. Something had to be under her control.

"Very well. Stand by the fireplace to warm yourself, and I'll be right back with a clean, dry dress for you." Catriona exited the room.

Moments later, Shauna entered.

"Thank God. You have to tell me how to get back to the future. I can't take it here."

Shauna locked a shrewd gaze on her for a long moment. Erin didn't try to hide her desperation.

"Okay," Shauna said. "For me, there were two objects that apparently caused me to travel through time. Did you touch or have two objects from this time period?"

"The key! I was in this castle in the future, doing a photo shoot. I actually entered this room and found an old key on the floor. When I held it, I felt strangely wonderful and warm, in a supernatural kind of way. A little gray-haired lady who worked here said I could have it and—oh dear God—she said it was the key to my future." Erin felt her face go white and cold.

"Aha! She was probably a ghost. In my case, a little white-haired man convinced me I'd enjoy holding a four-hundred-year old sword. Plus, I was wearing an antique brooch I'd inherited."

Erin replayed her conversation with the elderly lady in her mind. Strange. She should've never taken the key.

"Where is this key now?" Shauna asked.

"I have no idea. I was holding it when I went to sleep, but when I ended up on that rock in the ocean, I was empty-handed."

"Was there a second object?"

Erin shook her head. "Just the whisky."

"What do you mean?"

"I drank three mini bottles of Farspag Tower whisky because I was getting the flu. My roommate convinced me it would help me recover quickly. I lay down in bed holding the key and drifted in and out of vivid dreams involving Brodie. I thought I was asleep. I experienced a sharp pain in my head. Then suddenly, I was on a rock in the ocean."

"The sharp pain, yes. I felt the same thing when I traveled. And the dreams beforehand. If you really want to go back to the future, my suggestion would be to find the key and then drink some of the Farspag whisky."

"I bet Brodie has the key. He locked me in this room twice." Erin would swipe it from him at the earliest opportunity. He probably kept it in that sporran thing around his waist. "Do you think you could find some whisky made here?"

"I'll try." Shauna observed her with speculation. "Are you sure you want to leave Brodie?"

"Umm. Yes, I think so." She ignored the tightness in her chest and the heavy dread that filled her stomach.

"Don't want to give it a few days? 'Cause he is a real cutie, if you ignore the scowl."

Erin had to agree. He was far more than a cutie. He was intense and addictive. And she knew some part of her needed him, just as he needed her. But her right place was in the future, becoming a doctor.

A knock sounded at the door.

"Think about it more. If you decide you have to leave, I'm glad we got to meet." Shauna hugged her. "I'll go look for that whisky."

She opened the door to leave and Brodie stood in the corridor holding a blue velvet dress, probably one of his mother's hand-me-downs.

"Be sweet to her," Catriona said and smacked his arm.

Brodie merely flicked a glare her way, then entered and shut the door.

Erin bit her lip to keep from grinning at the way he held the dress, as if it were a poisonous snake.

He threw the garment on the bed and propped his hands on his kilted hips. "The lads who poured water on you will be doing twice as many chores this week."

She supposed they'd gotten off easy, considering this was not far from medieval times when people were whipped or tortured for less. "Seems I'm destined to wear a wet dress in 1621."

He frowned, studying her.

She dropped her gaze to that pouch-like sporran that hung from his waist and rested over his package. She pointed. "What do you keep in there?"

"Where? My sporran?"

"Yes."

"Why?"

"The key to this room, perhaps?"

"I'm no' giving you the key, if that's what you're hinting."

"I need it, but not for unlocking the door."

He crossed his arms over his broad chest and looked less tolerant by the second. "What for, then?"

She let out a long breath, knowing he was going to laugh in her face. "To go back to the twenty-first century."

But he didn't laugh. His scowl darkened and he searched her eyes.

"You aren't laughing. Did you already know?"

"Gavin mentioned it might be possible, but I didna believe him. He says his wife is from the twenty-first century."

"Yes, she is. And I didn't realize it was 1621 until Shauna told me at dinner. I mean, my God, I could've been killed today by MacPeter. I thought this was just a giant, very authentic Renaissance-Faire-type Celtic Festival where everyone was acting."

Brodie leaned back against one of the tall bed posts and watched her with a guarded expression.

"I have no idea how this happened to me or why, but I have to find a way to go back."

"Why?"

"How can you ask me that? If you'd time-traveled to the twenty-first century, wouldn't you want to come back here where everything is familiar? Where you have your family, friends, home and your position as chieftain?"

He shrugged. "Being chieftain is no' as delightful as it sounds."

"You don't like it?"

"Doesna matter if I like it or no'. 'Tis what I am."

"Where I come from, everyone gets to choose what they want to do for a career. The sky is the limit. I'm a fashion model, but I want to be a doctor." She truly might never get to live out her dream. "I have an eighteen-year-old sister in college. Who's going to watch out for her and pay her tuition if I don't return to the future?"

"What of your mother and father?"

Tears filled Erin's eyes. She wasn't sure whether from the barrage of nostalgic memories or Brodie's compassionate tone. Was it possible he had a soft spot after all? "I haven't seen my dad since I was a little kid." Her voice caught, but she forced the words out. "And my mom passed away seven years ago with cancer. She fought the disease for years and I always swore I'd become a doctor, find a cure and save people's lives. I promised her."

Abruptly, Brodie pulled her into his arms, a warm hand at the back of her neck. His body was hard and unyielding, but his embrace comforting and gentle. This was something she had not experienced in the twenty-first century. No man had ever held her when she was upset. Unable to believe how good it felt, she laid her head on his shoulder and simply breathed him in. His sexy body exuded an enticing masculine fragrance, spicy, musky with a hint of sea air. If some modern-day cologne maker could bottle that irresistible combination, they'd be rich.

Her nose and lips brushing his neck, she inhaled his aroma several times and almost hyperventilated.

His hot breath against her ear sent tingles through her body. Strangely, she was content right here. Being in Brodie's arms felt warm and cozy, like home. But it wasn't. She was stranded four hundred years away from home.

Chapter 9

I should not have come into this bedchamber, Brodie thought. Hell, he should've left Erin with his sister and sought solitude himself to wrestle with his demons. A woman in tears always perplexed him. He knew not what to say or do and, worst of all, he was far more aroused than he should be.

"Erin?" He sat on the bed and drew her onto his lap.

Her tears increased. She held tight 'round his neck and cried against his shoulder.

Och, more than anything he wished to ease her pain. "Shh. All is well." He stroked her back, absorbing the wondrous feel of her into himself. Her tall, lithe body with its feminine curves snatched his reasoning ability. She felt unlike any woman he had thus far touched. She felt somehow right.

"No, all is not well." She sniffed.

"You didna cry when a witch chased us. You didna cry when you were leaving MacPeter's castle. You fought your way out."

"But this is far worse. I have to get back to my time period. Will you give me the key?" Her red, tear-filled eyes beseeched him, tore at his resolve, and he glanced down, taking her hand, rubbing her palm.

Aye, he should give her the key. He knew he should. But he was not quite ready to let her go.

Something thumped hard against the door.

"What the devil?" Brodie set her on the bed, strode forward and tried to open the door. Locked? He dug into his sporran for the key. "The key is gone."

"You're joking!"

"Nay. Open the damnable door! Now!" he yelled at those in the corridor.

A faint giggle sounded.

"Catriona, I shall thrash your backside for this!"

Several more laughs sounded. Male. His so-called friends, no doubt.

"Damn them all," Brodie muttered, turning.

Erin stood by the bed, her reddened, moist eyes wide. "Why did they lock us in?"

"If you knew, you'd think them all lunatics." He did not need their imprisonment to fall for Erin. 'Twas already happening. He found her strength exceedingly appealing. Indeed, she cried and screamed at times, but the way she'd fought her way out of MacPeter's castle was remarkable. She had the heart of a female warrior. Add to that how he craved naught but having her naked in bed under him or on top, riding him, and he was near mad with longing. He fought it down and forced himself to concentrate on their conversation.

"How did they steal the key?" she asked.

"'Twas likely Finnian's magic that removed it. I've no' taken off my sporran since my return, except during…." Their heated tryst. Which he didn't want to think about or talk about now, else he'd become highly aroused again. "The aged coot is determined to drive me insane." Brodie strode to the window and stared out at the ocean far below and the waves breaking on the rugged coastline. Sharp yearning pulled at him. He craved the cool caress of water on his skin. "'Slud!" he growled. He could escape this trap easily enough, but what would he do about Erin? He couldn't take her back to the island with Wilona on the loose. Too dangerous.

"I need that key to return to the future." Erin pounded on the door. "Shauna! Help me! See if you can get the key for me."

No response.

Erin turned, fear and desperation in her eyes. "Where did she go? She said she'd help me."

He wanted to tell her not to be afraid, that he would take care of her and protect her, but he could not quite bring himself to utter the promise. What if she didn't want his protection? "If Gavin has aught to say about it, Shauna willna be helping you return to the future. They're determined to—"

Brodie couldn't say it. Every time he thought of giving all inside himself to Erin, his stomach ached. God, he wanted to. But what if she didn't choose to give all to him? Clearly, she wished to go back to her home, her time period, and he couldn't fault her for that.

"I know. They want us to fall in love and get married. We've only known each other a couple days." She tucked a lock of short blond hair behind her ear and sent him a confused glance from those mesmerizing fairy-blue eyes.

"Aye."

"They're expecting the impossible. I don't know you that well."

Do you want to? He almost asked. Nay, he would not expose himself to rejection.

"What do you think of all this?" she asked.

He shrugged, unable to put into words the thoughts and feelings warring inside him. The irritation at his clan and friends for wanting to control him. The confusion about her and how she'd burst into his life like a blazing fallen star. Had she been sent to save him from himself? Though he loved being a selkie, deep down something told him it wasn't his true destiny. He only fit into the selkie world because of the black magic curse that had been placed on him.

Erin moved toward him. "Come on, Brodie, tell me something. Talk to me. I can't read the thoughts going on behind your wicked dark eyes."

Wicked? He yearned to do very wicked things to her, indeed.

He glanced away, out the window again.

"What do you want, truly, deep down?" she persisted.

He no longer allowed himself to think about what he truly wanted deep down. He had half of what he wanted when he lived with the selkies. Acceptance, respect, friendship. But still, he knew his life wasn't complete. What he wanted most was acceptance, respect and friendship among his clan. And, yes, even love.

"I think you're afraid," Erin said softly and touched his arm.

He glanced back at her.

"Don't give me that hostile glare. I know what you're afraid of."

"Indeed?" Facing her, he crossed his arms over his chest.

"Yes. Catriona told me about your fiancée who broke your heart and left you last year for another man. You loved her, and now you're afraid to trust another woman."

Aye, he knew he was transparent. Everyone was aware of his failures and disappointments, so it was only natural for someone to tell Erin about it.

"'Tis no' fear. 'Tis wisdom," he said, his stomach clenching into a tight knot. "Why should I trust? I havena yet encountered a woman who wishes to stay with me. You're trying to return to the future. I'd be a madman to nurture feelings for you or trust you."

She nodded, giving him a vulnerable, emotional look. He hoped she wouldn't break into sobs again. He could not abide it.

"You have a point," she finally said, dropping her gaze. "Perhaps the woman for you is right here, a native of Scotland and your time period."

Heaviness weighted his chest. Everything in him shouted she was wrong. Something about her ignited his every nerve ending like a lightning strike. Could she be the one?

The possibility was there, in her. The potential. It could be….

"Will you please help me return to the future?" The soft tone of her voice and her pained expression proclaimed this was her fondest wish.

How could he not, when she asked in that way? He would miss her intensely, but to make her stay here against her will was not the answer. Suddenly he yearned to give her anything she wanted. He wished her happy. And if he and his time period did not make her happy, she did not need to be here.

"Aye." Although he didn't know how, he would do everything in his power to help her. For once in his life, he allowed himself to believe in destiny. What should happen would, whatever was best for her and for him. It was out of his hands. He was naught but an instrument of fate.

"Great!" Erin bounced on her toes. "Okay, how will it work? How will I get back?"

"I dinna ken. Magic brought you here, so I'm thinking magic can take you home."

"Are you a magician or wizard?"

"Nay, and Finnian willna help us. But the selkies have a wizard. 'Haps he can give us some advice or a spell."

"Sounds great. How do we get out of this room?"

"Gather up all the clothing and blankets you can find. I'm going to investigate."

"Investigate where?"

He approached the bookshelf between the fireplace and the door. "Here." He moved a wooden latch and pulled the bookshelf open much like a door on hinges. A metal secret passage door waited behind it.

"Neat trick," Erin said.

"I'll be back soon. Stay here and wait."

"Why can't I go, too?"

"I have ne'er followed this passage to the end. I dinna ken where it emerges. I'll return within the hour for you. Gather the things. Bring the wine, bread and cheese, too." Whoever had planned their imprisonment hadn't wanted them to starve, at least.

Erin nodded. "I'll get everything ready. And thanks."

They made a good team, he realized, observing her. Her plump, sensual lips tempted and tormented him, but a kiss would not help their situation. Trying to ignore her, he lit a candle from the hearth fire, took his sword and descended the steps, clearing away the cobwebs. He had only been down this spiral stone staircase once in his life, when he was twelve and his father had shown it to him in secret. He'd never told anyone about it. The stairs seemed to descend three stories. Warm, moist air filled the tunnel beneath. The floor and walls turned to solid rock. He was now underground.

After a few hundred feet of twisty tunnel, he entered a cavern filled with steam. Glancing around, he recognized this as a deeper part of the cave he'd claimed near the shore. Hot water bubbled up in a small pool and flowed out. He wished he'd known earlier this connected to the castle. He could have put it to good use.

Sheathing his sword, he ventured to the front part of the cave and lit a torch on the wall. He'd left his sealskin hidden beneath a pile of rocks. He shoved the stones away, but the sealskin was not underneath. Where was it?

Brodie searched behind and beneath other rocks, then exited the cave to look along the windy shore. The moon gleamed in the dark sky. Tide was in, and if the sealskin had been out here, it would have washed away.

Returning inside, he took a new torch he'd stored there and lit it. In the deeper cavern, near the hot spring, he placed the torch into a crack between rocks and searched this chamber as well. Nay! The sealskin was gone. "Damnation!" He could not survive without it. Someone had stolen it. Finnian! The aged miscreant. Or maybe Torr. They were trying to force him to give up his selkie life. He would not be forced into doing anything!

"Brodie?" a female voice called from far away. He growled. Erin did not obey a single thing he said.

Bending so as not to hit his head, he strode back along the rock passage. A flame glowed in the distance. Erin's candle.

"I'm here," he called and kept moving forward.

Soon they met within the narrow tunnel and she set down the bundle of clothing and food she'd brought. Because of her height, she had to bend slightly, as he did.

"You were gone a long time. I thought you'd left me." She looked a bit too wide-eyed and frightened for his peace of mind.

"Nay. Wait here."

"Promise you'll come back?"

"Aye, of course." Bypassing her, he climbed the steps to the bedchamber, closed the bookshelf and the secret passage door so no one would follow or guess where they'd gone. He would beat his friends at their own scheme.

"Did you find a way out?" she asked when he rejoined her.

"Aye. This is the cave at the shore. We'll stay here tonight. I'll find a galley and ready it for sailing across to Ròncreag Isle in the morn."

Later that night, Brodie returned from hiring a fisherman with a galley who'd transport them in a few hours. He turned up the bottle of spiced wine and took a long sip to refresh himself, then undressed and slipped into the hot spring pool. Erin slept on a bed of blankets not far away, covered up to her ears. She looked vulnerable lying that way, with her knees drawn up. He felt in that moment he was meant to be her protector. Ridiculous. But that damnable instinctive feeling would not go away.

Indeed, she was like a mermaid out of water, this lass from the future. Was she sent for him alone, as Finnian believed?

Blocking the thought from his mind, Brodie closed his eyes and absorbed the pleasing heat of the water. His skin felt tight and his muscles itchy and restless. He longed for the ocean. Or her. He couldn't be sure which. They seemed one and the same, and produced a gut-wrenching yearning. But when arousal followed, swelling his cock, he knew it was her that he craved.

"Damnation," he muttered. He had to stop wanting her. She was leaving.

She stirred on the pallet, sat up and rubbed her sleepy eyes. "Brodie? Did you find a boat?"

"Aye. We set sail an hour before dawn." He drank another swallow of wine, hoping that would appease his carnal thirst. No such luck. The longer she observed him in silence, the more he ached. He ground his teeth.

"Is something wrong?"

"Nay," he said, not wanting her to know. But the itchy, achy feeling intensified in his bones. He scratched his shoulders and back.

She rose and hunkered at the edge of the small hot pool. "Can I have a sip?"

He gave her the wine and she drank. "Mmm, that's good."

An implausible feeling of possessiveness overcame him. *She is mine. Nay!*

Aye, she is.

She replaced the cork in the bottle top, her curious blue eyes examining him. "You don't appear to feel well."

He cursed in Gaelic. "I yearn. And ache."

"For what?"

He did not want to talk of this to her. She would not understand. Hell, he did not even understand it himself.

"Brodie? What's wrong?"

"'Tis only… during the past year, I have not gone so long without shifting. Finnian or someone stole my sealskin, and now I canna change form."

"I see." Her gaze trailed down over him and back up. "Is it part of the curse?"

"Aye. I crave the sea, and swimming like a seal. I know you canna understand that, but I enjoy being a selkie. If I had never been one, I wouldna know the difference."

"So you're trapped. You love your prison, even though it is harmful to you."

"'Tis no' harmful to me," he snapped. She was starting to sound like his family.

"I think it is. You're lonely. I recognize that in you because I'm lonely most of the time in my profession. People think models are shallow and spoiled, nothing more than a beautiful empty vase. But I'm a person in here, with dreams like anyone else."

Or 'haps she knew well what it was to be misunderstood and a misfit. "What are your dreams, Erin?"

"I want to be a doctor."

He remembered now. Her mother had died from a certain illness and Erin had sworn to find a cure. "I'm sure you can do it."

"Seriously?" She sent him a pleased but shy look.

"Aye, you're a strong, brave woman with great intelligence."

"Thank you. You're the first person who's said that to me since my mom."

Indeed she was a woman unlike any he'd ever met. "You're perfect." His own words startled him. What the hell was wrong with him? Why had he blurted that out?

"Oh, no. I'm not perfect by a long shot."

Some part of him knew she was perfect for him. Not self-centered as one would expect, given her beauty. But another part of him felt paralyzed, afraid to claim her. What if she rejected him? While it was probably true he could bed any woman he set his mind to have, claiming a woman's heart was another matter entirely. Women were fickle creatures.

"Have you forgiven her?" Erin asked.

"Who?"

"The fiancée who left you."

He shrugged. He hadn't considered forgiving Elspeth. Besides, she hadn't asked for his forgiveness, and he was too caught up in the anger of betrayal to forgive.

"You should."

"Why? You dinna even ken who she is." He tried to keep his voice calm, despite his irritation.

"For your own sake. Holding a grudge is like keeping poison in your body. When you don't forgive, it hurts you more than the other person."

He said naught. 'Twas a glaring truth, he knew, but what caught his attention was Erin's wisdom in this.

"You must have loved her a lot," she said in a soft tone that distracted him. She flicked a brief, potent glance at him.

"I dinna wish to speak of it."

"If Elspeth were here, what would you say to her?"

"'Tis no' fit for a lady's ears, what I wish to say," he muttered.

"That's a big grudge. Don't let Elspeth imprison you."

"She ripped my heart out." Hell, why had he said that? Could he no longer control his own tongue? He muttered a string of Gaelic curses.

Erin observed him with compassion. Or pity. Either way, he hated it.

"That's good," she said. "Let all the anger out."

He shook his head, unable to release the anger. "Nay."

"I'm sorry she hurt you," Erin whispered.

Brodie had thought he and Elspeth would have a wonderful life together when they married. They would have children and lead the clan. Maybe travel sometimes by galley and see other places. He'd wanted to show her.... "It doesna matter. My love for her is dead. She's in the past, another life. I am no' the same person now."

"Can you forgive her and move on?"

He must have, for he was not thinking of Elspeth anymore. In truth, he did not give a fig about her at the moment. All he could focus on was the shape of Erin's lips, pink, parted, lush. And her big blue eyes, dark but sparkling in the torchlight. So intent upon him. She looked at him as no other woman ever had, as if she saw the real Brodie. No pretending. No shyness or fear. To her, he was not a chieftain. Not a selkie. He was just a man. And she understood what it was not to fully belong to the family or group you were supposed to. She did not demand things from him or expect anything of him, except when it came to their intimate encounters. Then all was effortless. Such overwhelming pleasure.

"Mind if I join you?" she asked.

If she did, he could not promise to keep his hands to himself. He craved her too intensely. "Nay. Careful, there are loose stones on the bottom."

She removed her clothing and his gaze consumed the beauty of her slender, naked curves. His erection pulsated and lust seared him deep inside.

Lifting a brow, she stared at the water. "You're happy to see me."

He glanced down to find the tip of his cock protruding from the water. "Indeed."

She slid into the hot spring, sank down to her neck and sighed. "This is so nice. Wish I had some of my mango bubble bath."

He did not give a damn about mango bubble bath, whatever in blazes that was. One second more and he would launch himself at her. He swallowed hard and restrained himself.

Rising again with water glistening and streaming down her ivory skin, she waded toward him. Losing control with temptation so near, he yanked her to his chest. She sucked in a sharp breath. Her silky skin against him felt like heaven, soothing to the ache. His greedy cock pressed against her taut lower belly. A moan slipped out before he could prevent it. Hell, he had done a stupid thing and allowed himself to need her.

Her sensual lips brushing his, she teased, then kissed him, wanton and erotic. The kiss turned bonfire hot and he found himself devouring her mouth, unable to get enough. He hugged her tighter, grinding his erection against her. He had to be inside her. Just one more time before she left.

Bittersweet regret stabbed at his gut. But not enough to dissuade his intense arousal.

And then she did something unexpected, placed sweet, hot kisses down his chest, down his abdomen. A tremble of anticipation shook him. Damnation. He thought he would ignite like gunpowder when she took his cock into her mouth. He groaned, watching the head disappear between her sensual lips, then move in and out. She sucked hard and stroked her tongue over the especially sensitive spots. Even her teeth teased him.

"Och." He gently gripped the strands of her hair, unsure whether to hold her in place or pull her away. He could not endure much of this temptation. When she glanced up, her dark blue, aroused eyes meeting his, he almost went off like a canon.

He yanked her up. "I want you," he said against her mouth.

"Yes."

Placing his hands on her arse, he lifted her as she spread her legs, opening herself to him. "Wrap your legs around my waist." His cock strained toward that paradise. He positioned and lowered her, sliding in slowly. He thrust his hips, driving his cock to the hilt with a bit too much enthusiasm.

She gasped, then moaned. "Oh my God, Brodie!"

"Aye," he rasped. Never had a woman felt so good, so tight, hot and wet. Tingles raced through him such as he had never felt before. 'Twas a magic she held over him. "What manner of spell have you cast upon me?" he demanded through clenched teeth as he fucked her deep.

She shook her head, crying out at each thrust. Wild with lust and need.

The sensations drowned out his suspicions and he no longer cared. In that moment, she tightened around him in climax, her arms around his neck, her legs around his waist, and her tight pussy milking him. Och, he could not withstand it. Pleasure pounded through him, through his cock. His seed rushing from him and into her produced an intense bliss such as he had never fathomed.

He heard himself groaning and cursing, but it did not seem like him. He relished her cries in his ear as they rode a wave as intense and violent as one from the ocean. It lifted them together, then all seemed suspended, hovering at the crest of that wave. Finally, he came back to himself, trying to catch his breath, listening to her harsh breathing in his ear.

"Brodie," she whispered. "Wow."

He could say naught. She had turned him speechless. And further, when she sweetly kissed his ear, his neck with such affection, an ache latched onto his chest. Though he did not want to, he withdrew from her and set her to her feet. He dropped his hands to her waist and tried to regain his reasoning ability. His control. For a moment, he forced himself to concentrate on the bubbling hot water flowing around them. But all he wanted to do was yank her against his chest where his heart beat so hard, and never let her go. After a moment's hesitation, he gave up the struggle and drew her tightly into his arms. He brushed his lips and nose against her silky fair hair. She wrapped her slender but strong arms about him.

God, he did cherish her.

After her, he had a sense no other woman would ever satisfy him. No other woman would ever arouse him as she did. So why was he willing to let her go? Because he cared too much to force her to stay. He wished to give her whatever she most desired.

She kissed him tenderly near his collarbone, then laid her head there, her breasts flush against his chest. She made a contented little sound, and he felt he could stay like this forever.

How could that have been the last time for them?

Chapter 10

The fishermen's lantern illuminated the chilly, damp predawn darkness as Brodie helped Erin board the boat. The galley might be large enough to hold a dozen people, she decided. Though ancient-looking, the wooden boat felt solid and sturdy beneath her feet.

A sharp wind off the Atlantic penetrated her clothing, which included a wool blanket and furs. "Brrr." She shivered.

Once he boarded, Brodie took off his wool cloak and wrapped it around her.

"No. You need that."

"I'm no' cold."

How could he not be? She would never understand him.

"Selkies feel no cold at this temperature," he murmured in her ear. His deep, enticing voice in the darkness soothed her, but also made her want to rub up against him and beg him for more seduction. His warm breath against her ear teased her and she recalled vividly the sumptuous erotic things they'd done a few hours ago. He pulled the cloak and hood tighter about her and she relished the gentle way he took care of her. She would miss him, if the wizard's magic worked and she was able to return to the future. Tears burned her eyes and the wind chilled them.

A part of her wondered what would happen if she stayed a few more days, as Shauna had suggested. But she was afraid she might fall completely in love with Brodie in that short time, then like Shauna, be unwilling to leave. Erin couldn't break her promise to her mother to find a cure for cancer and take care of her little sister. Arabella was only eighteen and completely immature, not to mention penniless. Their grandma who'd helped get them through their teens was gone now, too.

Minutes later, four men shoved the boat from the beach, then jumped in and rowed, the waves tossing it gently. The wind had shifted, and the odor of fish was strong. It almost turned her stomach. But she buried her nose in Brodie's cloak, inhaling his sexy, comforting scent.

When he placed an arm around her shoulders, warmth emanated through her. And she felt something more when he held her, something she hadn't felt since she was a child—a sense of safety and belonging. They fit together.

While it was still dark, they arrived on the island where she'd first appeared in this strange world. They disembarked and Brodie carried her through the shallow water to deposit her on dry sand. He returned to the boat and talked for a moment to the fishermen.

Aside from the lantern on the boat, the only light radiated from the moon, stars and the faintest predawn glow at the horizon. Three silhouettes, men wearing kilts, emerged from the cliff shadows. They might be selkies, some of Brodie's friends, for they hastened toward him in the shallow surf. But no, each of them held a drawn sword.

"Brodie!" she yelled. "They have swords!"

He withdrew his own and—

Someone grabbed Erin's arms from behind and flung her to the sand. On impact, her breath whooshed out. *Oh my God, don't pass out.* Drawing in a deep breath, she screamed and kicked, planting her foot hard into one man's groin. When he doubled over, she threw two good punches to another man's face. She tried to scramble away but the first one caught her.

"Dammit! Turn me loose!"

Speaking to each other in Gaelic, they shoved her onto her stomach, bound her hands behind her back, and tied her feet.

"Brodie, help!"

"He canna help you now, lassie." The man threw her over his massive shoulder. She squirmed and kneed his chest. Grunting, he slapped her butt, hard.

"Ouch! You asshole!"

Following behind, his crony laughed. "MacPeter will love having this hellion back."

"MacPeter?" she asked. "You work for that bastard?"

"Shut your filthy mouth, whore! He's my kin."

Oh dear God, what was she going to do? MacPeter wanted to rape her. She would neuter him if he tried it. She was not a proponent of violence, but she had to protect herself and find out where Brodie was.

Upside down, she glanced around and saw they'd tied him up and carried him further along, toward three boats she hadn't noticed before in the edge of the surf. Oh God, Brodie. Was he alive? Conscious? Icy fear paralyzed her. Her captors headed her in the same direction along with two screaming women who had to be selkies. In the distance behind her, swords clashed and men yelled. Why were they doing this?

The man tossed Erin into the boat, slamming her hip and shoulder against the solid wood bottom. The pain almost blinded her, along with the dizziness from being upside down. She held her breath until the pain lessened.

Moments later, she opened her eyes in the dimness. Brodie lay in the same boat, about five feet from her. Something dark—blood—smeared one side of his face. He lay so still and unmoving, a cold fear slithered through her.

"Brodie?"

No response.

A bound and gagged female selkie sat near him.

"Is he alive?" Erin asked.

The female nodded.

Thank goodness. Erin had to free herself so she could help him. With tied hands, she felt behind herself but could locate no piece of metal or wood to saw the ropes against.

A half dozen of MacPeter's clansmen pushed each boat from the shore and into the surf, then hoisted themselves aboard and started paddling. A sudden panic seized her. What if they threw her overboard? She remained quiet and pretended to be semiconscious so as not to provoke their captors while on the ocean. Instead, she studied them to discern who was injured and what kind of weapons they carried. Each had a sheathed sword dangling from his hip, along with knives and daggers secured to their belts. One man held a bundle of spears, while an archer stood guard, his gaze darting about over the ocean.

Another of MacPeter's men was bleeding heavily from a cut on his shoulder. One of the rowers had a shallow slash on his calf. Apparently the male selkies had fought hard. Why were MacPeter's men kidnapping selkie females? Did they see them as less than humans, as animals with no rights? Brodie appeared to be the only male captive on this boat and the only unconscious one. Why? If she knew their motives, she might find a way to stop them.

"Here they come!" the archer yelled, notching an arrow into his bow and letting it fly. More shouts went up in Gaelic. Each man grabbed a spear and held it at the ready. Who was threatening them? When a wave tilted the boat to the side she saw. The animals were coming to their rescue, just as when the witch-shark had chased her and Brodie. Dolphins, orcas, seals, large fish and other marine animals chased them, jumping through the waves. Water splashed all around them in the chaos. Erin couldn't believe the breathtaking spectacle, especially the huge black and white orcas. Clearly, these animals loved the selkies and would risk their lives to protect them.

Stay back, animals! She would just die if one of them got speared.

A hefty animal thumped underneath the boat, lifting and tossing it slightly. Oh crap! If it capsized, she'd be dead. And so would Brodie. MacPeter's men stumbled and some fell into the bottom of the boat. One toppled overboard with a scream. She cringed. They didn't call those beautiful creatures killer whales for nothing.

One of the females who wasn't gagged keened out a loud, high-pitched song. At least Erin assumed it was song, or some kind of ancient, melodic vocal music. It was beautiful, eerie and haunting. Chills dotted her skin.

All the men halted and stared at her, and when she finished, nothing but the waves and the creaking boat made a sound. The animals were gone. She must have communicated with them.

The leader of MacPeter's men yelled a command in Gaelic. Several men sat and began rowing furiously again.

When the dawn light grew brighter, she saw that Brodie's head injury had stopped bleeding and no blood pooled near him. She was relieved that his chest rose and fell with each breath.

Her arms were numb because she was lying on them, her hands crushed beneath her butt. She needed to shift position but didn't want to draw attention.

A short time later, with much shouting from the men, they approached a shore that looked unfamiliar to her. Steep cliffs and small sections of sandy beaches. The castle at the top was not Farspag. It had to be Dunwield, MacPeter's castle, though she'd never seen it from this side.

Once they'd dragged the boat into the shallows, the men hoisted the female captives onto their shoulders and carried them, one by one, to dry land. Two men lugged Brodie between them. And another man threw Erin over his shoulder, almost knocking the breath from her lungs. Her stomach ached. He groped her butt through her clothing. Ugh! He stank worse than week-old dead fish. But at the moment, stench was the least of her worries. Once at the base of a cliff, he set her onto her feet and cut the rope binding her ankles. She should kick him in the teeth and run like hell, but her hands were still tied and she couldn't leave Brodie.

"Walk!" the grizzled man yelled into her face. His breath was worse than his body odor.

Ten female selkies lined up in front of her. The men with swords prodded them up the narrow trail toward the ancient, dreary-looking castle at the top.

"Brodie, wake up," Erin said.

A couple of hours after their arrival, they all waited in two dank dungeon cells with only a smoking torch in the corridor providing wavy, dim light. Iron bars separated the long row of cells. Erin was imprisoned with several female selkies, and Brodie lay in his cell alone. Erin and the rest of the women had been untied, but Brodie hadn't.

He stirred and muttered slurred words.

"Brodie? Are you okay?"

He moaned and moved his head.

Erin wished she could touch him, smooth his hair back and get him some medical help. Damn that barbaric MacPeter.

"You have to be okay, Brodie. Please." She sat on her knees, watching him through the bars.

"Erin?"

"Yes."

He opened his eyes. "Where are we?"

"MacPeter's dungeon."

"God's bones." He sat up, though this was difficult with his hands secured behind his back. "What the devil did they do to me?"

"Hit you on the head. Are you dizzy?"

"Aye." He blinked as if trying to focus. "Who's in there with you?"

"Several selkie women. I don't know their names."

"MacPeter was the one kidnapping them? Hell. We have to get out of here."

A distant door slammed and several heavy footsteps approached. Erin held her breath, afraid to imagine what would happen next.

Wilona, in her youthful guise, strode along the passage wearing a flowing green gown and carrying a candle. Three of MacPeter's henchmen followed her. She stopped at Brodie's cell.

"Ooh, the poor laddie," she taunted. "See what you get for betraying me with that whore?"

"You bitch!" he pronounced between clenched teeth as he forced himself to stand. "You betrayed the selkies and sent MacPeter after them."

Erin wanted to yell curses at Wilona and help ease Brodie's obvious pain.

"Aye, well, there were too many females around. When it comes to men, I'm a wee selfish." Wilona chuckled. "And I do enjoy those virile, handsome selkie men."

"You will get what's coming to you," Brodie promised.

"Of course. I shall have everything I desire." She turned to the guards. "Take them to the great hall."

"Why?" Brodie asked. "What are you and MacPeter planning?"

"'Tis a surprise, my sweet."

Ten minutes later, Erin stood beside Brodie, still bound, and the female selkies in the malodorous great hall, guards at their backs. Erin was thankful that they hadn't tied her hands again. She must find a way to free the prisoners.

MacPeter sat at his elevated table littered with bones and meal remains. His beard equally littered with crumbs, he beamed a satisfied smile at them. "Young Brodie, 'tis too bad you showed up on the isle when you did. I have no choice but to relieve you of your head."

Erin almost choked upon hearing that last word. She latched her hand on Brodie's arm. What the hell was he talking about, execution? Icy prickles raced over her skin. Brodie's jaw was clenched tight and his eyes narrowed as if, despite his bound hands, he was ready to kill MacPeter.

"Nay!" Wilona said. "He is mine."

"Humph. You canna control him, witch. And I willna have anyone ken about my selkie wench plunder."

"Who would believe him? Selkies dinna really exist. At least, that's what most folks believe."

"Aye, but without their sealskins, they look human. I wouldna have others think I am abducting women either." MacPeter shook his head. "Brodie has caused me naught but trouble. I want him out of my way."

"If you kill Brodie, I shall kill the white-haired whore you are so fond of." Wilona glared at Erin.

Erin could scarcely breathe. How were they going to escape these two maniacs?

MacPeter laughed, then whispered into the ear of one of his men. The man nodded and strode away. "Stand back!" MacPeter commanded everyone.

Now what? Erin squeezed Brodie's forearm. If MacPeter tried to kill him, she'd strangle the bastard with her bare hands.

Much shuffling and murmuring ensued among MacPeter's clan. One of MacPeter's guards withdrew his sword and strode toward her.

"Oh shit," she muttered. Maybe she could surprise him with a drop-kick to his groin and he'd lose his grip on the weapon.

Brodie stepped in front of her. "You willna harm the lady," he commanded.

"Nay, I willna," the guard said.

"Step away," MacPeter ordered Brodie.

Erin peered around Brodie, and the guard offered her the basket-hilt of his broadsword.

"What the hell?" she whispered, not hesitating to accept the deadly looking weapon. This was their ticket out.

She grinned at Brodie, but he merely frowned, his confused gaze darting to MacPeter.

Another guard gave Wilona a similar sword and pushed her toward the center of the floor.

"This shall be fine entertainment," MacPeter said.

What? They wanted her and Wilona to duel with swords?

"Nay!" Brodie roared.

"Shh. I can do this," Erin whispered to him, then turned to MacPeter. "If I win, all of us go free—Brodie, all the female selkies and me."

"Aye." MacPeter laughed, his belly jiggling.

"Do I have your word of honor?"

"Indeed, my lady." But his malicious grin said his every word was a lie. And, of course, he had no honor.

Erin didn't care. She would win, dammit! Never had she been more determined.

"Fire sweet, fire red, warm his heart and turn his head," Wilona murmured in English, along with words Erin couldn't understand while they circled each other, swords at the ready.

Erin tried to quickly get a feel for the basket-hilt sword, which was much heavier than the foil she'd used for fencing.

When Wilona raised her arms to continue the chant, Erin lunged, slicing the blade through her sleeve. Blood appeared, seeping dark through the green fabric. Wilona spun away at superhuman speed and disappeared.

"Erin!" Brodie yelled. "Behind you."

Erin whirled to face Wilona, her evil grin and her blade, and parried just in time, knocking the sword tip away. But it returned again and again, and sliced the edge of her hand. Erin jumped back.

Wilona laughed and Erin, ignoring the stinging pain, charged forward in a fleche move, hoping to catch her off guard. Wilona stumbled back and Erin grasped the wrist of her sword arm. They fell, Erin on top, and Wilona's sword clattered away.

"I win!" Erin said.

More strange words poured from Wilona's mouth, then she screamed and yanked her injured arm away. Erin glanced down to see blood dripping from her own hand into Wilona's wound. Damn, she had to stop the bleeding and apply pressure. She rose and shrank back toward Brodie. This place was full of germs. She needed strong whisky to clean her cut.

Wilona writhed upon the floor, then fell silent and still. And she was no longer in her youthful form. How could she have died from such a shallow wound?

"Nay! She canna be dead!" MacPeter dropped to the floor and held Wilona in his arms. "My love, wake up."

"Get off me!" Wilona grumbled, shoving at him.

"Thanks be to God, you're alive," he gushed.

"Aye. Let me up, you rank beast."

"I'll carry you." And MacPeter proceeded to do so.

"Release me!"

"You shall live in my bedchamber from now on, my bonny lass. I'm hard with wanting you."

"What about us? Are you releasing us as you promised?" Erin called.

"Aye. Leave! Get out of my sight, all of you." MacPeter proceeded up the stairs with his prize.

Wilona raised her arms and chanted more unusual phrases, but they had no effect on MacPeter or anyone else.

"You caused her to lose her magical powers," Brodie said in Erin's ear as one of the guards cut the ropes from his wrists.

"How?"

His hands free, he tore off one of his shirt sleeves and wrapped it around her hand. "Your blood dripped into her wound. I have heard of this but didna ken 'twas true. The blood of a kind, good and benevolent person can cause a witch's dark powers to vanish if that blood enters their body."

"Kinda weird and gory."

"Come. We must leave before MacPeter changes his mind." Taking her hand, Brodie led her out the entry door and down the steps outside, behind the two dozen or more female selkies who'd been captured over the past several days.

Weak sunlight filtered through the heavy clouds, revealing piles of horse dung littering the cobblestone-paved barmkin they crossed.

"I'll have one of the selkies apply a healing balm to your hand once we are back at Ròncreag Isle," he said. "I'm proud of you for besting Wilona. You are a skilled swordswoman."

"Thanks. What was up with MacPeter?" Erin said as they passed through the gates. "He was acting strange."

Brodie grinned, which momentarily distracted Erin. It was such an unusual expression for him to wear. "During the swordplay, did you hear Wilona's words? She was casting a love spell."

The gates clanged shut behind them and they headed down a trail toward the shore. "So, she wanted MacPeter to fall in love with her?" Erin grimaced.

"Nay, I think it was directed at me. But it missed and struck MacPeter."

"Ah. Thank God you didn't go all moon-eyed and carry her upstairs. She's finally getting what she deserves—a lifetime of sex with Stinky MacPeter."

Brodie chuckled. Once they reached the edge of the cliff overlooking the ocean, he stopped and turned her to face him. "Erin, if you wish to stay here, in this time, 'twill be safe now."

The look in his soulful midnight eyes made her feel as if her legs had been knocked from beneath her. Her throat tightened, and for a long moment she couldn't speak.

"I can't." She forced the words out. "I have to return to the future."

Chapter 11

When Erin and Brodie arrived at Ròncreag Isle with all the female selkies who had been kidnapped, dozens of excited seals scuttled along the shore and splashed into the water to greet them at the galleys. What a beautiful and magical place, Erin thought. The distant gray islands and mainland in the evening mist were breathtaking. She might grow to love it here, but this wasn't her home. Brodie almost made her feel she could belong. She certainly felt closer to him than she had to any other man, or to anyone, for a long time.

But her true home was in the twenty-first century, and hopefully his wizard would help her return.

Brodie took her hand and led her away from the tiny beach of the protected inlet and up a steep rocky pathway to a high grassy area. "We have no horses here on the isle," he said. "We must walk to the wizard's home. And I suspect he will have the best of healers there to look at your hand."

"Okay. What about your head injury?"

"It no longer pains me. Selkies heal quickly."

She was very much aware of his dismal mood while they walked. She wanted to cry. Instead, she focused on the feel of Brodie's warm hand around hers and how confidently he led her. Thank God, he didn't make it even harder on her by begging her to stay.

An hour later, they approached a large cave higher up on a cliff. She knew she would never forget this moment—the sound of the waves crashing on shore far in the distance, sea gulls and other birds calling. The frigid wind off the ocean was chilling in the dusk, but she always felt cozy and warm when Brodie touched her.

They entered the large dark cave. Torches flamed on the walls here and there.

A guard strode forth, halted in their path and spoke to Brodie in Gaelic.

"We have come to speak with Muirfinn," Brodie told him in English. "Erin has traveled through time and wishes to return to her home. We seek Muirfinn's magic."

"Wait here." The guard disappeared into the cave passage.

Erin's stomach gnawed. "I'm nervous," she whispered. "How does this magic work?"

"I dinna ken. 'Tis a closely guarded secret even I am no' privy to."

"Have you met this wizard before?"

"Aye. He is an honorable and wise selkie."

The guard returned minutes later. "Muirfinn will see you now."

Brodie led her deeper into the cave, into a well-lit but small cavern. A fire burned in a pit the center of the floor.

A gorgeous and noble-looking man with long dark hair and neatly trimmed dark beard waited there. He wore a shimmering blue silk robe with pearls down the front.

Brodie made introductions and the man bowed.

This was the wizard, Muirfinn? She'd imagined another Finnian.

"You are injured, my lady?" He motioned them toward a sitting area near the fire.

Erin nodded.

"Please bring wine to refresh our guests, Rhona, and the healing balm," he said to a female selkie who waited in another doorway. She hastened away.

Brodie explained how Erin had come from the future through magic and wished to return.

"Selkie magic is a closely guarded secret," Muirfinn said, his dark eyes deadly serious. "We have ne'er shared it with humans. I must have your word you will not reveal the secret to anyone."

"Of course," Brodie said. "You have my word."

"I promise not to tell anyone," Erin said. "Will it hurt?"

"I dinna ken. I have ne'er traveled through time." Muirfinn smiled. "But 'haps I should like to try it sometime."

The beautiful, dark-haired Rhona served the wine in jewel-encrusted silver goblets fit for a king. She then unwrapped Erin's hand and applied an aromatic salve that soothed and cooled the pain. The cut had stopped bleeding.

"Thank you. That feels better."

Rhona gave a brief bow and left.

"How does selkie magic work?" Erin asked the wizard. Would he simply chant a spell the way Wilona had? Or would he touch her with a magic wand?

"Selkie magic is sex magic," Muirfinn said with grave seriousness.

Okay, that was something she hadn't expected. A fit of nerves seized her, making her hand shake as she took a small sip of wine. "What do you mean, sex magic?"

"Sometimes selkies want to accomplish more with their sexual unions than pleasure," he went on, looking more like a sex god than a wizard, with all those muscles. "Sometimes they wish to work a magic spell, or conceive a child. That is when they seek my help."

Selkies needed his magical help to conceive? How bizarre.

"Traveling through time will require a strong magic." His eyes seemed to gaze through her soul. "And a strong arousal. 'Twill depend upon you and

Brodie."

"We will—um—have sex? Brodie and I?" Erin asked.

"Aye. Though you share a profound bond, you are opposites in many ways. Extreme opposites generate strong attraction. This bodes well for the magic to work."

Erin's heart thumped hard. "How, exactly, does it work?"

"I will explain the intricacies of the ritual later." Muirfinn frowned, studying her. "Are you certain you wish to leave this time period and Brodie?"

No, she didn't wish to. "I have to."

When he continued to stare at her with such intensity, it seemed he was reading her mind. "I hope your soul and Brodie's will come together again in the future. 'Haps in another lifetime."

Erin's throat ached. How could she wait a lifetime to be with Brodie again?

"'Tis your decision," Muirfinn said calmly and sat back, releasing her from his powerful scrutiny. "When you are both ready, come into the ritual chamber." He motioned toward a curtained doorway, then proceeded through himself.

"Oh my God," Erin whispered. She guzzled the last of her wine, hoping it would make her pass out.

Brodie stood and waited. "Are you ready?"

No. But she forced herself to be. She couldn't look at him for fear she would burst into tears. Carefully, she placed her goblet on a small table, stalling, she knew. Gathering her courage, she rose.

Brodie took her hand and led her toward the doorway. She savored the hot, rough texture of his hand. Abruptly he pulled her aside, into a dark alcove and into his arms, tight against the hard muscles of his chest. His embrace was strong and secure. And for the longest moment, it seemed he clung to her desperately.

This was the end. This was goodbye.

But he said nothing.

"I wish…." What could she say? *I wish I could stay. I wish my chest didn't ache when I think of leaving you. I wish you could come with me.*

"Shh. There is no need to speak," he said against her hair. "But know I want to give you what you wish for most. I would ne'er ask you to stay where you dinna want to."

"It isn't that I don't want to. It is that I can't."

"Aye. 'Tis the way of things."

She stroked his back, realizing fully that this might be the last time she could hold him. She might never know all his thoughts or the turmoil that went on inside him, but she felt it and sensed it just beneath the surface. Maybe it was best he refused to share the most hidden parts of his soul with her.

He drew back a little. "Erin, I have enjoyed our time together. And I hope you will remember it fondly."

"Of course." She looked into his shadowed face but could not discern the expression of his eyes. "You're amazing, Brodie. No matter what anyone says, you're an awesome man. And you'll be a great leader of your people."

With warm, rough fingertips, he stroked her cheek in a caress so gentle it almost broke her heart. Then he drew her closer and kissed her lips, first tenderly, then with fierce possession and erotic heat as his tongue teased hers. Her body warmed, growing moist and aching for him.

He pulled back. "You must mentally and physically prepare yourself for what we will do inside, for we will not be alone."

Not be alone? Oh crap.

Having sex with Brodie was certainly no hardship. But considering that five other scantily clad people—Muirfinn and four female selkies—were present in this torch-lit cavern with Erin, chances were good Brodie had been right. They wouldn't be having sex in private.

"Prepare her," Muirfinn told his female assistants.

What did that mean? Erin glanced at Brodie, and he gave a slight nod. Trusting him that this was safe, she followed the four female selkies behind a wide screen of red silk. Steam rose from a large hot spring in the floor.

"What kind of preparations are we talking about here?" Erin whispered.

"We will remove clothing, then bathe with oil of heather," one said in halting English along with some Gaelic words.

Well, of course. It was some kind of sex ritual, so naturally nudity was expected. And from what she'd seen—and smelled—the selkies valued cleanliness.

They quickly removed their clothing and stepped into the hot spring pool. These women were all dark-haired, dark-eyed and olive-skinned, as most of the selkies were, and their bodies voluptuous and beautiful. Erin knew she looked skinny and pale in comparison, but tried not to be self-conscious about it.

Once they'd bathed in the sweetly fragrant oil of heather and dried off, Rhona bowed to her. "Come."

Erin followed her to the main room again, which was now empty.

"Lie." The females helped her onto a dais covered by a white linen sheet. "Calm." Rhona whispered to her. "Feel desire,"

"Right." Were these people nuts? Desire wasn't something she could turn on and off with the flick of a switch. Nerves seized Erin's stomach. Performance anxiety. She felt like a sacrificial virgin. Well, she was no virgin, but still… what would happen? She almost asked but decided she'd rather not know.

"Where's Brodie?" she asked.

"Behind screen." Rhona pointed to the opposite side of the room.

"Okay." Erin had to relax and feel arousal for this to work, or so they said. Closing her eyes, she imagined Brodie undressing and bathing behind the screen. She imagined his amazing body and recalled his scrumptious kiss of a few minutes ago.

Movement close by distracted her and she opened her eyes. The nude females stood beside her, one at each of her legs and arms. Muirfinn waited a short distance away, also naked. His sculpted muscles were impressive. And like the other naked male selkies she'd seen, he was well endowed. His cock appeared to be swelling and inching upward by the second.

"Rhona." He bowed and held out his hand.

The female smiled and hurried to him. Muirfinn took her mouth in an extended erotic kiss and gently fondled her breast, tweaking the nipple. Moaning, Rhona stroked his huge cock, now standing at attention. Then she dropped to her knees and took him into her mouth, stroking and sucking as if he were the most delicious thing on earth. Wow, they were hot together. Erin averted her gaze and stared toward her feet instead.

"Must watch," the female to her right said. "They perform… your pleasure."

What? Was she serious? Erin inched her gaze back to the two. Rhona was now standing upright again, practically passing out with arousal and begging for it. Muirfinn lifted her into his arms. She wrapped her legs around his waist and he slid his impressive cock up into her. Rhona cried out, her head thrown back as she rode him. His hands on her butt, he lifted her, thrusting up into her in a highly arousing display. Erin ached, getting wetter by the second, but kept her thighs pressed together.

Given their frenzied movements and moans, it appeared they might climax at any moment. But he withdrew and set her on her feet again. She could hardly stand. He smiled and teased her while she gasped for breath. He helped her back to Erin's side, then led another giggling female toward the center of the room.

He was soon fondling her, kissing her, and stroking her curvy body. He turned her back to him, bent her over and drove his massive, primed cock inside her. Which she gladly accepted with arched back and eager gasps.

The man had a harem!

Both of them moaned, continuing the thrusting for several minutes. It seemed the female was almost ready to climax when he withdrew and repeated the process with the third and fourth female selkies. The man must be made of iron to have so much sex and not come.

By the end of this "performance," Erin was drenched and almost desperate for sex herself. The females stood at each of her limbs again, and Muirfinn by her side. The arousing, musky scent of sex was all around her. Sexual energy pulsated in the air. He said something to the females in Gaelic and the two by her thighs spread her legs.

"What—!"

"Easy," he told her in a calm voice. "We ne'er do anything you dinna wish. But I must see that you are ready for the ritual and for Brodie. Do you agree?"

Unsure how he would do this, Erin nodded and held her breath.

Muirfinn reached a hand down, spread her sex lips and stroked a finger slowly over her sensitized clit and her wet inner lips. Gasping, she almost jumped out of her skin. His finger felt fantastic. And again he stroked her. She moaned.

"Aye. She is ready." He took his hand away and moved to stand a foot or so above her head. "Brodie. Come."

Fighting back her arousal, she lifted her head. Naked, Brodie walked slowly toward them. He did not appear fully aroused yet, perhaps only halfway. But as he stood between her legs, his gaze moving over her, his cock grew erect. She focused on his eyes because she could see his soul there, his emotions, revealed to her now more clearly than ever before.

"Now, we begin. Hold her down," Muirfinn said.

"What? You don't need to—"

"Shh." Brodie said. "'Tis part of the ritual. Relax, Erin. I shall make it good for you."

Well, of course. He always did.

The females did as Muirfinn asked. Two held her arms and two held her legs wide apart. Brodie stepped closer, placed his hands at her hips and tugged her toward the edge of the dais. The female to his right took his huge cock into her hand, guided it toward Erin, and placed the tip at her opening. She didn't want anyone else touching his cock, but the move did send arousal sizzling through her veins. Her back arched involuntarily.

Looking into her eyes, Brodie thrust his hips, sliding into her a few inches. Oh, he felt extraordinary. And she was so horny, she was ready to beg for it.

Brodie's body was a sculpted work of art, and she never wanted to have sex with anyone but him. She was addicted to the way he looked at her with dark wickedness blended with soulful emotion.

"Traveling through time is a difficult thing to conjure," Muirfinn said. "Instead of the ninety-nine strokes required for a normal ritual, Brodie, you will need to use twice that number, 198 strokes. Then both of you climax at the same time while thinking of the intention, sending Erin back to her time."

What? Was he insane? She could never last that long. She was already on edge.

"Count them, Brodie."

"Aye," he breathed. His pace was quick and deep.

"We also will focus on the intention," Muirfinn said, placing his palms lightly against either side of Erin's head, preventing her from moving it. Nor could she move her arms or legs, held in place by the females. She couldn't believe it when her arousal climbed even higher. Suddenly she knew why— arousal was flowing into her from the selkies. Was that why Muirfinn had brought all of them almost to climax, then stopped?

Erin felt wetter than she'd ever been and Brodie's cock glided easily in and out. Each thrust was a sexual feast as he forced apart her pussy walls, stroking in a most pleasurable way. Soon sweat glistened on his face and chest, but he did not take his gaze from hers.

"Think of the future, Erin. Think of what you want," Brodie said. He clenched his jaw hard as if barely stopping himself from climaxing. "Focus on it, Erin. Think of your home. Your time."

She nodded.

He closed his eyes, sucked in a deep breath and said, "One-ninety-five...."

Her orgasm started with a tingle deep inside her. It spread outward. She closed her eyes to better feel it. A wet finger stroked her clit. It was all she could take. She didn't know if it was too soon, but she started coming and forced herself to think of the future, her home. Brodie thrust harder, pounding into her. Pleasure engulfed her in spiral after spiral of ecstasy and wrung out her whole body.

Shoved to the hilt, Brodie dropped over her, his face against hers. The heat of his cum drenched her, filling her. He growled, deep in his chest. "I love you, Erin. I love you," he whispered.

"I love—" A pain lanced through her head, turning her words into a scream.

Chapter 12

An exploding force of energy propelled Brodie back from the dais and away from Erin. The bright light that had near blinded him disappeared. So had Erin. He glanced around, searching. The selkies remained, but Erin was gone.

"The magic worked!" Muirfinn said. "She is returned to the future."

Brodie couldn't respond.

Pain and loneliness filled him. His heart felt torn from his chest. He fell to his knees before the empty dais.

God, what had he done? Sending her away, the only woman he would ever love.

He wanted to curse all the fates. With the hard stone biting into his forehead, he surrendered, allowing the pain to rip through him with a vengeance. A roar of rage escaped his throat.

A while later, he emerged from what seemed a maelstrom of pain and looked around the empty, dim cave at the torches. The wizard and his assistants had gone. Something was wrong. Brodie couldn't see very well. The dark corners were indeed dark. He pushed himself up and went outside. Damnation it was cold, the wind far more icy than normal. How dark it was, even with the moon shining.

"Saints. I am no longer a selkie," he whispered. "The curse is ended." He did not care.

He returned to the cave in search of his plaid and shirt. Naught mattered without Erin to share it. Once he was dressed, he picked up his cloak and the furs she'd worn and put them on himself. He caught a whiff of her scent and loneliness floored him, sucking away his breath. He forced air into his constricted chest.

How could he have sent her back?

Nay, it was the right thing. It was what she wanted.

He strode outside and along the cliff's path to the windy beach, where he found a rock to sit on to wait for morn. And a boat to take him home. Ròncreag Isle was no longer his home. Mayhap it had never been. The curse and his time as a selkie now seemed like a long dream. Mayhap he had never truly belonged with the selkies, no matter how much they accepted him.

Erin had broken the curse and given him back his life. His real self.

"Erin, I thank you," he whispered, gazing up at the bright stars. "Where are you? When are you?" He imagined her in some future location, four hundred years distant, though he knew not how it would look. She would be glad to have her regular life back.

A short time later, dawn gleamed at the horizon. A light shone on the ocean from an approaching galley. Who was that? Not MacPeter returning, surely.

Brodie stood by the water, waiting. Once the galley entered the shallows, two kilted men jumped off and tugged the boat closer to shore.

"Gavin and Torr," he muttered, watching them splash through the surf.

"Are you well, Brodie?" Torr called.

"Aye."

"Finnian sent us," Gavin said, stopping beside him. "He said your curse is broken and you might need a way home."

"Aye, 'tis true."

"How do you feel? Where is the lass?"

Brodie could not rightly say how he felt. Numb? "Erin is gone. To the future."

"How the hell did that happen?" Gavin demanded.

"I sent her. Selkie magic."

"Why in blazes would you do that?"

"'Twas what she wanted most. I would not keep her here against her will."

Gavin stamped about, muttering curses.

"But your curse is broken," Torr said, frowning. "That doesna happen without the exchange of love."

"Aye. It all happened at near the same time."

"I can imagine how you must feel, my friend," Gavin said. "I tried to convince Shauna to go to the future to save her own life. 'Twas what she'd wanted from the first. But in the end, she wouldna do it. If she had, I know 'twould have been devastating for me."

Brodie nodded. He sure as hell felt devastated himself. But he could not focus on that now or it would suffocate him. He strode toward the galley. "Let us go." He did not wait for his two friends, but waded through the icy sea water.

Erin bolted upright in bed. The pain that had shot through her head slid away as did the waning pleasure from her orgasm. *Where am I?* She was no longer on the dais under Brodie. Squinting through the dimness, she saw she was in the inn room where she'd been when she time-traveled.

"Brodie?" A feeling of silent emptiness filled her. He was gone. Long gone. Four hundred years in the past. In essence, he was dead. Her throat closed and she could not breathe.

"Oh God, what have I done?"

Tears ran down her face and she sucked in a great gulp of air. Maybe she hadn't time-traveled. But when she saw the glowing red numbers on the digital clock, she knew she had.

"I'll never see Brodie again," she whispered, covering her head with the pillow. It was her own fault. This was what she'd chosen, to leave him.

She'd always been good at controlling her emotions, but now they would not be restrained. Though she was crying like a heartbroken child, she didn't care. She'd just given up the best thing that had ever happened to her. But she'd had to. She must keep the promises she'd made.

Minutes later, she pushed herself up and looked out the window at the dawn light glowing over the Scottish landscape.

This was what she'd wanted. Right? Her old life back. To be with her sister. Following her dream of becoming a doctor. A plane to take her home.

After a trip to the bathroom, she searched the cold room. Nothing. Her luggage and clothes were gone. How much time had passed since she'd left?

She wrapped a cool white sheet around her naked body and loneliness threatened to drown her. She missed Brodie and his heat and arms surrounding her. Almost in a daze, she went out into the carpeted hallway and downstairs to the lobby.

"May I help you?" The exhausted-looking man with bushy hair at the inn's front desk eyed her sheet curiously.

"When did Kincaid's group leave?"

"Kincaid? That fancy clothes designer?" He asked in a thick Scottish accent. "About a week ago. Say, are you the model that went missing?"

"Yes."

"Where have you been, lass? We searched everywhere."

"You wouldn't believe me if I told you. Did my group by any chance leave my luggage?"

"Aye. 'Tis in our office. I'll get it."

Thank God! At least she'd have her clothing, passport, and the things she needed to get home.

But she wouldn't have the person she needed most.

A month later, Erin lay in bed in her tiny apartment in New York. Lethargy weighed her arms and legs. It was around noon and she didn't have the energy or motivation to get up. God, what was wrong with her? She'd never felt so miserable in her life. Her career was fine. She had jobs booked for the next few months and income flowing in so she could save for medical school. Her sister was doing well at college. But Erin felt her life was over.

Why couldn't Brodie be here? Why hadn't he time-traveled with her? They'd been physically connected, after all. It wasn't meant to be. He was the leader of his clan and they needed him. He was where he belonged. But she suddenly felt she didn't belong in her own life. Maybe because she'd discovered her sister wasn't as immature and helpless as she'd thought. She'd become more independent in the last few months and had a good job to support herself. And what about Erin's dream to become a doctor? Even without formal training, maybe she could become a healer and save lives in 1621.

Was it possible to go back to the past?

Erin jumped out of bed and paced. What if she was too late? What if Brodie had already married someone else?

"Oh God." Slumping on the chair, she decided to call her lawyer.

Two weeks later, Erin arrived at the Highland Inn at Dunmory where all the craziness had happened. In her own way, she'd said goodbye to her sister and left her all of her worldly possessions, though she would not know this for a while. Because, who knew? Erin might not be able to travel to the past again. But with everything in her, she knew she had to try.

Brodie was who she wanted more than anything else in life.

She wheeled her suitcase into the lobby and checked in.

"'Tis you again, lass?" the bushy-haired front desk clerk said.

"Yes. I can't get enough of this place." She grinned.

"A wee bit of the Highland magic has gotten into your blood." He laughed.

"You're right about that."

After leaving her luggage in her room and raiding the mini-bar for three tiny bottles of Farspag whisky, she headed out to walk the short distance to Farspag Tower. The evening was misty, and heavy clouds rolled through the sky. A sharp breeze blew off the Atlantic. On the way north, she'd seen frost and snow on several of the mountains. Winter was definitely here, even though it was supposed to be late fall.

"Oh crap, the castle's probably closed," she muttered, realizing it was already after five. The castle gate was closed but not locked. She pushed through and headed toward the entry door. It opened easily. Inside, the great hall was cold and empty. She couldn't believe she'd dined in this room four centuries ago with a boisterous group of Highlanders.

Her footsteps echoed in the hollow space.

"Anyone here?" She was afraid to say that too loudly, but unsure why. She remembered so clearly sitting at this scarred wooden table and glancing down the length of it toward Brodie. His dark eyes had always heated her from the inside out. Such secrets he hid within himself. He'd loved her. If she could reach him again, would he love her still?

"Brodie?" she whispered, standing still for a moment. Silence. She headed up the spiral stone staircase to the floor above and the bedchamber. She stepped through the open doorway. The old brass key lay on the floor, like an invitation to come home. A chill went through her.

She scooped up the key and warmth flowed into her.

"Oh yes," she whispered. It had to work. She removed the tiny bottles of Farspag whisky from her pocket, sat on the ancient high bed and took a sip. She drank a whole bottle and nothing happened. Oh darn, she wasn't supposed to do this here. She was supposed to be at the inn. No, it would work. It had to. Now it was raining outside, and she didn't want to take time to go back to the inn.

She opened the second bottle and drank, the whisky scalding her throat. "Ack!" She couldn't get used to it. She reclined on the bed and stared at the canopy overhead.

Nothing.

Moments later, she forced down the third bottle. Okay, she was starting to get a major buzz and her veins were burning. She'd be falling-down drunk in a few minutes. Could she get under the covers? How long since they'd been laundered? She pressed her nose against them. They smelled fresh. Keeping her shoes on because she'd need them in the past, she crawled beneath the covers.

"Brodie, where are you?" she whispered. "Come get me. I want to be with you. I love you." She held the key between her palms.

She remembered him so clearly. His seductive eyes. His big warm hands sliding roughly along her skin. His silky dark hair and his powerful body. The memory of their lovemaking was so vivid, arousal radiated through her.

She could almost feel him. Almost.

The sharp pain exploded behind her eyes. She cried out. "Oh God! Brodie?"

The bed shook violently in the darkness and someone else jumped from it. "What the devil?"

"Brodie? Is that you?" Only a dim glow came from the fireplace, and she couldn't see.

"Erin?"

"Yes! Where are you?" Her eyes frantically searched the darkness for his form or movement.

Before the hearth coals, a candle flared to life, illuminating Brodie's face. She'd made it!

He carried the candle to the bedside table.

She crawled to the edge of the bed and flung herself into his arms. "Hold me, Brodie. Oh God, I missed you." The hardness of his chest and his warmth seeped into her. His wonderful masculine scent was home to her.

"Erin?" He embraced her so tightly, he almost crushed her. "Is it truly you?"

"Yes." She pulled back.

He gazed at her in awe, his midnight eyes going a bit glassy. Tentatively, he cupped her face in his palm. "Is this a dream?"

"No. It's real." Her tears trickled down and he brushed them away with his thumb.

She relished the warmth of his hand and stroked her fingertips over his face, the whisker stubble of his jaw and chin.

He swallowed hard. "Why? How?"

"I came back to stay with you." Her throat constricted. "I love you."

He whispered a Gaelic curse, or was it a prayer? "Erin, I love you," he said with a fierceness that thrilled her. He took her face in his hands and kissed her with reverence, tasted her as if he couldn't get enough. "God, I have missed you."

"I missed you, too."

He laid her on the bed and they indulged in a long, thorough kiss that left her craving lots more.

He ran his hand up her leg. "What's this you're wearing?"

"Jeans."

"Take it off." He tugged at the tight denim. "I must have you now."

"Wait." She struggled out of her clothing and flung it all to the floor. Fortunately for her, he was already naked. And aroused.

Within seconds he was inside her. She relished his every powerful thrust and growl of satisfaction. It was a scorching, urgent quickie, and he showed her exactly what making hot, passionate love meant.

"Oh, wow," she whispered afterward.

"Aye." He breathed hard, lay back on his pillow and pulled her close. "Saints, I'm glad you're here, lass," he whispered against her forehead. "I didna think I could go on."

"Well, I couldn't go on. That's why I had to return to you." She laid her head on his hard shoulder. "What have you been doing since I left? Partying with the selkies?"

"Nay, I'm no longer a selkie. The curse is broken, thanks to you, and I've been leading the clan."

"Oh, that's good! I'm so proud of you. Are you enjoying it?"

He shrugged, making her head rock on his shoulder. "I missed you too much to enjoy anything."

She sweetly kissed his prickly jaw.

He faced her and trailed his fingertips over her brows, her cheeks, her lips, while looking into her eyes. "I canna believe you came back, princess. 'Tis my dream come true. What made you change your mind?"

"I was miserable, sad and lonely without you. You are my life."

"You will stay with me, Erin? Forever?" His gaze turned especially intense, as if he were demanding she make a vow, now.

"Yes. Forever."

"Promise you will never leave me again." His voice grew stern and gruff, the fearsome warrior surfacing. And she loved it.

"I promise."

Releasing a breath, he asked, "Will you marry me?"

Her throat was so tight she could hardly answer. "Yes, I will," she whispered.

Holding her tight, he pressed his face against hers and murmured Gaelic words. "I thank you. Lass, you dinna ken how I've yearned for you by my side."

He proceeded to make love to her for the rest of the night. Just as a hot scoundrel should.

About the Author:

Nicole North's erotic romance novellas have been described by reviewers as *"exciting, high octane, captivating, scintillating, sinfully delicious and pure romance."* Her stories contain *"heart and heat, killer love scenes, magic and extraordinary characters."* Her works have finaled in over a dozen writing competitions and won several awards. She is a member of Romance Writers of America and three chapters. She teaches online workshops about various aspects of writing, including sexual tension and how to write great love scenes. Though she has a degree in psychology, writing romance is her first love. She and her husband live in the Southeastern US, but she wishes she lived in the Scottish Highlands at least half the year.

Cox Club

❧✦❦

by Alice Gaines

To My Reader:

The great thing about writing is the ability to portray the world the way it ought to exist. There really ought to be clubs where women can go to fulfill every sensual and sexual fantasy. I've created such a club in this story. Enjoy the fantasy!

Chapter 1

The cab stopped in the absolutely last place you'd expect to find an exclusive sex club. One lone light bulb barely made a dent in the drizzle, but you wouldn't want to see too much in this neighborhood, anyway. Nothing but run-down warehouses, some with forklifts sitting outside. From the peeling paint on others, it appeared they hadn't held any merchandise for years.

The driver looked back over his seat. "You ladies sure you want to get out here?"

"Thank you, yes." Andi Crawford's friend, Carol, fumbled in her purse for a few seconds and then passed the man several twenties. "Keep the change."

He took them briefly and then grunted his approval. "You'll pardon my saying so, but this block don't look safe."

Andi sat in the darkest part of the cab, back between the seat and the rear window. The place *wasn't* safe. In fact, he had no idea how unsafe it was, but not for the reason he thought.

Carol opened the cab door, grabbed Andi's arm, and hauled them both onto the street. She continued holding onto Andi as she closed the door again and the cab drove away. Obviously, she thought Andi would bolt, and she could very well be right. But in this part of town, wearing three inch heels and a short skirt, Andi wasn't going anywhere without the cab.

Why had she let Carol talk her into this?

Oh hell, she knew damned well. She hadn't had an orgasm in six months— except for the ones that woke her up from a dream sometimes. Not since Blake, damn him, anyway.

She scanned the dilapidated building in front of them and found nothing but painted windows and the number 316. "Shouldn't that say sixty-nine, or something equally suggestive?"

"This is the right place. Don't worry about it." Carol searched around in her purse again and pulled out what looked like a credit card, blank except for the magnetized strip. She inserted it in a slot in the door, and when she pulled it out again, the metal slid aside with a soft whoosh.

"Beam me up, Scotty," Andi said.

"It's another world, all right," Carol said. "Come on."

With no place better to go, Andi followed her friend inside. For a moment, they stood in near darkness until Andi's eyes adjusted enough for her to make out soft light up ahead. That turned out to be a reception area complete with a coat check. A man stood behind the counter, naked from the waist up. He had a finely muscled chest with a butterfly tattoo just above one nipple. Not a hair marred his perfection.

As they approached him, Andi became more and more aware of her lack of panties. Carol had insisted, and it seemed deliciously wicked at the time. Now, barelegged and with nothing covering her mound, wicked turned to downright sinful as she approached the man.

Carol took both purses and handed them over to him. "You won't need this. Everything's already paid for. My treat."

Smiling, the man turned to put them in a cubbyhole, and… holy shit… he wasn't just naked above the waist. He wasn't wearing anything at all. He was fully erect and very impressive.

He caught her staring and turned so she could get an even better view. "Your first time?"

She swallowed and nodded.

"Welcome to Cox Club," he said as though he exposed himself to strange women every day. Come to think of it, he probably did, on the job, anyway.

Lord help her, she couldn't look away from him, couldn't even raise her attention to his face. She hadn't seen a tool so beautiful since….

"Hi," she said, although it didn't come out much louder than a whisper.

Carol laughed. "Forgive my friend. She's been sheltered."

He wrapped his fingers around his shaft and pumped. As if it needed to get any bigger. "I'd be happy to… um… broaden your horizons. In fact, someone will take over for me in a few minutes."

"I wouldn't want you to work through your break," she said.

This time, he joined Carol in laughter.

Carol grabbed her arm again. "I'd better get a few drinks in her."

"My name's David, if you change your mind." He reached under the counter and produced two small velvet sacks. Carol took both and handed one to Andi. As they moved off, David called to them. "Enjoy yourselves."

"We will." Carol wiggled her fingers at him over her shoulder and led Andi into what appeared to be the club proper.

The sounds hit her first—the band onstage playing something Latin with a driving beat, the normal buzz of conversation. There was more, though. Almost as an undercurrent. Moans and labored breathing. The sounds of lovemaking, punctuated by an occasional soft cry. It all took her back to her bedroom. Not the one in her apartment, but before that. The one where she'd found satisfaction and then lost it.

Her body responded, her nipples tightening and the inner muscles of her sex constricting. Damn it. She shouldn't react like that. Not to someone else's exhibitionism. She shouldn't be here. Shouldn't want to be here, but she couldn't go back to the emptiness without at least giving this a try.

A waiter came by with a tray of glasses. He wore a starched collar and nothing else except an erection. She grabbed a glass and drank half of the contents in one swallow. Champagne. The good stuff.

"Are they all like that?" she asked.

"Most of them," Carol answered. "You can ask any of them to undress. You can ask any of them to do anything you want."

"Do they like it?"

"It's their job." Carol shrugged. "I guess they couldn't get hard if they didn't."

"It's prostitution."

"We've talked about this. It's pleasure."

Andi downed the rest of her drink. "Right."

"Come on. Let's get you something stronger." Carol found a table near the bar, and the two of them sat, facing the main area of the club. The band had started a slow song, and couples moved together, most twined around each other. A kiss here, a squeeze of a breast there, a woman's hand rubbing over her partner's crotch. The music's rhythm thrummed in Andi's blood—a deep thump-thump that made her heart beat faster. She crossed her legs, but the action only created friction against her clitoris, so she uncrossed them and shifted in her seat.

Another man approached—clothed, thank heaven, although his snug jeans looked as if he'd lived in them long enough to show off every muscle as he moved. He put one hand on the back of each of their chairs and leaned between them. "Can I get something for you ladies?"

"Scotch for me," Carol answered. "Margarita for you, Andi?"

She glanced from her friend to the stranger and immediately lost herself in the brown depths of his eyes.

"Andi," he said. "Sweet name."

"And you're…."

"Jeff," he offered his hand, and she shook it.

"I'm Carol." She tipped her face up, and Jeff bent to kiss her. The two continued for a moment, their lips touching, retreating, and then savoring each other again. Much like the dancing on the floor.

Finally, Jeff straightened. "I'll be right back with what both of you want."

As soon as he was out of earshot, Carol leaned toward Andi's ear. "I bet he will, too."

"Are you going to…. "

"Fuck him? Probably. If he knows how to use this right." She opened the sack and pulled out something shaped like a lipstick. She tore the protective plastic wrap away, and when she turned the bottom, it hummed to life.

"A vibrator?" Andi whispered.

"Small but powerful. You have one, too."

"You're going to let Jeff use that on you?"

Carol set the toy aside and took both of Andi's hands in hers. "Look, hon,

I know how you feel about these things, but I couldn't stand to see you so miserable."

Andi stared down at their intertwined fingers. "I know."

"You're a beautiful woman, approaching your sexual prime. Don't let the best time of your life pass you by."

"I've dated," she answered.

"Slept with anyone?"

"A few."

Carol's hand went to her chin and lifted her head so she'd have to look into her friend's face. "Have any of them satisfied you?"

"It's not easy. I can't seem to open myself up to anyone."

"Since Blake," Carol said.

Andi didn't answer. She had no answer to that.

"He might have been a titan in bed, but he's not the only one in the world," Carol said. "You just need to learn how to relax."

"Easier said than done."

Carol picked up Andi's velvet bag and shoved it into her hand. "Use this. I want you to have at least one orgasm before we leave here tonight."

"What's this about orgasms?" Jeff said as he leaned over their shoulders to put their drinks in front of them.

"You have big ears," Carol said as she slid into the next seat so that Jeff could sit between them.

"The better to… well… something," he said.

"Aren't you having anything?" Carol asked.

"Nope," he said. "I have other things to keep my hands busy."

Carol laughed wickedly and took a sip of her drink. Andi tried her margarita and found it excellent. Tangy and sweet with its rim of salt to set off other flavors. She drank some more, letting the liquor slide down her throat in hopes it might relax her.

"What brings two such lovely ladies to Cox tonight?" Jeff asked.

"It's my friend's coming out party," Carol answered.

Jeff lifted an eyebrow and studied her. "You're new to this?"

"Untouched," she answered.

"We'll be gentle," he said. "Or whatever you prefer."

"Look, Jeff, I…. "

Carol glared at Andi, the warning clear in her eyes. Carol would be pissed if she left now. She'd agreed to this in the first place, and part of her ached to stay and find out if she could finally get some relief from the constant need between her legs.

She ached now, and if she was truthful with herself she knew damned good and well that her clitoris had already hardened. She needed this, damn it, and she couldn't let some nerves stand in her way. She finished her margarita and put the glass on the table. "Would you mind?"

"Another?" He picked up the glass. "I'd be happy to."

"Just tequila this time."

Carol turned and watched as Jeff went back to the bar. When Andi followed her friend's gaze, she got a good look at the man's ass. He had a glorious butt—firm and rounded. The jeans helped the view, faded as they were in just the right places. Her palms itched, imagining how his muscles might feel as they pumped.

"What do you think?" Carol asked.

"He's prime, no doubt about it."

"Would you rather have him or David?" Carol asked. "I can find another guy."

"I'm not going to have sex in the middle of a club," she answered.

"That's what the private rooms are for, dummy. Unless…. " Carol nudged her and motioned with her head toward a table not far away.

When Andi looked, she couldn't help but gasp. A man sat there with a dazed, happy expression on his face. She didn't have to search for the reason. A woman knelt in front of him, her head bobbing as she slid her lips over his cock.

"Is that allowed?" Andi asked.

"If she wants to do it." Carol shrugged. "Some patrons like to do it in the open. Others like to watch."

"Ah, you've spotted them." Jeff set a tumbler of tequila and a small plate with lime slices and salt in front of Andi and sat down. "She's a regular."

Andi took a swig of her tequila and then coughed. "Does she always do that?"

"Sometimes." He leaned close enough that his hot breath blew into her ear. "Does watching make you hot?"

She stared at the couple, much the same way she hadn't been able to look away from David earlier. The table obscured her view a bit, but she could clearly make out part of his shaft moistened by the woman's mouth. After a bit of sucking, she pulled his member from her mouth and then circled the head with her tongue. The man had closed his eyes, and his chest rose and fell raggedly.

"Yes," she said. "It makes me hot."

"Me, too." Jeff nibbled on her earlobe for a moment and then bent to do the same for Carol.

A small shiver went through Andi—partly at the loss of Jeff's body heat, but more at the certainty that she was watching a man become so aroused he'd climax soon.

Sounds came back to her. Memories so vivid she might actually be hearing them. The sweet noises Blake made when he'd satisfied himself that he'd satisfied her and allowed himself to climax. Precious because they'd been so much in love. Still precious, even though she'd deny it to herself if she could manage.

Smiling, Carol turned on her vibrator and handed it to Jeff. He smiled, too as he slipped it under Carol's skirt. Already, a hard ridge of flesh showed under the button fly of his jeans, and Carol sighed and pressed her palm against it.

For a moment, his eyes closed, and when he opened them again, he reached with his free hand to pick up the velvet pouch with Andi's vibrator in it. He held it in front of her in invitation.

"No… uh… thanks," she answered in an unsteady voice, but when he set the vibrator down and then let his hand fall to her knee, she didn't push him away.

When Carol's gaze went fuzzy and out of focus, Andi did her best to find something innocent to look at, but it seemed that every man around her had a visible erection, either barely concealed behind some clothing or not hidden at all. The place was called Cox after all. The whole point was to choose one and enjoy him. No promises and no guilt. She could search the club for the biggest and have that. She could have two or three lovers at once if she wanted. She could certainly allow Jeff's hand to move farther up her inner thigh as it was doing right now, stroking the sensitive flesh and sending the message of what he'd do when he got to the top.

She finished her drink in one swallow and sat there gripping the glass as he came closer and closer to her sex. She shouldn't want this, but, oh God, she did. It had been too long since someone touched her with any expertise at all, and the care he took with teasing her, the deliberate movements of his fingers, told her he knew what he was doing. He could make her come, sitting in this chair. The knowledge made her clitoris throb, and the first discharge of moisture collected between her legs.

He leaned toward her again. "Feeling better?"

"Uh-huh," she managed to croak.

"Good." He touched her, at first a light press against her mound, but then he parted the lips and found her most sensitive flesh.

She shuddered and swallowed a whimper of need.

"Good girl," he whispered. Then he straightened. "Well, ladies, how about a threesome?"

"No," Andi said. Not with Carol looking on. She'd never be able to face her friend again. "I… I can't."

"Still shy," Carol said. "You two go on. I'll find someone else."

"No, you two go. Enjoy yourselves," she answered.

"You're sure?" Carol said, standing.

Just then, the man at the other table climaxed. He started with a low moan that built. Then, his body went stiff, and he jerked a few times. Under the table, the woman pumped his cock until he finished and collapsed against the back of his chair.

"I'm sure," Andi said.

Still holding Carol's vibrator in one hand, Jeff took her other hand and started to lead her away. Carol stopped him long enough to bend over and stare into Andi's face. "Find David."

"Just go on, please."

The two of them left, finally, and Andi sat there, still throbbing from Jeff's touch. What in hell did she do now? She could leave—retrieve her purse and call a cab from her cell phone. As excited as she'd become, walking would probably make matters worse, so she'd have to sit here a while and calm down. If she could. Another waiter with another impressive member came by, so she signaled to him.

"Ma'am?" he said.

She handed him her glass. "Another tequila, please."

"Sure thing."

"The drink only," she added.

"Be right back."

She never drank this much, and she'd probably regret it later, but a few more sips might calm her nerves. While she waited, she picked up the velvet pouch and held it in her fist. If she found one of those private rooms, she could use the vibrator to give herself some relief and then get the hell out of here.

Instead of the waiter, David appeared with her drink—dressed in jeans and a club t-shirt this time. He set it on the table but made no move to join her.

"This place looking any less weird yet?"

"A little. Thanks." If only, he knew what was going on in her pussy and how wet she'd become between her legs, he wouldn't be standing there with a pleasant smile on his face.

"Some of the women here are freaks," he said. "I like the shy ones. Makes me feel all manly to protect them."

"Are you any good at it?"

He laughed. "I haven't had any complaints."

She sipped her tequila slowly. If she concentrated on the liquor she could deal with his face and not dwell on the image of his engorged cock.

"I'm still available, if you've changed you mind," he said.

She couldn't stop herself before she'd glanced at the front of his pants. No sign of a bulge.

"I can manage again, easy, if you're interested," he said.

"Sorry. I shouldn't stare."

He shrugged. "I'm used to it."

She took a little bit more tequila. It warmed her belly and sent a signal lower. She needed a man to ease the fire Jeff had started—hell, the fire she'd brought into the club with her. David was nice. He had the sort of member a woman dreamed of. Carol had spent a lot of money so she could enjoy herself. Why not? Why in hell not?

She set the drink aside. "I think I have changed my mind."

Blake Crawford went from the back entrance of Cox Club up the narrow stairs to the control room. If an employee—now a former employee—hadn't acquired a place like this, he would have never set foot in it at all. He sure as hell wasn't going to risk any of the patrons or staff recognizing him and alerting the media that Crawford Hotels and Entertainment, Inc. owned a sex club, even one as exclusive as this one.

A small man with a balding head and a bit of a paunch over the belt of his slacks greeted him at the top of the stairs, extending his hand. "You the new owner?"

Blake shook. "Temporarily."

"Don't know why Becker sold. This place practically mints money," the man said. "I'm Howard, by the way."

"Blake Crawford."

"I recognized you. Come on in."

The man led Blake into a dimly lit room full of control panels and video screens like the ones used in high-tech security. One showed the front of the building and another the dance floor. Various other monitors captured more remote corners of the club.

"You tape your customers?" he asked.

"We don't tape anyone, but we watch."

"In God's name, why?"

Howard laughed. "You're the first guy ever to ask that. Everyone else just volunteers."

"Seriously, don't the customers complain?"

"They agree to it for their own safety." The man rubbed the back of his neck. "You see, not everyone who comes to work here has the best interests of the clients at heart. We select the staff as carefully as we can, but someday, we might make a mistake."

Blake stared at a screen that showed a couple necking. The man had opened her blouse and was fondling her breast. "What a world."

"We need to make sure all our ladies have the experience they want."

"I'll bet there's a lot of competition for your job," Blake said.

"Nah. Watching gets old really fast. Mostly, I just listen for sounds of distress."

One of the images went black to be replaced by another. A man lying on a bed while a woman rose and sank onto his cock.

"Shut that off, would you?" Blake ordered.

"It's that switch right by your hand."

Blake flipped the little lever and the entrance into the main room came into view. A face registered in his brain. Carol Redman, a friend of Andrea's. A tall blonde stood next to her. Oh, no… it couldn't be. She turned to face the camera. She might have punched him in the gut.

"Damn it all to hell," he said.

"You recognize someone?"

"My wife."

"Your wife goes to sex clubs?" the man said.

"My ex-wife." The ex didn't matter except in a legal sense. Andrea was his wife and would always be. She did not belong here.

"Oh, yeah, I remember," the other man said. "The artist or something."

"Sculptor."

"Your divorce was in the papers."

"Yeah." Without him willing it, his hands closed into fists by his side. "Can you keep a camera on her?"

"Not one, but I can follow on different cameras as she moves around."

"Do it."

Carol led Andrea into the bar and to a table, where they sat. His wife kept looking around her at all the male flesh—the very aroused male flesh—as if it fascinated her and frightened her. It probably did. She had a passionate nature, but she hid it both for personal and professional reasons. Probably none of the men cruising by realized they had the country's most brilliant young sculptor in their presence. Maybe she'd only come to do research in the masculine form for some project.

But, when Carol changed seats to make room for a man to sit between them, Andrea didn't move away. She let him sit there, as close as if they were on a date. Most likely she didn't realize the guy was looking down the front of her dress.

"Who's that man?" Blake asked.

Howard squinted at the screen. "Name's Jeff. He's been with us a while. Nice guy."

Blake would shove his nice guy teeth down his nice guy throat if he did anything to harm his wife. In fact, he ought to do it, anyway, on general principle. But, starting a fight in a place like this would land him in the media in ways that could ruin his company's reputation. So, he just stood there, his gut roiling, and watched another man leer at the only woman he'd ever loved.

"Is he going to….?" Blake asked.

"F… um… have sex with her?"

"Yes. Have sex with her."

"If she wants," Howard answered. "That's what the club's all about."

Don't do it, baby. Don't do it.

The man got up again, only this time he came back with a tumbler of whiskey and a plate. Limes and salt. Not tequila, please. She could never handle straight liquor. She'd do something stupid, and she had the perfect opportunity sitting right next to her.

Thank heaven the guy—Jeff—seemed more interested in Carol. She handed him something that looked like a lipstick, but when he turned the control at the bottom, no red goo appeared.

"What is that thing?" he asked.

"A vibrator," Howard answered. "All the clients get one when they come in."

Sure enough, when Jeff slid it under Carol's skirt her smile turned silly.

"Handy little gizmo," he said.

"Yeah, I guess," Howard said. "Makes the guys' work easier."

"I imagine so."

Down in the club, Jeff picked up a velvet bag and seemed to offer it to Andrea. No doubt promising the same service to her that he was giving her friend. She shook her head but took a healthy drink of her tequila. Or unhealthy, depending on how you looked at it. She didn't stop him, though, when his hand went to her knee and then inched upward. She kept drinking, grasping the glass as if she could crush it between her fingers. After a moment, she jerked in her seat, and her eyes went wide.

The bastard had touched her. Oh, shit. Blake squeezed his eyes closed. He deserved this. For all the times he'd put his own career over hers, for all the demands he'd made, for the final stupid thing that had made her leave him. He'd lost her, and he deserved this.

"You okay?" Howard asked.

He opened his eyes to find Andrea sitting alone. Carol and Jeff were walking away, and Andrea wasn't following.

Good girl. He managed to breathe. "I'm fine."

But then, another man approached her. Sandy haired and pleasant looking. He didn't sit down next to her, but gave her yet another drink. Damn it. He stood, his fingers slipping into the back pockets of his jeans while he talked to her. She sipped this drink slowly and engaged the man in conversation. This time she smiled, seeming at ease with him. Finally, she got up, grabbed the bag with her vibrator in it and walked away with him.

Blake fought the urge to put his fist through the screen. "Follow them."

"Do you really want to watch?" Howard asked.

"No, I don't *want* to watch," he snapped. "Do it."

"Your funeral." Howard flipped a few switches, and a corridor came into view. Without the crowd noises the sound of their footfalls came through clearly, even against the oriental carpeting. The man led Andrea to a door, opened it, and let her cross the threshold before he went in and shut the door behind him.

"Is there a camera in that room?" Blake gritted.

"There's cameras everywhere."

"Turn it on."

For a moment, Howard didn't move. Blake glared at him. "Turn it on."

Howard shrugged, and threw another switch. A smaller enclosure appeared on the screen. A room with little more than a bed and an antique table and chair next to it. All very plush and all very functional.

"I'll leave you alone," Howard said. "I don't really need to watch the boss's wife…. "

"Ex-wife."

"Whatever. If you need anything, call me." With that, Howard left the room, and Blake stood alone with a wall of video screens, one of which showed his wife getting ready to have sex with a stranger.

They didn't talk, thank God. And then, when the man tried to put his lips to hers, she burrowed her nose under his chin and laid a path of caresses along his jaw line and then up to his ear. Great. She wouldn't let him kiss her, but she was going to let him fuck her. *Oh, baby.*

At least, the guy took the hint and didn't press her. He did turn her away from him and pulled her dress over her head in one motion. Her blonde curls feel back in place around her chin and neck as she stood, naked, facing the camera.

In an instant, he grew rock hard, staring at her body after so many months. With her small, firm breasts, she could go braless easily enough, but she always wore panties. Jeff had touched the bare skin of her sex. Felt its softness and heat. Jeff hadn't made her come, though, and neither would this guy. He was the only man who could do that. That couldn't have changed.

The new man pulled her back against him and ground his pelvis into her ass. Unless he was both a fool and blind, he would have noticed its glorious dimensions. Andrea thought herself fat there and her hips too broad. She exercised constantly, but that only managed to make her firm as well as plush. As the stranger closed his eyes in bliss, Blake could sense the pressure of her butt against his erection. Wiggling. Rubbing him because she knew what it did to him.

"You're making me hot, Andi," the guy crooned into her ear.

"Don't talk," she whispered back. "Just touch me."

The man obeyed, now nibbling on her earlobe and his hands went wandering over her body. If Blake's film studio did porn, which it never would, the director could hardly have gotten a better camera angle to show him every inch of her and where the man's fingers went.

As the guy continued, now nibbling on her shoulder, his hands cupped her breasts. After squeezing them for a bit, he tugged at her nipples. She squirmed, but not with pleasure and pushed his hands away.

Don't yank on them, idiot. Gently. She's trying to show you what she wants.

The fool got the message, cupped her breasts and rubbed them until she sighed with delight.

Damn, he shouldn't watch this. She didn't know he was and wouldn't approve. But as much as he hated to admit it, even to himself, the sight of his wife becoming aroused had him throbbing in his pants. He could so easily imagine he was doing it for her and that, in the end, he could sink inside her and feel her muscles clenching around him in orgasm.

She groaned and leaned against the man, so he supported her with one arm around her ribs as his other hand crept downward. Over her belly and below. Into the golden hairs that covered her mound. When he parted the lips there and rubbed, she arched her back, pressing her head against his shoulder.

He'd found her clitoris. Damn it. That should be Blake's fingers, giving her just the right touch until she coated them with her honey. He should be caressing that small bundle of nerves that could make her purr. He should be readying her to take his cock inside of her. Not some stranger.

The man kept working her. First fast, then slow as her gasps turned to whimpers.

"Come for me, honey," he murmured into her ear. "Let go."

"Can't," she cried. "Need to."

"That's okay. There's another way." The man helped her—half-carried her, actually—to the bed, where she lay on her side, her arm tucked beneath her and her head on her elbow. If the lighting were better, he could no doubt make out that the green of her eyes had turned to emerald in arousal.

The man fairly strutted for her as he removed his clothing. There wasn't much of it. He toed out of his loafers, tossed his t-shirt onto the chair, and then unzipped his jeans and bent to remove them. When he kicked those aside, her eyes widened, and she bit her lip in approval. The guy was well endowed with a thick shaft and a prominent head.

"Condom?" she asked.

"Sure thing." He pulled open the drawer, found a foil packet, and unfurled the rubber over his erection. Then, he bent to search his jeans pocket and removed the velvet bag. After carefully setting the vibrator on the corner of the table, he tossed the pouch aside and turned toward the bed. "Let's try doggie style."

Andrea rose on all fours, lifting her spectacular ass into the air. Blake's knees almost buckled as he pictured taking out his stiff member, guiding the head between her lips, and impaling her with one thrust. Though he knew better... knew he was playing with fire... he grasped his shaft through the layers of his clothing and squeezed. If he'd thought to strangle his cock into submission, the action had the exact opposite effect. Agony, but he couldn't stop.

The guy climbed onto the bed, took his position between her legs, and guided his cock between the lips of her pussy. Holy Christ. He was watching another man fuck Andrea—his wife. Divorce be damned, she was his wife. He shouldn't have to stare at another man's member sliding in and out of her precious body. He shouldn't have to listen to her breathing turn to moans. Most of all, he shouldn't have a hard-on becoming so insistent it wouldn't go away without some help.

In that room, wherever it was in this pit, his wife arched her back and moved in time with the man's thrusts. Heating up, the way she did as he'd increased his pace inside her all those times. At least, this guy couldn't see her expressions changing as she became more aroused. How she'd wince when he went really deep. The first time she'd done it, he'd feared he'd hurt her. But then, she'd only begged for more.

One thing the man wouldn't do, though—he wouldn't make her climax. Only Blake had done that. No man before him had, and his heart insisted no other man had since. Even though she moved faster now and her juices coated the condom, she wouldn't come. Not with a stranger, no matter how well endowed.

The guy was straining against her now, holding her hips and slamming into her. He'd climax soon, and the whole ordeal would end. If only Blake didn't feel exactly the same way that man did. Andrea's muscles could grip like a velvet caress. His poor cock ached for that sensation now. Just once more to feel her tense and then explode into orgasm.

"Oh, God," the man groaned. "You gonna come?"

"More," she whispered.

"Ah, shit… so good," the man said.

She moaned. "Vibrator."

The man stopped thrusting long enough to reach to the bedside table and grab the little toy. When he twisted something on the base, it gave out a soft hum. Well, hell, that would do it. She'd gotten hot enough that the machine would finish her off.

Sure enough, when the man circled his arm around her midsection, she stiffened and let out a high, keening cry. He'd found the right spot. After a few more hard thrusts—both of them moving in time with the other—she tipped her head back and shouted.

Deep inside her, she'd be sending powerful spasms all along the length of the man's cock. Impossible, but Blake felt it on his own rod—around his shaft and squeezing at the head.

"Damn it," he growled as he fumbled with his fly. Frantic, he got the zipper down and reached inside, into his shorts, to free his cock. The orgasm hit him like a wall slamming into him. After no more than a few strokes, he came, spraying semen everywhere. It went on and on—so long that when he finally finished, Andrea lay alone on the bed, her partner had already left the room.

Reclining on her back with one hand between her breasts, she looked so vulnerable and alone. He should be there with her, stroking her hair and telling her how beautiful she was. Instead, she rested on a strange bed, having just given herself to a man she'd never seen before and might never see again. What a screwed up world.

He found his handkerchief in the inside pocket of his jacket and cleaned himself up. He'd even managed to hit the control board, so he wiped that up, too and then stuffed his handkerchief back into his pocket and his cock into his pants. The zipper sounded as loud as a buzz saw as it went up.

Finally, he took one more look at his wife before fumbling with the controls to turn the image off.

"Well, Andrea, if you want a sex club, I'll give you one."

Chapter 2

The express delivery arrived at ten. Andi wiped her hands on a towel before she opened the door, but traces of clay still clung to her fingers. The guy presented her with one of those gawd-awful electronic signature screens, and she made enough of a mess with her name that no one could possibly decipher it, then closed the door and leaned against it.

Inside the package, she found nothing more than a business-sized envelope. It held something hard and shaped like a credit card. Sure enough, when she pulled it out, that's what it was, complete with the magnetic strip on one side. Only, nothing on the other side indicated what kind of credit card. What in hell?

She checked the return address on the envelope. 316 Olive Street. Cox Club. Carol had used something similar to get them in the night before.

Okay, friendship was grand, but she had no intention of going back there again, and certainly not on the very next night. She'd needed the sex. She'd had it. David had made it very good. End of story.

She went into the kitchen and set the card and all its packaging on the counter. After pouring herself a cup of coffee, she picked up the phone and dialed Carol.

The machine answered, but it always did, so she let it go to the beep and started talking. "Carol, it's Andi. Did you send me—"

The phone on the other end picked up. "Hi, hon? How you doing?"

Andi took a sip of her coffee and made a face. Old and bitter. "I'm good."

"Only good?" Carol said. "If I'd shtupped that guy David, last night, I'd feel more than good."

"Didn't you have fun with Jeff?"

"That boy has a wicked mouth," Carol answered. "But, don't change the subject. I want to know about you."

"It was great."

"'Great.' That's all you said on the cab drive home. Didn't you have a good time?"

"Of course, I did. It was wonderful." She didn't have to lie about that. David had had all the right equipment, and he'd used it with skill. He'd been almost as good as Blake, and that meant he'd been a hell of a lot better than most men. The fact that she'd fantasized about Blake the entire time had helped things along, too.

"Did you climax?" Carol asked.

"Carol!"

"Well, did you?"

"I did, and it was great. Really, really great," Andi said.

"Oh, honey, I'm so glad. You needed that."

Andi dumped the coffee in the sink and set the mug on the counter. "Did you send me a card to that place? If so, I'd rather you have it. I don't need a repeat performance."

"Not me," Carol answered. "You know I love you, but that place costs an arm and a leg."

Andi picked up the card and searched it for more information. Nothing. "At least, I think that's what this is."

"Andi, what's going on?"

"A messenger delivered something this morning. It looks like the card you used to get into the club last night."

"No clue who sent it?"

She glanced at the envelope where it lay on the counter. "Just the address, 316 Olive."

"That's it."

"Who would send this to me if you didn't?"

Carol laughed. "Isn't it obvious? David did."

"No." Andi grabbed a strand of her hair and twirled it around her finger. "There must be some rule against fraternizing with the patrons."

"Fraternize?" Carol laughed even harder. "Do you think what you did with him last night was fraternize?"

"That was professional." Andi groaned inwardly. "At least for him. Oh, hell. You know what I mean."

"I don't know what kind of rules they have," Carol said. "But he obviously liked what he saw in you. Didn't he climax, too?"

"Well, yeah." If she was any judge of men's orgasms—an unlikely proposition—he'd come as hard as she had. He'd been wonderfully rough at the end, as if he'd put off his own pleasure for as long as he could stand. So like Blake, she hadn't had to work too hard to picture her ex-husband's thrusts and groans as he neared orgasm. Unless he'd faked all that. Who knew with men in his profession?

"Hmm. It must've been something," Carol said.

"I'm sorry…. "

"Your end of the line went dead for a while. You must have been thinking evil thoughts there."

"I was thinking that David shouldn't be spending so much money on a stranger, and don't tell me we're not strangers. We fucked for a few minutes. That's all."

"Maybe they give him an employee discount," Carol said. "Maybe he wants to build a base of regular customers."

"He can count me out. As a once-in-a-lifetime experience, fabulous. As a way of life, no."

"Are you going to tell him that?"

"Nicely but very firmly," Andi answered.

"You'd better do it tonight. That card's only good for twenty-four hours."

Shit. She had a meeting with a dealer from the gallery downtown bright and early the next morning. She didn't need to go out clubbing tonight. She could simply stay away and hope David would get the message, but she had fucked the guy the night before. It would be cold to simply stand him up. Besides, he might waste his money on more cards for her when she had no plans to use them.

"You are going to go, aren't you?" Carol asked.

"Just to clear things up with him," she answered.

"Sure. While you're there, see if he'd like to send me some freebies."

"You're incorrigible," Andi said.

"That's why you hang out with me."

"Talk to you later."

"Hey, fill me in on all the details tomorrow," Carol said.

"Good-bye, Carol."

Laughing again, Carol hung up. After setting the phone back in its cradle, Andi stood, tapping the card against her lips. Could a man who did *that* for a living really have enjoyed her enough to want more? Intriguing idea, but one for her diary. Not for real life.

David wasn't behind the counter at the entry to Cox as he had been the night before. A tall African American man stood there instead. Sleekly muscled and—of course—wearing nothing but a very impressive erection.

"Is David here?" she asked, as he took her purse and gave her a claim ticket.

He thought for a moment. "Haven't seen him. I don't think he's working tonight."

"But, he sent me… that is, I thought…. are you sure?"

He shrugged. "It's a big place. I might've missed him."

Damn. For some idiot reason, she'd expected him to be working reception. Instead, she'd have to search the club for him.

"I guess I'll go look for him." She started toward the entrance to the main part of the club.

"Hey, wait," the man called.

When she glanced back, she found him holding a velvet pouch up.

"Don't you want this?" he asked.

"Not tonight. Thanks."

The Latin band was playing again as she walked past the dance floor into the bar area. People danced in pairs and threes, twined around each other. Many of the men wore nothing. One man in particular had draped himself all over his partner, and the muscles of his butt and thighs bunched as he ground his pelvis against her. If the woman hadn't been wearing a dress, they'd be fucking in front of dozens of people. Andi would have watched, too, just as she watched them now.

Well, shit. She wasn't getting anywhere this way. If David hadn't greeted her out front, he'd probably look for her in the bar. She sure as hell wouldn't go looking for him in all the private rooms.

She probably stood out among the others as the passed the tables. In jeans and a t-shirt and with her hair pulled back in a pony tail and no make-up, she probably looked as if she'd just come from a touch football game. Good. She hadn't come for seduction, but only some conversation.

Just as she reached the bartender and leaned over to get his attention, a woman's voice came from nearby.

"Oh. My. God." The sound of feminine admiration, even awe. What could a man do to get that kind of attention in a place like this where all the men impressed with their beauty and sexual availability?

She didn't have to search long before she found the answer. A new man had entered. Fully dressed, unless a shirt open to nearly the waist counted as part naked. He stood taller than everyone around him, commanding space with the breadth of his shoulders. And, he moved—how he moved—with an almost predatory grace. A mask covered his forehead and eyes, creating a sense of mystery, but something about him tugged at primal memories inside her. She knew him somehow, although if she'd met him before, she'd surely remember him.

He looked her way, and a dark, blue gaze met hers. No wonder he seemed familiar. He might have been Blake's lost twin. The dark hair, strong chin, and remarkable blue eyes. Good Lord, who would have imagined the world could produce two men who looked like that?

He headed her way, and her knees turned to elastic. She groped for a bar stool, found one, and sank onto it before her legs failed her.

"Can I get you something, miss?" the bartender said from behind her.

She stared at him as if the question hadn't registered. "Sorry?"

"Would you like something to drink?"

"Tequila. A double."

While the bartender filled her order, Andi felt the other man coming closer and closer. The air around her took on a charge, crackling with tension. Anticipation.

When she turned back, he was standing close enough to her to surround her with the scent of his cologne. Her hand trembled as she lifted her drink to her lips. She only got a sip before he took the glass from her and tasted the liquor.

"No," he said, using the short o of Italian and Spanish. He set the tumbler on the bar and came even closer. So like Blake—to make her decision for her and then overpower her with his physical presence. Blake would never enter a place like this, and he'd never wear pants so tight. Oh, God, the pants. How in hell was she going to keep from staring at his crotch? Blake had patches of silky hair on his pecs, while this man's chest was naked and smooth and only inches away from her palms.

He leaned down toward her, placing his lips to her ear. "*Señorita.*"

"*Señora,*" she corrected.

He very pointedly picked up her left hand, staring at the place where she used to wear a wedding ring. Smiling, he kissed that spot and then took each finger, starting at her pinky, and kissed the tip. When he got to the thumb, he trailed his tongue along the pad underneath and then all the way to the tip, which he sucked into his mouth.

No mistaking that signal. He'd done it exactly the way a lover would trace the length of her pussy lips and then lap at the sensitive nub at the top. Her clit hardened, and she shifted against the stool. That only made matters worse, of course, so she sat as still as the rapid beating of her heart would allow.

His mouth still close to her ear, he pressed a kiss to the lobe. "*Favor de ayudarme.*"

"Help you?" she breathed. "How? Um…*como*?"

"*Esa mujer.*" He tipped his head toward a woman at the end of the bar. A red head staring at him with frank admiration. "*Me quiere.*"

Clever. He'd used the verb that meant both love and want, and he'd made his accent unremarkable. Neither Spanish nor Mexican but more like speaking in a way that an American would understand.

She looked him straight in those amazing eyes. "Then, you'd better do what she wants, don't you think?"

He raised an eyebrow. Arched it, rather, in a regal way that said he didn't care what anyone else wanted. "*Prefiero usted.*"

Her eyes widened at the formality of his address. "*Usted?*"

"*Tu,*" he answered, his voice as rich as chocolate in her ear. "*Te quiero.*"

Again. He loved her, he wanted her. For a moment, she forgot how to breathe and had to command herself to take air into her lungs. In, out, in time with the throbbing in her pussy. Already, her panties had grown wet, expecting satisfaction of the kind she hadn't had since she'd left Blake.

Her poor sex couldn't know that this wasn't Blake. This man hadn't spent years learning how to touch her for maximum pleasure. He couldn't fill her as perfectly as her husband had and make her come for a second time before giving in to his own orgasm. This man might amount to no more that the mechanical fuck she'd had the night before. Efficient and thorough, but not the stuff of dreams.

Still, when he took her hand and helped her off the stool, she went with him without resistance. And when he put his hand at the small of her back to guide her through the bar, she let him lead her as if in a dance. Blake had always done this, too, and though it emphasized his dominance over her, it also made her feel cherished and protected.

They went down the same quiet hallway David had led her down the night before. As David had done, this man stopped at one of the doors and pulled a key from a pocket of his pants. He let them both in, threw the lock, and caught her hands and brought them to his mouth and kissed her knuckles. Sweet. Even an innocent gesture. He opened one hand and kissed the palm. The image of what he'd done with her thumb came crashing back to her. This man was the closest she'd ever get to Blake without crawling back to her ex-husband and surrendering to his compulsion to control every aspect of her life and mold it to his own desires.

As he pulled her closer and bent to her ear, she melted inside.

"*Te quiero*," he repeated, the sound of his voice traveling along her nerves to the backs of her knees. Why not stay—take her chances that this man could fill the emptiness that had hollowed her out since she'd left Blake?

He took her moment of hesitation to turn her around and pull her back against him. Sure enough, her buttock met hardness behind his fly. A shaft as thick as Blake's—so big, he'd had to ease it into her slowly the first time. The sort of instrument that you wondered for a moment on waking what you'd done the night before to earn such a pleasant tingle in your sex.

Oh, God. How could she walk out and leave that behind?

Besides, he'd cupped her breasts and squeezed with just the right pressure while his tongue traced the outline of her ear and then dipped inside for a second. Her bones seemed to melt, turning pliant, and if he didn't hold her firmly, she'd probably waver and fall. He didn't let that happen, though, but laid a trail of kisses along her neck while his fingers toyed with her nipples through the layers of her Tee shirt and bra.

She groaned aloud, to hell with the fact that she didn't know this man. She was only human, after all, and he seemed to find her every hot button.

"*Suave*," he whispered into her other ear as more liquid pooled between her thighs. The thought of what he'd do with that huge cock had sent her fantasies into overdrive, and now his hands went lower, over her ribs to her belly. He'd touch her clit soon, or she would. She wouldn't need that vibrator to come tonight.

Instead of moving to her pussy, he grasped the hem of her t-shirt and pulled it upward. After lifting her arms so that he could pull it off, she turned toward him and ran her palms over the smooth skin of his chest.

Quickly, he bent to brush his lips over hers. Just a taste to make her want more. It worked. Though she hadn't kissed David the night before, she'd allow this man to take her mouth. He groaned and did it, and the sound tugged at something in her memory. She'd heard that before. As his lips traveled over hers, their softness stealing her breath, that something broke, full-blown into her consciousness.

Of course, she knew him. For the love of God. He wasn't *like* Blake. He *was* Blake.

She pulled back, holding him away from her, and stared into his face. Every feature fit. This was the man she'd said her vows with, the man who'd shared her bed for five years. He'd changed his clothing and his cologne. He'd even waxed his chest. But, she wasn't about to mistake her own husband, ex or no.

"You," she whispered.

He stiffened, and pure fear shone in his eyes. She'd spotted him, all right, and he knew it. And yet, she maintained the act.

"That is, *tu*," she said. "*Quien eres?*"

His features softened, and his shoulders relaxed. She'd asked him who he was. A normal enough thing if she hadn't recognized him. "Ramón."

"Ah," she sighed. "Ramón. *Te quiero.*"

He kissed Andi again, fitting his mouth to hers the way he'd practiced for years. Blake. She could have Blake without any promises or demands or guilt. She could have his body—his fingers, he lips. His gorgeous cock that filled her so well.

Sliding her tongue along his lower lip, she kissed him the way that most inflamed him. She'd practiced on him, too, although she'd never quite cracked his tight control. Tonight, it slipped just a little as he growled deep in his throat and his fingers dug almost painfully into her waist. No wonder. Passion always ran like a current between them. And then, it had been so fucking long.

Still nibbling at her lips, he pushed her inches away from him and worked his hands to the front closure of her bra. He unfastened it with his usual skill and bent to circle one nipple with the tip of his tongue. Arching her back, she offered herself to him as a happy groan escaped her chest. Her husband—the man who knew her body better than she did herself—could play her like a master. For these moments, the arguments didn't matter, the divorce had never happened. She could let him fuck her until she begged for mercy and not have to face any consequences. As long as he pretended to be Ramón, she could have him any way she wanted. She could let him put his face between her legs and use his tongue against her clit until she came then return the favor, sucking his member deep into her mouth. She could mount him and ride him until they climaxed together.

Now his hands splayed over her ribs, he half-lifted her from the floor and sucked her nipple into his mouth. Pinpricks of light flashed against the insides of her eyelids, each a dart of pure pleasure that raced through her to her sex. Already, she'd dampened her panties, and now she couldn't have stopped the flow if she'd wanted to. She wouldn't have any trouble taking his bulk tonight. In fact, if he stripped her now and rammed his erection into her, she'd probably just explode into orgasm around him.

"Ramón," she whispered. "*Por favor. Quiero...*"

"*Esto?*" He slipped a hand between her thighs and pressed against her most sensitive flesh. Even through the jeans and panties, the pressure sent a shock through her, and her body jerked in response.

"*Pobrecita*," he said.

To hell with Spanish or anything that took conscious thought. "Please. Oh, please."

Chuckling, he removed his hand and then guided her to the bed. In truth, he almost carried her as her legs could hardly support her. After her stretched her out on top of the spread, he kissed her briefly.

She opened her eyes for a moment to study him. Behind the mask, she found the same dark, almost midnight hair and blue eyes she'd encountered so many times as she'd awakened and found him watching her. The same eyes went hazy with passion as they'd made love, at the moment that he'd entered her. He closed a hand over her breast and kneaded the flesh, and she let her eyes drift shut again. No time for reflection now. Just sensation.

He helped her to sit up long enough to rid her of her bra and then guided her down again. She really ought to do something to help him undress her, but he did it so very well. Her running shoes hit the floor with soft thuds, and then, her socks slid off one foot and the other. He massaged her arches for a few seconds, his strong fingers stretching muscle. Such carnality. The man could turn her feet into erogenous zones.

Still, she lay in a trance of lust as he popped the button on her jeans and pulled the zipper down. He tugged the pants past her hips and then dipped his fingers into her panties. Those, too, yielded to his touch, and after a second or two, she was completely naked. Exposed and ready for whatever came next.

She managed to open her eyes a crack to watch him undress. After bending to remove his shoes and socks, he remained sitting on the bed to yank off his shirt and send it flying across the room. The mask slipped, but he pushed it back into place. When he stood to unfasten his fly, she got a clear view of his ass. Tight, just like the rest of his flesh. Those muscles would drive him into her with long, solid strokes, never tiring until he'd made her come at least once.

Then, when he turned—oh, when he turned—that amazing cock. Long and swollen, it stood straight out from his body, crowned by a thick head. She could hardly breathe staring at its beauty, and her pussy clenched, closing around the emptiness he'd soon fill. She covered her mound with her hand and pressed into the wetness there. Her clit responded with a jolt of sensation that set her teeth on edge. He'd scarcely touched her, and yet she'd already become completely aroused.

"*Yo lo hago*," he snapped. He wanted to touch her, to take control. Fine. No consequences.

So when he lay beside her and moved her hand away, she let him. Soon enough, he fingers replaced hers, parting the seam of her pussy lips and stroking upward to find the nub of flesh that most craved his touch.

When he found it, she gasped and then moaned. Damn, but she was going to come, and hard. He could make her do it now, if he wanted, but he'd draw out the pleasure until she couldn't stand to wait another instant. He could read her so well, he knew somehow when to make her linger and when to show mercy and finish her.

Clever man. Clever, wicked man. His mouth went back to her breast while his fingers feathered over her clit. Now faster. Now soft, but lingering. Between that touch and the tugging at her breast, she lost any connection to reality. Stretching like a cat, she reached her arms over her head and searched for some anchor to grip as he turned her world upside-down with lust. Her fingers met wooden post or bars of some sort, so she gripped them in her hands as her body took on a life outside her control.

No longer content with only teasing her clit, he slid a finger into her and probed. Arching, she pressed against his hand, silently begging—more, faster, harder. Instead, he pulled out and smoothed her own moisture over her throbbing nub in circles that made her wild.

"I'm ready," she gasped. "Please. Oh, God."

He repeated the process, pushing into her and then rubbing the tip of his finger over her clit. Every nerve inside her stretched to the breaking point. He didn't stop. Plunge, stroke, circle. Again and again.

"Damn you," she cried. "You know what… do it. Do it."

Finally, he gave her what she needed. He rubbed her hard, pressing the sensitive flesh with enough force to throw her past the boundary. The orgasm rushed through her, catching every part of her up in its power and squeezing. She opened her throat and shouted as the spasms began deep in her belly and coursed along her inner walls. He didn't ease the pressure but demanded more and more, and her body responded. No climax had ever shaken her so roughly, and when he finally released her, she had to fight for breath. Moaning, she sank into oblivion so profound she almost didn't notice as he stretched out next to her and took her into his arms.

Un-freaking-believable. Was it possible he'd become an even better lover in the months they'd been apart? If so, he'd practiced on another woman, and that possibility wasn't worth considering at the moment, as his warmth surrounded her and the evidence of his arousal pressed against her hip. No, he only seemed better because she'd been without for so long. Even on the two occasions when she'd tried to make love to another man, no one had moved her the way this one could. Not even David—with the assistance of a vibrator—came close to Blake's skill. Or his caring. No matter what had happened between them, she had to give him that.

He pressed a kiss to her temple. "*Bueno?*"

"Good?" She had to laugh. "*Bueno* doesn't even begin to describe it."

"*Quieres más?*"

"I do, and I know you'll give it to me." She rolled toward him, nestling her nose under his chin. Her fingers hit the smooth skin of his chest, not the hairs she'd normally encounter there. She could get used to that.

"I imagine you'd like *más*, too," she said. No point trying to drag Spanish up into her pleasure-curdled brain, especially when he understood English well enough.

"*Más*," he repeated.

Smiling to herself, she let her hands drift lower along his body, past his ribs to his flat belly. He made room for her explorations, no doubt realizing her destination. She found his cock easily, of course, and stroked it between her palms. He was rock hard, his skin the texture of warm velvet. When she petted his length, his body stiffened and shuddered.

He sucked in a breath. "*Dios.*"

She might not approach lovemaking in the same meticulous manner he did, but she'd had enough experience with this man to read his reactions. The tension of his limbs and his labored breathing gave away his state of full arousal. When she gave the head of his member a tiny squeeze, he grunted, and droplet of moisture appeared at his tip. If he'd been with other women, they probably couldn't do *that* to him so easily.

She glanced up into his face and stroked his shaft from the base to the tip. "*Bueno?*"

"*Cuidado*," he said from between clenched teeth.

"I'll be careful," she said. "I'll take great care with this monster."

Blake seldom lost control. He even climaxed when he decided the time was right. It'd be fun to tease him now and see how long he could maintain his fake identity as Ramón. Slowly, she trailed her fingers along the underside of his shaft to his sac. They'd been lovers for months before he'd let her touch him there, but once he had, she'd learned that a brush of her fingertips at the right spot could make him wild.

When she did it now, he let out a very American-sounding "Oh." Very satisfying after he'd commanded her responses so effectively. She repeated her strokes until he groaned and pushed her hand away.

Now, he took over again, rolling her onto her back and settling between her legs. The tip of his cock eased between her pussy lips and pressed for entrance.

Yessss. Oh, yessss. She opened for him, wrapping her legs around him to urge him deeper. For months, she'd done without this. She'd tried to push the feelings out of her memory for fear of wanting him so badly she'd call him and say something really stupid like "I can't live without you" or "I was wrong. Take me back."

The images had come to her in dreams, though—a poor imitation of the reality. Reality returned as he pushed his hips forward, sliding his cock inside her as far as it would go.

Now with their bodies joined, he stared down at her. Passion glazed his eyes, but a light of triumph shone through, too. Even through the mask. He thought he'd won something from her with this charade. Let him. That didn't matter as long as his sex was inside hers. No matter how they'd come together, this was where the belonged. United in something bigger than the two of them apart.

Then, he began to move, slowly at first. An easy glide, especially because she'd grown so wet for him. Neither of them spoke. They didn't need to. A sigh here, a stretch there. Labored breathing, a random kiss or touch. All spoke louder than words would have. All told the same story—about hunger and need and completion.

"*Mira*," he whispered. Look.

He owned her body, and so, she obeyed. For a moment, she could see him as if his mask had fallen away. The same face she'd watched so often as they made love. His total concentration on the moment, driving himself to push her higher. Propped up on his elbows, he moved faster. Angling himself so that each thrust brought a jolt of excitement against her clit, he pushed deeper inside her. The combination sent her senses reeling. Nothing else in the world felt like this—the fullness of the passage of his cock and the pressure at the seat of her arousal. She had to close her eyes now and focus all her energy on simply feeling him.

They'd join each other in orgasm this time. He'd push her to the point of no return and then allow himself to come with her. Already, the tension coiled tight in her pelvis—so sweet, so undeniable. Her breaths came out as moans now. She'd signal to him if she had to that she needed more, but Blake would know that. He always did.

Still, he pushed her harder, bringing her closer with every movement. Any more force, and he could push them completely off the bed. She reached for her anchors again and found them. Gripping the posts for all she was worth, she held herself in place for his assault. Too long, they'd been apart, and now she couldn't get enough of him. She strained against him. More friction. More pressure against her bud. More. More.

In the next moment, she wasn't struggling any longer. Her body took over as her sex clamped down on the hardness inside her. Her whole being contracted to the place between her legs where the wave had built and now crested. Her hips jerked upward as the spasms started. This time when she came, she clutched at his cock, gripping it rhythmically.

She let loose a half-cry, half-sob as it continued, and Blake responded with a deep growl that built to a roar. Still in that perfect place, she held him as he made his last, frantic thrusts, battering his cock into her. His body went rigid in her arms, and he emptied his lust inside her. For those few seconds, she owned him instead of the other way around. He was human and vulnerable and so very, very dear.

Finally, with a soft moan that became a sigh, he rested the side of his face against hers. "*Mañana?*"

She took a deep breath. "*Sí.*"

"*Te quiero.*"

I love you, too. I love you.

Chapter 3

Blake stared at the decanter for a long, long time before he pulled the stopper, hefted it, and poured a stiff belt of Scotch into the crystal tumbler in his hand. Then, he added another shot to the glass, put the whiskey away, and went with his drink into the living room. He'd built a small fire in the grate. The weather didn't require it, but staring at the flames always rid him of distractions so that he could think. Tonight, he had distractions by the boatload, and he would have turned on the air conditioner if he'd had to—his normal instinct to conserve be damned. If he couldn't get his mind to settle down soon, he wouldn't get much sleep. He'd performed with little sleep in the past, but how much easier to face his day with at least some rest.

Andrea had come with another man. Damn. Blake sank onto the coach and set his drink on the glass top of the coffee table. Of course, he'd been the other man, but she hadn't known that. For a minute, she'd seemed to recognize him, but in reality, she'd only been curious about Ramón. How easily she'd gone with him. How easily she'd climaxed for him. He'd worked so hard when they first met to bring her to orgasm, holding off his own release for what felt like hours to make sure he pleased her first. Now, she took the results of his efforts—his love for her, damn it—and given it to a stranger with tight pants and a phony accent.

Oh, hell. If that wasn't a reason to drink, what was? He took a swig of Scotch and almost choked. Expensive stuff and smooth, it still burned his gut going down.

The knowledge that his wife could go to a place like that and let another man touch her had ruined his stomach before the liquor got there. She liked the place too damned much. Two nights in a row. Two strangers. Now, she'd agreed to another night. Maybe he shouldn't have invited her, but what if she'd gone on her own? He'd keep going back there and making love to her as Ramón until he figured out a way to use that club to get her back.

In the meantime, he had to stop deceiving himself. He wasn't just using the club for a strategic reason. He'd do anything to touch that woman again. To kiss her and hold her and watch her face as she reached orgasm. Staring into the fire only reminded him of the way she moved beneath him—a sinuous dance to meld her body to his. Then... poof... she'd go up in flames and take him with her. She probably didn't even hear the sounds she made as she burned hotter and hotter. He did. The most erotic music in the world—his wife, ecstatic because of something he'd done.

He'd do it all again tomorrow night and the night after and the night after that if she'd let him. The woman was a narcotic. He'd thought he'd broken her hold on him, but the scent of her arousal brought the cravings back. Even now, her perfume clung to his skin and clouded his brain. His fingers had dipped into her wetness, and he sure as hell wouldn't wash them for a while.

The house phone rang, a sharp sound that made him jump. He went to it and picked up the receiver. "Crawford."

"You have a visitor, sir," the security man said.

He checked his watch. Eleven twenty. No one came around this late. His bastard heart lifted with hope that it might be Andrea. She'd figured out he was Ramón, and she'd come to tell him she couldn't live without him.

"… Wolfe," the man on the other end said.

"I'm sorry…."

"A Mr. Kenneth Wolfe to see you."

"Ken?" His CFO ought to be in bed now in his own house in the suburbs with his wife. "Send him to the house."

While Blake waited, he searched for his cell phone and found it on the dining room table. He'd turned it off before leaving for the club. Still off. He'd been too distracted to think about such trivial things as… say… running his business. When he flipped it on, the voice mail message blinked at him. Great. Ken had needed him, and hadn't been able to contact him.

Back at the front of his house, he opened the door just as Ken got out of his car in the driveway. "A little late, isn't it?"

Ken climbed the steps and walked past him into the living room without so much as a hello. "Don't you ever read your e-mail, check your IM, or answer your cell?"

"Of course, I do."

"You haven't for the last three and a half hours," Ken said.

"I've been busy." Dressing up as a gigolo to seduce his own wife.

Ken reached into his pocket and pulled out a few papers. "If you had been available, you would have seen this."

"What is it?"

"Figures." Ken handed the sheets to Blake. "About the Paradise. Nothing earth-shattering but things a detail guy like you might want to know before closing a deal."

"Thanks." Blake opened the pages and sat on the couch. When Ken joined him, he glanced pointedly at the drink sitting there.

Blake ignored him, or tried to, and scanned the numbers. "We knew the Paradise runs in the red."

"We didn't know how far in the red."

"Doesn't matter." Blake set the spreadsheets on the table and leaned back.

"It'll never make a profit for us, but the place is a jewel. Old luxury—the kind no one can afford to build anymore."

"So, you have to have it."

"I have more money than I can count," Blake said. "I've made you pretty rich, too."

Ken raised his hands in a surrender gesture. "I'm not complaining."

"I want to have something beautiful. Something unique." Like Andrea. Unfortunately, no amount of money could buy her.

"If the new numbers don't change your mind about buying the hotel, at least, you can use them to get a better price."

"Haggle?"

"Something like that," Ken answered.

"Not for a gorgeous lady like the Paradise," Blake said. "I plan to treat Hsu like the poobah he thinks he is."

"Then, it'll be black tie tomorrow night?" Ken asked.

"Tomorrow?" He couldn't have anything scheduled for the next night, could he? Aside from sex with Andrea. He never had to consult a calendar. He always remembered anything important.

"The dinner party for Hsu to celebrate our latest acquisition." Ken stared at Blake for a moment. "The one Jo and I are hosting for you."

"Ah, shit."

"Swearing, too?" Ken said.

"What's that supposed to mean?"

"Out of touch with the office for hours. Swearing." Ken paused briefly. "Drinking on the night before a meeting."

"I'm not turning into a booze hound," Blake snapped.

"Of course you're not," Ken answered. "I doubt you've even touched that… what is it… Scotch?"

Blake's stomach twisted into knots again. "Does it matter?"

"Look, you run the company. No, you are the company. None of us would want to work for anyone else, but I have to ask as a stockholder—"

"What?" Blake snapped.

"Are you… well… yourself?"

Blake didn't answer. He not only didn't have an answer, he didn't even know who 'he' was any longer. Was he Blake Crawford? A man who'd built an international hotel and entertainment corporation? Or was he Ramón? The tight-pants-wearing male prostitute who hung around a sex club waiting for one particular woman?

"It was a rough divorce, what with the publicity and all," Ken continued. "You seemed okay, but maybe you're having a delayed reaction."

He didn't say anything to that, either. Everyone thought they knew about his break-up with Andrea, but they didn't know shit. And yes, he'd use that term. Sometimes only profanity got the job done. Bad enough that he'd lost her. Even worse that it obviously broke her heart to leave him, and the whole disaster had been his fault.

"Look, I'm sorry I mentioned it," Ken said. "None of my business."

"It is if my behavior affects your stock portfolio," Blake answered.

"Don't worry about it." Ken clapped him on the shoulder. "I'm in good shape."

"Then, maybe you can do me a favor."

"Anything. Name it."

Blake took a deep breath and released it. Delegating had never been the easy part of the job for him, but Ken had earned his trust over and over during their years together. "I have to get out of any after-hours demands for a while."

"How long?"

"I don't know." Damn it, why didn't he? He had a plan for everything. Why did all his plans go to hell where Andrea was concerned? "Maybe a few weeks. Maybe months."

"Months?" Ken repeated.

"Can you handle it?"

"I can, but…." Ken's voice trailed off. "What's going on with you?"

Not having a good answer, Blake remained silent as he twirled his glass around on the coffee table.

"A woman," Ken said finally. "Be careful, friend. Rebound relationships are usually disasters."

"I won't end up in the papers again. I promise."

"I'm more worried you'll get yourself hurt," Ken replied.

"There are never any guarantees, are there?"

"Okay. Anything after five is now my responsibility." Ken rose. "Just be careful, Blake."

Blake got up, too. "I will."

That was a lie, of course. He'd already thrown careful out the window. His heart might very well go after it.

As he had the night before, Blake sat at the farthest table from the bar, back in a corner where he might disappear in shadows. If one of the female clients demanded his services, he'd have to find some reason to decline, which would be mighty awkward. He could have stayed up in the control room, but if he didn't get to Andrea on time, she might go off with one of the other men. At least, tonight she knew who'd sent her the card to get in, but he still wouldn't take any chances.

Another couple had found the same hidden corner, and for good reason. The woman had opened the guy's fly and was now happily stroking his cock under the table. Blake should have looked away before his member swelled in his snug pants. Too late now. As he watched the woman's hand moving along her partner's shaft, all his brain could register was how the muscles of Andrea's pussy had gripped him the night before. He must have had the same dazed look on his face as his excitement had built.

He shifted in his seat, but that only rubbed his balls against his pants. At least, here he didn't have to worry about having an erection. It was expected. Again, he had a drink in front of him, and again, he'd hardly touched it. Now, he took a swallow and forced it down. Nowhere as good as his own liquor at home, but anything that might slow his libido down could give him some control when Andrea finally showed up.

What if she didn't? Could Cox Club have been a diversion for her and not a lasting attraction? Maybe she'd come to her senses and wouldn't keep the sex date she's made with a faceless stranger. If that was true, he'd thank heaven, but it also meant that he'd have to find some other way back into her life. Moving on and trying to forget about her was no longer an option.

The woman nearby stopped working her partner's rod and held it, gripping the base. His eyes half-shut with pleasure, the guy reached into his pocket and pulled out a condom. While he kicked out of his shoes and stood to remove his jeans, the woman tore the packet open. Now naked except for a tight t-shirt, the guy watched as she unrolled the protection over him. Great. They were going to fuck right here, and Blake would have to watch.

Just as the woman bent over the table and the man lifted her skirt to slide his cock into her, a hand came down on Blake's shoulder. He jumped and looked up to find Andrea watching the couple. Her fingers dug into him as she stood with a half-smile on her face.

"*¿Te gusta eso?*" he asked. If she had a voyeuristic streak, he could use the information.

She bit her lip. "I've never actually…. Oh my, they're really fucking, aren't they?"

"*Sí.*"

"You understand English," she said.

Damn it all. The image of a cock moving in and out of a wet pussy had distracted him. No real harm. Ramón had only been fibbing about speaking Spanish only.

"Good," she continued, her grip on his shoulder still tense. "It'll make things easier."

That could have meant any number of things, but the low, wicked tone of her voice promised mischief or worse.

At the other table, the man bent over and circled his arms around his lover's waist. Little doubt where he'd buried his fingers, and sure enough, her moans turned to cries.

Andrea cleared her throat and kept staring at the couple. She'd worn slacks, damn it, or Blake could stroke her nether lips and find her clitoris. He could make her climax right here and catch her if she fell. Hell, another minute of this, and he'd have her in the same position as the other woman, and he'd have his distended member inside her.

He inched his hand up the inside of her leg past her knee and to her thigh.

"Not here," she whispered. "I have other plans."

"*Bueno*."

"Very good," she said. "At least, I hope you'll think so. Come on."

She turned and took a few steps away before he could get out of his chair. Walking with this crowbar in his pants wouldn't be easy, but at least, now a club patron had claimed him, and he wouldn't have to worry about some other woman demanding to give him the same treatment that other man was receiving. Behind him, that woman climaxed with a muffled shout, and her partner followed right after. Good for them. He'd have Andrea making the same noises soon.

Instead of going toward the room they'd used the night before, she led him down a different corridor. Smiling, she stopped in front of one door and used her card to let them in. Candles by the dozens gave off a flickering glow, the room's only illumination. They made enough light to show off the props along the walls, though. Whips, leather straps, even knives. To one side stood a huge frame with cuffs at the corners. The thing could accommodate a man's size, even one as large as his six-foot-one.

He glanced at her. "*¿Para ti o mi?*"

"Neither of us," she answered. "We'll use the bed instead."

Given the other features of the room, he hadn't even considered the bed. It was narrow, not much wider than a twin, but the reason for that became clearer as he took a few steps toward it and studied it. Cuffs hung from all four corners. Once a person had been fastened into them, she'd lie spread-eagled and helpless—open to anything her partner did to her. Or 'his' partner. The bed could hold him as well.

"Take off your shoes and socks," she ordered.

Because he no longer had to pretend he didn't speak English, he bent and followed her instructions. When he straightened again, she was standing nearly on top of him. If his cock had softened any since they left the bar, her nearness had its usual effect on him. So, when she placed her palm against the front of his pants, she found him fully erect.

As she gripped him though the fabric, she smiled up at him. "Already hard. Well done, Ramón."

"*Gracias*."

"Here's the only rule for tonight. I can do anything I want to you, but you're not allowed to come until I have."

"*Sí*." She couldn't possibly think that requirement odd, as no decent lover would finished until he'd made his partner happy. Still, if she bound his hands, that might be difficult to accomplish. And what, exactly, did she plan to do to him first?

While he pondered that, she opened his shirt and pulled the tails from his pants. Now, she ran her hands over his ribs to his back while she tipped her head back to nuzzle the flesh under his chin.

"Mmmm," she murmured. "You're sweet enough to eat."

He closed his arms around her, but she pushed them apart. "No. I'm in control here. Stand still and take whatever I give you."

Okay, this was not his usual Andrea. Though never timid in bed, she always let him take the lead. The arrangement had worked for them, so neither of them had questioned it. Now it seemed she had other ideas. His member didn't mind. It remained stiff and eager to find out what she'd do.

She began by laying kisses along his neck to his collarbone. After that, she used her tongue to trace the furrow down the center of his chest. In the candlelight, she resembled a cat as her fingers curled into his flesh as she worked. She reached a nipple and teased it with her thumb before circling it with her tongue. He'd read that male nipples responded as hotly as women's did, but he'd never experienced the sensations before. Nerve endings he hadn't known existed responded, sending a zing of excitement all the way to his balls. He couldn't stop a groan. With any luck, it came out with a Spanish accent.

She straightened. "Remember, you can't climax until I have."

"*Sí*," he answered. "Uh, *no*."

"Good boy."

She gave his other nipple the same treatment, stroking it with her tongue until even the backs of his knees felt the jolt. Normally, he'd be touching and kissing her, too. He'd bend to take the tip of her breast into his mouth while his hand sought the treasures between her legs. Tonight, she hadn't removed any of her own clothes, and she'd ordered him to do nothing but stand there and allow her free access to his body. It would be liberating if it weren't so damned frustrating. If he had control, he'd have them naked and coupling within a minute and climaxing shortly after that.

She continued her maddeningly slow explorations, now kissing his ribs. Who in hell kissed ribs? His cock thought that a splendid idea. Either that, or his swollen flesh expected that her mouth would land there soon. Heaven help him if she did. She'd already driven him near the breaking point, and it wouldn't take much oral sex to push him past.

Sure enough, she sank to her knees in front of him and reached to the pull of his zipper.

"*No*,' he said.

"No?" She stared up at him. "Don't tell me no."

"*Favor de...por favor no...*" No use. He could hardly form the words in English. His Spanish had gone out the window minutes ago.

"That's better." She unzipped his fly and reached into his pants to curl her fingers around his shaft. When she pulled it out, the ruddy color betrayed his high state of arousal.

"What a fine, big tool," she said. "I bet it'd like to be fucking me right now."

"*Sí*." He could manage that simple word.

"Later," she said. "Right now, I want to suck on it."

He groaned. "*No*" wouldn't stop her. From the look of victory in her eyes, it was clear that nothing would stop her. He could only brace himself and hope for the best.

He got the best when she closed her mouth over the head of his cock, but not what he'd been hoping for. She knew how to manipulate his member. She'd spent years learning all the most sensitive spots and what kind of pressure to use. For now, he'd have to deal with the fact that she was doing this for a stranger and concentrate on something that got his mind off how her mouth felt as she flicked her tongue at the spot on the underside, just below the ridge that circled the tip of him.

Damn, she was good. She stroked his shaft with her fingers while her lips took more and more of him. His hips pumped slowly, completely out of his control. No man could withstand such an assault without shooting right to orgasm. He—the man who loved her and who'd let her learn with his body— stood no chance at all at resisting. And yet, he had to obey her orders or she might stop coming here.

Holding her head to steady himself, he thrust farther into her mouth. Not because he wanted to but because his body gave him no choice. Without language, he growled a warning. A primitive cry. *Enough. No more.*

Finally, she took her mouth off him but continued to grip his shaft in her fist. "What an animal you are. I do believe you want to eat me up."

"*Sí,*" he managed between gritted teeth.

"If you're a good boy, I'll let you do it," she said. "Get on the bed."

He would have obeyed instantly, but she tugged his slacks down and helped him step out of them. That took some effort as they were so damned tight. He managed to get rid of his shirt without help, though, and went to the bed and lay on his back. As soon as he'd settled into place, she joined him and cuffed one ankle and then the other.

"Now, you can't run away," she said.

As if he would. His poor cock needed to get into her pussy, and it would one way or another before they left this room.

"I'm going to undress now, and you can touch yourself while you watch," she said. "But, don't climax, or I'll have to leave you here until you can get hard again."

He almost laughed at that. Some punishment. It wouldn't take him long after one orgasm to get ready for a nice, slow fuck. Not with this woman. Andrea inspired him to new heights every time they made love.

By now, she'd removed her shoes and socks and unsnapped her jeans. When she pushed them over her hips, she revealed the tiniest thong of black satin he'd ever seen. He wouldn't even have to remove them to penetrate her. He could simply push the strap aside and expose her sex for anything he wanted. Maybe in the future, he'd do exactly that. Right now, he reclined against the mattress, his fingers clutched around the base of his shaft as he desperately tried to strangle it into submission. He'd only come all the harder for the effort and the delay.

Now, she shucked out of her panties and stood facing him, her mound partially covered by the tails of her blouse. "Would you like to watch me touch my pussy?"

His mouth suddenly dry, he shook his head in answer. What little Spanish he could muster wouldn't explain watching her wasn't good enough. He needed to touch her, lick her, fuck her. So, he lay where he was in silence.

She reached between her legs, moving her fingers rhythmically. Her eyes half-closing with arousal, she let out a long coo of pleasure. "I'm wet already. You made me that way, you naughty man."

Probably his imagination, but he could have sworn he could detect her perfume—the scent she gave off when fully aroused. It always went right to his gut. Tonight, it went right to his sac.

She stroked herself harder. "I could come this way, you know. If I did, you could come, too. Would you like that?"

He growled his disapproval.

"I didn't think you would," she answered. "You'd rather be inside me, wouldn't you?"

He nodded again, still gripping his cock.

"All right. You can eat me first." She removed her blouse and then the scrap of black satin that acted as a bra. Somewhere, he'd have to find her matching sets in every color of the rainbow so that he could take them off of her.

She approached the bed slowly, her hips swinging in a frankly sexual dance. After she climbed on, she didn't bother to kiss him, but knelt with her thighs on either side of his head. She'd pinned his arms, so when she lowered herself to his face, he couldn't use anything but his mouth to caress her.

He'd been right about her arousal. She gave off her usual musk of soap and hot, wet woman. He could use his hands on her buttocks to guide her to him, and she didn't object. When he finally had her in the right position, he drew his tongue along the crease of her pussy lips in a long swipe that ended at her clit.

Her turn to groan, and she did, loudly and lustily. After years of making love with this woman, he'd learned what could hold her at that high plateau between excitement and bliss. He'd do that some other time, and soon. Now, he needed to make her hot enough to need his cock inside her while he finished her. He continued teasing her, stroking her lips for a while before returning to her hot spot to roll it and then flick at it with the tip of his tongue.

"Oh, Ramón." She groaned. "Where did you learn to eat pussy like that?"

Hell and damnation. She thought another man was doing this for her. The knowledge might have dimmed his arousal if she hadn't made him so damned hot. He'd known he'd have to face this when he dreamed up his alter ego, but he hadn't imagined that she'd fasten the man to the bed and act this uninhibited. She'd never done anything remotely like this during their marriage.

"You stopped," she cried. "I didn't say you could stop."

He'd have to worry about her behavior later. Right now, she needed to approach orgasm so that she'd take him inside her and ride him until they both climaxed. He licked her again, letting his tongue linger on her hot button. Pass after pass until she stopped talking except for oohs and ahhs of pleasure. When he pursed his lips around her clit and sucked, she shuddered. Another sign that she'd come soon.

Instead, she climbed off him, breathing hard, and bit her lip for a moment. "You thought you could make me climax that way."

He didn't say anything. Who knew what the right response to that was?

"You could, but that isn't what I want." She grabbed his hand, pulled it to the corner of the bed, and fastened him into the cuff there. "I want you stretched out and helpless when you climax."

"*Señora?*"

She repeated the process with his other hand and then rested back. "Wonderful. You're at my mercy now."

She didn't exaggerate. By straining against his bonds, he could move a few inches here or there, but for the most part, he was fully secured. He'd have to trust her to satisfy both of them. A total reversal of their usual roles. Had he dominated her so thoroughly that she'd repressed this side of her sex drive?

Another thing he'd have to worry about later, because now, she moved her leg over him to straddle his pelvis. One of hands grasped his member, and the other one parted the lips of her pussy as she positioned him between them and lowered herself slowly onto his cock.

What a sight she made as she closed her eyes and took him one slow inch at a time. Her moisture closed around him, her muscles gripping him, tight enough to make him climax on the spot.

He held off, barely, by biting the inside of his cheek. Nothing in her rules said that he couldn't thrust. More likely the opposite—that anything he could do to make her come was allowed, even encouraged. Bound at hands and feet, he only had his cock to use on her, so he did. Slow and hard, he moved, stroking her inner walls, giving her the best he had.

That must have been what she wanted, because she moved with him. Up and down, back and forth, taking his rhythm as his own.

"So good." She cupped her breasts, massaging them, the perfect image of a woman claiming her own pleasure. If he could take some part in that, all the better. Teasing the nipples now, she drew them into hard points. Normally, he'd do that with his mouth, but watching her made for an erotic display he'd never get out of his head.

When she increased her pace, he matched it, shoving himself upward to impale her.

"Oh, God," she gasped. "You're so big."

For you, baby. Just for you.

"I need to… oh!… more. Please?" she cried.

He worked harder, slamming his cock into her pussy. The heat, the wetness, the velvet of her walls. No more. He couldn't last. And he couldn't touch her clit to make her come.

She did it, instead. With the fingers of one hand, she parted her pussy lips and rubbed at the sensitive bud.

Immediately, her cry went up. "Now. Don't stop. Don't stop!"

Yes, now. Her sex tightened around his shaft and then bursts into spasms. Powerful. The world went red and then blazing white as they came together. His hips jerked wildly as he gave her everything he had. Both of them shouted as she continued to milk him for everything he could give her. At that moment, he would have given her his soul if she didn't already have it. His woman. His mate. His life.

After long seconds of ecstasy, she rested against his chest, a limp but cherished burden. Even if he'd been freed of the restraints, he couldn't have moved. The orgasm—the loving had sapped him of everything except for the joy from being inside his wife again. The second time now since the divorce, and even sweeter than the first.

"Ramón," she said after a while. "You sure know how to fuck."

Another man's name again. Even though he was the other man, the sound soured his stomach. She should only talk to him after lovemaking. Only, how in hell could he accomplish that?

Maybe the time had come for him to tell her the truth and make her see reason. She needed to give their love a second chance if either of them were to be happy again. If he did, though, she might stop coming to Cox. He hadn't had time to truly win her. Besides, if things didn't work out, he could still have her body a few more times before he lost her for good.

She propped herself up on her forearms. "You said something?"

He must have made some noise. No surprise there. The thought of really losing her always hit him like a punch to the groin. Even in the darkest days, after he'd left the courtroom and the final realization had settled in—that they were no longer bound to each other—even then, he hadn't been able to give up hope. Hopeless sap that he was, his world view had her in it. Permanently.

"No wonder," she said. "I should have untied you minutes ago."

She got up, separating them. His member had remained hard enough to stay in her all that time. It missed her immediately and went flaccid. The cravings would return soon enough, and as long as he kept playing her mystery lover, he could have her again.

When she set him loose of the bed, he sat up and rubbed his wrists.

She studied him with some alarm. "Too tight?"

"No."

Her features settled into the smile that used to brighten his mornings. "Good."

"*Mañana?*"

"*Mañana.*"

Chapter 4

Andi spread all the cards from Cox out in front of her on the dining room table. Six of them. She hadn't been back to the club in almost a week. Blake kept sending cards, though. How long would he continue before he did something else to get to her?

She picked up her mug and sipped at her coffee. A few yards away in what would have been a living room but served as her studio, her latest work sat incomplete. The collection of geometrical patterns had made sense when she sketched them, but now, the coherent whole she'd envisioned escaped her. She'd had plenty of time to work on the piece, but every time she approached it, her mind went wandering into dimly lit rooms and a pair of blue eyes behind a mask. One way or another, the man was death to her career, even without trying. And she couldn't give him up.

She sighed and pushed the cards into a pile. At least she'd thrown him a curve for a change by not showing up for repeat performances. He wouldn't let the thing between them go. Not her Blake.

Right on cue, the doorbell buzzed. For the last few days, she'd jumped every time it did. She did again now. Taking a steadying breath, she rose and went to the front. A glimpse through the peephole showed him, dressed in all his corporate splendor, standing in the hallway outside.

Her fingers fumbled with the lock, but when she got the door open, she gave him a confident smile, or the best impression she could do with her heart racing. "Blake."

He fiddled with his collar. "Andrea."

"Is there something you need from me?" *Aside from the obvious.* She almost slapped herself.

"It's kind of silly," he said. "I've been thinking about Bandit."

"You came to see the cat?"

"I miss the patter of little, feline feet around the house."

"You hate the cat," she said.

"I don't hate it. I'm allergic to it."

"Her," Andi corrected. "You used to call her Cat-hole."

"Term of endearment. Can I see her?"

This didn't have anything to do with the cat, and they both knew it. But she couldn't miss what he'd do next, so she made a sweeping gesture that he should go inside.

"Here, kitty," he called as he walked by. "Where's my girlfriend?"

Andi stifled a laugh. Bandit was a mean-tempered little beast who deserved to be called something obscene. She'd been the cutest kitten at the shelter when they'd picked her out. Her evil disposition had only appeared later. The fact that she made Blake sneeze was an added bonus.

"There she is," he declared as he scooped her off her place on the couch. Little floozy that she was, Bandit started purring and kneading his coat with her paws. Claws, too, no doubt.

"How's my sweetheart?" he went on.

"Sweetheart?" Andi repeated. "She bit you once."

"She'd had her shots."

"That makes everything okay, I guess."

He didn't answer, but smiled at her while scratching Bandit behind the ears.

"Why are you here?" she asked. "Really."

"I wanted to see how you are." After a moment, he inclined his head toward her work. "New piece?"

"Yeah." She hugged herself, partly because of the awkwardness of making small talk with him and partly to keep her hands to herself. He looked so damned good.

"Nice," he said.

"No, it's not. It's horrible."

"It'll be great when you finish. I've always loved your work, you know that."

She shrugged. First hugging herself, now shrugging. Bandit saved the moment by hissing and twisting to get out of his grip. He dropped her and brought the back of his hand to his mouth.

"She scratched you."

"Nothing," he mumbled. Then, he sneezed. Twice.

She went to him. "Let me see it."

He showed her his hand. The scratch was, indeed, nothing. "Looks like Bandit's losing her killer instinct."

"She misses me."

"She didn't miss your jacket. It's covered with her fur," Andi said.

Dark charcoal with pinstripes, the garment fit his broad shoulders perfectly. She'd loved watching him get dressed in the morning, knowing this stunning example of the male gender belonged to her.

"Honestly, Blake," she said. "Who wears a suit to visit his ex-wife?"

"I came from a meeting." He stood up, looking down at her with that 'I mean business' glint in his eye. Oh, no. Making love with 'Ramón' was one thing. Making love with the real Blake was quite another.

She put a hand on his chest and physically pushed herself away from him. "Come into the kitchen, and I'll de-fur you."

He followed her closely enough that she could feel him behind her. When she grabbed a paper towel and moistened it in the sink, he stood nearly on top of her, pinning her against the counter. This time, she pushed him, and he backed up, but only a foot or so.

"Don't you have one of those lint rollers?" he asked.

"This'll work." It didn't, though. The paper towel just pushed the hairs around on the wool of his jacket. He used the opportunity to inch closer to her, nearly burying his nose in her hair.

"New cologne?" he murmured.

"Shampoo," she answered softly. This near to him, she could hardly get enough breath to push that word out.

"Flowers." He inhaled unsteadily. "Nice."

She put both hands on his chest, but this time to touch him, not to put distance between them. "Blake, you're crowding me."

Instead of backing off, he took her touch as a cue to press his lips to her ear. "How do you think that happened?"

Half a whimper got out of her before she could stop it. "What?"

"How did I manage to pin you here against your own sink?"

"Cat hairs."

"Good ol' Cat-hole." He nibbled at the spot just below her ear, and suddenly, her head grew so heavy, it titled to one side. He knew she loved to have her neck kissed. So many times, he'd come up behind her at the sink, and kissed her until she nearly melted into a puddle. Never at this particular sink, but there was a first time for everything.

Good God, if she didn't do something soon, she'd end up making love to her ex-husband in her bachelorette apartment.

He continued his onslaught on her nerves, of course, now sliding his lips downward to where her neck met her shoulder. "Do you what I miss the most?"

"Cat-hole?" she breathed.

"The noises you make when you come. I'll never forget the first time I heard them."

Of course, he wouldn't. He'd worked so hard to satisfy her. Before Blake, she'd thought orgasms were impossible for her without a vibrator. He'd stroked her and kissed her, pushing her past her shyness to have his mouth *there* and turned her to an addict who could never get enough of him. He was working the same magic now.

He pulled her against him, pushing her breasts into the firm wall of his chest. And letting her feel his erection against her belly.

"You gave me the greatest gift in the world that day," he said. "No, the second greatest. The best was the day you married me."

Damn it all. In another moment, he'd have her crying and begging him to help her find a way they could be together. After he short circuited her brain with his special brand of sex. This man could twist her into knots, and she should never have let him near her, not even as Ramón.

Then, he caught her lips with his and captured a tiny bit of her soul. No mask, no disguise. Just the man she'd love until she died, gentling her mouth with his. He took such care to kiss her thoroughly, methodically dismantling her resistance until she answered, demanding more. And receiving it. He sighed, or she did. Sounds didn't penetrate the haze he'd created around them.

He broke off the kiss and put his mouth to her ear again. "I want my face between your legs."

"Blake…." Breathe, damn it, breathe. "I…. "

"I want to make you come so hard the neighbors hear you scream." As he spoke, he ran his hands under her Tee shirt and upward to cup her breasts. Another defense fell away, and when he found the front closure of her bra and unfastened it, her aching flesh fell naturally into his palms. Flicking his thumbs over the nipples, he worked them into tight peaks.

Enough. This far and no further, or she'd lose control completely. "Don't! Oh God, I can't."

He took a step backward, removing the warmth of his body. She had to lean back against the sink to steady herself.

"You want me to stop?" His face was flushed, and his breath came hard. The look in his eyes squeezed her heart in her chest. Loss, hurt. For a moment, this big, bad CEO looked like a little boy.

"No," she answered. What else could she say? She couldn't deny herself any more than she could deny him.

So, like a fool, she walked into his arms and offered her mouth up for another heated kiss.

"Oh, baby." He touched his lips to her forehead, to each eyelid, and then to the tip of her nose. "I love you so much."

Damn him, why had he used that word? They might be safe if they didn't say love to each other. Just a roll in the hay for old time's sake. Now, he'd made it love.

She should have stopped it right there, but when he bent and swung her up into his arms, she coiled her fingers together behind his neck and let him carry her into the bedroom.

The queen size bed wasn't as large as the king they'd shared in marriage, but it had plenty of room for him to deposit her in the middle and sit down to remove his shoes and socks. That done, he took hers off too, and methodically went about stripping every bit of clothing off her body. After tugging her jeans down and sweeping them past her feet, he repeated the process with her panties. Next, he helped her to sit up and did away with her Tee shirt and her bra, which was already open.

He let her back down onto the coverlet and started in on his own clothes. His jacket went flying in one direction and his tie in another. He almost popped some buttons in his shirt before he had that off, too. His pants and shorts only took another second or two. Before she could take in his beauty—and the rigid state of his sex—he joined her on the bed, pushing her upward against the headboard so that he could part her legs and place his mouth over her pussy.

Nobody else did oral sex the way Blake did. He sucked on her nether lips, tugging at them gently, which put pressure on her clit with every movement. Sighing deeply, she reached down to stroke his hair to tell him that he was doing it right, that no one but he could make her come alive with his touch. That she loved him.

A sob caught in her throat. She did love him. She'd never stopped and she never would stop, and if he promised to treat her to this heaven, he'd always have a place between her legs. He was her curse, her poison, and her life.

As the tension built in her pussy, he played her clit like a master. Hard and fast enough to start a fire and then backing off to let it smolder. Over and over, he repeated the pattern until her every breath became a gasp or a whimper and she thought she'd die if he stopped and knew she'd die if he continued.

Now, he grasped her hips to pull her against his mouth, angling his tongue to hit the most sensitive part of her body. Here, too, he used a maddening touch to bring her to the edge and hold her there. Impossible to take more of this and not fly apart, but he demanded, and she obeyed. The coil wound tighter inside her. His every movement jangled at her nerves. Even the coverlet beneath her seemed to burn her skin as her body went wild with need.

Just when she couldn't tolerate another second without begging for release, he pressed his tongue against her clit, rubbing it hard enough to shoot her into orgasm. Her hips jerked upward, but he held on and kept up the pressure as explosions rocked her from the inside. She did scream then, even her voice beyond her control. The climax kept coming, and he kept urging her on. Wave after wave, crushing the air out of her chest.

When he finally let her finish, he rested her hips against the bed and then moved up beside her to gather her against him, her nose under his chin. Even in the peace that settled over her, the spasms continued in her sex. Softer now, but real. A reminder of what this man meant to her that no other man ever would.

"I think the neighbors did hear that one," he said after a moment.

"You bastard." The words came out like a caress.

He chuckled, the sound reverberating in his chest. "I'm the bastard who knows where all your buttons are."

"Egotistical bastard."

"Egotistical bastard with a raging hard-on," he said. "Do you know what it does to a man to have his woman climax like that?"

I'm not your woman. No force in heaven could make her mouth form those words, though. She'd fought so hard to put this man out of her present and into her past, and she'd failed. Damn Cox Club, and damn whatever fate had made him show up there. She'd landed back on square one—naked in his arms after an unbelievable climax. And, in another moment, she'd take him inside her, and he'd make her come again. No amount of phony will power could prevent it.

"Baby, are you okay?" he whispered.

"Fine."

He put his hand under her chin and tipped her face up so that he could gaze into her eyes. "You sure?"

"Why don't you shut up and make love to me?"

He grinned. "That's what I like to hear."

Somehow, the man managed to look cute. And vulnerable. His dark hair—normally with every strand in place—had grown a bit shaggy behind the ears, and some fell over his forehead almost into his eyes. Blake Crawford, CEO of Everything, needed a haircut. She reached up and pushed the rebellious strands back, smiling back at him despite herself.

All that tenderness changed in a heartbeat, though, as he positioned himself between her legs. Again, the dominant male, taking his rightful place. He kissed her briefly before entering her in one smooth glide.

As always, the total possession took her breath away. After all these times, she ought to have become used to how they fit together as if created for each other. As her hips rose up to meet his entry, she wrapped her legs around him to keep him where he was.

He began to move in slow, even thrusts. "How I've missed this."

He hadn't missed her at all. He'd fucked her thoroughly only a few nights before. This was different—more honest—Blake and Andrea, husband and wife, lovers before that.

The sounds of sweet sex filled her small bedroom. Breathing in unison—his soft grunts, her sighs. Already, he filled the space with his presence while his body reclaimed hers. His chest rubbed against her nipples as his sex plundered hers. Such luxury, the pleasure of their coupling while she trailed her fingertips down the furrow of his spine.

"Baby," he whispered. "Come for me."

"I will."

He ought to have known by then that her body would never deny him. Since that first night, when he'd taken the time to give her pleasure, holding off his own release until he'd made her climax.

He repeated that care now as his thrusts came faster and went deeper. She joined him in the climb toward fulfillment. Now, she clutched his shoulders and she angled her pelvis so that on each forward movement, he hit her most sensitive spot. Her sex tightened around his, creating friction that sent a current of fire through her.

He groaned. "You make me so hot."

"Blake… oh, yes."

She let her mind become suspended in the moment. By herself, absorbed in her mounting arousal. And yet, Blake was in her, around her, on her. He was her world, his body claiming hers. Pounding into her now, he'd retreated into his own reality as well, and still, they'd united again in a way they'd never truly break.

Her body couldn't wait any longer, and the frantic pace of his movements told her that he'd reached the end of his control. Too soon, and yet at the perfect moment, she shot upward into orgasm. The pressure built inside her as he continued pumping. In the end, they came at the same moment, grasping at each other. Hanging on as the madness took them. He released his essence inside her as her sex contracted around his.

It ended, as it always did, with sweet lethargy as they both went limp with spent lust. Somehow, she ended up with her back against his front, spoon-fashion, as he curled a protective arm around her, his palm covering one breast.

"There's no one else like you, baby," he murmured into her ear.

She could have said the same thing, of course, if she could have done anything but take a breath and let it out on a sigh.

"The world thinks I'm some kind of playboy," he went on. "When there's only one woman I want."

True enough. Blake had always been strictly faithful, no matter how many women—most more glamorous than Andi—had expressed interest. That part had always amused her and given her a sense of feminine pride. He did everything with such determination, though, and he put all that effort into wanting her, as well. In the end, he'd wanted too much.

"I'm convinced we could have made it, Andrea. Until death did us part," he added.

"Divorce isn't the end of the world," she answered.

He stiffened ever so slightly behind her. "No."

In fact, it seemed divorce hadn't even managed to end their relationship. Lots of formerly married couples fell back into the sack from time to time. Or so the stories went. She'd done it—what?—three times now? And she hadn't finished. She'd either go back to Cox and have "Ramón" again, or she'd have Blake some other way. Her body had overruled her mind. So had her heart. Damn that place, anyway.

His palm drifted lower until his fingers splayed over her belly. "Is there any chance…"

The meaning didn't register for a moment. When it did, she pushed his hand away. "I'm taking pills. Real ones."

He lay absolutely still behind her for a second and then rolled over. When she glanced in that direction, she found him sitting, clutching the edge of the mattress in his fists. His back made one rigid line.

Tough shit. What did he have to be angry about?

"Want some eggs?" he said lightly. As if they hadn't just waded into the waters that had finally ended their marriage.

"I'd love some eggs."

Andrea's kitchen was stocked with only enough food to convince a visitor that someone camped out there occasionally. Instant coffee and creamer. Who drank that? Ramen noodles, canned soup. He briefly studied a tin of that processed ham-food and put it back again. Not even in his most desperate moments would he put that into his eggs.

Eggs. What if she didn't have any of those? In the refrigerator, he found a carton. Avoiding the sell-by date on the side so he wouldn't have to know how old they were, he lifted the top and counted. Five. Barely enough, but they'd have to do. The vegetable crisper had half an onion and a bell pepper, so he took those out and went in search of butter and cheese. He found both—neither too geriatric in appearance. No ham, no bacon, no sausage. No bread, either, for toast.

"Don't you ever go shopping?" He looked over his shoulder and caught her staring at his butt. He only wore his shorts and suit pants. She'd always said pin stripes emphasized the curve of his ass. Doing his best to hide a smile, he went back to his work.

"I had to fire the maid," she answered. "She got into the good brandy."

"You have enough money of your own," he said. "I would have given you more. You don't have to live this way."

"Are you going to cut that bell pepper, or aren't you?"

She'd come up so close behind him, he jumped at the sound of her voice. She'd put on a simple nightgown that fell below her knees. Not a negligee or a peignoir, just a pink cotton thing with lace for straps. She'd pulled her hair back into a pony tail held together by what women called a scrunchie. An innocent look for the woman who'd just been liquid heat beneath him.

She raised an eyebrow. "The pepper?"

"Right." With the sole knife he'd found, he removed the top and cut off a thick slice, which she immediately grabbed and brought to her mouth for a bite. Some things never changed, thank heaven.

While he beat the eggs with a fork and then grated cheese—or rather peeled off strips with a vegetable parer—she grabbed a carton of orange juice from the fridge, found some glasses, and went to the table where she sat, nibbling on the pepper.

He deliberately turned his back to her in an effort to appear nonchalant. "So, seeing anyone seriously?"

A long silence followed until he remembered to scramble the eggs some more.

"Would I have just fucked you if I were?" she answered finally.

He glanced back at her. "We don't fuck, Andrea. We make love."

She raised her bare feet to the rung of her chair and hugged her knees to her chest. The gesture said more than any words could. She wasn't going to answer to him.

Suddenly, his gut turned to water. As stubborn as she could be, she might have refused to give him any information on general principle. The other alternative didn't bear even considering—that she'd taken her encounters with his persona at the club seriously. She wouldn't be having sex with three men, not the Andrea he knew, but how could she have feelings for a man who did *that* for a living?

The aroma of browning onions pulled him back to the present. If he didn't pay more attention, the whole thing would burn. After adding the eggs, he stirred them with the only thing he had, the fork. She could worry about the non-stick surface.

"What about you?" she asked. "Any of the tabloid stories true?"

He had to smile at the tinge of jealousy in her voice. "You know how they are."

There had been women since the word got out he was single. He'd gone home with a few, had stayed the night with one. Completely unsatisfying, at least for him. No one's orgasms felt like Andrea's.

"That's not exactly an answer," she said.

"No one."

He could have mistaken it, but he might have detected a sigh of relief. So, she wanted him. She obviously wanted Ramón. What went on here?

When he held out the pan with the finished eggs, she got up and found plates and forks and allowed him to serve her.

They sat and ate, much as they'd dozens of times before, but usually in the middle of the night. Even before they'd married, one of them would awake the other for sex, and they'd fill their other appetite with a snack afterwards. Mrs. Morehouse had always complained about the mess in the morning, but they'd kept to their ritual. It wasn't the same in this empty apartment in the afternoon, but it was the closest he'd had in much too long. So, he savored the rubbery eggs and overcooked vegetables as if they were his last meal.

Still, one thing teased at the back of his mind. "There's really no one in your life?"

"Besides Bandit?"

"You know what I mean."

"It's really none of your business," she said as she pushed a piece of onion around on her plate.

"Even if…. " He stopped himself before he blurted out something unfortunate like 'even if I didn't love you' or 'even if we didn't just make love' or something relatively innocent like 'even if we hadn't been married.' If he was planning a way back into her heart and her life—which he was, he might as well admit it—he'd need to be more subtle than that. He'd tried to control her once and lost everything as a result. This time, she'd have to come to him.

"I care about you," he said finally. "I want you to be happy."

"Thanks, Blake. I am." She got up, stacked his plate on top of hers. With her glass in the other hand, she went to the sink. Less than an hour before, he'd cornered her there and convinced her to let him make love to her. His cock could manage again, even so soon. He could probably seduce her a second time, too. If only they could have sex twenty-four/seven, he could keep her with him forever. Short of that, he'd have to find some other way to make her want to keep him around. Maybe Ramón could help him to gather information on how to do that. At the very least, his Latin counterpart might find out how she felt about him.

He sipped his juice and watched her as she rinsed off the dishes and then sloshed water in her glass. The fabric of her nightgown didn't do much to hide the curve of her buttocks or the slight swing of her breasts as she worked.

Yes, indeed, his cock could have performed again with very little provocation. He'd save that for her lover at the club. All he had to do was get her back to Cox.

Chapter 5

The note worked. Andrea appeared at Cox at her usual time and headed to the place at the bar where he'd first introduced himself to her as Ramón. Blake stayed in the shadows for a moment just to watch her. In her jeans and a baggy sweater that went to half-thigh, she might get less attention than the more brightly and scantily dressed female patrons. He knew the body beneath the cable-knit, though, and he'd better get to her before some other man decided to go exploring.

He pushed away from the wall and approached her. When she spotted him, she smiled and then bit her lip in a way that made his cock stiffen. For just a moment, he could forget that she was greeting another man, and he could bask in the welcome.

Smiling back, he lifted his fingers to check his mask and then closed the remaining distance to take her hand.

"*Bienvenida, cara mia.*" He brushed his lips over her knuckles.

"You said it was *muy importante* that I come."

"*Mi cuerpo quiere el tuyo*"

"*¿Es lo todo importante?*" The corner of her mouth curled upward as if she didn't believe him.

He bent to whisper to her. "*Tengo más.*"

"I'm sure you do." She took a step away and crooked a finger to order him to follow. "This way."

She took him to a room along the same hallway as she'd chosen the first night. Most likely, she didn't have any more kink in mind. His member didn't much care. Merely going with her through the crowd, surrounded by pulsing music and muffled sounds of sex had given him a substantial erection. But then, with this woman, his sex didn't need any help. He might have imagined it, but she seemed to be swinging her hips more than usual, which made her tight little butt move under the sweater. Who knew cable knight could be so erotic?

Once she had him inside, she pushed him up against the door and pulled his head down for a kiss. In an instant, her mouth was everywhere on his, sucking, licking, even nibbling. Damn, but the woman was on fire, and in another moment, she'd have him so hot, he'd forget the purpose of tonight's visit… to find out how she felt about her ex-husband.

"*Cara, despacio.*" He had to fight to get a breath. That meant to slow down, didn't it?

"Can't," she gasped. "It's been too fucking long."

Wrong. First, she'd ignored the cards to Cox he'd sent for days. Second, they'd made love at her apartment only yesterday. How did she have any reason to act neglected?

Still, when she tore at the buttons of his shirt and then pushed the garment off his shoulders and down his arms, he didn't even try to stop her. And when first her hands stroked his chest and her mouth found his nipples, he only groaned in response.

He somewhere found the strength to push her back. Not far, just enough to shake his head to clear it. "*Tengo algo...*"

"I know. *Muy importante.*" Her hand went to the front of his pants, covering his erection. "*Esto es lo más importante.*"

Holy hell. He nearly came out of his skin. Maybe he should let her have her way with him. He could ply her for information later, even another night. Because if she kept doing that, he might not have any choice in the matter.

"What did you do while we were apart?" she murmured into his ear. "Did you have other women?"

"*No. Solamente tu.*"

"You must have gotten really horny alone so long." She squeezed him through his pants. "God, you're big. And hard."

"*Ay.*"

"Did you stroke yourself until you came?" she said. "Did you imagine you were fucking me?"

"*Cara...*" Damn, if he didn't stop her soon, he'd lose this battle before he ever got into it.

"Can I watch you do that now?" Up and down, she rubbed him, from the base of his rod to the tip.

"Andrea," he said from between clenched teeth.

She stopped dead, her hand still over his shaft. "You know my name."

"*Sí.*"

She stepped away and flicked the switch to the overhead light. The room grew so bright it nearly blinded him.

"You know my name," she repeated. "Why? This place is supposed to be anonymous."

"*Escúchame.*" He struggled for breath and succeeded a bit. "*Tu esposo.*"

"My ex-husband," she corrected. "What about him."

"*El sabe.*"

"About us?" she asked.

"*Sí.*"

"Really?" She crossed her arms over her chest. "And how would he find out?"

Damn. This was not how she was supposed to react. She ought to be horrified that her husband, even a former one, knew that she'd been coming to a place like Cox and having anonymous sex with strangers. She should be begging for details—did he know about the leather straps and how she'd sucked so eagerly on another man's erect member? She ought to appear horrified, not resemble the female spider about to creep across her web toward her unsuspecting mate.

"*No se*," he answered.

"I think you do know. I think you know very well." She approached him slowly until she stood only inches away. Quickly—before he caught her intent—she reached up and snatched off his mask and stared up at him. "Don't you, *Ramón*?"

"What the hell?" He grabbed the mask back, but to no use. The damage had already been done.

He kept her gaze focused on her, her chin tipped up to do it. Nothing in her expression showed the least hint of surprise to discover his real identity. In fact, her eyes had a wicked glint to them, as if she'd played some grand joke on him.

But then… damn it all. . .. she had. "You knew I was Ramón."

She just kept on smiling at him, curse her black soul.

"When?" he demanded. "When did you figure it out?"

"The first time you kissed me," she answered. "I was married to you for five years. Didn't you think I'd recognize my own husband?"

"And yet, you let me make a perfect fool of myself?"

"No one's perfect." She smirked at him. Actually smirked.

"You let me wear these ridiculous shirts and tight pants?" He threw up his hands in a gesture of pointless rage. "You let me go on and on in broken Spanish."

She chuckled. "I didn't make you do it."

"For the love of God, I waxed my chest!"

"And very nicely, too."

"What did you think would go through my head when you suddenly stopped coming here? How did you think I'd feel?" Good God, that sounded like a soap opera, and he was shouting, too. He never shouted.

"I didn't know, but that was a very interesting visit you paid me at my apartment."

He bent over her, nearly pushing his nose onto hers. "You tied me up!"

She shrugged. "Seemed like a good idea at the time."

He started pacing, running his fingers through his hair as he did. All the idiotic things she'd put him through. He ought to do something to get back at her, but at the same time, a blossom of happiness unfurled inside him. She hadn't slept with another man, except for that first time. She hadn't worked out her bondage fantasy with a stranger. She hadn't come fast and hard for another lover's touch. She'd done all that with and for him. She'd known all along who he was and had come to him willingly.

He stopped and cross his own arms over his hairless chest, narrowing his eyes at her. "You've been dishonest with me since the first."

She let out a hoot. "I have? What about you?"

"I did it for your own good," he answered. "To teach you a lesson."

"Oh, yeah? What lesson was that?"

"Don't use that tone with me, young lady."

Her eyes widened. "I beg your pardon."

"I'm sorry to have to do this." He would have rolled up his sleeves if she hadn't stripped him of his shirt minutes ago. "I'm going to have to punish you."

Something crackled in the air between them. A jolt of understanding, charged with tension. Whatever followed, they were both in for it. It wasn't clear who had challenged and who had accepted, but they were about to turn a corner in their relationship. Never completely soft before, his cock came to full attention in his pants. Ready for action and straining against his fly.

She raised her hands in the air. "Oh, I'm so scared."

"You ought to be. You've pushed me too far, Andrea."

She licked her lips in a way that made his member twitch. Or it would have if it had had any room in his pants. The poor thing was doing its best to bust open the zipper.

"Just what it is you think you can do to make me behave?" She backed away from him but not so far that he couldn't grab her with one lunge.

"I can spank your pretty bottom until you can't sit down for a week." He would spank her, but she would sit afterward. She'd sit on his lap, taking his sex deep inside her how.

She grinned and made a great show of staying out of his reach, all the while signaling she'd surrender soon enough once he'd taken up the chase. They both knew he'd never hurt her, although things might get rough if he couldn't pull her down onto him soon.

"You wouldn't spank me," she said. "You wouldn't dare."

"Get out of your clothes and see if I don't."

She stuck her tongue out at him. "Make me."

"Do it," he ordered, slapping his hand against his thigh hard enough that the sound echoed around the room..

"What a beast you are."

She hadn't gotten far from him, so it didn't take much to close the distance and catch her by the waistband of her jeans. Fumbling, he pushed her Tee shirt up and popped the snap at the top of her zipper. "Enough playing around."

Though she pretended to squirm, he easily opened her zipper and shoved the pants over her hips. Then, he picked her up like a sack of flour and carried her to the bed where he sat and draped her over his knees.

She let out an "oof" and made as if it get up, but he held her with a palm between her shoulder blades. Now, he could stare at the curve of her buttocks. Smooth skin, sweetly round, just the right size for his hand. He stroked one cheek before raising his arm and bringing it down to smack her.

Because she'd turned up the lights earlier, he didn't have to search through darkness to see the effect of his blow. She'd turned a pale pink. Nothing livid just a healthy glow.

"Hey, what do you think you're doing?" she said, her voice breathless in that way it got as she became excited.

He swatted her again, on the other buttock this time. Instead of any hint of fear, she arched her back, offering her flesh for more of the same. And why not?

The next time he slapped her, she let out a little moan of pleasure. Her skin grew warm under his hand, so he let his fingers linger to savor her heat. Not far away, the lips of her sex seemed to swell and part, opening to him. He touched them, too, stroking softly until she sighed in approval.

He hadn't completely removed her jeans, though, and they kept her knees together. Next time he did this—and he might very well—he'd plan better. For now, he bent over and reached toward her foot. She lifted it to help him, and he soon had one shoe and sock off. The two of them bared her other foot, and now he could push the denim down her legs, taking her panties with it. One final tug, and he was able to toss the clothing aside. Now naked from the waist down, she lay completely open for his explorations.

"You act as if you want this," he said, his own voice grown thick with arousal.

"No," she gasped. "Don't hit me."

"This, then?" He cupped her mound, squeezing gently.

"Oh, God," she cried, wiggling her butt. Her hip hit is erection, rubbing. Even through the fabric, the contact sent a jolt through him that set his teeth on edge.

He smacked her again on both buttocks and then slid his hand between her thighs. She pulled her legs together, squeezing his fingers against the lips as a trickle of moisture coated his fingers.

"Spread your legs," he ordered as he pushed them apart himself and slid a finger into her wetness.

She gasped and stiffened as he probed with one finger and then two to stretch her. Heaven help him, she'd better be ready for all of him and quickly when his control finally evaporated.

Her breath came hard and fast, and she gave up all pretense of struggling. Instead, she surrendered, spreading her legs in a silent plea that he continue. This was his Andrea, the woman who trusted him enough to make herself truly vulnerable. He continued stroking her inner walls and then removed his fingers so that he could use the tip of one to spread her own wetness over her clitoris. She shuddered and let out a whimper. More. She wanted more, so he gave it to her. Another plunge into her body and another caress to her most sensitive flesh. He rolled it now, pressing it into her flesh until her whimpers grew louder and higher in pitch.

"Blake," she cried.

Just his name, and yet, it held so much meaning. It wasn't a cry for anyone but him. Now. She couldn't wait any longer.

He struggled with his fly. Cursed tight pants. The snap fought him, and the zipper balked at the violence of his pulling. Finally, he took a deep breath and struggled for patience. It gave way, and he pulled his cock free. Immediately, she lifted herself far enough that she could grasp his shaft and guide the head between the lips of her pussy.

Sucking in her breath with a hiss, she lowered herself onto him. "Damn, I thought I'd die."

"I think I will," he gritted back.

"Not until you've fucked me."

He didn't argue about the word. Who could with his cock in the grip of her inner heat?

She moved then, pushing herself upward and descending onto him. Her muscles grasped him firmly—tight—like the first time they'd made love. By now after so many times together, they fit together so perfectly even the months apart had meant nothing at all. Her body welcomed his with the combination of passion and innocence that made her so lethal to his heart. As she quickened her pace, he grasped her hips so that he could thrust up into her. Hanging onto his shoulders, she pressed the side of her face against his and crooned her pleasure into his ear. Soft sounds desperate with need. His heart threatened to burst with pride and love. She'd come to him, not some other man. She'd always known his hands touched her, and she'd taken and given without reservation. Somehow, he'd make this permanent. Even if his mind came to accept their separation, his body never would.

"Blake." She followed that with a sigh that almost sounded like a sob.

"I'm here, baby."

"Don't stop." A tremor rushed through her body as she arched her back and kept moving. "Don't ever stop."

"Never."

"I can't... oh, God... now... Blake!" Her orgasm claimed them both. He felt it in his bones as she turned to fire in his arms. Another sob, and she opened her throat to release her cry of completion. As her sex sent spasms along his length, he held her hips fast, pumping into her as he climaxed. Another voice joined hers. His own, but foreign enough that he hardly recognized it. They hung suspended in their own reality for long seconds before reality returned. When it did, she sagged against him, her face buried in the crook of his neck as her breath came hot and ragged against his shoulder.

He held her, stroking her hair and then running his palm down her back. He had his Andrea back, the wife he'd cherished and always would. She'd come to him willingly all these times. She couldn't walk away again. No one could risk losing this perfection once she'd found it again.

Sighing, he lowered them to the mattress, although he kept her right where she was against his chest. Somehow, his face had spread itself into a silly grin that would not go away and probably made him look like a damned fool. He had been a damned fool to lose her. The crawl back into her life started right now.

She made a fist and swatted at his chest with it with no more force than an infant would use. "You have your nerve spanking me."

"You tied me up, remember?"

"You liked it," she answered.

"You liked this."

"Never mind any of that," she said. "It's the principle of the thing."

He kissed her forehead. "I want to ask you something, and I'd like an honest answer."

She tensed. "All right."

"The other man you were with here…. "

"David?" she said in a tiny voice.

David. Somehow, knowing his name made the guy more real. "Did he satisfy you?"

"He was sweet. Considerate."

Blake took a steadying breath. "You climaxed."

"With the vibrator." She pulled back and stared at him. "Hey, wait a minute. How do you know about him?"

"I watched you."

"What?" She sat straight up. "What in hell are you talking about?"

"Closed circuit television. I was in the control room."

"What the fuck? There are cameras?" She covered her breasts with her arms and glanced around.

He sat next to her and pulled her against him. "Don't worry. I told the guy who runs them to turn off the ones where we are."

"But you watched me with David. Why? How? How did you even find out about Cox?"

"I own the club."

"You." She stared at him as if he'd grown another head or turned green and sprouted antennae. "You own Cox Club?"

"Someone in my company acquired it. I was visiting it before selling it the night you walked in."

"You?" she repeated and then clapped her fingers over her mouth and dissolved into laughter. "You… oh, my God… you own a sex club?"

"I didn't mean to buy it." Women, would he ever understand them? Never mind the plural—only this woman mattered. He'd just told her that he'd watched her with another man. He'd had a security camera on her while she'd had sex with a stranger, and now she was laughing.

"You…. " She gasped in a breath between guffaws. "Mr. High and Righteous, Entrepreneurs' Circle Man of the Year. The great and prosperous Blake Crawford. Lord have mercy! Owns a sex club."

"One that you frequent, so I don't know what makes you so virtuous," he said.

"To visit… damn, damn, damn… it's too funny." She dragged in a breath. "To visit you and your waxed chest."

"If you don't stop, I'll spank you again."

That did it. She rolled on the bed, clutching her ribs. Oh hell, it was funny. And she was here and laughing and naked. With him. He really couldn't ask for anything better.

He lay down again and pulled her into his arms as her laughter subsided with a hiccup and an unladylike snort. "I'm glad you're happy."

She sighed. "I'm going to miss Ramón."

"I'll keep waxing my chest if you like."

"Blake… "

He kissed her before she could say anything that might hold their past reality in it. Months of that had been quite enough. She yielded, her lips softening under his. They could make love again. He knew it and she knew it. He savored her mouth, letting the heat build until his purpose sunk in. No going back. Only forward.

Finally, he pulled away, and she gazed up at him, moistening her lips. "What do we do now?"

He caught her hand in his and brought it to his mouth to kiss the knuckles. "I want a chance to win you back. You don't have to agree to more than that. Just one real chance."

"All right," she said finally. "Do your damnedest."

Andi scanned the crowd for the twentieth time. The gallery was softly lit, making each of her pieces resemble jewels against a backdrop of clinking glasses, expensive perfume, and Mozart. *The Times* had sent an art critic—a small man with bulbous nose whose whole vocabulary seemed to consist of "hmmm" and "I see." The fact that they'd covered her exhibit at all meant a great deal to her career. Everything was perfect and should have satisfied her. It would have, a month ago.

Lost among her own creations, she wandered toward the nude. Call-in programs had played on the radio as she'd worked on it in her studio. Then, she'd worn her grubby fleece, her hair tied up in a bandana. Now, she teetered on three-inch heels, and crimson satin ruffled around her legs. Mother of pearl combs had replaced the bandana, sweeping her curls up to the top of her head. The successful sculptor, surrounded by her admirers, all drinking champagne and eating canapés. What a sham.

The entire studio took an inward breath as Blake Crawford entered, or at least, it seemed that way to Andi's ears. A definite ripple of female interest floated around as he walked from the entrance toward her. No doubt some of the men had taken an interest, too. He was simply spectacular, and only a stone could have ignored him.

Déjà vu could hardly describe how she felt watching him come toward her. Another gallery in a different city. Not quite as grand as this one, but it had filled with magic the moment Blake had entered. A lowly worker then—an art student with a day job—she'd hardly believed he'd noticed her until he'd stood only feet away.

He looked the same now, his impeccable formal wear fitting his broad shoulders. He might have found exactly the same tux just for her—to remind her. His blue eyes held the same interest, the same promise of something wonderful, out of reach but not impossible. Something no one else would share.

A passing waiter held out a tray, and Blake took two glasses. Smiling, he walked to her and offered one. The same way he had on the night when he'd found a pumpkin and turned her into a princess. After touching the champagne flute to hers, he lifted it in a toast. "Beautiful."

She took a sip of her drink, doing her best to remember how to breathe at the same time. "They did a wonderful job with the show."

"I didn't mean that."

Somehow, he could still make her blush, or maybe the heat in her cheeks came from no more than standing close to him. "I thought you liked my work."

"I do."

"You're not looking at it."

"I can do that later." He bent closer to her. "I love you in that color."

"I chose the dress for you." Heat flared on her neck now. In a moment, her skin would match the color of the satin.

"Lovely," he said softly. "Although the neckline could be a little higher."

She tilted her head, slanting a glance up at him. "You disapprove?"

"It makes me want to kiss you silly in front of all your fans."

"You can do that later, too."

"I'll hold you to that." His smile told her he'd hold her to a great deal more than mere kissing. A flutter started in her stomach and moved south. His presence alone was enough to create delightful confusion in the general vicinity of her heart. Add to that the fact that she'd agreed to let him try to win her back, and the whole situation took on the feel of the prom with the captain of the football team. Of course, she'd never experienced such a thing, having been a shy girl with braces who always got good grades. If she'd ever had that sort of fantasy, he was fulfilling it right now.

"Thank you for inviting me," he said in the low, sweet voice that he used in their bedroom.

"I'm glad you came." She put her free hand on his. "Truly."

He lifted her hand to his mouth and kissed her knuckles. "Would you do me the honor of showing me around?"

"Sure." She stepped aside to give him a better view of the nude. "I think you remember this one."

"Of course." He eyed it for a moment. "I'm still don't think you should have done a study of my mother *au naturel*."

"Silly." She swatted at his arm.

"She's a holy terror, I'll admit, but I'm not sure she deserves this."

"Blake! Someone might overhear."

"No one would believe you'd do a nude of your mother-in-law, surely."

"None of the patrons," she answered. "But a reporter... you know the kind."

"I had my security check before I got out of the car. None of those leeches in the vicinity," he said.

"Thanks." She walked him toward another piece, the one she'd been working on when he'd dropped in to visit the cat he despised.

"I definitely remember this one." He leaned toward her. "Was I the inspiration for the obelisk?"

"You're impossible." She put her fingers over her mouth to stifle her laughter. "What's gotten into you?"

"I'm happy. For the first time in six months." His blue eyes filled with emotion. Joy tinged with uncertainty. And love. The combination almost tottered her off her heels.

Her vision misted over, and she couldn't keep her stupid chin from wobbling.

He touched the side of her face. "Aww, baby, don't."

"Sorry." She brushed her eyes, taking care with the damned make-up, and gave him an uncertain smile. "Better?"

"I'd kill to put my arms around you right now."

The string quartet came to life behind her, although they might have been playing all along. She would never have noticed. Rather than their usual fare, they launched into a waltz. Something Viennese, rich and lilting.

"Here's my excuse." He took her glass and set both of their drinks on the pedestal of the sculpture. Probably against the rules, but who cared. "May I have this waltz?"

"It's only background music. No one's supposed to dance to it."

"We will."

"There's no room. We'll knock something over."

He looked around, spotted the French doors that led to the small terrace, and inclined his head toward it. "Out there."

"All right."

He twined her arm around his, the exact way men did in historical romances. But then, that was how he'd always made her feel—the Regency miss, the Victorian spinster, both trying to protect their hearts and failing in the attempt. Finally, succumbing to his seduction only to have their happily-ever-afters. Wonderful for fiction, but sadly, modern reality required for a woman to have her own life, independent from her mate's. That part, they'd never quite managed, but the rest of it... oh, the rest of it... how perfect he'd made it.

When they arrived at the tiled terrace surrounded by a wrought iron railing he didn't bow exactly, but he paused before settling one palm at the small of her back and curling the other hand around hers to bring both of them to his chest. She went to him naturally, like breathing, and he led the two of them in a simple box step—one, two, three, one, two, three. There seemed no other place in the world to rest her gaze than his face. In the dimmer light, his eyes shown a crystalline blue, and his lips parted as if he could whisper to her without words. He should have worn a sash across his chest, a sword and scabbard dangling at the corner, but honestly, that wouldn't have made him any more perfect.

A devil's glint entered his gaze. "Been back to Cox lately?"

"No desire. My favorite staff member left," she answered. "You?"

"Not at all. My only client disappeared."

"I wonder if they ran off together."

"Very likely," he said. "I heard they were in love."

She chuckled again. "I still can't believe you did that for me."

"I haven't had my full revenge yet."

"Should we go back some night?"

"No longer mine. I managed to unload it." He used their joined hands to tip her head up towards his. "Besides, I'd rather go forward."

"Mr. Crawford, would you look this way, please?" It was a man's voice, harsh and crude. Blake turned toward it, and a barrage of lights flashed. At one time, they would have confused her, but now, she'd had enough experience with paparazzi to know what to expect.

"This is a private party," Blake shouted. "Go away."

"Is it true that you and Mrs. Crawford are getting back together?" A woman this time.

Blake pressed her face into his chest, using his arm to shield her. "Damn you, leave us alone."

"So, that is Mrs. Crawford, then." Yet another reporter.

"Would the two of you pose with one of the sculptures?"

"Come on, Mrs. Crawford, give us a shot."

"The public wants to know."

How many of them were there? How many fucking cameras had they brought? How were she and Blake going to get out of here? They could all boil in hell for spoiling such a perfect night.

"This way, quickly," another man whispered nearby. He must have been one of Blake's employees if Blake had let him get that close.

"The back way," the man went on. "We've brought your car around."

Blake nodded, his grip tightening around her. "Come on."

"Why tonight? Of all nights, why this one?"

"Come on, baby. We'll get you out of here."

"But it's my show." All right, she'd wailed that, but who wouldn't when a bunch of bastards had ruined not only her big show but the fantasy Blake had created for her? She couldn't even be angry with him about it. He didn't control these vultures.

Now, four arms, four pairs of hands guided her. With Blake's arm still covering her head, the world came through as bright, buzzing light and questions that might have been in Old Church Slavonic for all she understood them. They moved slowly, arms shoving, elbows thrusting. A few oophs from the crowd sounded as sweet as the waltz had earlier. Maybe if the 'reporters' all died horrible deaths the others would find a different way to make a living.

They made it to a loading dock finally. Henri, the gallery owner greeted them there. Even in near darkness, his skin was pale, his eyes perfect circles.

"I'm so sorry, Mr. Crawford," he said. "I don't know how they got in."

"It's my fault. I shouldn't have come," Blake answered.

"No." She gripped his lapels. In a moment, she'd stop acting hysterically, but right now, she had a right. "You should have come. I wanted you here."

"Poor thing." Henri patted her arm. "Did they hurt you?"

"They ruined your show, Henri. How will I ever make it up to you?"

"Not your fault, cherie. We'll do others."

"Of course, you will," Blake said. "Her work is magnificent, isn't it?"

"The best," Henri answered.

Bless them both. She could kiss the two of them and would, although Blake's might be a bit more intimate.

"Next time, I'll help with security," Blake said. "No repeats."

"There, you see?" Henri declared. "All fixed."

This time, she put her hand on Henri's arm. "No damage?"

"*Mais, non.* If they hurt anything or anyone, we'll put them into jail."

"Thank you," she breathed.

"Here's the car," Blake said.

"*Bon soir,*" Henri called after them as they left. It was anything but a good evening, especially for Henri, the dear man. She and Blake would make it up to them.

The Bugatti sat several feet below the loading dock in an empty galley. In her heels, she'd have a hard time scrambling down, so Blake helped her to fall into the arms of the man who'd driven the car and then dropped down beside her. After helping her in, he sprinted around to his side, jumped into the seat, and started the engine. The man stepped clear as Blake made a broken U turn and then let the powerful engine take over with a low rumble that accelerated into a roar. No paparazzo in hell could keep up with this beast.

Chapter 6

Andrea didn't blanch when he pulled up to the security kiosk they'd passed together hundreds of times, but then, she must have realized from his route that he was taking her home. Not to the apartment, but to her real home. The one she'd shared with him. He'd taken a risk bringing her here. She might see it as another attempt to control her. He'd make up an excuse if he had to—the paparazzi might have figured out where she lived and surrounded her building. Probably, the truth would work better. He'd seen her again, no masks, no insincere interest in the cat. He just couldn't be without her again so soon.

She said nothing as he guided the Bugatti along the quiet streets, the lamps whizzing by creating a rhythm of light and dark inside the car. When he turned into the driveway and stopped the car, she climbed out before the garage door opener could do its work.

He took a breath to steel himself, turned off the engine, and got out after her. Clutching her ribs to hug herself, she stood there, staring up at the house as if she might go inside and never come out again.

He touched her elbow. "I hope you don't mind."

"Why did you bring me here?"

He searched for a clever answer and only found the truth. "I wanted to talk."

"We could have done that at my apartment." She didn't move, and her tone gave nothing away. If angry or fearful, she didn't show it.

"I'll take you there if you want."

"No." She dropped her arms to her sides. "This is fine."

"I promise not to bite," he said. "Unless you ask me to."

She glanced up at him. "I'm not afraid of you."

"Famous last words." He gestured toward the front staircase. "After you."

After all the nights they'd come home to this house, it shouldn't seem like such a blessing climbing the stairs ahead of him. The material of her dress clung to her hips as she went. An invitation almost too powerful to ignore, and yet, he'd shackle his hands before he'd reach for her. This time, she had to come to him. Somehow, he had to conquer his instincts to control, order and manipulate. Still, as he used his key in the lock and opened the door ahead of her, he almost slipped when she reached for the light switch herself. She belonged here, and how easy that would be to demonstrate by pressing her against the wall of the entryway and kissing her until she took his hand and led him to the bedroom.

By clenching and unclenching his fingers, he managed to keep his hands to himself and only closed the door behind them and dropped his key onto the tray on the little table.

"Wine okay?" he asked. "I have a decent cab."

She gave him a half-smile over her shoulder. "Sounds great."

"Have a seat."

While she took a place on the couch, he went to the bar and selected a bottle of cabernet. The remote for the stereo sat inches away, so he used it to turn on some music. Soft jazz filled the room—a quartet featuring a breathy sax. The sounds created a tension in the room. Not unpleasant but risky, given that he had no idea how far her could go with her. Damn, why couldn't this be like a merger or a sale? Something he could understand and predict.

Instead, he found the corkscrew, opened the wine, and took it and two glasses into the living room area. He joined Andrea on the couch. Not too far away and not too near.

She took a sip and then sat, running her fingers down the stem of her glass. "You wanted to talk."

"Yeah." He took some of the wine for fortification. "Mostly, I wanted to apologize."

She didn't answer but sat, watching him as if she didn't know whether to come nearer or back away.

"I've had a long time to think, and pretty much everything you said about me is true."

"Such as?"

He took some more wine and then set his glass on the table. "I always thought I was a pretty liberated guy. I wanted a mate who had her own life. Dreams, ambitions, that sort of thing."

"That sort of thing," she repeated.

"That pretty much sums it up. I wanted you to have your career, but only if I didn't have to pay too much attention to it."

"You weren't all that bad," she said softly.

"I was bad enough." *I lost you.* How many nights had he lain upstairs in the bed they'd shared, gazing up at the ceiling in darkness, telling himself that very thing? *You lost her, you stupid bastard. How are you going to get her back?* He'd never had an answer.

"All the times I took you away from your work to play the corporate wife," he said. "I knew you hated it."

"I married a CEO."

"You were supposed to marry the man not the position."

"I knew what I was getting into." She paused. "Sort of."

"I still need to explain about the pills. I don't think you completely understand."

"What's not to understand? You wanted me pregnant."

"I wanted your baby." The words came out more sharply than he'd wanted. More vehement. She straightened, and her eyes widened.

"It's hard to make this clear when I don't fully understand myself," he said. "I wanted to do all the caveman things—hover over you and protect you. Slay lions and bring you mammoth meat."

"Mammoth?"

"I can't force this to make sense. It's so basic to me."

She drank the rest of her wine and put the glass on the table next to his. Then, she turned toward him, her arm resting on the back of the sofa. She looked so beautiful, even in the bright light. Some of her hair had worked its way free of the pins and hung in curls around her face. Her skin looked like powdered heaven above the low bodice of her dress. If he could only press his face into the curve of her throat and breathe in her perfume, he'd be truly at home. But he didn't dare, so he sat there, fear and joy warring inside him.

"I wanted to make a child with you," he said after a moment. "I wanted to feel the baby kick and watch you nurse. I wanted to cherish both of you and make sure you had everything wonderful in life."

"That sounds pretty sappy," she said.

"It's true. All the books are full of motherhood, but fathers matter, too. And we can't have babies, damn it all."

She lifted her knee up onto the couch, now facing him full on. If she'd been a potential business partner, the posture would have shown that he'd closed the deal. He nearly vibrated with an ache to hold her next to him, but he held off.

"Did you buy the movie studio to get the props department?" she asked.

"No, but it proved handy."

"If they hadn't addressed the package to both of us, I wouldn't have opened it," she said. "The counterfeit pills were nearly perfect. It took me forever to figure out what you'd done."

"And only a few minutes to pack and move out."

"I didn't understand. I thought you were just trying to control me."

"Only natural when you consider my history." He sighed. "And you weren't really wrong."

The music ended, and the room became so quiet, the hum from the refrigerator in the kitchen came in loud and clear.

"I'm sorry, baby. I needed too much," he said finally.

"At least, now I understand."

He picked up the wine and refilled her glass. When he put it down again without pouring any for himself, her eyebrow went up.

"You're not having any more?" she asked.

"I'm driving."

"Where?"

"Taking you home."

She sat for a bit, nibbling at her lower lip. "I don't... have... to go home."

His heart stopped for a full second and then restarted with a lurch. "You want to stay here?"

"If you'd like that."

"I would."

She leaned toward him. He had permission now to kiss her. He had permission to do a great deal more than that, and he would. In a moment. In their bedroom. Right now, he sat and watched her approach him, her lips parting. Almost shyly, she rested her palm on his chest and brought her face up to his. He held himself perfectly still—or as still as he could manage with his heart pounding in his chest—as she set about destroying him with a kiss. First, at the corner of his mouth and then along his lower lip, she tasted him slowly. The tip of her tongue came out to tease him. As she took more and more, she opened his jacket and slid her hands over his ribs, massaging his flesh through his shirt. When she let out a tiny whimper, he gave in to his rising need and turned her, bending her over his lap.

Her hair fell free of its restraints and fell across the cushions of the couch as he deepened the kiss. Their breath mingled, harsh to his ears and sweeter than any music. Angling his head, he probed her mouth with his tongue and shuddered when she answered with a soft stroke of her own. She was sweetness and fire, and she was his for the night. Then more days and more nights, if he could convince her. He would. He had to. Somehow.

In the haze of rising lust, he'd pushed down the strap of her gown without realizing he'd done it. He'd trapped her arm against her body, but exposed her breast. Small and firm, she didn't need a bra, and now he could circle his tongue around her nipple until it tightened into a hard nub. When he took it into his mouth, she arched her back, pushing herself up to meet him.

He could have her now. Right there on the couch. He could slide off her pantyhose and the silk panties beneath, stroke her at her most sensitive spot until she writhed and begged for him. He could unzip his fly and guide his cock into her. They could couple out of desperation. But this time when she came, he could listen to the sounds of her orgasm bounce off the walls of their bedroom as they had so many times. The most beautiful music in the universe, the echoes of his lovemaking with his wife.

Though the effort made a physical ache inside him, he pulled back and gazed down at her. She'd half-closed her eyes in arousal, and her chest rose and fell, her nipple peaking stiff. He slipped her shoes from her feet and let them fall to the carpet. "Come on. Let's go to bed."

She smiled at him fully, her eyes still not focusing completely. But she got up from the couch and extended her hand to him. He took it and, like a lovesick puppy, let her lead him off.

They didn't say a word or stop even for a second before they reached the bedroom. Here they wouldn't need light but would find their way with their hands and mouths. Undressing her in the dark took skill and brought joy. He'd never forgotten the feel of her body, how far down her back the zipper of her dress would go, where he'd find the waistband of her panty hose. She removed his clothes as he worked, their hands sometimes at cross purposes, earning him a giggle here, a sigh there. Garments fell who knew where, exposing skin for exploration. Small, strong fingers tugged at the buckle of his belt, pulled down the zipper, and pushed his pants and shorts over his hips. With uncertain balance, he stood and let her rid him of shoes and socks so she could get him naked from the waist down. She paused on her way back up, her hand placed against his cock. Already swollen, it responded with a force that stopped him in the act of shrugging out of his shirt. She knew how to touch him for maximum effect, and she did so now, circling the head with her thumb.

He stopped her before she could pump his shaft or—God help him—put her mouth on his sex. This was no time for half-clothed fumblings, no matter how wickedly delicious. He needed her naked and beneath him, opening her legs to give him entrance while their bodies slid against each other. Skin to skin, breath to breath, completely exposed. So, after guiding her upward, he finished removing his clothes and helped her with her last scrap, finding the clasp of her bra effortlessly, even in the dark and tossing it aside.

Now, he could take her to the bed, help her onto it, and follow her down into the comforter and the mattress beneath. He let her feel his weight, as if he could pin her here forever, and she accepted it. Her hands clutched at his shoulders as her mouth sought his and found it. The room filled with the sounds of lovemaking. Ragged breathing, punctuated by moans and soft cries. The rustle of skin against silk as she moved beneath him. Everything he'd taken for granted for too many nights. Everything he'd memorize in case fate took her away from him again.

Her hands traveled everywhere on him—across his back, to his sides, down toward his buttocks. Her palms stroked him, followed by her fingertips pressing into him. Catlike. Pushing and massaging.

While she touched, he tasted. Her mouth, the space under her chin, the furrow between her breasts. Without sight, he had to search to find the right spots, and the hunt made her all the more mysterious—a foreign land of citrus and honey. And heat. Enough to burn the edges of his soul.

When he found her nipple and pressed it with his tongue, she let out a cry of delight that went straight to his heart and to his member. Now, her claws came out. Short fingernails, but strong enough to scratch scored the skin over his ribs. Her signal that she'd become ready and would welcome the intrusion of his sex in hers.

Sure enough, when he pressed her legs apart and settled between them, she reached between their bodies to grasp him and bring the tip of his cock to that spot of heaven between her thighs.

He made himself go softly. Even when he'd found his place at her entrance, and she'd removed her hand to allow him passage, he held off. Just for a moment… a second, if that was all he could manage. He held himself there, his heart sending up a prayer of thanks for the miracle that would now happen between them.

She wasn't having any of that. With a sigh, she pushed her hips upward, taking him deeper. Still, he went slowly, savoring each inch as he penetrated. Her muscles closed around him, hot and insistent. And wet. Sweet, so sweet.

Fool that he was, he'd imagined himself in control when, in truth, this woman owned him. If she wanted him to thrust, he'd thrust. That's what he'd been created to do. To please her.

Even so, he began slowly. Long steady glides into her and back, almost but not quite retreating so that he could surge forward again as deep as she'd take him. Cooing her approval, she rose to meet him at each pass. Now, they rocked together, faster and with more urgency. Already, they approached the boundary, the moment of not turning back where nothing lay ahead of them but the final upward shot to oblivion. Soon, nothing would keep them stuck in reality. Nothing would hold them back from perfection. They'd shatter together and come back rearranged, made more whole by what they'd shared.

She arrived first. His Andrea. His love. She let out a strangled moan that built to a wail as her body shuddered beneath his. Her hips jerked upward as the tremors raced through her. Gritting his teeth for control, he continued pumping his cock into her to give her one more jolt of pleasure before he had to surrender to his own need.

In the end, he had no choice but could only slam into her as his own orgasm claimed him. He stifled a roar against her shoulder as his body released his essence into her wet heat. At that instant, each lost in their own release, they clung together in love that surpassed even this passion.

So, when he finally went limp, falling on his side and pulling her against him, his cheek met wetness on hers, and he couldn't tell if the tears were hers or his own.

Andi might have wondered why the grin refused to leave her face if the pleasant tingle between her legs didn't constantly remind her of how she'd spent the night. Blake had outdone himself, and not even the protein in his eggs could give her enough strength to lift anything heavier than a coffee mug.

She contemplated her latest work in progress, but the lump of clay might have been a sphinx for all she could make of it in the light of day. Though he'd left her an hour ago… safe in her own apartment and with her car in the garage below… he still filled her senses as well as her thoughts. She didn't have to lie to herself any longer that she was over him. She didn't have to pretend she didn't love him. Things between them weren't perfect yet, but they were mending. Soon, she wouldn't need this barren place any longer.

She studied her drawings and then stared at the clay a bit more. Someone had obviously put some thought into how the piece would eventually come out, but that someone had existed before the gallery party, Blake's sweet confessions, and then the sex had scrambled her brain. Maybe in a few hours she'd get her mind back to yesterday. Maybe she would tomorrow. Right now, she might as well forget about doing anything besides mooning over the man she'd married.

The phone rang in the kitchen, so she went to it and grabbed it from its cradle. "Hello."

"Hi, baby." Blake. The voice that still rang in her ears after the night they'd spent together. "How are you?"

"You saw me half an hour ago."

"Yeah, but how *are* you?"

"Kind of confused. Disoriented." She bit her lip for a second or two. "It feels good."

"I know what you mean." A longish silence played out at the other end. "So... can I see you tonight?"

Something warm blossomed in her chest, squeezing her heart. "Sure. That'd be fun."

"Your place or mine?"

"Why don't you pick me up here after work and take me home?"

Home. The word hung between them, a physical presence.

"Sounds great," he said with an almost audible sigh of relief. "I'll call when I'm ready to leave."

"I'll be here."

"I love you, baby."

"I love you, too, Blake," she answered.

They both mumbled good-byes, but the important words had been said. I love you. Damn, but that felt good.

Oh, hell... now she really wouldn't get anything done, but she'd have to find something to pass the hours until evening. Bandit showed up out of nowhere with a wail of disapproval that could wake the dead. Even that couldn't sour her mood, so when the cat circled her feet, rubbing against her ankles, she edged the beast to the side so that she could get to the cabinet with the canned kitty treats. She'd chosen Meaty Bits 'n' Sauce and was searching the drawer for the can opener when the phone rang again.

Bandit complained loudly again, like the diva she was, as Andi put down the can and picked up the phone.

"Andi, it's Mel," her business manager said from the other end. "Do I have news for you."

"Something good?"

"The best. A fabulous sale to an outfit in Hong Kong."

"Hong Kong?" she repeated. "No one knows me there."

"They do now. Someone's renovating an old luxury hotel. Four stars. Something called... " Papers rustled at Mel's end. "The Paradise. They want to commission half a dozen works or more."

"Hong Kong," she said yet again. "Breaking into the Asian market. This could be big."

"You bet. Let's see they want something huge for the main lobby. More for the restaurants. Hell, they probably want something for the executive gym."

"How long do I have to do all this?"

"Months," he answered. "They won't reopen for a year, but get this… they're paying up front."

"Whoa." She leaned against the counter for support in case her legs wouldn't hold her up. A job like this could shoot her career into the stratosphere. "Who do I meet with and when?"

"I'm going to set something up for next week. A guy named Ken Wolfe."

"Wait a minute… Ken Wolfe?" She knew a Ken Wolfe. So did Blake. "What's the name of the company?"

More papers rattled. "Oh… here it is…Blandrea Properties."

Damn it. Damn it all to hell. "Blandrea as in Blake and Andrea?"

"Hey, yeah. What a kick. Coincidence, huh?"

"No coincidence. My husb… ex-husband owns the company."

"That's his outfit?" Mel asked.

"One of them. The son of a bitch."

"You're mad because he's sending some business your way?"

She clutched the phone with enough strength to turn her knuckles white. "You wouldn't understand."

"Maybe, he's trying to help your career, kid."

"Or control it," she said. "Direct it and contain it so it doesn't get in his way."

"That sounds kinda harsh."

"You haven't seen Blake Crawford in action."

Mel didn't speak for a moment, and Andi couldn't form much more than pure, hot anger in her brain. After all the sweet things he'd said the night before. Slaying lions and mammoth meat. He only wanted her baby so he could cherish them both, he'd said. Cherish, protect, and order around. Bastard. Scum-sucking bastard. And she'd swallowed it all.

"You want I should turn the offer down?" Mel asked finally.

"Let me do it," she said. "In person."

"Are you sure? Can it be so awful working for your ex? It's a great opportunity."

"Good-bye, Mel. I'll take care of this." With that, she hung up the phone. Carefully so that she didn't slam it hard enough to break it.

Maybe the leopard couldn't change his spots, after all. Maybe Blake's DNA made him behave as if he could tell everyone and everything what to do. Maybe they'd never find a way to fit their lives together. One way or another, she'd find out the answer in the next hour.

Andi stalked into the anteroom of the inner sanctum without knocking. Blake's secretary's office would out-do some CEOs', with its leather couch and original artwork. Blake was quite the connoisseur of paintings and sculpture, but he didn't own this particular sculptor, no matter how good his commissions were.

Virginia rose from behind her gleaming mahogany desk. "Andi. How nice to see you."

"Thanks."

Virginia picked up the phone. "I'll let Blake know you're here."

"Never mind. I'll do it myself." She walked to the huge pair of doors that marked this as the territory of a successful businessman and grabbed the knob of one of them.

"Remind him he has a meeting in five minutes," Virginia said from behind her. "Very important."

"I'll just bet it is." Without looking back, she let herself into Blake's office and closed the door behind her with more force than strictly necessary.

He glanced up, his expression turning from concentration to sunshine. "Andrea. What a great surprise."

"Yeah." She walked to his desk, slammed her purse into the chair opposite his, and stood with her hands on her hips.

His smile faded, his features settling into something non-committal. "What's up?"

"Do you own the Paradise Hotel?"

He leaned back in his chair. "I do."

"Then, you know that Blandrea Properties has offered me a commission to fill the place with statues."

"Oh, that."

"Damn it, Blake," she said. "What in hell were you thinking?"

"Lower your voice." His jaw tensed, a muscle twitching at the corner. "Someone might hear."

"Let them. They all know you're a controlling bastard. They might as well listen to someone say it out loud."

"Because my wife is the best in the business?" His own voice rose above the even tone he always used around his business. "Because I want to work as a partner with her?"

"Partnerships are for equals," she shot back. "A partner doesn't go behind my back to my manager with an offer too sweet to refuse."

His eyebrow went up. "And I suppose you would have accepted if I had?"

That stopped her. She would have said no without even considering his offer. She distrusted him that much. "Maybe."

He snorted softly.

"Don't put this on me," she said. "Last night… "

Oh God, last night. Had it all been a farce? She lifted her chin and glared at him. "All those things you said. That you realized you'd tried to fit me into your life instead of respecting my independence. You swore you knew you'd been wrong. You promised that would change. Now this."

"I meant every word."

She gestured helplessly. "Then, how could you do this?"

"I didn't."

"What?" she demanded.

The door opened, and Virginia poked her head inside. She glanced from Andi to Blake, clearly feeling the tension in the room. "They're all in the conference room. Waiting for you, Blake."

He rose, pushing away from his desk. "I'll be right there."

"No, he won't," Andi said. "He's busy here."

Virginia stood like a statue, her hand closed on the edge of the door.

"Tell them I'll be along in five minutes," Blake said.

"He won't be there then, either," Andi answered.

"Go on, Virginia, and thank you."

The door closed softly, and Blake circled his desk to stand in front of her. "That was quite a display."

"What did you mean you didn't set up my commission?" she demanded.

"I didn't. I only found about it this morning."

That took some of the wind from her sails, and she took a step backward. "If you didn't then who…. "

"Ken did. He got some crazy idea that the publicity about our marriage might create business for the Paradise."

"He was going to use the paparazzi who follow us around to sell hotel rooms?" she asked.

"Something like that. I was going to tell you about it tonight and see what you wanted to do. I'd like to have your work in the Paradise."

"Oh." One stupid syllable, but the only one that came into her brain at the moment.

"I haven't been taking care of my business very well in the last few weeks," he said. "I'm sure you know why."

She didn't answer but stood, her arms around her ribs. She was not the villain of this piece, and she wouldn't let him put her on the defensive.

"Ken's been working without my input most of the time," he said.

"I didn't invent Ramón. You did."

"I did a lot of things I'd usually never consider. I did them for you,"

"Yeah, yeah," she said. "Waxing your chest and all that."

"And you still don't trust me." He leaned toward her. "What in hell do you want me to do to prove myself?"

The phone rang. He muttered something under his breath, leaned over his desk, and snatched up the receiver. "Crawford."

After a moment, he ran his fingers through his hair. "Tell them I'm on my way."

"Don't, Blake. Don't you dare leave now."

He covered the mouthpiece with his fist. "The Morrison people came all the way from London."

"Then they won't mind waiting a little while longer."

"We can talk tonight."

"I don't want to talk." She glared at him while an insane idea flashed into her mind. Crazy but perfect. "I want you to fuck me."

He stared at her as if she'd lost her mind. "What?"

"I want you to bend me over your desk and fuck me."

"Right now?"

"What's the matter?" she said. "Think you can't do it?"

"That's never a problem with us, and you know it."

She toed out of her shoes and unzipped her slacks. His mouth dropped open. "You can't be serious."

"I mean it. Do this now, and I'll never question you again."

A voice sounded on the phone. Virginia calling his name. Andi got out of her slacks and pushed her panties over her hips. After a moment, Blake shook himself and put the phone to his ear.

"Give me fifteen minutes."

"Half an hour," Andi said.

He covered the mouthpiece again. "Half an hour?"

"Do it."

He put the receiver to his ear again. "Tell them I'll be down in half an hour. Until then, no interruptions. Not for anything. Understood?"

Now naked from the waist, she knelt before him as he hung up the phone. By the time she unfastened his fly and pulled out his cock, he'd already begun to swell and harden. In this state, his whole member fit into her mouth, so she could take him all and feel him grow hard against her tongue.

He groaned and dug his fingers into her hair. "Damn, that shouldn't feel so good."

As he became fully erect, she continued to swirl her tongue around him while she stroked his length. His hips pumped in a slow rhythm as she sucked at the head, pulling on the ridge that circled it.

"Enough, baby." The words came out as a harsh whisper. "I'm ready."

She released him and rose, gazing up into blue eyes gone hazy with arousal. He'd made himself vulnerable for her, and now, she'd have her triumph over everything that could keep them apart.

She had to push aside a few things to make room on the top of his desk—including a picture of them from their honeymoon. Something toward the other side fell to the floor, but before she could worry about that, he'd spread her legs apart and pulled up her hips to guide the tip of his sex between her folds.

Maybe it was the fellatio, or maybe the position, but he seemed even larger than usual as he pushed his way into her. She stretched to accept him, savoring the passage of his cock into her sheath.

In a moment, he was plunging into her, gripping her hips to hold her in the right position. Even through her bra, her breasts pressed into the wood of his desk, making them feel achy and full. But nothing compared to the sweet invasion of his tool in her body.

As her arousal mounted, she breathed in and out through her mouth so that she wouldn't cry out her pleasure. Grasping the other edge of the desk, she held herself still for his penetration and she offered herself for more. Faster, harder, until their bodies slapped together on each forward surge.

Her clit had begun to throb, so she worked a hand under her body and down to her mound. He bent, pushed her fingers away and replaced them with his own. Tugging and rolling, he worked the scrap of flesh into a prick of fire between her legs. All the while, he kept fucking her in a hard, steady rhythm. Now, she balled her hand into a fist and bit down on her knuckles. She was going climax, and it would be good enough to make her scream. Somehow, she had to keep quiet.

And... there. Oh, yes, now. Fuck, yes. She swallowed the cry, forcing it down into her throat while her fist covered her mouth. Her whole body shook with the force of the orgasm, squeezing him over and over with her inner muscles.

He stiffened behind her, gripping her almost painfully, as he came with a muffled shout. Holding her hard against him, he let loose his semen in waves she could almost feel. The powerful male at his ultimate moment. Her lover, her husband. The man who'd done this ridiculous thing to win her heart.

When they'd finished, he lowered them to the floor and sat with his back to the desk, cradling her against him. After a moment, his chest rose and fell on a huge sigh. "We should do this again some time."

"We didn't need the full half hour."

"Just as well we took it," he said. "I won't be able to think straight for a few minutes."

She snuggled her cheek against the wool of his suit jacket. "Thank you, Blake."

"I'm always happy to oblige my lover."

"Not for the sex." She looked up at him and ran a fingertip along the line of his jaw. "Although it was great."

"I'd do anything for you."

"I guess you just proved that." She hesitated. "So... do you think... should I move back in with you?"

This close to his chest, she easily caught the tiny catch in his breath. "I'd like that more than anything."

"Can I bring Bandit?"

He chuckled. "What would life be like without Cat-hole?"

"I'm sorry I put you through so much."

He rubbed her arm. Up and down, up and down. "Just don't make me go looking for you in any more sex clubs."

"Why would I do that when I have the only man I want at home?"

About the Author:

Aside from reading and writing, I love to garden, cook, and knit. I also love reptiles and have a pet corn snake named Casper. Visit my blog at www. AliceGaines.blogspot.com or email me at AuthorAliceGaines@yahoo.com.

Check out our hot eBook titles available online at eRedSage.com!

Visit the site regularly as we're always adding new eBook titles.

Here's just some of what you'll find:

A Christmas Cara by Bethany Michaels

A Damsel in Distress by Brenda Williamson

Blood Game by Rae Monet

Fires Within by Roxana Blaze

Forbidden Fruit by Anne Rainey

High Voltage by Calista Fox

Master of the Elements by Alice Gaines

One Wish by Calista Fox

Quinn's Curse by Natasha Moore

Rock My World by Caitlyn Willows

The Doctor Next Door by Catherine Berlin

Unclaimed by Nathalie Gray

Men you've been dreaming about!

Secrets

Satisfy your desire for more.

*F*eel the wild adventure, fierce passion and the power of love in every **Secrets** Collection story. Red Sage Publishing's romance authors create richly crafted, sexy, sensual, novella-length stories. Each one is just the right length for reading after a long and hectic day.

Each volume in the **Secrets** Collection has four diverse, ultra-sexy, romantic novellas brimming with adventure, passion and love. More adventurous tales for the adventurous reader. The **Secrets** Collection are a glorious mix of romance genre; numerous historical settings, contemporary, paranormal, science fiction and suspense. We are always looking for new adventures.

Reader response to the **Secrets** volumes has been great! Here's just a small sample:

"I loved the variety of settings. Four completely wonderful time periods, give you four completely wonderful reads."

"Each story was a page-turning tale I hated to put down."

*"I love **Secrets**! When is the next volume coming out? This one was Hot! Loved the heroes!"*

Secrets have won raves and awards. We could go on, but why don't you find out for yourself—order your set of **Secrets** today! See the back for details.

Secrets, Volume 1

A Lady's Quest by Bonnie Hamre
Widowed Lady Antonia Blair-Sutworth searches for a
lover to save her from the handsome Duke of Suther-
land. The "auditions" may be shocking but utterly
tantalizing.

The Spinner's Dream by Alice Gaines
A seductive fantasy that leaves every woman wishing
for her own private love slave, desperate and running
for his life.

The Proposal by Ivy Landon
This tale is a walk on the wild side of love. *The
Proposal* will taunt you, tease you, and shock you. A
contemporary erotica for the adventurous woman.

The Gift by Jeanie LeGendre
Immerse yourself in this historic tale of exotic seduction, bondage and a concubine's
surrender to the Sultan's desire. Can Alessandra live the life and give the gift the
Sultan demands of her?

Secrets, Volume 2

Surrogate Lover by Doreen DeSalvo
Adrian Ross is a surrogate sex therapist who has all
the answers and control. He thought he'd seen and
done it all, but he'd never met Sarah.

Snowbound by Bonnie Hamre
A delicious, sensuous regency tale. The marriage-shy
Earl of Howden is teased and tortured by his own
desires and finds there is a woman who can equal his
overpowering sensuality.

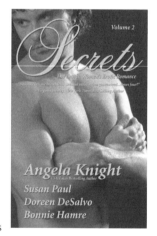

Roarke's Prisoner by Angela Knight
Elise, a starship captain, remembers the eager animal
submission she'd known before at her captor's hands
and refuses to become his toy again. However, she has
no idea of the delights he's planned for her this time.

Savage Garden by Susan Paul
Raine's been captured by a mysterious and dangerous revolutionary leader in
Mexico. At first her only concern is survival, but she quickly finds lush erotic nights
in her captor's arms.

Winner of the Fallot Literary Award for Fiction!

Secrets, Volume 3

The Spy Who Loved Me by Jeanie Cesarini
Undercover FBI agent Paige Ellison's sexual appetites
rise to new levels when she works with leading man
Christopher Sharp, the cunning agent who uses all his
training to capture her body and heart.

The Barbarian by Ann Jacobs
Lady Brianna vows not to surrender to the barbaric
Giles, Earl of Harrow. He must use sexual arts
learned in the infidels' harem to conquer his bride. A
word of caution—this is not for the faint of heart.

Blood and Kisses by Angela Knight
A vampire assassin is after Beryl St. Cloud. Her only
hope lies with Decker, another vampire and ex-merce-
nary. Broke, she offers herself as payment for his services. Will his seductive powers
take her very soul?

Love Undercover by B.J. McCall
Amanda Forbes is the bait in a strip joint sting operation. While she performs, fellow
detective "Cowboy" Cooper gets to watch. Though he excites her, she must fight the
temptation to surrender to the passion.

Winner of the 1997 Under the Covers Readers Favorite Award

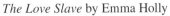

Secrets, Volume 4

An Act of Love by Jeanie Cesarini
Shelby Moran's past left her terrified of sex. International film star Jason Gage must gently coach the young
starlet in the ways of love. He wants more than an act—
he wants Shelby to feel true passion in his arms.

Enslaved by Desirée Lindsey
Lord Nicholas Summer's air of danger, dark passions,
and irresistible charm have brought Lady Crystal's
long-hidden desires to the surface. Will he be able to
give her the one thing she desires before it's too late?

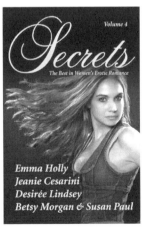

The Bodyguard by Betsy Morgan & Susan Paul
Kaki York is a bodyguard, but watching the wild,
erotic romps of her client's sexual conquests on the
security cameras is getting to her—and her partner, the ruggedly handsome James
Kulick. Can she resist his insistent desire to have her?

The Love Slave by Emma Holly
A woman's ultimate fantasy. For one year, Princess Lily will be attended to by three
delicious men of her choice. While she delights in playing with the first two, it's the
reluctant Grae, with his powerful chest, black eyes and hair, that stirs her desires.

Secrets, Volume 5

Beneath Two Moons by Sandy Fraser
Step into the future and find Conor, rough and masculine like frontiermen of old, on the prowl for a new conquest. In his sights, Dr. Eva Kelsey. She got away before, but this time Conor makes sure she begs for more.

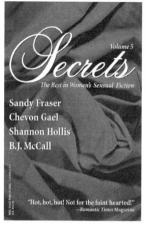

Insatiable by Chevon Gael
Marcus Remington photographs beautiful models for a living, but it's Ashlyn Fraser, a young exec having some glamour shots done, who has stolen his heart. It's up to Marcus to help her discover her inner sexual self.

Strictly Business by Shannon Hollis
Elizabeth Forrester knows it's tough enough for a woman to make it to the top in the corporate world. Garrett Hill, the most beautiful man in Silicon Valley, has to come along to stir up her wildest fantasies. Dare she give in to both their desires?

Alias Smith and Jones by B.J. McCall
Meredith Collins finds herself stranded at the airport. A handsome stranger by the name of Smith offers her sanctuary for the evening and she finds those mesmerizing, green-flecked eyes hard to resist. Are they to be just two ships passing in the night?

Secrets, Volume 6

Flint's Fuse by Sandy Fraser
Dana Madison's father has her "kidnapped" for her own safety. Flint, the tall, dark and dangerous mercenary, is hired for the job. But just which one is the prisoner—Dana will try *anything* to get away.

Love's Prisoner by MaryJanice Davidson
Trapped in an elevator, Jeannie Lawrence experienced unwilling rapture at Michael Windham's hands. She never expected the devilishly handsome man to show back up in her life—or turn out to be a werewolf!

The Education of Miss Felicity Wells by Alice Gaines
Felicity Wells wants to be sure she'll satisfy her soon-to-be husband but she needs a teacher. Dr. Marcus Slade, an experienced lover, agrees to take her on as a student, but can he stop short of taking her completely?

A Candidate for the Kiss by Angela Knight
Working on a story, reporter Dana Ivory stumbles onto a more amazing one—a sexy, secret agent who happens to be a vampire. She wants her story but Gabriel Archer wants more from her than just sex and blood.

Secrets, Volume 7

Amelia's Innocence by Julia Welles
Amelia didn't know her father bet her in a card game with Captain Quentin Hawke, so honor demands a compromise—three days of erotic foreplay, leaving her virginity and future intact.

The Woman of His Dreams by Jade Lawless
From the day artist Gray Avonaco moves in next door, Joanna Morgan is plagued by provocative dreams. But what she believes is unrequited lust, Gray sees as another chance to be with the woman he loves. He must persuade her that even death can't stop true love.

Surrender by Kathryn Anne Dubois
Free-spirited Lady Johanna wants no part of the binding strictures society imposes with her marriage to the powerful Duke. She doesn't know the dark Duke wants sensual adventure, and sexual satisfaction.

Kissing the Hunter by Angela Knight
Navy Seal Logan McLean hunts the vampires who murdered his wife. Virginia Hart is a sexy vampire searching for her lost soul-mate only to find him in a man determined to kill her. She must convince him all vampires aren't created equally.

Winner of the Venus Book Club Best Book of the Year

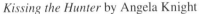

Secrets, Volume 8

Taming Kate by Jeanie Cesarini
Kathryn Roman inherits a legal brothel. Little does this city girl know the town wants her to be their new madam so they've charged Trey Holliday, one very dominant cowboy, with taming her.

Jared's Wolf by MaryJanice Davidson
Jared Rocke will do anything to avenge his sister's death, but ends up attracted to Moira Wolfbauer, the she-wolf sworn to protect her pack. Joining forces to stop a killer, they learn love defies all boundaries.

My Champion, My Lover by Alice Gaines
Celeste Broder is a woman committed for having a sexy appetite. Mayor Robert Albright may be her champion— if she can convince him her freedom will mean they can indulge their appetites together.

Kiss or Kill by Liz Maverick
In this post-apocalyptic world, Camille Kazinsky's military career rides on her ability to make a choice—whether the robo called Meat should live or die. Can he prove he's human enough to live, man enough… to make her feel like a woman.

Winner of the Venus Book Club Best Book of the Year

Secrets, Volume 9

Wild For You by Kathryn Anne Dubois
When college intern, Georgie, gets captured by a
Congo wildman, she discovers this specimen of male
virility has never seen a woman. The research possibilities are endless!

Wanted by Kimberly Dean
FBI Special Agent Jeff Reno wants Danielle Carver.
There's her body, brains—and that charge of treason
on her head. Dani goes on the run, but the sexy Fed is
hot on her trail.

Secluded by Lisa Marie Rice
Nicholas Lee's wealth and power came with a price—
his enemies will kill anyone he loves. When Isabelle
steals his heart, Nicholas secludes her in his palace for a lifetime of desire in only a
few days.

Flights of Fantasy by Bonnie Hamre
Chloe taught others to see the realities of life but she's never shared the intimate
world of her sensual yearnings. Given the chance, will she be woman enough to
fulfill her most secret erotic fantasy?

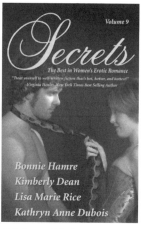

Secrets, Volume 10

Private Eyes by Dominique Sinclair
When a mystery man captivates P.I. Nicolla Black
during a stakeout, she discovers her no-seduction rule
bending under the pressure of long denied passion.
She agrees to the seduction, but he demands her total
surrender.

The Ruination of Lady Jane by Bonnie Hamre
To avoid her upcoming marriage, Lady Jane Ponson-
by-Maitland flees into the arms of Havyn Attercliffe.
She begs him to ruin her rather than turn her over to
her odious fiancé.

Code Name: Kiss by Jeanie Cesarini
Agent Lily Justiss is on a mission to defend her country
against terrorists that requires giving up her virginity as a sex slave. As her master
takes her body, desire for her commanding officer Seth Blackthorn fuels her mind.

The Sacrifice by Kathryn Anne Dubois
Lady Anastasia Bedovier is days from taking her vows as a Nun. Before she denies
her sensuality forever, she wants to experience pleasure. Count Maxwell is the perfect man to initiate her into erotic delight.

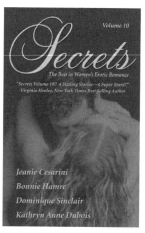

Secrets, Volume 11

Masquerade by Jennifer Probst
Hailey Ashton is determined to free herself from her
sexual restrictions. Four nights of erotic pleasures
without revealing her identity. A chance to explore her
secret desires without the fear of unmasking.

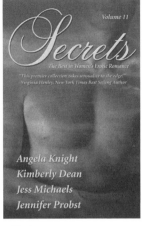

Ancient Pleasures by Jess Michaels
Isabella Winslow is obsessed with finding out what
caused her husband's death, but trapped in an Egyp-
tian concubine's tomb with a sexy American raider,
succumbing to the mummy's sensual curse takes over.

Manhunt by Kimberly Dean
Framed for murder, Michael Tucker takes Taryn
Swanson hostage—the one woman who can clear him.
Despite the evidence against him, the attraction is strong. Tucker resorts to uncon-
ventional, yet effective methods of persuasion to change the sexy ADA's mind.

Wake Me by Angela Knight
Chloe Hart received a sexy painting of a sleeping knight. Radolf of Varik has been
trapped there for centuries, cursed by a witch. His only hope is to visit the dreams of
women and make one of them fall in love with him so she can free him with a kiss.

Secrets, Volume 12

Good Girl Gone Bad by Dominique Sinclair
Setting out to do research for an article, nothing could
have prepared Reagan for Luke, or his offer to teach
her everything she needs to know about sex. Licen-
tious pleasures, forbidden desires… inspiring the best
writing she's ever done.

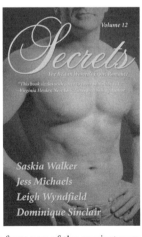

Aphrodite's Passion by Jess Michaels
When Selena flees Victorian London before her evil
stepchildren can institutionalize her for hysteria,
Gavin is asked to bring her back home. But when he
finds her living on the island of Cyprus, his need to
have her begins to block out every other impulse.

White Heat by Leigh Wyndfield
Raine is hiding in an icehouse in the middle of nowhere from one of the scariest men
in the universes. Walker escaped from a burning prison. Imagine their surprise when
they find out they have the same man to blame for their miseries. Passion, revenge
and love are in their future.

Summer Lightning by Saskia Walker
Sculptress Sally is enjoying an idyllic getaway on a secluded cove when she spots a
gorgeous man walking naked on the beach. When Julian finds an attractive woman
shacked up in his cove, he has to check her out. But what will he do when he finds
she's secretly been using him as a model?

Secrets, Volume 13

Out of Control by Rachelle Chase
Astrid's world revolves around her business and she's
hoping to pick up wealthy Erik Santos as a client. He's
hoping to pick up something entirely different. Will
she give in to the seductive pull of his proposition?

Hawkmoor by Amber Green
Shape-shifters answer to Darien as he acts in the name
of long-missing Lady Hawkmoor, their ruler. When
she unexpectedly surfaces, Darien must deal with a
scrappy individual whose wary eyes hold the other half
of his soul, but who has the power to destroy his world.

Lessons in Pleasure by Charlotte Featherstone
A wicked bargain has Lily vowing never to yield to the

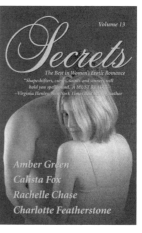

demands of the rake she once loved and lost. Unfortunately, Damian, the Earl of St.
Croix, or Saint as he is infamously known, will not take 'no' for an answer.

In the Heat of the Night by Calista Fox
Haunted by a curse, Molina fears she won't live to see her 30th birthday. Nick, her for-
mer bodyguard, is re-hired to protect her from the fatal accidents that plague her family.
Will his passion and love be enough to convince Molina they have a future together?

Secrets, Volume 14

Soul Kisses by Angela Knight
Beth's been kidnapped by Joaquin Ramirez, a sadistic
vampire. Handsome vampire cousins, Morgan and
Garret Axton, come to her rescue. Can she find happiness with two vampires?

Temptation in Time by Alexa Aames
Ariana escaped the Middle Ages after stealing a kiss
of magic from sexy sorcerer, Marcus de Grey. When
he brings her back, they begin a battle of wills and a
sexual odyssey that could spell disaster for them both.

Ailis and the Beast by Jennifer Barlowe
When Ailis agreed to be her village's sacrifice to the
mysterious Beast she was prepared to sacrifice her vir-

tue, and possibly her life. But some things aren't what they seem. Ailis and the Beast
are about to discover the greatest sacrifice may be the human heart.

Night Heat by Leigh Wynfield
When Rip Bowhite leads a revolt on the prison planet, he ends up struggling to
survive against monsters that rule the night. Jemma, the prison's Healer, won't allow
herself to be distracted by the instant attraction she feels for Rip. As the stakes are
raised and death draws near, love seems doomed in the heat of the night.

Secrets, Volume 15

Simon Says by Jane Thompson
Simon Campbell is a newspaper columnist who panders to male fantasies. Georgina Kennedy is a respectable librarian. On the surface, these two have nothing in common... but don't judge a book by its cover.

Bite of the Wolf by Cynthia Eden
Gareth Morlet, alpha werewolf, has finally found his mate. All he has to do is convince Trinity to join with him, to give in to the pleasure of a werewolf's mating, and then she will be his... forever.

Falling for Trouble by Saskia Walker
With 48 hours to clear her brother's name, Sonia Harmond finds help from irresistible bad boy, Oliver Eaglestone. When the erotic tension between them hits fever pitch, securing evidence to thwart an international arms dealer isn't the only danger they face.

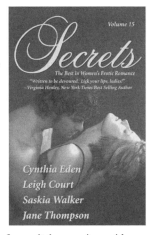

The Disciplinarian by Leigh Court
Headstrong Clarissa Babcock is sent for instruction in proper wifely obedience. Disciplinarian Jared Ashworth uses the tools of seduction to show her how to control a demanding husband, but her beauty, spirit, and uninhibited passion make Jared hunger to keep her—and their darkly erotic nights—all for himself!

Secrets, Volume 16

Never Enough by Cynthia Eden
Abby McGill has been playing with fire. Bad-boy Jake taught her the true meaning of desire, but she knows she has to end her relationship with him. But Jake isn't about to let the woman he wants walk away from him.

Bunko by Sheri Gilmoore
Tu Tran must decide between Jack, who promises to share every aspect of his life with her, or Dev, who hides behind a mask and only offers nights of erotic sex. Will she gamble on the man who can see behind her own mask and expose her true desires?

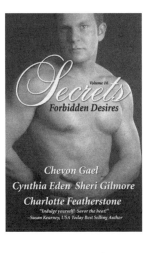

Hide and Seek by Chevon Gael
Kyle DeLaurier ditches his trophy-fiance in favor of a tropical paradise full of tall, tanned, topless females.
Private eye, Darcy McLeod, is on the trail of this runaway groom. Together they sizzle while playing Hide and Seek with their true identities.

Seduction of the Muse by Charlotte Featherstone
He's the Dark Lord, the mysterious author who pens the erotic tales of an innocent woman's seduction. She is his muse, the woman he watches from the dark shadows, the woman whose dreams he invades at night.

Secrets, Volume 17

Rock Hard Candy by Kathy Kaye
Jessica Hennessy, descendent of a Voodoo priestess, decides it's time for the man of her dreams. A dose of her ancestor's aphrodisiac slipped into the gooey center of her homemade bon bons ought to do the trick.

Fatal Error by Kathleen Scott
Jesse Storm must make amends to humanity by destroying the software he helped design that's taken the government hostage. But he must also protect the woman he's loved in secret for nearly a decade.

Birthday by Ellie Marvel
Jasmine Templeton's been celibate long enough. Will a wild night at a hot new club with her two best friends

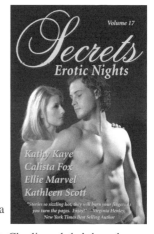

ease the ache or just make it worse? Considering one is Charlie and she's been having strange notions about their relationship of late… It's definitely a birthday neither she nor Charlie will ever forget.

Intimate Rendezvous by Calista Fox
A thief causes trouble at Cassandra Kensington's nightclub and sexy P.I. Dean Hewitt arrives to help. One look at her sends his blood boiling, despite the fact that his keen instincts have him questioning the legitimacy of her business.

Secrets, Volume 18

Lone Wolf Three by Rae Monet
Planetary politics and squabbling drain former rebel leader Taban Zias. But his anger quickly turns to desire when he meets, Lakota Blackson. She's Taban's perfect mate—now if he can just convince her.

Flesh to Fantasy by Larissa Ione
Kelsa Bradshaw is a loner happily immersed in a world of virtual reality. Trent Jordan is a paramedic who experiences the harsh realities of life. When their worlds collide in an erotic eruption can Trent convince Kelsa to turn the fantasy into something real?

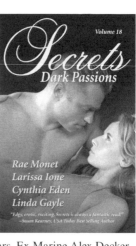

Heart Full of Stars by Linda Gayle
Singer Fanta Rae finds herself stranded on a lonely Mars outpost with the first human male she's seen in years. Ex-Marine Alex Decker lost his family and guilt drove him into isolation, but when alien assassins come to enslave Fanta, she and Decker come together to fight for their lives.

The Wolf's Mate by Cynthia Eden
When Michael Morlet finds "Kat" Hardy fighting for her life, he instantly recognizes her as the mate he's been seeking all of his life, but someone's trying to kill her. With danger stalking them, will Kat trust him enough to become his mate?

Secrets, Volume 19

Affliction by Elisa Adams
Holly Aronson finally believes she's safe with sweet Andrew. But when his life long friend, Shane, arrives, events begin to spiral out of control. She's inexplicably drawn to Shane. As she runs for her life, which one will protect her?

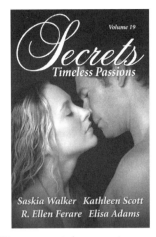

Falling Stars by Kathleen Scott
Daria is both a Primon fighter pilot and a Primon princess. As a deadly new enemy faces appears, she must choose between her duty to the fleet and the desperate need to forge an alliance through her marriage to the enemy's General Raven.

Saskia Walker   Kathleen Scott
R. Ellen Ferare   Elisa Adams

Toy in the Attic by R. Ellen Ferare
Gabrielle discovers a life-sized statue of a nude man. Her unexpected roommate reveals himself to be a talented lover caught by a witch's curse. Can she help him break free of the spell that holds him, without losing her heart along the way?

What You Wish For by Saskia Walker
Lucy Chambers is renovating her historic house. As her dreams about a stranger become more intense, she wishes he were with her. Two hundred years in the past, the man wishes for companionship. Suddenly they find themselves together—in his time.

Secrets, Volume 20

The Subject by Amber Green
One week Tyler is a game designer, signing the deal of her life. The next, she's running for her life. Who can she trust? Certainly not sexy, mysterious Esau, who keeps showing up after the hoo-hah hits the fan!

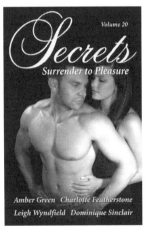

Surrender by Dominique Sinclair
Agent Madeline Carter is in too deep. She's slipped into Sebastian Maiocco's life to investigate his Sicilian mafia family. He unearths desires Madeline's unable to deny, conflicting the duty that honors her. Madeline must surrender to Sebastian or risk being exposed, leaving her target for a ruthless clan.

Amber Green   Charlotte Featherstone
Leigh Wyndfield   Dominique Sinclair

Stasis by Leigh Wyndfield
Morgann Right's Commanding Officer's been drugged with Stasis, turning him into a living statue she's forced to take care of for ten long days. As her hands tend to him, she sees her CO in a totally different light. She wants him and, while she can tell he wants her, touching him intimately might come back to haunt them both.

A Woman's Pleasure by Charlotte Featherstone
Widowed Isabella, Lady Langdon is yearning to discover all the pleasures denied her in her marriage, she finds herself falling hard for the magnetic charms of the mysterious and exotic Julian Gresham—a man skilled in pleasures of the flesh.

Secrets, Volume 21

Caged Wolf by Cynthia Eden
Alerac La Morte has been drugged and kidnapped. He realizes his captor, Madison Langley, is actually his destined mate, but she hates his kind. Will Alerac convince her he's not the monster she thinks?

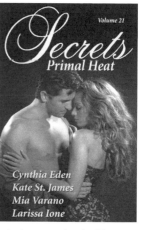

Wet Dreams by Larissa Ione
Injured and on the run, agent Brent Logan needs a miracle. What he gets is a boat owned by Marina Summers. Pursued by killers, ravaged by a storm, and plagued by engine troubles, they can do little but spend their final hours immersed in sensual pleasure.

Good Vibrations by Kate St. James
Lexi O'Brien vows to swear off sex while she attends grad school, so when her favorite out-of-town customer asks her out, she decides to indulge in an erotic fling. Little does she realize Gage Templeton is moving home, to her city, and has no intention of settling for a short-term affair..

Virgin of the Amazon by Mia Varano
Librarian Anna Winter gets lost on the Amazon and stumbles upon a tribe whose shaman wants a pale-skinned virgin to deflower. British adventurer Coop Daventry, the tribe's self-styled chief, wants to save her, but which man poses a greater threat?

Secrets, Volume 22

Heat by Ellie Marvel
Mild-mannered alien Tarkin is in heat and the only compatible female is a Terran. He courts her the old fashioned Terran way. Because if he can't seduce her before his cycle ends, he won't get a second chance.

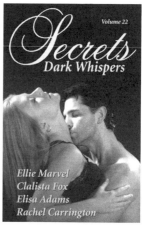

Breathless by Rachel Carrington
Lark Hogan is a martial arts expert seeking vengeance for the death of her sister. She seeks help from Zac, a mercenary wizard. Confronting a common enemy, they battle their own demons as well as their powerful attraction, and will fight to the death to protect what they've found.

Midnight Rendezvous by Calista Fox
From New York to Cabo to Paris to Tokyo, Cat Hewitt and David Essex share decadent midnight rendezvous. But when the real world presses in on their erotic fantasies, and Cat's life is in danger, will their whirlwind romance stand a chance?

Birthday Wish by Elisa Adams
Anna Kelly had many goals before turning 30 and only one is left—to spend one night with sexy Dean Harrison. When Dean asks her what she wants for her birthday, she grabs at the opportunity to ask him for an experience she'll never forget.

Secrets, Volume 23

The Sex Slave by Roxi Romano
Jaci Coe needs a hero and the hard bodied man in
black meets all the criteria. Opportunistic Jaci takes
advantage of Lazarus Stone's commandingly protective nature, but together, they learn how to live free...
and love freely.

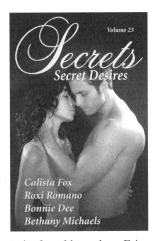

Forever My Love by Calista Fox
Professor Aja Woods is a 16th century witch... only
she doesn't know it. Christian St. James, her vampire
lover, has watched over her spirit for 500 years. When
her powers are recovered, so too are her memories of
Christian—and the love they once shared.

Reflection of Beauty by Bonnie Dee
Artist Christine Dawson is commissioned to paint a portrait of wealthy recluse, Eric
Leroux. It's up to her to reach the heart of this physically and emotionally scarred
man. Can love rescue Eric from isolation and restore his life?

Educating Eva by Bethany Lynn
Eva Blakely attends the infamous Ivy Hill houseparty to gather research for her book
Mating Rituals of the Human Male. But when she enlists the help of research "speci-
men" and notorious rake, Aidan Worthington, she gets some unexpected results.

Secrets, Volume 24

Hot on Her Heels by Mia Varano
Private investigator Jack Slater dons a g-string to
investigate the Lollipop Lounge, a male strip club.
He's not sure if the club's sexy owner, Vivica Steele,
is involved in the scam, but Jack figures he's just the
Lollipop to sweeten her life.

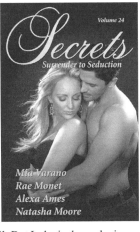

Shadow Wolf by Rae Monet
A half-breed Lupine challenges a high-ranking
Solarian Wolf Warrior. When Dia Nahiutras tries to
steal Roark D'Reincolt's wolf, does she get an enemy
forever or a mate for life?

Bad to the Bone by Natasha Moore
At her class reunion, Annie Shane sheds her good girl
reputation through one wild weekend with Luke Kendall. But Luke is done playing
the field and wants to settle down. What would a bad girl do?

War God by Alexa Ames
Estella Eaton, a lovely graduate student, is the unwitting carrier of the essence of
Aphrodite. But Ares, god of war, the ultimate alpha male, knows the truth and becomes obsessed with Estelle, pursuing her relentlessly. Can her modern sensibilities
and his ancient power coexist, or will their battle of wills destroy what matters most?

Secrets, Volume 25

Blood Hunt by Cynthia Eden
Vampiress Nema Alexander has a taste for bad boys. Slade Brion has just been charged with tracking her down. He won't stop until he catches her, and Nema won't stop until she claims him, forever.

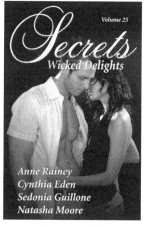

Scandalous Behavior by Anne Rainey
Tess Marley wants to take a walk on the wild side. Who better to teach her about carnal pleasures than her intriguing boss, Kevin Haines? But Tess makes a major miscalculation when she crosses the line between lust and love.

Enter the Hero by Sedonia Guillone
Kass and Lian are sentenced to sex slavery in the Confederation's pleasure district. Forced to make love for an audience, their hearts are with each other while their bodies are on display. Now, in the midst of sexual slavery, they have one more chance to escape to Paradise.

Up to No Good by Natasha Moore
Former syndicated columnist Simon "Mac" MacKenzie hides a tragic secret. When freelance writer Alison Chandler tracks him down, he knows she's up to no good. Is their attraction merely a distraction or the key to surviving their war of wills?

Secrets, Volume 26

Secret Rendezvous by Calista Fox
McCarthy Portman has seen enough happily-ever-afters to long for one of her own, but when her renowned matchmaking software pairs her with the wild and wicked Josh Kensington, everything she's always believed about love is turned upside down.

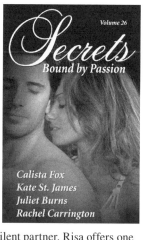

Enchanted Spell by Rachel Carrington
Witches and wizards don't mix. Every magical being knows that. Yet, when a little mischievous magic thrusts Ella and Kevlin together, they do so much more than mix—they combust.

Exes and Ahhhs by Kate St. James
Former lovers Risa Haber and Eric Lange are partners in a catering business, but Eric can't seem to remain a silent partner. Risa offers one night of carnal delights if he'll sell her his share then disappear forever.

The Spy's Surrender by Juliet Burns
The famous courtesan Eva Werner is England's secret weapon against Napoleon. Her orders are to attend a sadistic marquis' depraved house party and rescue a British spy being held prisoner. As the weekend orgy begins, she's forced to make the spy her love slave for the marquis' pleasure. But who is slave and who is master?

Secrets, Volume 27

Heart Storm by Liane Gentry Skye
Sirenia must mate with the only merman who can save
her kind, but when she rescues Navy SEAL Byron
Burke, she seals herself into his life debt. Will her
heart stand in the way of the last hope for her kind?

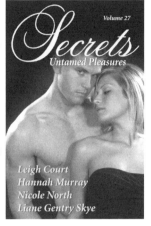

The Boy Next Door by Hannah Murray
Isabella Carelli isn't just looking for Mr. Right, she's
looking for Mr. Tie Me Up And Do Me Right. In all
the wrong places. Fortunately, the boy next door is just
about ready to make his move...

Devil in a Kilt by Nicole North
A trip to the Highland Games turns into a trip to the
past when modern day Shauna MacRae touches Gavin
MacTavish's 400-year-old claymore. Can she break the curse imprisoning this *Devil
in a Kilt* before an evil witch sends her back and takes Gavin as her sex slave?

The Bet by Leigh Court
A very drunk Damian Hunt claims he can make a woman come with just words. He
bets his prized racehorse that he can do it while George Beringer gambles his London townhouse that he can't. George chooses his virginal sister, Claire, for the bet.
Once Damian lays eyes on her, the stakes escalate in the most unpredictable way…

Secrets, Volume 28

Kiss Me at Midnight by Kate St. James
Callie Hutchins and Marc Shaw fake an on-air
romance to top the sweeps. Callie thinks Marc is a
womanizer, but as the month progresses, she realizes
he's funny, kind, and too sexy for words, damn it.

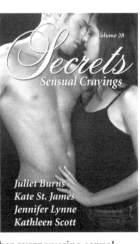

Mind Games by Kathleen Scott
Damien Storm is a Varti—a psychic who can communicate telepathically to one special person. Fear
has kept his Vartek partner, Jade, from acknowledging
their link. He must save her from the forces who wish
to see all Varti destroyed.

Seducing Serena by Jennifer Lynne
Serena Hewitt has given up on love, but when she
interviews for a potential partner she's not prepared for her overpowering sexual
attraction to Nicholas Wade, a fun-loving bachelor with bad-boy good looks and a
determination to prove her wrong.

Pirate's Possession by Juliet Burns
When Lady Gertrude Fitzpatrick bargains with a fierce pirate for escape, but unwittingly becomes the possession of a fierce privateer. Ewan MacGowan has been
betrayed and mistakenly exacts revenge on this proud noblewoman. He may have
stolen the lady's innocence, but he also finds the true woman of his heart.

Secrets, Volume 29

Sweet-Talking the Opposition by Saskia Walker
Journalist Eliza Jameson is on assignment when she
finds the perfect distraction on board—old flame,
Marcus Weston.

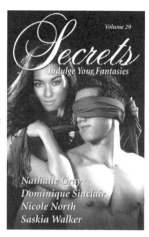

Chimera by Nathalie Gray
From the overcrowded slums of a future Earth, he rose
as the perfect tool of lethal justice and deception. But
when his next assignment involves a popular politician
who's as smart as she's attractive, the greatest betrayal
would be to deny his heart.

Edge by Dominique Sinclair
Catlina Demarco has left the agency and Noah Tyler,
her former partner and lover, is intent on bringing her
back. Forced into the jungle by armed banderos, they end up working as partners,
their thoughts as one, their bodies craving, their goals conflicting.

Beast in a Kilt by Nicole North
Lady Catriona MacCain has loved Torr Blackburn since she was a young lass. When
Catriona's family promises her in marriage to a detestable chieftain, she needs Torr
to save her. But he's been cursed by a witch and doesn't believe himself worthy of
the virginal Catriona. However, she's determined to seduce Torr and claim him.

Secrets, Volume 30

Kat on a Hot Tin Roof by Maree Anderson
Kat Meyer is clueless about the curse that turns her
into a cat at night. When Jace Burton wakes to find a
naked and distraught Kat in his living room, he's inclined to believe her bizarre tale of sleepwalking. But
how's he going to react when he discovers the truth?

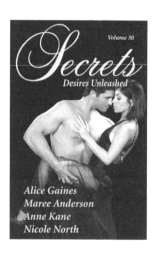

Kellen's Conquest by Anne Kane
Mia's most cherished dream is to settle down with a
family. Kellen may be the sexiest man in the known
worlds, but he's AlphElite and when they settle down,
it's with one of their own kind. When someone sets
him up to kill Mia, Kellen decides to kidnap her and
keep her by his side until he's sure she's safe.

Scoundrel in a Kilt by Nicole North
When a shape-shifting Highland chieftain and a modern day supermodel meet in
1621 Scotland, neither will ever forget their earthshaking erotic connection.

Cox Club by Nicole North
What if you went to an exclusive club for sexual satisfaction only to discover your
ex-husband owns the place?

The Forever Kiss
by Angela Knight

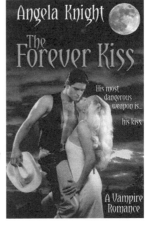

Listen to what reviewers say:

"*The Forever Kiss* flows well with good characters and an interesting plot. ... If you enjoy vampires and a lot of hot sex, you are sure to enjoy *The Forever Kiss*."

—*The Best Reviews*

"Battling vampires, a protective ghost and the ever present battle of good and evil keep excellent pace with the erotic delights in Angela Knight's *The Forever Kiss*—a book that absolutely bites with refreshing paranormal humor." **4½ Stars, Top Pick**

—*Romantic Times BOOKclub*

"I found *The Forever Kiss* to be an exceptionally written, refreshing book. ... I really enjoyed this book by Angela Knight. ... 5 angels!"

—*Fallen Angel Reviews*

"*The Forever Kiss* is the first single title released from Red Sage and if this is any indication of what we can expect, it won't be the last. ... The love scenes are hot enough to give a vampire a sunburn and the fight scenes will have you cheering for the good guys."

—*Really Bad Barb Reviews*

In *The Forever Kiss*:

For years, Valerie Chase has been haunted by dreams of a Texas Ranger she knows only as "Cowboy." As a child, he rescued her from the nightmare vampires who murdered her parents. As an adult, she still dreams of him—but now he's her seductive lover in nights of erotic pleasure.

Yet "Cowboy" is more than a dream—he's the real Cade McKinnon—and a vampire! For years, he's protected Valerie from Edward Ridgemont, the sadistic vampire who turned him. Now, Ridgmont wants Valerie for his own and Cade is the only one who can protect her.

When Val finds herself abducted by her handsome dream man, she's appalled to discover he's one of the vampires she fears. Now, caught in a web of fear and passion, she and Cade must learn to trust each other, even as an immortal monster stalks their every move.

Their only hope of survival is... *The Forever Kiss*.

Romantic Times Best Erotic Novel of the Year

Object of Desire
by Calista Fox

Listen to what reviewers say:

"*Object of Desire* was a very good book! The plot was fast paced, the adventure was thrilling, and the espionage angle added a whole new edge to the book. The developing relationship between Devon and Laurel was fun to watch, and the romance between them was intense! ... I loved it!"
— Romance Junkies

"James Bond move over! Calista Fox is romancing the stone with a sexy new spy and a sizzling hot story. With enough glitz for Jackie Collins and intrigue for Ian Fleming fans, Fox blazes a new brand of the sexy spy."
—Erin Quinn, author of *Haunting Beauty*

"*Object of Desire* delivers sizzling sensuality, emotional complexity, and an intriguing story—everything I've come to expect from Calista Fox!"
—Rachelle Chase, author of *The Sin Club* and *The Sex Lounge*

"A roller coaster of action and romance—you'll barely have time to breathe!"
—Leigh Court, author of the award-winning novella, *The Disciplinarian* (**Secrets Volume 15**)

In *Object of Desire*:

When treasure hunter and spy Laurel Blackwood raids Victoria Peak in Belize to recover a rare Mexican fire opal rumored to evoke dark desires and passions, she unwittingly sets off a sequence of dangerous events—and finds herself in the midst of a battle between good and evil... and lust and love. Being chased through the Yucatan jungle is perilous enough, but Laurel must also keep the opal from falling into the hands of a deadly terrorist cell, a greedy Belizean dignitary, and one particularly hot and scandalous treasure hunter named Devon Mallory.

For ten years, Devon has had his eye on the thirty-million-dollar prized opal and his heart set on winning Laurel for keeps. But her web of secrecy and now her betrayal over recovering the legendary stone without him has Devon hell-bent on stealing the opal from her and collecting on the massive pay-out. Unfortunately for Devon, there is much more to Laurel Blackwood than she lets on. And soon, he's caught in the eye of the storm—falling under her sensuous spell, willing to put his own life on the line to help her protect the mystical jewel.

But Devon will eventually have to decide which gem is his true object of desire...

It's not just reviewers raving about *Secrets*. See what readers have to say:

"When are you coming out with a new Volume? I want a new one next month!" via email from a reader.

"I loved the hot, wet sex without vulgar words being used to make it exciting." after *Volume 1*

"I loved the blend of sensuality and sexual intensity—HOT!" after *Volume 2*

"The best thing about *Secrets* is they're hot and brief! The least thing is you do not have enough of them!" after *Volume 3*

"I have been extremely satisfied with *Secrets*, keep up the good writing." after *Volume 4*

"Stories have plot and characters to support the erotica. They would be good strong stories without the heat." after *Volume 5*

"*Secrets* really knows how to push the envelop better than anyone else." after *Volume 6*

"These are the best sensual stories I have ever read!" after *Volume 7*

"I love, love, love the *Secrets* stories. I now have all of them, please have more books come out each year." after *Volume 8*

"These are the perfect sensual romance stories!" after *Volume 9*

"What I love about *Secrets Volume 10* is how I couldn't put it down!" after *Volume 10*

"All of the *Secrets* volumes are terrific! I have read all of them up to *Secrets Volume 11*. Please keep them coming! I will read every one you make!" after *Volume 11*

Finally, the men you've been dreaming about!

Give the gift of spicy romantic fiction.

Don't want to wait? You can place a retail price ($12.99) order for any of the *Secrets* volumes from the following:

① online at **eRedSage.com**

② **Waldenbooks, Borders, and Books-a-Million Stores**

③ **Amazon.com or BarnesandNoble.com**

④ or buy them at your local bookstore or online book source.

Bookstores: Please contact Baker & Taylor Distributors, Ingram Book Distributor, or Red Sage Publishing, Inc. for bookstore sales.

Order by title or ISBN #:

Vol. 1: 0-9648942-0-3
ISBN #13 978-0-9648942-0-4

Vol. 2: 0-9648942-1-1
ISBN #13 978-0-9648942-1-1

Vol. 3: 0-9648942-2-X
ISBN #13 978-0-9648942-2-8

Vol. 4: 0-9648942-4-6
ISBN #13 978-0-9648942-4-2

Vol. 5: 0-9648942-5-4
ISBN #13 978-0-9648942-5-9

Vol. 6: 0-9648942-6-2
ISBN #13 978-0-9648942-6-6

Vol. 7: 0-9648942-7-0
ISBN #13 978-0-9648942-7-3

Vol. 8: 0-9648942-8-9
ISBN #13 978-0-9648942-9-7

Vol. 9: 0-9648942-9-7
ISBN #13 978-0-9648942-9-7

Vol. 10: 0-9754516-0-X
ISBN #13 978-0-9754516-0-1

Vol. 11: 0-9754516-1-8
ISBN #13 978-0-9754516-1-8

Vol. 12: 0-9754516-2-6
ISBN #13 978-0-9754516-2-5

Vol. 13: 0-9754516-3-4
ISBN #13 978-0-9754516-3-2

Vol. 14: 0-9754516-4-2
ISBN #13 978-0-9754516-4-9

Vol. 15: 0-9754516-5-0
ISBN #13 978-0-9754516-5-6

Vol. 16: 0-9754516-6-9
ISBN #13 978-0-9754516-6-3

Vol. 17: 0-9754516-7-7
ISBN #13 978-0-9754516-7-0

Vol. 18: 0-9754516-8-5
ISBN #13 978-0-9754516-8-7

Vol. 19: 0-9754516-9-3
ISBN #13 978-0-9754516-9-4

Vol. 20: 1-60310-000-8
ISBN #13 978-1-60310-000-7

Vol. 21: 1-60310-001-6
ISBN #13 978-1-60310-001-4

Vol. 22: 1-60310-002-4
ISBN #13 978-1-60310-002-1

Vol. 23: 1-60310-164-0
ISBN #13 978-1-60310-164-6

Vol. 24: 1-60310-165-9
ISBN #13 978-1-60310-165-3

Vol. 25: 1-60310-005-9
ISBN #13 978-1-60310-005-2

Vol. 26: 1-60310-006-7
ISBN #13 978-1-60310-006-9

Vol. 27: 1-60310-007-5
ISBN #13 978-1-60310-007-6

Vol. 28: 1-60310-008-3
ISBN #13 978-1-60310-008-3

Vol. 29: 1-60310-009-1
ISBN #13 978-1-60310-009-0

Vol. 30: 1-60310-010-5
ISBN #13 978-1-60310-010-6

The Forever Kiss:
0-9648942-3-8
ISBN #13
978-0-9648942-3-5 ($14.00)

Object of Desire:
1-60310-003-2
ISBN #13
978-1-60310-003-8 ($14.00)

Red Sage Publishing Order Form:

(Orders shipped in two to three days of receipt.)

Each volume of *Secrets* retails for $12.99, but you can get it direct via mail order for only $10.99 each. Novels retail for $14.00, but by direct mail order, you only pay $12.00. Use the order form below to place your direct mail order. Fill in the quantity you want for each book on the blanks beside the title.

_____ *Secrets* Volume 1	_____ *Secrets* Volume 12	_____ *Secrets* Volume 23
_____ *Secrets* Volume 2	_____ *Secrets* Volume 13	_____ *Secrets* Volume 24
_____ *Secrets* Volume 3	_____ *Secrets* Volume 14	_____ *Secrets* Volume 25
_____ *Secrets* Volume 4	_____ *Secrets* Volume 15	_____ *Secrets* Volume 26
_____ *Secrets* Volume 5	_____ *Secrets* Volume 16	_____ *Secrets* Volume 27
_____ *Secrets* Volume 6	_____ *Secrets* Volume 17	_____ *Secrets* Volume 28
_____ *Secrets* Volume 7	_____ *Secrets* Volume 18	_____ *Secrets* Volume 29
_____ *Secrets* Volume 8	_____ *Secrets* Volume 19	_____ *Secrets* Volume 30
_____ *Secrets* Volume 9	_____ *Secrets* Volume 20	Novels:
_____ *Secrets* Volume 10	_____ *Secrets* Volume 21	_____ *The Forever Kiss*
_____ *Secrets* Volume 11	_____ *Secrets* Volume 22	_____ *Object of Desire*

Total _____ *Secrets* Volumes @ $10.99 each = $_____

Total _____ Novels @ $12.00 each = $_____

Shipping & handling (in the U.S.) $_____

US Priority Mail: UPS insured:
  1–2 books .... $ 5.50   1–4 books $16.00
  3–5 books .... $11.50   5–9 books $25.00
  6–9 books .... $14.50   10–28 books $29.00
  10–12 books .... $16.00   29–32 books $35.00
  13–24 books $24.00
  25–32 books .... $36.00   **Subtotal** $_____

Florida 6% sales tax (if delivered in FL) $_____

TOTAL AMOUNT ENCLOSED $_____

Your personal information is kept private and not shared with anyone.

Name: (please print) _____

Address: (no P.O. Boxes) _____

City/State/Zip: _____

Phone or email: (only regarding order if necessary) _____

You can order direct from **eRedSage.com** and use a credit card or you can use this form to send in your mail order with a check. Please make check payable to **Red Sage Publishing**. Check must be drawn on a U.S. bank in U.S. dollars. Mail your check and order form to:

Red Sage Publishing, Inc. Department S30 P.O. Box 4844 Seminole, FL 33775